For Ke[n]

Hope you enjoy the read

MAGGIE'S
MECHANICS

& that you find it
mysterious + heart-
warming.

Best regard,

Sheila J. Connolly

MAGGIE'S MECHANICS

Mystery & Mayhem

Mixed with Love

SHEILA J. CONNOLLY

Clover Valley Press, LLC
Duluth, Minnesota

Clover Valley Press, LLC
6286 Homestead Road
Duluth, MN 55804-9621
USA

This book is a work of fiction. Any resemblance between characters in this book and actual persons is coincidental.

Cover design by Stacie Whaley, i.e. design
Cover illustration © 2013 Kimberly Dunn

Printed in the United States of America on acid-free paper.

ISBN-13: 978-0-9846570-5-6

Library of Congress Control Number: 2013947055

For Mom, who knows me through and through
and loves me still and always.

25 February 1915 to 5 July 2003
Still alive in my heart and mind and soul.

CONTENTS

CHAPTER 1.

I Got Trouble

THE LIGHT WAS IMPRESSIVE. Exhilarating even. But the sound was terrifying. The explosion changed everything. Immediately. And forever.

Bett raised her hands instinctively in defense. But there was no defense. The light flashed, and everything in its reach turned stark. It froze solid objects in startling brilliance and made shadows black; intensely, sharply black. In that instant, everything became two dimensional.

What the light flattened, the sound then overwhelmed. Muted and distant at first, its concussive *boom* drove out all other sound. For a moment, even the freeway was silent. But the silence didn't last. Screeching brakes and blaring horns answered the assault.

Bett was too stunned to move. But Maggie was out of the truck even before the light had spent itself, while the sound was still a booming terror. Bett felt her leave. And when she could tear her eyes away from the storm of fire on the freeway below, she saw Maggie in the headlights, running toward the overpass ramp, down to the burning car.

She wanted to call her back, but it was too late. All she could do was follow her, out of the pickup, across the bridge, down the ramp. And Bett could run, too, but she usually ran for pleasure. She'd never run to a fire before, or paced anyone with Maggie's long-legged gait. She didn't expect to catch her. She didn't know what to expect. And she didn't know what either of them could do. The fire seemed even bigger now than it had from the truck cab. Flames shot skyward, alternating with billows of black smoke. She saw Maggie, almost at the foot of the ramp, still running hard.

Time seemed to have stopped with the traffic flow. Bett saw everything clearly, singularly. A truck driver on the other side of the freeway climbed down from his cab, carrying a fire extinguisher. He jumped into the opposite lane, where oncoming traffic was stopped by a thin line of fire coursing from the wreck, threading its way across the road.

Heat waves from the blaze distorted the traffic beyond the burning car. The slow-motion effect was enhanced by the strange lighting. It was just past dusk, and headlights from the stopped cars barely permeated the dense black smoke. And when the air cleared, the light spun and danced through the heat.

Bett could just see Maggie on the dark side of the road. The light flickered over her in a strobe effect as she unfurled a blanket. It whipped in the fire wind like a banner. You can't smother it, Bett thought. No blanket can put out a fire that size! Then she saw Maggie move even closer to the car, bending out of sight. Bett wanted to warn her, but the words caught in her throat as Maggie straightened up, holding a sheath of flame.

Then Bett knew why she'd run so fast. They'd given a ride to a guy carrying gas back to his car. Maggie knew him. Knew something must have happened to him, not just to his car!

The fire towered over Maggie, diminishing only when the blanket fell into place around the young man's body. Bett saw her wrap an arm around his waist and cradle his head, carrying him instead of dragging him. Maggie stepped back, feeling for the edge of the road, struggling for balance with the awkward load. One corner of the blanket protected her face from the flames, but it fell away as she looked down. Then a second explosion *ka-phoomed* at her feet. The sound and the light struck simultaneously this time. Maggie stumbled in a tight circle and began falling back, into the flames.

Bett never broke stride. Never even faltered. Using the momentum of her run, she threw a bone-jarring tackle that cost Maggie her grip on the blanketed figure and tumbled the two women far beyond the burning car. They were separated as they rolled along the edge of the freeway. Even from yards away, Bett knew that Maggie was unconscious by the way she lay prone and unmoving.

As Bett scrambled to her side, she sensed two strong odors: the bitter smell of singed hair and the nauseating stench of burned flesh. Without thinking, she turned Maggie over. Her long sleeves had protected her arms from the fierce flames, but heat simply poured off her hands. Bett gasped at the burn streaks. The left hand looked worse than the right, but both were marked by patches of seared and blackened skin.

She remembered Maggie's hands as they had rested on the bar the night they'd met. Strong, capable hands. No jewelry dressed them. Tendons grooved the backs, where blue veins crossed like rivers on a map. The map was obliterated now. Even in this light, Bett could see blisters forming.

Questions filled her mind. There were new categories within major burn degrees now, and she tried to remember the symptoms for each. Third degree meant muscle involvement. Or was it bone protrusion? Oh, god! She fought hysteria.

"Novice doctors always assume the worst," her father had stressed to her. "They hope to avoid surprises that way. You must bring your knowledge to the moment. Not your fear!" The memory of her father's drill calmed Bett. She continued her examination more coolly and crossed Maggie's hands over her chest, shifting her to lie flat on her back. That was when Bett saw the right side of her face. It was a bloody mess.

Bett realized that she'd neglected even basic first-aid procedures. She felt the carotid artery for Maggie's pulse. It was steady, if somewhat rapid. Bett knew then that she'd have to stop thinking of Maggie in personal terms, or she'd never be able to treat her.

Pulling a handful of tissues from her jacket pocket, she cleaned the cheek. The source of the bleeding was a cut on the right eye: a jagged, irregular slice that crossed the lid vertically. Bett was puzzling over what could have caused that kind of wound when a hand grabbed her wrist.

"Hey! That smarts!"

Maggie was conscious again. Bett breathed a sigh of relief, then felt her trying to sit up. Bett pressed her down. "No. Lie still now. Are you cold? Do you hurt anywhere?" Keeping her voice calm in unconscious imitation of her father's, she mentally listed things to check for: shock, broken bones, blood loss, pupil dilation.

Maggie reached for her eye. Bett caught her before she could touch it.

"Youch!"

"I'm so glad you can feel that!" Bett knew that severe burns left little nerve sensation in the affected area. "It means you aren't hurt too badly."

Maggie's good eye narrowed. "For somebody who used to study medicine, you've got mighty funny ideas of good and bad hurt!"

Bett smiled thinly as she squared a tissue. They didn't know each other very well yet, but she recognized that soft drawl and was pleased Maggie remembered some of what they'd talked about when they first met two weeks earlier. She put the makeshift pad over the damaged eye.

"Hold that in place there. Don't rub, though. Your eye is cut, and I want you to keep it covered while I make sure you're all in one piece."

She checked Maggie's head first, running her fingers through her short red hair and watching her face for signs of pain. Maggie didn't show any discomfort, but her gaze grew unfocused. Bett wondered if what had cut her lid might have also caused a concussion. Her collarbone was intact. Her ribs were fine, too. Then Maggie startled her.

"Bett! Something's wrong!"

"What? Where does it hurt?"

"No, I mean something else is wrong. I have to do something, but I can't remember what." Maggie's eye clouded with confusion. "What happened?"

Bett took off her own jacket to cover Maggie. "Do you remember the explosion?" At Maggie's negative murmur, Bett added "mild concussion, partial amnesia" to the list of injuries to give the paramedics. And where were they, anyhow?

She looked around. The truck driver was foaming the back of the car with his fire extinguisher. It seemed like hours, but only minutes had passed since the explosion. Maggie had been unconscious only briefly.

Suddenly, sirens sounded from every direction. Bett saw a squad car cross the overpass and started to relay that news to Maggie, but the cacophony of engines and horns was compounded by the thunderous clapping of a helicopter. There was too much noise to shout over. And Maggie's eye had closed.

thing she expected from a cop, especially a female cop, was to be laughed at. This one had done it twice in the space of a minute.

"Address?" She acted as if Bett hadn't said anything.

"Don't you want me to spell 'Holman' for you?"

"Nope. Took a stab at that myself. Where do you live?"

Bett recited her school address. "But that's only good until June. Do you want my address after that?"

The woman gave Bett a long look. "Nice to have so much advance notice, huh?"

Bett wondered what the hell that was supposed to mean, and whether all police-women were so enigmatic and rude.

"Age?" Tebert was looking down at her notebook again.

"Twenty-two," Bett said promptly. Then added, "Almost."

That produced another sidelong glance. "Ah, would that be 'twenty-one-going-on-twenty-two'?"

Bett nodded sheepishly.

Suddenly the driver's door was yanked open from outside. "Ebert!"

"Yes, sir!" She stepped out with alacrity.

Traffic noise kept Bett from hearing more. She turned to look through the steel mesh screen of the squad car. The medics were putting Maggie on a gurney. One of them held up an IV bag while the other strapped her in place. A white splash of gauze was visible, a flag against her red hair.

As she watched, Bett's thoughts took her to the Oakland bar where she and Maggie had first met two weeks before. A campus flyer had announced the premier of an *All-Womyn Jazz Trio* at the Fox Borough. Her best friend Elise had gone home that weekend, so Bett hitched a ride with some women she'd met in a women's studies course.

They made it clear on the ride over that "The Hole," as they called it, was not where they hung out in the East Bay. "No class at all," they said. "Real diesel dykes and old closet fems hang out there. It's a trip back to the sixties."

"The fifties!" someone shouted. And they all laughed.

Bett wasn't going for the ambience, though. She was going because Ellen, her therapist, had suggested it. In their last session, Ellen asked how Bett's classes compared to the pre-med studies she'd recently quit.

"There's more to life than school!" Bett side-stepped the real question.

Ellen hadn't seemed to notice. "I agree. When was the last time you went out? Maybe you should try that instead of studying so much."

Bett had taken Ellen's advice. And on the ride to the Fox Borough, she began thinking of the Friday night jaunt as a kind of therapy. She laughed with the other women about the bar's regulars. It seemed harmless enough, until they got to the door. There a round-shouldered woman with pockmarked cheeks growled "ID!" at them as a group. When Bett showed her student card, the woman snorted. "Now listen! You snoots cause any trouble here, and I'll run you out personally. Got it?"

midnight. Her name was Maggie McIntyre, and she had been six-foot-four since she was fourteen years old. She hadn't measured herself since then. Other people had, she told Bett, but they were kind enough to only write their findings in medical journals.

Bett found her self-deprecating humor hard to take at first and kept expecting a bitter punch line. But that wasn't Maggie's way. That night she was simply attentive, funny, and later, wonderfully passionate throughout their lovemaking. Bett's only disappointment was that she hadn't stayed the night.

Maggie explained as she dressed to go that she had to work the next day. "Mornings after can be a little awkward, and I do my best awkward on the dance floor," she added in her now-familiar drawl, "not at breakfast."

As she heard Maggie drive away that night, Bett realized sleepily that she hadn't gotten her phone number. That didn't worry her then. Maggie had her number and, of course, knew where she lived.

Bett had fallen in love that night. She knew it was love, not just because of the warmth she woke up with the next morning, but because of the glow of joy that stayed with her all through the following days. Even when a week went by without word from Maggie, and her euphoria faded, her anticipation never dimmed.

Now, sitting in a squad car two weeks later, Bett realized just how little she knew about Maggie. Nothing at all about her past, and damn little about her present. Oh, they had talked plenty, but it was all about Bett—her family, her studies; all about leaving pre-med. She reviewed their conversations, knowing she must have asked dozens of questions. A memory surfaced: Maggie had said she was from Back East. Everybody said that. Bett hadn't given it a thought. It was just an expression people used if they weren't native-born Californians. Practically everybody she'd met since high school said they were from Back East.

That thought set off a ticking sound in her head, and she knew she hadn't remembered correctly. Usually that internal noise only came to her during an exam. It meant an error somewhere—a math mistake, or a wrong date, or something misheard.

She reviewed her thoughts. Back East was the trigger. But surely Maggie had said… The ticking grew more frantic. No. She'd said where she was from, and I said, "Oh, Back East." Bett relaxed as the rest of their conversation came to her. Maggie said she was from Michigan. The tick was less frantic, but still present. Bett thought about her occasional drawl. Missouri, maybe? She knew it was an *M* state because she had associated her name with it. Maggie McIntyre from M. Bett was relieved to have narrowed it down, until she began listing all the M states.

Maybe it was Maine? No, she only knew that accent from TV. She was sure she'd never met anyone from Maine. Maybe nobody lives there.

But that thought caused a chittering noise in her head. It was distinct from the ticking and meant a lapse in logic. It made her think of little field mice sitting on a fence rail in the back of her head, laughing and nudging each other: "Even mice know better than that!"

A full minute elapsed before Bett noticed that her question remained unanswered. She didn't mind, so long as she could look into those wonderful eyes. Even as she watched, the gray brightened, and a smile crept into the fine lines gathered there.

"Some say timing's the most important part," Maggie drawled.

Bett read her slow smile and returned it, equally slowly. "Even on cars?"

"Cars…?" Her eyes changed again as a bemused furrow knit her brows.

Bett wanted to erase the confusion in her face, then realized she was the one being teased. Her own smile broadened. "No, I guess I wasn't talking about cars." She would have pursued that opening, but the bartender returned, and *she* wanted to talk about cars.

"Did you give him hell for treating it like that?"

It seemed to Bett that Maggie turned from her reluctantly.

"Now, how could I do that to a guy with girlfriend trouble?"

"What kind of girlfriend trouble?"

Maggie sipped her drink. "Seems she's got a hearing problem."

Bett's medical interests were piqued even as Maggie's eyes lit up again.

"You mean she never heard all that racket?" asked the bartender.

"Oh, he says she heard it. But she didn't want him to think she'd caused it, so she turned the radio way up. That way neither of them could hear it!"

The bartender slapped a towel on the bar, laughing with her. Then she was called away again.

"That's not a true story, is it?" asked Bett.

"Sure."

"That's really sad."

"No sadder than him deciding to sell it instead of getting it fixed. But that's 'poor-man thinking' for you."

"Poor man? Doesn't it cost more to buy a new car than to get one fixed?"

"Yup. But you can't tell some people that. Not folks who've been ripped off all their lives. They only know how to buy on credit. Most garages don't work that way, so they junk what doesn't work and go back to the finance office." She smiled. "But you don't want to keep on talking about poor people and bad timing, do you?"

Bett shook her head, then declined Maggie's offer of a cigarette and sent the pack she'd bought to her table with the waitress, avoiding her original party and spending the rest of the evening at the end of the bar with Maggie. By 10:30 the jazz trio still hadn't shown up, and the women Bett had come with created a scene complaining about that. When they finally got up to leave, Maggie nodded toward them.

"Is that the last train to Berkeley, or do you accept rides from strangers?"

Bett looked around. "Do you see any strangers applying for the job?"

"Only me, ma'am." Maggie bowed slightly. "I can be stranger yet, but I don't like doing it in a crowd."

They laughed a lot that night. Laughed and talked and drank together until after

All right, people do live in Maine, she thought. Just because I haven't met them doesn't mean they don't live there. Maybe they never *leave* Maine. All was quiet inside her head now. She thought that was a far-fetched conclusion, but she wasn't about to reawaken the mice.

Then the driver's door opened again. It wasn't Tebert who got in, but a burly policeman.

"What happened to Tebert?" she asked.

"Who?"

"The other cop. Hey, aren't women supposed to question women?"

He gave her a look as he put his hat on the dashboard. "You must mean Ebert. She's going to ride with Maggie." He hadn't seemed to hear Bett's implied criticism, but then asked, "Are you a hostile witness?"

Bett thought Tebert had said some funny things. Maybe all cops did. She'd have to ask her friend Elise. Cops were her hobby. "No. Why?"

He thumbed through a notebook. "Policewomen usually interview hostile witnesses, juvenile delinquents, mass murderers, and idiots. Theory has it... Well, never mind that. You expected her, so I just guessed your category."

He said all that solemnly, leaving Bett with her mouth half open. She recovered quickly, though.

"Which category does Maggie fit?"

He chuckled and stuck out his hand. "Guess we're both friends of Maggie. I'm Brian Kessler."

Bett shook his hand warmly. "How do you know her?"

"Hmm?" He was turning pages again. Finally he patted a shirt pocket, pulled out a slip of paper, and read it silently. "I'll tell you about that another time." Then he tucked the slip back in his pocket. "Now, why don't you tell me what happened tonight?"

CHAPTER 2.

Put Away

MAGGIE FADED IN AND OUT of consciousness without knowing it. She just felt distant from all the confusion. No one event stood out as particularly odd. Everything had its own moment and then vanished entirely from memory, like a dream that went on and on, as dreams do.

Tracy Ebert appeared in the dream. Maggie hadn't seen her in a long time. She wanted to talk to her, but then a stranger began asking questions. She answered lucidly: "It's Friday. This is Oakland, or maybe Emeryville?" She tried to check on that, but strong arms prevented her from even raising her head. A sense of urgency, coupled with a feeling of wrongness, welled up in her. Before she could react to that, she had to tell the interviewer her name and where she lived. She didn't mind such simple questions, but wasn't she supposed to be doing something else?

"No, nothing hurts," she said. "Ouch! That does!" Another memory came to her. She'd said that before when someone touched her hands. Why would her hands hurt?

"My eye? No, it doesn't hurt. Just itches." She wanted to rub it, but she was stopped again. And her head felt funny. It didn't really ache, it just felt fuzzy. A sudden light made her close her other eye. Then a sudden pain in her arm surprised her, but the pain disappeared quickly, replaced by a sense of motion.

"Maggie, can you hear me?"

She recognized the voice, but she was sleepy and tired of questions. The feeling of something being out of sync returned. A memory darted by, vanishing in the daze. She turned to follow the thought, but it was gone. She rolled her head back to center, and sounds cleared. Words emerged from a distant murmur. Tracy Ebert's voice came through to her.

"Are you awake?"

Maggie's mouth was dry. She licked her lips, then thought to nod.

"Here," another voice said, "this might help."

She felt the inside of her cheeks and lips being swabbed with a cool, minty substance that drew saliva. She swallowed and cleared her throat. It felt raw, and she wondered why. She looked up, squinting in the strong overhead light until Ebert leaned over her, blocking the brightness. She relaxed then, knowing Tracy would take care of things.

Her eye itched. She tried to reach it but couldn't move her hands. Raising her head, she saw she was strapped in and took a horrified breath. Tracy came into view again.

"Get me out!" Maggie rasped.

Ebert touched her shoulder gently. "Take it easy. Do you remember what happened?"

Maggie shook her head and lay back. Then the nameless fear returned. She looked around more deliberately. "Where's Bett?"

"She's talking with Kessler. What else do you remember?"

"Is she okay?"

"She's fine," Ebert said brusquely. "Do you want to talk now?"

"Something's wrong!" Maggie closed her eye. "That's all I know."

Tracy brushed her cheek. "Don't worry about it. Just rest now, okay?"

Maggie nodded. Rest sounded like a good idea. She'd worry about her eye later. She'd remember what she was supposed to be doing then, too.

❖ ❖ ❖

Sergeant Kessler reiterated Bett's statement. "So you and Maggie left the M & M yard about 6:30 and started cruising the freeway, right?"

Bett was dismayed by his brief summary. "This is all so foreign. Maggie and I just met a couple weeks ago. I don't know much about cars, or why we were looking for broken ones." She spread her hands. "I just thought I should tell you everything, in case it was a clue."

His expression softened. "You're doing fine. I know Maggie, and your details fit what she'd be doing here."

Bett was encouraged by his mild praise.

"So then what happened?" he prompted.

"Maggie saw this car," Bett pointed at the smoking wreck, "and pulled up behind it. Nobody was around, but she went and looked it over, then came back, saying she thought she knew whose it was. We drove up the ramp, and a couple of blocks further, she honked her horn and said, 'That's him!' Then she hollered at this guy across the street and offered him a lift."

"Did she call him by name?"

"Yes, but I can't remember it." Bett knew that was going to be important, especially if Maggie didn't remember anything. But knowing that didn't help. She still couldn't get the name right in her head.

"Can you describe him?"

"Sure. He was young, my age or a couple years older. About five-ten or so. Real skinny. His hair was what I remember best. It was pure white. I've never seen hair that color before."

Kessler looked at her sharply. "You mean blond?"

13

"No. Well, I suppose you might say that if you'd never seen really white hair like his."

Kessler made a note. "What happened next?"

"He was carrying a gallon milk jug, but it was yellowish, sort of amber-colored. And opaque, so I couldn't really see what was in it, but I could smell gas."

"You're sure?"

Bett shrugged. "Maggie had him put the jug in the back of the truck, and when he got in she said, 'You're just supposed to buy gas, not swim in it!' I was glad they weren't smoking. And he was mad about the whole thing. Said the station charged a buck for the gas and five more for the jug. He called it a racket, making you pay a big deposit so you'll bring back the jug and then end up buying the rest of your gas there, too. Maggie said they were probably laughing all the way to the bank."

"Did Maggie introduce you?"

"No. And that's kind of strange, too."

"Why?"

"Well, she was real formal about introducing herself when we met. She said 'How do you do' and told me her whole name."

He smiled. "Sounds like Maggie."

Bett thought it was all right to pursue a tangent now. "Have you known her long?"

"Since the first day she hit town." His grin flashed again. "What else did they talk about?"

Bett tried to remember the details of their ride back down the hill, but she hadn't paid much attention to their conversation. "She asked how things were going, and he said something about being on the road again. He'd crossed the border for the last time, and California income tax was going to set him free."

"Income tax?" he repeated.

"Well, it sounded like that," she hedged, "but it might've been something else." She shrugged. "You know, I never believed that thing about having one sense work so well it blocks all your other senses, but I guess it's true." Bett saw his curious look. "I have real good eyesight. Apparently I don't hear very well because of it."

Kessler grunted. "Sounds pretty weird to me."

"It's true. A group did research on disabled people. That was one of their findings."

"So how do you know about it? You look pretty able-bodied to me."

The light in his eyes contrasted with his serious expression. She smiled. "I am. But I read medical journals. I used to, anyhow. My dad's a doctor."

Kessler nodded. "Did this guy say what border he'd crossed?"

"No, but I think he meant Nevada, not Mexico. Maggie asked if he'd been playing with loaded dice again. He just laughed and said he'd tell her all about it later. Then they got out and went to the back of the truck for a minute. She came back, and I saw him in the truck's headlights. For the last time," she added quietly.

Bonnie didn't answer that. Instead she asked: "What shop?"

"A garage. We do basic engine repair and tune-ups, but one of the guys used to work in tool-and-die, so we subcontract some work. Reboring cylinders and stuff."

"You lost me already. All I know about cars is 'turn the key, honk the horn, and go!'"

"Most of my customers are like that. The hard part is getting people to trust our work. Almost everybody's been burned pretty bad somewhere…" Maggie was shocked by her tactless choice of words. But Bonnie's dark eyes were crinkled with laughter.

"Look at how much we have in common! Lie back now. I'm going to debride your hands."

"What's that mean? And how can I see what you're doing if I'm lying down?"

"Curious, are you?"

Maggie shrugged. "I just think I'll be able to deal with whatever you do if I can see what's going on."

"Debriding can be quite painful," Bonnie cautioned. "If you can't see what I'm doing, you won't jerk away at a critical moment."

"So tell me what you're going to do. Then it won't bother me. I'm the strong, silent type, remember? No-jerk model!"

Bonnie smiled. "The body responds to pain with nausea or dizziness. If I let you watch, you have to tell me if you feel any of that. Agreed?"

At Maggie's nod, Bonnie explained that the burn area was restricted to a flash-fire effect on the backs of her hands. "The fact that you can feel the burns means you're a lot better off than victims who don't feel any pain at all. They're the ones we have to worry about the most." Bonnie looked at the chart again. "It says here you were given a painkiller, but only a mild one because of your head injury. That can make you woozy." She smiled. "A technical term I learned from my patients. Are you feeling anything like that now?"

Maggie took a moment before answering. "Huh-uh."

"How's your head feel?" she asked more directly.

"Thick. Like I'm off balance." At Bonnie's look, she quickly added: "Because I can only see out of one eye. Can we take this bandage off?"

"Not yet. Your eyelid's cut, and you're going to have a real shiner in a day or so. It's best if you don't use it until the trauma subsides. Just leave it alone. The ER doctor will tell you when it's okay to use it again."

Maggie nodded, but she was distracted by Bonnie's remark. Someone else had said "Your eyelid is cut." A sweeter voice. Memory drifted on the edge of the blankness in her mind. Then it was gone.

"Close your eye now," Bonnie directed. "Tell me if you feel dizzy."

Maggie didn't sense any change in balance. She heard the click of a lamp switch and fought the instinct to move her hands from the heat it cast. When she opened her eye, Bonnie was moving the lamp back.

"Sorry. I should've warned you: Even a slight change in temperature will register on your wounds." She picked up one of Maggie's hands. "Debriding is how we get rid of dead skin, like this blister. Eventually it would slough off by itself, but that could take weeks. See where it's burned over your knuckles here? Dead skin isn't flexible like living tissue. We remove it so it won't act like shrink-wrap on your joints."

"I was always taught to leave blisters alone. Did they change the rules?"

"No, that's still true for small blisters, ones that haven't broken. New skin would grow underneath here, just like when you get a blister on your foot, but your hands are burned too badly. We have to clean the new skin to ward off infection. That's the biggest danger with burns like these."

Maggie watched her take a pair of delicate scissors and a tweezer-like instrument to pick up the loose, blistered skin. The first cuts exposed the extent of the burn damage, and Bonnie's actions grew much finer as she reached the edge of the burn. The debrided surface glistened in the light, looking raw. Maggie asked if the fluid there was a bad sign.

"No. That's actually good news. It means your system is functioning; trying to heal itself by sending extra liquid to the wounds."

Bonnie checked her IV, which was empty, and removed the bag but left the needle in. "You might get another IV tonight," she explained, clipping the tube and capping the short end. "No sense getting stabbed twice. But whether you get a second IV or not, be sure to drink lots of water and juice over the next few days. Gatorade is best if you can stand the taste. It's got potassium, and you need that to replace the fluids and get your electrolytes back up. Hand burns, especially on the backs, need special care. Tendons are close to the surface, so any excess heat can damage them. I'll show you some hand stretches you can use, too."

She straightened from her task, allowing Maggie a brief rest before starting on her other hand. "How do you feel? How's the pain?"

"Not too bad."

"You're holding up very well. Are you left-handed?"

"No. Why?"

"Just a guess. The more-used appendage usually suffers the greater injury." She glanced at the chart again. "No clue here, either."

"Does it say what happened?"

"No. We only get details, if we get them at all, during patient follow-up. Or from the police or paramedics. All it says here is 'gasoline fire.'"

"You mean it wasn't an accident? Jeez, why can't I remember?"

"Don't worry about that now," Bonnie said. "When we finish here, you can ask the police that. One of them is waiting to talk to you."

Maggie nodded. Mention of the police brought a memory fragment. Ebert in uniform, hovering over her. It was like a dream, but not a dream. She held the fragment in her mind, trying to find other memories that fit around it. Sudden pain made her suck in her breath sharply.

"Are you all right?"

"Yeah." Maggie wet her lips. An odd, minty taste brought her another memory: the ambulance ride. She remembered asking, "Is she okay?" An image of Bett surfaced. It was Bett who had said: "Your eyelid is cut."

Pain brought her back to the present. She concentrated on keeping her hand still as Bonnie trimmed burned skin close to healthy, live tissue. Hot and cold rushes of pain jolted through her, and she felt her strength draining, along with the final effects of the drugs. At last, the trimming was finished. She kept her eye closed, letting the pain subside.

Bonnie applied a balm to the burns, and Maggie spread her fingers, anticipating a stinging sensation. But the salve itself was painless; the sharp tingle came from a new level of sensitivity. When she opened her eye, she saw Bonnie watching her closely. Her eyes were an even deeper brown now. Empathy showed in tiny lines at their corners.

"I'm fine," Maggie replied to the unspoken question. "Can I get up now?"

Bonnie shook her head and wiped Maggie's face with a damp paper towel scented with lemon or some kind of spring flower. "We have to wrap your hands first. Hospitals are full of germs, you know."

New skin needed to breathe to heal, Bonnie explained. The salve she applied would keep it free of bacteria, and the first layer of gauze covering the debrided area would be easy to remove for more cleaning later. She wrapped each finger of the left hand separately before binding them all together with a final layer of densely woven gauze.

Maggie had almost no finger movement in her left hand, but she knew it wouldn't help to complain. And she was relieved when only the back of her right hand needed bandaging; those fingers weren't burned at all.

"Ready to try your legs now?" Bonnie asked.

Maggie swung them over the side of the table in reply.

"Wait, now. Just sit for a minute. We'll do this in stages."

She recognized Bonnie's wisdom as a buzzing noise filled one ear.

Bonnie moved to stand in front of her. "Put your hands on my shoulders and slide toward me when you're ready. It won't be much of a drop with legs as long as yours."

She slipped off the table. Despite the discomfort of Bonnie's touch on her hips, Maggie leaned on her briefly before shifting her stance.

"In stages," Bonnie cautioned before letting her move forward.

Maggie's first steps were hesitant, but she quickly gained confidence, lengthening her stride around the room. Suddenly her ankle turned on her, and she hobbled briefly, protecting the weakened foot. Bonnie grabbed her to keep her from accidentally swinging her hands into something solid.

"I'm all right. Please let go."

Bonnie released her but stayed within easy reach.

Maggie rotated her injured foot. "That surprised me. I don't remember twisting it, but that's what it feels like. You'd think something like that would come back to me."

Bonnie nodded encouragement. "Having one eye covered might take some getting used to."

Maggie tested her ankle before putting her full weight on it again. She stepped forward slowly, checking her balance and testing her vision. She needed sight to make her escape and found she could compensate for her visual limitations by keeping her head turned slightly to the right. It slowed her standard pace, but by the time she'd circled the perimeter of the room in both directions, she didn't have to study each step. She stopped a few feet short of Bonnie.

"So long as nobody asks me to chew gum, I should be okay." She started to slip her hands into her back pockets, a natural gesture.

Bonnie shook her head. "You're just well enough to get into trouble!" Then she nodded at a wheelchair. "Time to take you to ER for your eye."

"I'd rather walk," Maggie suggested hopefully.

"Hospital rules," Bonnie countered.

"Okay. But can I stop in the bathroom first?"

Bonnie pointed to the far end of the room. Maggie had seen the restroom on her walk around the room, but it was the door next to it that she really wanted. Marked "Authorized Personnel Only," it had a vertical window, paper-covered from the other side.

She entered the bathroom, flipped on the fan/light switch and pulled the door to, but not all the way. Through the narrow opening, she watched Bonnie go to the phone at the other end of the room. As soon as she picked up the receiver, Maggie left the bathroom, silently shut that door, and entered the next room undetected.

Experience served her well. "Authorized Personnel" enjoyed a lounge/kitchenette in their off hours. The room was empty now. Maggie had counted on that. More important, the lounge had an exit to the hallway. Signs indicated the way to ER or the Burn Unit. Nothing pointed to an exit, but she set off, following the ER arrow. Voices around the next corner stopped her, and she backed up a few steps to a door marked "Laboratory" and tested the knob. It turned, and she ducked inside. But the sign was missing a directional arrow. Maggie found herself in a stairwell. She hurried down the steps toward the glowing red EXIT sign below.

❖ ❖ ❖

At the squad car, Brian Kessler waited for a reply to his radio request. When it came through, he went in search of his only available witness to the events that led up to the inferno. He was surprised to find Bett at the top of the ramp instead of at Maggie's truck. She seemed to be studying the corner of the exit.

"What's up?" he asked.

"Oh, nothing, really."

"Might be a clue…?" he prodded.

Bett dismissed that. "It's no mystery."

He raised an eyebrow. "Oh? What caused the explosion then?"

"You're kidding!" she scoffed. "That's a Pinto, isn't it?"

"A Pinto?" Her reply baffled him.

"Yeah. Aren't Pintos the cars that are always blowing up?"

"Not as a matter of course." Brian stifled a smile. "And that happens to be an Impala. What did you lose up here?"

"Nothing. I just remembered seeing a pickup truck stopped here when I was chasing Maggie down the ramp."

"Why?"

"Why was I chasing her?"

He couldn't hide his smile this time. "No. I mean why did you notice that truck? Wasn't all the traffic stopped then?"

Bett turned to keep from revealing herself further. "Yeah. I just can't figure out why they stopped here. Two guys were looking out the back window. I only saw them for a second, and I'm sure this was where they were stopped, but the hill would've blocked their view of the freeway. They couldn't possibly see the fire from here."

Brian went over to verify her conclusion. The hill rose steeply at the corner of the ramp, and a shrub grew at an obstinate angle, making any view of the bottom of the ramp impossible, even from the cab of a pickup. "I see what you mean. What do you suppose they were doing?"

Bett shrugged. She didn't even know where they'd come from. They hadn't gone by her as she crossed the overpass. For all she knew, they'd just never seen women running before. "Can we go to the hospital now?"

"As soon as Hudson gets here to take Maggie's truck."

They walked over to the truck then, and Bett picked up a tool from the step on the driver's side. "Funny the things you notice," she mused. "I heard this hit the step when Maggie pulled the blanket from behind the seat. I didn't see her do it, and I would've said it was too noisy to hear yourself think, what with the explosion and horns and everything." She slipped the tool beneath the seat and got in, scooting across to the passenger seat.

Brian settled behind the wheel and took out a notebook. "What happened after the guy left?"

"Well, Maggie didn't seem to be in any hurry to go. I figured we were just waiting to see if he got started. The next thing I knew, it looked like World War III was starting. She ran down there but couldn't do anything. I couldn't, either. Not then."

"How did she get hurt?"

Bett took a breath. "The fire was huge. She covered him with a blanket and was trying to carry him away from the fire. The second explosion came out of nowhere."

"There were two?"

"Yeah. The second one wasn't as big, of course, but she was right there when it hit. I ran into her. Them. She was falling back into the fire. It was all I could do."

Just then a tow truck pulled up. "Here's Hudson," Brian announced.

Bett saw a sandy-haired man get out of the passenger side. "Like the butler in the old TV series?"

"More like the car." Brian nodded at the driver.

Bett followed Brian out of the truck. She'd been about to ask why Hudson brought a car to mind, but when she saw the short, thick-necked driver, she decided it had something to do with his build. Even climbing down from the cab seemed to cost him more energy than he could afford. Once on the ground, he hitched heavily belted pants over an enormous belly and spat on the pavement.

"Where is she?" he growled.

Kessler explained that Maggie had been taken to the hospital.

"What happened? Her truck looks all right."

Bett wondered what the connection was between Maggie's truck and her health.

"She went to help somebody down on the freeway."

"Again?" Hudson shook his head. "Serves her right then. She's always 'helping people out.' Never charges 'em a thing for it, either. I told her. Warned her. She didn't even quit it when that loco pulled a knife on her." Rubbing a thick finger up the side of his nose, he cleared a nostril and spit the accumulation over the railing, as if direct- ing it on those hapless people Maggie was always rescuing. "Soft heart, soft head," he concluded. "Hurt bad?"

"Nah," Brian said easily. "Banged her head. Got her hands singed."

Bett couldn't stand it any longer. "How dare you talk about Maggie like that, you son of a bitch! Who are you to spit on her? She was trying to help out some poor guy…" Bett took a breath. "She only tried to save a man's *life* and nearly got herself blown up in the process!"

Then she turned on Brian. "I thought you were her friend! What do you mean 'banged and singed' like some kind of pop-up toaster snack? She was practically standing in the fire when she pulled him…" Bett sobbed in outrage, then gasped for breath, but she couldn't stop crying. She turned from them, furious for Maggie, humiliated by her own tears. She stalked to the back of the truck and sat on the bumper to compose herself.

Moments later, Brian followed and silently offered her a handkerchief.

She took it with distaste. He had betrayed Maggie. Not that she needed defending from anyone, but she didn't need trashing from that jerk Hudson, or such offhand treatment from the police. She said as much to Brian. To her surprise, he agreed.

"Sometimes you have to let people talk, Bett. They say things they don't always mean, but if you listen between the words, you'll hear what they're really saying. And I *do* care about Maggie. She's one of my best friends."

Bett nodded acceptance.

"Good." His voice hardened then. "As for you, you have to learn to hold your tongue sometimes. Do you know who you were talking to back there?"

"I don't have to…"

"Yes, you do. Hudson's very important to Maggie. He's…"

"That bastard doesn't deserve to wipe her boots!" Brian's rebuke brought Bett's rage back with renewed force. "You heard him!"

"Not now," Brian said firmly.

Bett closed her mouth tightly, as if trapping unspent anger, then wiped her face and blew her nose. "I'll get this back to you." She stuffed the used handkerchief into her pocket. "Why don't you finish with Hudson, and I'll meet you…" She faltered, aware again that she had no place to go, that this was foreign ground.

"Down at the squad car," Brian suggested.

He joined her a few minutes later and stuck his head in the window. "I have to check on the victim's personal belongings. It'll just take a minute."

Bett remembered Maggie's blanket then and followed him to retrieve it. She heard Brian ask if they had found any identification on the victim.

"Nope," came the reply. "And bad as this guy's burned, his own mother wouldn't know him."

"I might recognize him." Brian unzipped the bag and turned out the flap.

Bett rounded the back of the Medical Examiner's car and stopped mid-stride, gasping in shock at the sight of the victim. The face was a featureless lump of coal. Only the gaping eye sockets gave it human definition. And the teeth grinned grue-somely where lips had been. Nothing remained of the white-haired pretty-boy she'd met so briefly, just minutes ago.

Brian led her back to the squad car. "I'm sorry," he said gently.

Bett spoke as if in a daze. "His name was Scotty. That's what Maggie called him." The shock of seeing the body so changed—so ruined—prompted the memory of Maggie calling out to him, so eagerly. So gladly. "None of this was real before. It was just… fireworks and loud noises." Then her eyes widened. "But he's *dead!*" The finality of those words shook her as much as the sight of the body had.

"Please take me to the hospital," she urged. "I've got to know that Maggie's all right!"

CHAPTER 3.

Where Do We Go from Here?

THE DOOR TO THE EMPLOYEES-ONLY entrance clicked shut behind Maggie as she surveyed her surroundings. The hospital was built on a hill, and she'd gone down a flight of stairs to exit. Since her gurney ride hadn't included any elevators, the Emergency Room—and the parking lot that adjoined it—had to be up the hill.

Her hands felt the exertion of the climb first. They stung with a prickling sensation until she got to the top, where they started to throb in earnest. She held them up instinctively, reducing the pressure. That pain eased but seemed to move to her eye, reminding her sharply of her visual limits. Slowing her pace, she continued along the hospital's dark wall.

As she turned the corner of the building, a lighted, nearly vacant parking lot came into view. Smiling, she crossed to the white-curbed border. A parking lot meant an entrance. And a hospital entrance meant taxis.

She stepped up on the curb to look for one, dislodging a small stone as she did. Sudden dizziness made her step back, just as the pebble rattled on the pavement. She stood a moment, adjusting her balance, then put her foot on the curb again, preparing to step over it and cross the lot. Some inner sense made her hesitate. There was something odd about that pebble. It didn't sound right. No. It took too long to make any sound at all.

She looked down and caught her breath. The curb wasn't a curb, but a retaining wall! The parking lot was five feet below. She'd nearly walked head-over-heels onto it. That shook her even more than her loss of memory. Other people could remember for her. They had before. And while the near-psychic sense of something being wrong made her uncomfortable, this meant not being safe, even on foot. What did it mean about driving?

She stared at the concrete, willing herself to see it as a wall edge, willing her one-eyed focus to be true. Then she moved back, taking stock of what she knew for sure. Everything would sort itself out as soon as she remembered what happened. She patted her pockets for cigarettes but came up empty. She did discover the IV needle, though. She removed it and wrapped the sharp end with the tape that had held it in place.

Then she set off along the wall's edge, trying to measure distance as she went. Her judgment seemed to improve with effort, but she didn't know if that was wishful thinking or reality. Then she came to a short set of steps leading to the parking lot and the Emergency Room entrance. She sat on the top step to plan her next move.

First things first. She'd come here to find transportation, but where did she really want to go? Closing her eye, she concentrated on bringing the blank past to consciousness. Parts of the ambulance ride came to her, but all she could fix on was Ebert and the voice of the medic. There was someone before that... Bett. Tracy had told her Bett was all right. Maggie touched on other bits of memory, trying to put events in order. The sound of a helicopter was mixed with Bett's voice, but no other short-term memories surfaced. It was as if her mind had a sharp corner she couldn't see around.

The great blank space was only so deep, though. The afternoon at the garage was clear: full of phone calls and scheduling next week's work. It had gone smoothly for a Friday. Jack was the last of the crew to leave. He picked up four customers from the BART station, and she'd sent him home to an early supper while she processed them. She remembered setting her watch on the desk before going to clean up. It was just past six o'clock.

Her hands were covered with cleaning goop when the yard bell sounded a weak bleat, barely a ring at all. That made her curious. A car usually crossed the cable twice, giving off two quick rings. But she hadn't heard the gravel-sorting noise that a car would make pulling into the yard. She crossed the office to the doorway and chuckled at the scene before her. A bike rider had rolled in and was jumping up and down on the black cord, trying to make it ring again.

Maggie entered the yard quietly and put the heel of her boot on the cable, balancing herself on that pivot point to ring the bell continuously. The failed bell-ringer turned, and Maggie nearly lost her balance.

"I found you!" Bett crowed.

"So you did." Maggie regained her composure, but it wasn't a quick recovery. Bett was just the way she remembered her: young, pert, and absolutely beautiful. Sparkling black eyes looked up at her through long, thick lashes. Her wavy hair was dark brown, not black, as Maggie had thought the night they met. Windblown from her bike ride, Bett's cheeks glowed a natural pink. If anything, she looked even younger than she had two weeks ago. The only lines in her face were in the curve of her smile.

"Was I lost?" Maggie kept her voice light, wondering where her stomach had gone. Even with several feet separating them, her sense of Bett was tactile. She turned her thoughts from the young woman's physical features with an effort.

Bett smiled. "Of course not! How come it rings when you stand on it, but not when I do?"

"You probably don't weigh enough." Maggie put Bett's weight at about 110.

"But it rang when I rode over it on my bike...?"

The bike was lying in the dirt, and Maggie scowled at its maltreatment.

"Why?" Bett insisted.

"Sharp rims," she said briefly. "You shouldn't leave it like that."

Bett shrugged but picked up her bike and rested it against the garage wall. "You're very hard to find," she went on. "Do you know how many M & M Mechanics there are in the phone book?"

"Did you call them all? Or just ride through and ring their bells?" Maggie smiled then, as delighted by Bett now as she had been that night at the Fox. She searched her association of names to keep from dwelling on anything else. Bett Jakes? No. Jake Holman. Bett Holman. No relation to the hero in the *Sand Pebbles*. She remembered how amazed Bett had been to learn that she'd read the book but hadn't seen the Steve McQueen movie. Maggie told her she didn't go to movies much, but Bett gave her such a strange look at that remark that she decided not to tell her it was one of the few books she'd ever read.

"I called almost all of them," Bett said as they walked to the office. "It was really weird. When I asked for you, nobody said, 'Maggie Who?' They just said, 'She's not here. Is she supposed to be?' or 'Is she on her way?'"

"What's so weird about that?"

"None of them seemed surprised. Like they all knew somebody named Maggie. The third or fourth guy I talked to said I'd find you here."

"But you didn't call here, did you?"

"Huh-uh!" Bett confirmed gaily. "I wanted to surprise you." She looked around the office quickly. "It's okay, isn't it? Nobody's here...?"

"Don't worry. Everyone's gone home. I even get to leave early tonight. Feel like going for a ride?"

"Sure."

Maggie went to the cubicle under the stairs to finish cleaning up. As she rinsed the goop off her hands, she realized just how consciously she had avoided thinking about Bett. Now she was here; had tracked her down for some reason. Well, maybe she just dropped by to say hello. No big deal. They could go for a ride. Have something to eat. Dinner would be okay. Maybe Bett just wanted to have a good time once in a while, the way she did. Just because their first night together had been so fantastic...

"Are you decent?"

Bett was peering around the corner, and Maggie felt herself blush. She quickly splashed water on her face, then toweled it roughly. "Uh, sure. You hungry? We could get something to eat later."

Bett continued to gaze at her from the doorway, a smile playing at the corners of her mouth. "Dinner, you mean?"

Her reply was so suggestive that Maggie knew she had to act before Bett added to it. As she steered her through the office, an electric charge seemed to pass between them. Bett turned incredibly soft eyes on her, with a look that spoke more than words ever could.

"I, um, have to lock up first. We'll take my truck, okay?"

The moment passed with Bett's nod, and Maggie sent her to the white pickup with her bike while she locked up the office and activated the bay doors. She found herself smiling, grinning really, as she went through her evening routine. It wasn't how she usually closed up shop. She flipped one last switch, cutting power on the revolving neon sign of double M's, then joined Bett at the truck. She pulled a tarp from under the sidewall-mounted Servis box.

Bett asked: "What's in these, anyway?"

"Old dreams and road dust." Maggie gave her standard reply, and they laughed together.

She remembered driving through the gate and getting out to roll the wheeled section closed, snapping the heavy-duty padlock on the chain to secure the yard. All that could have been just the memory of habit, but then she knew it was real: She'd glimpsed Bett in the side mirror and given her a thumbs-up.

Finally, memory failed her. No matter how hard she tried, she couldn't remember getting back into the truck. It shocked her all over again to come upon such a monstrous vacuum. Then she smiled at her exaggeration. We're talking hours here, she thought. It's not like before. Still, she had no idea what happened after that. For all she knew, her truck had blown up right in her own driveway. But Bett wasn't hurt. Only she was. Where had they gone from there? What *did* happen? The questions chased one another in her mind until she had to look away to stop them.

Just then a squad car pulled into the parking lot, lights flashing, siren off. As it drove out of sight to the other side of the entrance, Maggie wondered if her head injury had sent her around the bend. She could've sworn Bett was in the car.

Must be love. She scoffed softly, letting herself dwell a moment longer on the girl who had tripped her heart so unexpectedly. She smiled at the way her thoughts kept going back to Bett. But half the universe has short dark hair these days. It was just a cop, wearing a regulation jacket. The bulk of the shoulders and the patch on the sleeve told her that. She thought for sure that Bett had been wearing a gray corduroy jacket.

And besides, she told herself, it simply wouldn't work. Bett was rich, for one thing. Her father was a doctor. She was studying to be one, too. Or had been. It didn't matter. They were worlds apart. Much too different. Even as those thoughts came to mind, she knew they weren't the reasons she refused to think about her seriously. She liked Bett: too much, too soon. She had to be especially cautious when someone affected her like that. Not that she regretted their time together...

Maggie headed down the steps, knowing that movement would clear her mind. Maybe these cops could find Tracy, and she wouldn't have to risk reentering the hospital. At the bottom of the stairs, she heard the electric doors to Emergency open. She looked around the corner just as they closed. One of the cops had gone in, but the cop riding shotgun was still in the car.

She walked straight out into the lot, as if she'd just left the ER, then swung around to where the police car was parked. Using the heel of her hand to tap the passenger-side fender, she announced her approach: "Evening, officer!" Then she stopped dead and blinked.

Bett's look of mild surprise turned to the shock of recognition. She threw the door open and leapt out, wrapping her arms around Maggie and spinning the two of them in a circle until they landed, none too gently, against the side of the car.

"You're all right!" she said, over and over again. "I was so worried you were hurt worse than I thought. Are you okay?"

"Yes!" Maggie held her at arm's length. "But what are you doing here?" She tugged her jacket sleeve. "I thought you were the Oakland Police."

"What? Oh, this is Tebert's. I used mine to cover you..." Then she hugged Maggie again, repeating what she'd said five times already. "I can't believe you're all right! When did they release you? What did they say about your eye? Your hands?" With each question, Bett touched her bandages gently.

Even with those acting as buffers, Maggie's blood ran a little faster. She backed away. "Don't!"

Bett was startled. "Did I hurt you?"

"No," Maggie said quickly. "I meant, um, don't ask me so many questions all at once." She smiled then. "Who's Tebert?"

"That policewoman who rode to the hospital with you." Bett looked for the nametag on her jacket before remembering where she'd seen it. "The name on her shirt said Tebert. Brian went to find her. And you. Why didn't they come out with you?"

"You must mean Ebert. The T is her first-name initial. And if that's her jacket, check the pockets for cigarettes, will you? I feel like I haven't had one in days." She took the box Bett found in one of the slit pockets. "Brian went to get her? Brian Kessler? What's he doing here?"

Bett watched Maggie fumble to take out a cigarette and extract matches from the cellophane wrap. "Did they check your lungs and throat for burns? Is it all right for you to smoke so soon?"

Trying to light up without catching her bandages on fire, Maggie replied through tightened lips. "They looked up my nose, down my throat, and in my ears." She puffed ineffectively when the match went out. "Shoot! And they said if I could get somebody to light it for me, I could smoke."

Bett took the matches from her. "Huh! They probably said, 'Go find someone who'll do anything you ask.'" She struck a match awkwardly, and it nearly blew out, but Maggie shielded it, taking a deep drag when it caught.

"Let's go get Brian." Bett started for the entrance.

Maggie held her back. "You must not travel smoking class very often." She led her to a bench. "Let's just sit here for a minute."

"All right, but where have you been? Why are you here instead of in the ER?"

Maggie explained that she'd been in the Burn Unit. "Then," she evaded, "I checked myself out."

"What did they say about your eye?"

"Not much. The lid's cut. I have to keep it covered to let it recover from something."

"Trauma?" Bett guessed, checking the bandage. Before she had a chance to ask more, they were interrupted.

"So you're not lost after all! Half the hospital will be happy to hear that." Ebert's tone was simultaneously arch and sarcastic.

Maggie greeted her with a nod, "Tracy," and gave guarded responses to her questions.

"What's the last thing you remember?"

"Locking down the yard." Maggie turned to Bett. "About 6:15?"

"Nothing after that? Are you sure?" Without letting Maggie reply, she shook her head. "Never mind. I'll go get Sergeant Kessler. Don't either of you leave. Got it?" She could have been anyone in uniform saying that. Then she left.

Before Bett could react to Ebert's officiousness, Maggie said, "Can you tell me what happened? Was anybody else hurt? Was my truck wrecked?"

Bett told her story again. But Maggie didn't feel any stirring of memory. Bett could have been relating a news broadcast. None of it touched her. Not until the end.

"Then I remembered you calling his name: Scotty."

Maggie stared at her. "You don't mean Scotty Fenn?"

"I… We don't know."

"But where is he now? If it *was* Scotty, what hospital did they take him to?" She started to rise, as if to go there.

Bett stopped her, but in the end she was helpless to do anything except confirm Maggie's worst fears.

"He's not dead?" Maggie vehemently refused Bett's nod. "No! No, he can't be! Not Scotty!"

"I'm sorry," was all Bett could say.

Maggie shook her head. "I suppose they did all they could." She sat forward, elbows on knees, staring past her bandaged hands.

Kessler and Ebert returned then, and Bett explained that she'd told Maggie what had happened.

"Did she say it was Fenn?" Kessler asked.

"No, she doesn't remember anything herself. Only what I told her: that Scotty is who I think we picked up."

Kessler nodded and went to Maggie to try to console her, but he couldn't reach through her grief, either.

Ebert tapped Bett's shoulder and offered a corduroy jacket in trade. "That jacket's too big for you."

Bett made the exchange without comment, still focused on Maggie, who seemed even more drained. The two of them got into the backseat of the squad car.

"You should eat something," Bett suggested. "Do you want to stop on the way home? Or maybe go to my place?"

Maggie put a bandaged hand to her good eye, rubbing gently. Wearily. "Doubt if they'd let me in anywhere," she said wryly. "Did Hudson say where he was taking my truck?"

Bett sniffed. "He probably drove it off the Bay Bridge."

Kessler related the highlights of Bett's exchange with Hudson.

Maggie looked at her. "Told him off, did you?"

"He's a pissant," Bett declared.

Ebert snorted, evidently enjoying that description of Hudson. "You can't tell Maggie that. She hates to admit when she's wrong."

"Even more than you do?" Maggie retorted.

Kessler turned to the backseat. "One thing I don't get. When I called the Burn Unit, the woman up there told me..."

"Oh, no!" Maggie said quickly. "Don't get me started on hospitals and how they can lose everything but mice and roaches without even trying. I suppose X-ray said I was never there, too. And Emergency said something like, 'Yes, we have her entered here, but not formally admitted. We'll need some proof of insurance. Are you the financially responsible party?'" The acid edge in her voice wasn't entirely acted, but Maggie had to distract him, knowing he'd readmit her if he knew how she'd left. "Let's just get out of here. Can you take us to my truck?" She stabbed at her only certitude: that her truck was all right. From there the world would sort itself out again.

Kessler gave her a look, then told Ebert: "Natchez Place."

Ebert acknowledged his order with a nod, but Maggie caught her glance in the mirror and was sure Tracy had recognized her elaboration for what it really was—a cover-up. Maggie had learned that kind of angry B.S. approach from Ebert years ago. She turned to Brian then, relieved that he hadn't detected her dodge.

"Your truck's back at M & M," Brian was saying. "You're going home now. By the way, Hudson claimed the tow on the wreck. Some foul-up with City tows not being available."

"Leave it to Hudson to make a buck whenever he can," she said.

"Have you got an extra key for your place?" Kessler asked.

The question surprised Maggie, and she patted her pockets distractedly. "Now where did I leave..." The enormity of her memory loss struck home again. She waited for a familiar scene to play in her mind, probing further into the emptiness, drawn to the darkness like a child to a cave. But there weren't any handholds there. No means of penetrating the void.

Bett said gently, "You left them in your truck."

Maggie shook her head, then looked away. Finally she said, "I keep a spare hidden on the Buick. But you could take us to the garage, and I could get my truck. Hudson will bring the tow there, too."

"Huh-uh. Report from the hospital said—how'd they put it—'probable concussion'? What kind of cop would let somebody like that drive? Nope. You're going home. Bett said she'd stay with you tonight. And what do you care about the tow, anyway?"

"I might remember something if I see it. You need a statement, don't you?" Then she added firmly: "And I can take care of myself."

He laughed, not unkindly. "You're as bad as the rookies I teach on Wednesdays. Bett helped by telling us what she saw. We'll never use a lot of her details, of course, since she doesn't know what's wheat and what's chaff. But hell, you don't even know where the field is!"

Maggie only shook her head, dismayed by the accuracy of his analogy.

"You ought to get some rest," he continued. "Take a few days off and sleep in. Get away from M & M for a while and give your brain cells a chance to reconnect."

"We'll see." Maggie's tone didn't offer much promise.

He opened the back door to let them out. "Why don't you go up to the mountains for a few days? You can do paperwork up there if you have to."

"And what if it *was* Scotty? I could…" She only hesitated a moment, "identify the body for you."

Brian shot a glance in Bett's direction. "And just how long do you suppose I'd keep my job if I let you civvies do all my work? No, you can't try to ID the body. Not until you remember more about tonight." Then he added: "Listen, I don't want to raise your hopes, but there wasn't any identification on the victim. We don't know for sure who you and Bett picked up tonight. Or even if it was the same guy you threw that blanket over. From what Bett said, it could've been Scott Fenn, but for now the ME considers him a John Doe." He rested a hand on Maggie's shoulder. "Remember, I know him, too, and I couldn't tell if it was Fenn. We'll run some prints and let you know what we find out. Does that satisfy you?"

She didn't answer his question. "I know you don't like him, Brian. But he *has* straightened out. I know he has." She turned then. "I'll get that key."

❖ ❖ ❖

As Maggie walked to the back of the duplex, Bett asked him, "Someday you'll tell me how you know her so well, won't you?" She was genuinely glad to shake his hand again.

Brian smiled back at her. "Try to keep her quiet for a couple days. I think she's hurt worse than she says."

"Yeah, she seems really disoriented, too." Bett frowned. "I don't know how they could have released her in that condition."

"They didn't. She just walked out the door."

Bett was astonished. "Why didn't you bring her back?" Then she shook her head. "I just thought she'd had a run-in with somebody at the hospital. How did you know?"

"I just know Maggie."

"Giving away my secrets, Brian?"

Bett turned, answering for him. "No secrets. Just some insights."

Maggie didn't reply. Nodding good night to Brian and Ebert, she led Bett up to her apartment.

CHAPTER 4.

Time I Spent with You

Bett woke slowly Saturday morning, and it took her a moment to register whose bed she was in. She called to Maggie, but got no answer. The Big Ben alarm clock read 8:30, and when Bett searched the apartment, she found a ring of keys and a note on the kitchen table.

> *One of the guys is picking me up. Your bike is still in the back of my truck at the shop, but if you can drive a standard and need to get someplace, here are the keys for the Buick. See you later.*
>
> *Maggie*
>
> *P.S. The clutch is tight.*

Bett puzzled over the P.S., then decided the endearment was an odd one but much warmer than "Have a nice day." She found tea bags in the silverware drawer and brewed a cup, smiling about the meal they had shared last night.

When they came in, Maggie invited her to make herself comfortable, and Bett looked around briefly. The rooms were spacious, if few. Like her own studio, the living room was also the bedroom. But unlike her place, Maggie's apartment contained very little furniture. A bed, nightstand, chest of drawers, and overstuffed chair were the only real furnishings. A small wall-mounted bookcase held half a dozen paperbacks, and an ancient TV stood in the corner, but it looked too old to be functional.

Maggie stretched out on the bed, saying she needed a short rest. She kept her feet on the floor, and Bett went to help her lift them onto the bed.

"No shoes on the bedspread," Maggie protested.

Smiling at the familiar childhood maxim, Bett unlaced the heavy boots and tugged them off, then announced that she would fix them something to eat and went to explore the kitchen. She was back moments later.

"Do you know you have exactly four cans of beer and a pound of lard in the refrigerator?"

"Oh, yeah. I forgot to tell you. Help yourself."

"But that's all there is!"

"That's okay. I don't want any. You go ahead."

Bett couldn't believe how thoroughly Maggie had misunderstood her. She sat on the edge of the bed. "What were you going to eat for dinner tonight, Maggie?"

Maggie opened her good eye, and Bett read dismay in it.

"We were going out for dinner, weren't we?"

"Yes, but I didn't mean that. I just wondered what you were going to eat if you planned on eating at home."

"Oh. Well, usually I eat pizza on Fridays. Do you like real Italian food?"

"As opposed to *fake* Italian food?"

That brought a smile to Maggie's face. "I mean something besides pizza or spaghetti and meatballs."

"I like all kinds of Italian food, but you don't have any of the fixings!"

Maggie was still smiling. "No, I've got Guido's." She dialed a familiar number and ordered a small pizza for herself, then gave Bett the phone, saying: "Watch out! Guido's always trying to sell me on his specials."

The food was delivered piping hot thirty minutes later, and Bett brought the packages to the kitchen table. After sampling her special, a garlic tomato sauce served on spinach noodles, she insisted on sharing it.

"Is this good?" Maggie asked after a couple of bites.

"It's fabulous! Don't you think so?"

She shrugged. "Tastes okay. I just never ate green noodles before."

Bett had taken Maggie's lack of enthusiasm as a reflection of her physical condition. But in the morning light, she decided her indifference was from lack of food experience. A quick survey of the cabinets revealed as meager a supply of foodstuffs there as she'd found in the refrigerator. She'd never seen such empty cupboards. It made her angry to think that someone who worked so hard could be paid so little. No wonder Maggie was so thin.

It was Bett's first glimpse of poverty. And it wasn't just the lack of food that appalled her. There was no personality in the apartment, either. Unless neatness counted. Maggie was very neat. The rooms looked like they'd been recently cleaned, too. Still, the walls were bare, and there wasn't so much as a single plant, even in the kitchen where greenery would flourish.

Worse even than the apartment's bareness was its lack of music. There was only an old, plastic-cased AM radio on the windowsill. It worked, but the only stations Bett could tune in were country-western or talk shows. All in all, it was pretty depressing to be in Maggie's apartment without her.

But the sunroom effect in the kitchen was pleasant. One wall consisted entirely of sash windows. Two of them were open at the top, letting in the spring breeze. Bett looked around again, seeing where a plant stand would fit at one end of the windows, and how the space over the sink would be a great place to hang a rack of mugs. She shook off her dismay. There were dozens of little ways she could help Maggie make her place more livable.

Cheered by her plans, she checked the time. She would have to hurry to make her ten o'clock therapy session. Fortunately, Ellen held Saturday hours at home in Oakland rather than in her San Francisco office. Bett could bike there in no time.

Then she remembered where her bike was.

She picked up the keys from the table. She'd never driven anything bigger than a golf cart before, but that hadn't been hard. How different could driving a car be? She'd watched people drive all her life. And she wasn't going far. After her session with Ellen, she'd drive down to M & M and surprise Maggie for lunch.

But as it turned out, she didn't go anywhere in the car. As soon as she turned the key, the Buick sprang forward with a jerk. She turned it again and again, but the engine never caught, and she finally had to stop. Not only was she running out of time, but with each turn of the key, the car moved closer to the garage door. As a last resort, she looked for a gear indicator like the one in her father's car. Nothing resembled the P-R-N-D-2-1 she'd seen in other cars, though, and she finally gave up and set off on foot.

✧ ✧ ✧

Brian Kessler arrived at M & M just as mid-morning break was ending. Maggie was in her usual place, giving instructions to what seemed like a roomful of boys. There were only four, but their shrill voices competed so well with the whirr and scream of tools in the adjoining bay that Brian could barely hear himself think. Maggie never seemed to notice the noise. He waited at the door, thinking the sound might not bother her today, but it couldn't help how she felt, either.

Her skin was still far too pale. Mottled freckles, usually invisible in her weathered face, stood out. White lines, like painted brush strokes, accented her uncovered eye. And Brian could see her forehead discoloring. A yellow-purple bruise had formed above her injured eye, continuing below the patch. It looked like she'd been hit with some kind of pipe or crowbar. If it weren't for her grin, he wouldn't have recognized her.

She dismissed the kids, who spilled past him to race one another out the door. She waved Brian in. "Hey, guy!"

"Hey guy, yourself. Thought I'd stop by and see how you made it through the night. How're you feeling?"

"Not bad." She shrugged, dismissing his concern. "But it sure was tough getting up this morning."

Brian raised an eyebrow. "She *is* awful cute. What crib did you steal her from?"

He was surprised to see color rising in her face. They always teased each other this way, but she seemed more sensitive than usual.

He raised his hands in apology. "She seems like a nice kid."

Maggie nodded, then changed subjects. "I saw that car Hudson towed in. Some fire. Any word on identification?"

"Ran the plates. Vehicle owner is Scott John Fenn. But, no," he answered her real question, "nothing positive on the victim yet. Did you remember anything when you saw it?"

"Not so much as a ripple. Might've been any old wreck Tony or Phil brought in. Did you schedule a pickup for it? Or do we get to charge the city twice by delivering it, too?"

"Buck-monger," he muttered, making a note to himself.

"Why don't you take me over to where it happened? I might remember something there."

Brian couldn't see any harm in that, but as they headed for the car, he broached the subject he'd brought up last night. "Thought you were going to take some time off?"

"You did say something like that, didn't you?"

"Did you mention it to Bett?" He saw Maggie's warning look but went on anyway. "I just thought she'd be good company for a few days. She's had some medical training, and besides…"

"I've got eyes." Maggie cut him off before he could warm to the subject. She turned to look at him and had to walk sideways to do that. "Well, I've got one eye, anyway."

He didn't bother to hide his grin. "That ought to be enough."

"As for taking time off, let's just say I've got it under consideration."

❖ ❖ ❖

Bett was resting on a collection of gaily printed pillows in her favorite corner of Ellen's office. "I only missed one appointment. Didn't you get my message?"

Ellen nodded. "Yes, but a no-cause cancellation isn't like you. You aren't thinking of terminating therapy, are you?"

Bett shook her head. "No. I just thought I might have a date and wanted to be available." She told Ellen about meeting Maggie two weeks earlier, and then not hearing from her again. "Elise threw my cards for me, but they kept coming up the same: great joy and terrible danger. Weird, huh?"

Ellen smiled. "I thought you didn't believe in the tools of the Wicca?"

"Well, no, I don't. Elise was a big help in other ways, though. She borrowed a car, and we went back to the Fox Borough the next weekend. But Maggie wasn't there either night. I talked to the bartender and the bouncer, and they said she doesn't come in very often. Then Elise interviewed me like a witness on a cop show, and that's how I remembered the M & M emblem on Maggie's truck. We looked it up in the phonebook. Did I tell you she's a mechanic?"

"Do they list women mechanics in the yellow pages these days?"

Bett smiled back at her therapist. "Well, there were quite a few listings for M & M, and I called a bunch of them before somebody told me which one Maggie worked at. It was really strange."

Ellen chuckled. "I'm sure it was. Those poor guys are probably still wondering about your call." She shook her head in mock disapproval. "It's bad enough you're confounding all the studies again. Lesbians don't have one-night stands, you know."

"Are those the same studies that say we have penis envy and mother worship?" A change in Ellen's face made Bett add: "No, I don't want to talk about my mother. I'm fine. Really."

"Good." Ellen let the ensuing silence lengthen a moment. "So, did you call her? Or is the moral of this story all about one-night stands?"

Bett smiled. "It's not the moral of *this* story!" She told Ellen about last night's events, focusing more on Maggie's injuries than the fatality. Even so, the memory of seeing the victim in the body bag made her shudder. She saw Ellen register that and explained its cause, adding, "I could never work with dead bodies like that."

Ellen nodded. "You always hated the thought of pathology."

That comment surprised Bett, but before she could respond, Ellen continued.

"Despite the tragic aspect, it sounds like things are looking up. You've got a new lover, a renewed interest in medicine…"

"I quit that," Bett interjected.

"Okay, so you're just going to do private-duty nursing, not surgery. When will they discharge her?"

"Oh, that's another story!" Bett explained Brian's theory about Maggie just walking out on her own. "You have to know something about hospitals to be able to do that, but I didn't think to ask her about it. Last night she just needed taking care of."

She told Ellen about checking Maggie's eye when she said it itched. The gauze was stuck fast, and Bett had to soak it with a warm washcloth for a few minutes. As they waited for it to loosen, Bett talked about her mother, recalling all sorts of nursing lessons she had shared over the years.

When Bett removed the patch, she saw that the eyelid was lacerated and still swollen. The welt on Maggie's forehead and cheekbone indicated that those features had taken the brunt of the blow. Not knowing what to look for under the lid, Bett had just covered it again with clean gauze and tape.

Ellen agreed that caution was warranted, then said, "I don't usually give away anybody else's time, but maybe your dad could take a look at it?"

"Great idea!" Bett smiled with sudden self-awareness. "You know, it was so natural to talk about Mom the way I did last night. I guess it's easier to talk about both of my parents when I'm not just dealing with her death." She paused. "And maybe if my dad looks at Maggie's eye, she'll listen to what he says and then take Brian's advice to rest for a few days."

"Who's Brian? You mentioned him before."

"One of the cops I met last night. He's a friend of Maggie's and really terrific." She contrasted him with Ebert, who was, in Bett's opinion, giving gay women a bad name.

"How do you know she's gay?"

"She knew Maggie's name without me telling her. And I got the impression they might have some… connection."

"That's a little vague, coming from you. What do you mean?"

"I think they might've been lovers."

"Oh?"

"Well, maybe just friends. I'll have to ask her."

"You don't know Maggie very well, do you?"

"Not yet, but I will." Then Bett added in a rush: "I think I'm in love." She saw Ellen's gaze turn thoughtful. "You look like you're going to give me some therapy."

Ellen smiled. "Just some advice. Lovers haven't been your problem. You're pretty together, compared to some of my clients your age, but you never claimed to be in love before."

"It's wonderful," Bett said. "I recommend it."

"Then I'll just suggest that you take it slow. You have a perfect opportunity to get to know her outside the bedroom. If all my clients had that kind of breathing space at the beginning of a relationship, I wouldn't have to keep Saturday hours!"

❖ ❖ ❖

Brian kept an eye on Maggie as they drove to the freeway, wondering if he'd misjudged her condition. Maybe he should have readmitted her last night. What worried him wasn't just her weariness, but her silence as well. She was usually full of talk about M & M and how all the little billies were working out.

"Little billy" was what she called all of her new hires, but not because she couldn't remember their names. She never forgot the name of anybody who worked for her, no matter what garage they ended up in. The term was foreign to Brian, but he figured it was one that she'd picked up in another part of the country before she found her way to Oakland. He asked her about it, but she only said that they all had something in common with a kid she once knew back home. Brian couldn't see any common denominator. They were black, white, Chicano; he thought one might even be Hmong. And they were all different ages, from Hiram to Hudson.

Hiram, the youngest, had been a fourteen-year-old dropout when he started. Maggie found out, and she nearly fired him just to get him back in school. He promised to finish by going at night, but she wouldn't listen. Stony had finally intervened.

Stony Jaeger was one of her first managers. He reminded her that she'd promised to trust his judgment when she gave him that title. Brian never heard the whole story, just that Stony had resolved it: Hiram stayed on the payroll, earning his place there and his GED at night. He'd changed a lot in his time at M & M.

Hudson had changed, too. He was another kind of little billy entirely. Brian recalled the altercation between him and Bett last night and wondered if Maggie had explained things. Even if she hadn't, Bett would learn soon enough what a miserable being Hudson was. Or had been.

That was another thing Brian never figured out. All the little billies Maggie hired changed after they'd been on board a while. They all started out motley and bedraggled, then they became eager. Maybe it had something to do with working on cars. It was a fascination he didn't share. As he pulled up on the Bridge Works overpass, he realized his familiarity with the wreck and ruin side of cars probably warped his view of them. He parked where Maggie's truck had been the night before.

Maggie glanced at him curiously. "Here?"

He shook his head and led her down the ramp. Her face stayed blank until they got to the scarred shoulder of the road. There her expression changed to bewilderment.

"I see the evidence." She pointed at the burn residue and track marks left in the foliage by the emergency vehicles. "But nothing clicks in my head." She moved up the incline a few feet and reached into the low greenery to pick up a distorted bit of metal. It was bright red on one side, soot-covered on the other. She rubbed a finger over the surface and sniffed it.

"Gasoline. This must be part of a gas can." She smelled the black sheen on her fingers again, then said, "I still don't remember anything."

"You wouldn't with that," Brian replied. "Bett says the guy didn't have a gas can. Must just be a piece of roadside junk."

"I thought she said Sc... that the guy was out of gas?"

"He was. But he carried it in a milk jug."

"I don't believe it!"

"She was pretty descriptive about that part."

"A *plastic* milk jug? Nobody could be that dumb."

"Hey, it was a short line the day God gave out brains."

"You know I'd never let anybody fill a gas tank from a plastic jug. It isn't safe. Besides, isn't there a law against selling gas..."

"Or filling any container not painted red and marked 'gasoline only.' That doesn't keep people from being stupid. It just explains the cause."

She turned away and moved further up the slope, using the jagged metal piece to brush back the ground cover.

Brian followed. "What are you looking for now?"

"Anything. This sure doesn't make any sense. Nothing about this whole thing makes any sense." Frustration made her swipe the plants savagely, causing the metal to bend unexpectedly. She lost balance and threw a hand out to catch herself, slamming it on the ground.

Brian grabbed her to keep her from hurting herself more, but he wasn't balanced either, and the two of them fell heavily. Then a horn blared on the freeway below. Someone shouted an obscenity, followed by ribald laughter as the car roared away.

They stared at each other a moment, then started laughing and slipping down the embankment. Maggie wiped her eye with a bandaged hand, not daring to look at

Brian yet. Finally she said: "Your wife's going to hear about this, and there'll be hell to pay!"

"No doubt," he agreed solemnly. "She hears the craziest things about me." He stood to help her up, but Maggie was feeling for something she'd landed on. She held up another bit of roadside junk: a short piece of flexible metal tubing. Brian took it from her.

"Seems sort of beat up," she understated. "But it might be the working end of a gas can."

He agreed with a nod, and they headed back up the ramp toward his car. He took the metal tube along, too, not noticing that he was the quiet one on the way back.

❖ ❖ ❖

The first thing that struck Bett as she entered the M & M yard was all the activity. Two pairs of kids were industriously washing cars at the far end of the garage, their shouts audible from across the wide yard. Inside one of the bays, two men were peering at the underside of a car on a lift. In the bay next to the office, she recognized a stodgy, short-necked man. Hudson was talking to a young black man with a wild afro who glowered at a car part as if he meant to break it. The muscles that bulged through his T-shirt made him look strong enough to do it, too.

Then he saw Bett, and his face changed dramatically. "Can I help you?"

She liked his look now. It was open and friendly. A moment before, she would have hesitated to approach him, even though it would have meant having to talk to Hudson. She was very glad the young man had spoken up. "Yes. I'm looking for Maggie."

At the sound of her voice, Hudson turned. "Thought you were bringing the Buick. What happened to it?"

"Nothing happened to it. It just wouldn't start. Is Maggie here, or don't you care?"

The younger man looked back and forth between them, then led Bett to the office to take her out of Hudson's range. "Maggie's gone out for a bit," he said, clearing off the visitor's chair. "You can wait if you like, or maybe I can help. My name's Stony. Are you having car trouble?"

"Not me. But Maggie said I could use her car." Bett told him about not being able to get it started, then added, "Kind of ironic, huh?"

"What is?"

"That it wouldn't start. Sort of like a fireman's house catching fire."

He nodded absently. "You say it 'jumped forward' when you turned the key? Did you put the clutch all the way in?"

A sound like an alarm clock that wasn't an alarm clock went off in Bett's head. Tick, tick, tick. She ignored it. "Uh, Maggie only left me the keys and a note. She didn't say anything…" The ticking grew louder, and Bett felt her way around that warning, even as she sensed mice gathering on a fence rail. "Oh, the clutch…" She didn't want to tell Stony about the P.S. in the note. She wanted to keep that just between her and Maggie. She hadn't even told Ellen, knowing she would have laughed at the phrase.

But Stony was waiting, his brow wrinkled in expectation, his mouth open slightly, as if to help her say the right thing.

Finally she said, "There was something about a clutch, now that you mention it."

He relaxed visibly, then nodded. "We just put a new one in. Sure, that's it. The clutch is tight." Then he looked Bett up and down. "And you've got short legs." Having solved that mystery for himself, he went out the door whistling.

Bett was sure she'd never heard the mice laugh so gleefully.

CHAPTER 5.

Family Promise

Bett was poring over a *Chilton's Auto Repair* manual when someone else asked if she was having car trouble. This voice held a hint of laughter, and she looked up to find Maggie in the doorway. The sun backlit her, enhancing her broad shoulders and angular stance. When she turned to answer someone's call, Bett could see traces of a smile still curving her lips.

"Be right back!" she said, then added: "Glad you're here."

Sunlight flooded the room again, but it didn't give Bett any of the warmth Maggie's short visit had. She was dwelling on that when Brian looked in.

"Earth calling Bett! Come in, Bett!"

"Hi! Where's your uniform? I wouldn't have known you!"

"I'm not on duty until this afternoon. Does Maggie know you're here?" He reversed the visitor's chair, leaning on meaty forearms to talk.

"She just popped in, then got called away. Will she have to work long? She probably shouldn't be here at all. I'm sure it's too soon for her to be doing anything with her hands."

He nodded. "Maybe we can talk her into going to lunch and not coming back. But first I want to ask you about last night. Tell me again what the guy was carrying when you picked him up."

Bett closed her eyes, mentally returning to the street they had driven up. She saw the young man in the distance wearing a blue shirt and jeans. His white hair… No, wait. It was a white T-shirt. But where did the blue come in? She opened her eyes. "He was carrying some kind of bag. Royal blue. It was slung over his shoulder like a knapsack. Did I tell you that before?"

"No, but I meant the gas can."

She shook her head. "It was a plastic jug, not a can."

"You're sure?"

"Yes! I told you about the five-dollar rip-off, didn't I?"

Brian nodded, then pulled out the flexible metal tube and toyed with it, bending it in the shape of a question mark and straightening it again.

"What's that?" Bett asked.

"What's it look like?"

"Like something I've seen before." She turned her head slightly. "Is that a clutch?"

"No!" He snickered spontaneously. "What made you ask that?"

"Promise you won't laugh?" Bett told him about the P.S. in Maggie's note.

Brian couldn't keep from chuckling. "You're a good sport, Bett. My wife would kill me if I ever laughed at one of her stories like this."

She tried to cover her embarrassment. "Well, that tube *did* look familiar!"

"How?" He was alert again.

"When you curl it down like that, it looks like a spout to a watering can. That's what the gas can looked like when Maggie put it in the back of her truck last night."

Brian led her to the back of the building where the pickup was parked and asked her to show him.

"There in the corner." Bett stood on the bumper and pointed, but the spot was empty, and she climbed into the truck bed to look further. "I swear she put it there. It was in the way when we put my bike under the tarp. Maggie took the can out while we covered the bike, then put it back in."

Bett lifted a corner of the tarp, but it was caught on something. Brian reached under a mounted toolbox for the cause and pulled out a milk jug, amber-yellow from its contents. They could both smell gasoline.

"See!" Bett felt vindicated. "And if this is here, that guy must have taken her can to the car, right?"

Brian set the jug on the bumper, trying to pull all the odd facts together. The fire had made sense when he thought it was caused by using an unsafe container. He had discounted Maggie's argument that she wouldn't *let* anybody fill a gas tank that way. Now none of it made sense.

Maggie joined them, and Bett showed her what they'd found.

"It could've been your can that blew up, Maggie. This could be a piece of it, right?"

She examined both ends of the spout, then shook her head. "Can't be mine. No screen on the flow end. The other end's gone, so there's no telling what size can it was, but my nozzles all have protective screens in the tip."

"But it was blown up," Bett protested. "Nothing's going to stay attached through an explosion. The rest of the can is gone. Why would a little screen stay put?"

"You're starting out wrong, Bett. The piece I mean prevents explosions. This end is supposed to have a very fine screen in it, as fine as a mosquito net. See, if a fire starts while you're pouring gas, your first reaction is to tip it back." She demonstrated with an imaginary can. "If you do that, the fire follows the trail of gas and jumps right into the nozzle. The next thing you know, you've got a ball of fire in the can: Ka-boom! But that little screen keeps the flame from getting into the can. You might still have a fire, but the can won't blow up in your hand." She spread her hands, palms up.

Bett gasped at the sight of her bandages. "What have you been doing?" She jumped down and pulled Maggie's hands from behind her where she was trying to hide them. "Look at this! You have to get these rewrapped."

Brian grinned broadly, echoing Maggie's earlier jibe: "Somebody's going to hear about this, and you'll catch hell!"

Bett was glad to hear them joking. Maggie had some sparkle in her eye now. Brushing Maggie's hair back to view the discolored swell on her forehead, she thought she detected a fever, but before she could say anything, the four car-wash kids arrived.

"Hey, Maggie! Look what we found!"

One of them plopped a furry brown bundle in her hands while the rest talked all over each other. "She was in the trash barrel where…"

"She's a he, you dummy! Don't you know nothin'?"

"Yeah, I know. But, Maggie, she never coulda' got in there by hisself, 'cuz…"

Maggie's look interrupted him, and he started over. "I mean *he* never coulda'… could *have* gotten in the barrel all by her… his… *him*self, because he can't jump that high."

Maggie rewarded the boy's careful wording with a wink and bumped him playfully, making him dance a quick step of pleasure. Another kid sniggered, and she gave him a look. Her face lightened at his apologetic nod, and she focused on the hungry pup, who was trying to suckle her thumb.

Just then a silver-sided catering truck pulled into the yard, blaring the first notes of "Dixie" followed by a musical call to *Charge!* Maggie asked Brian and Bett if they wanted coffee, then gave one of the boys some money. As they headed for the lunch wagon at a whooping run, she hollered for them to buy milk and corn flakes for the dog.

Lunchtime at M & M was pure bedlam to Bett's unaccustomed eyes and ears. The car-wash boys huddled around the puppy in the middle of the floor, watching him hungrily lap up the cereal they'd fixed in an upturned brass disk. Stony sat on a parts box at the foot of the stairs across the room and nodded hello to her before turning back to talk with the two men she'd seen working in one of the bays. Hudson had settled near the door and poured coffee from a thermos before unwrapping a homemade sandwich. He didn't speak to anyone, nor did anyone address him.

All the workers were eating except Maggie, who circulated and spoke to each of them, even talking to someone out of sight up the stairs.

Brian tapped Bett's shoulder. "Break will be over pretty soon. Where you going from here? Her apartment?"

"No, my dad's place, I think. She can rest there, and he'll check her eye and re-wrap her hands."

He glanced at Maggie. "She shouldn't be driving yet. If it's not too far, I'll give you a lift. But I have to get to work pretty soon."

"Oh, we don't need a ride," Bett assured him. "We'll take BART." She saw a twinkle come into his eye and wondered what caused it.

"How long did you say you've known Maggie?" he asked.

"Not long. Why?"

He sat back smiling. "Oh, I was just hoping you'd be able to spend some time with her this weekend. Make sure she doesn't overdo things."

"I was thinking that, too. Why does it matter how long I've known her?"

"No reason," Brian said offhandedly. "It's just that Maggie has some, ah, peculiarities. Odd kinds of ways, you might say."

It finally dawned on Bett that he was trying to tell her Maggie was gay. At first she was offended, but the longer she thought about it, the funnier it got. She knew she had to say something before she laughed aloud. "Don't worry, Brian. I'm a big girl now." She winced internally at that expression but knew it was one he'd understand. "So is Maggie. We can probably manage to deal with any, um, oddities that come up."

He shrugged. "Thought I'd offer my years of wisdom and experience."

They both smiled, each recognizing the other's real, if naive, caring for Maggie.

When Bett looked around again, the office had emptied out. Maggie came down the stairs carrying a cardboard tube that she gave to one of the kids, who sped off around the building. Bett saw him again through the window behind the desk as he put the tube in one of the storage boxes on the pickup.

"Break time!" Brian called to Maggie.

"Be there in a minute," she said, stepping out the door.

"God, she looks awful," Bett remarked. Her gaze followed Maggie, who had stopped Hudson to talk with him. After a moment, it became clear that whatever she was saying, Hudson wasn't buying it.

Brian nudged Bett. "Who's winning?"

She smiled, not taking her eyes off Maggie. "Are you a mind reader besides?"

He tugged his lower lip to keep from laughing. "Sure! Scored aces in that at the Academy."

Bett chuckled. "Then what are they arguing about?"

The discussion outside the door suddenly got louder as Maggie said, "A few days. For Pete's sake! Don't give me any trouble about it."

Hudson glanced in at Brian briefly, then at Bett. Finally he spoke to Maggie in a low tone, then hawked and spit in the dust beyond her.

Bett started to rise. Brian stopped her.

"She's a big girl, right?" Then he saw Maggie start to follow Hudson. "Hey!" he called to her. "Your coffee's getting cold."

She came in muttering to herself and sat in the chair he'd vacated for her. Then she turned to Bett. "I didn't mean to take this long. I was sure I'd be out of here by noon, easy."

"No problem." Bett went on to outline her plan to see Dr. Holman, adding that Brian had offered to give them a lift to the BART station.

Maggie sipped her coffee thoughtfully, looking at Brian over the edge of the cup.

"It wasn't all my idea," he protested.

Maggie tossed her head. "Hope he didn't embarrass you too much. Poor guy's been a cop so long, he doesn't know how to act around real people."

Bett looked on as the two of them drank coffee and bantered. Being in that male-dominated garage made her realize how rarely she personally interacted with men. It was interesting to watch Maggie do that. She looked genuinely comfortable in their world and seemed even more at ease with them than they were with her. When Stony came in to ask about schedules, he greeted Brian coolly but was seriously respectful of Maggie. So was the other guy who came clattering down the stairs just as they were about to leave.

Maggie introduced Jack, a pale young man with watery blue eyes and a shock of unruly black hair. Bett watched his inherent nervousness dissipate the longer he talked with Maggie. She had a real ability to put people at ease with a word, or more often, a quick smile or nod. Funny, Bett thought, how she could do that as easily here as at the women's bar the other night. She wouldn't have thought it possible for anyone to do that in both places.

"I didn't get those blueprints copied yet," Jack was saying.

"Tim already put them in the truck," Maggie answered. "I'll look at them over the weekend. Or will you need them?"

"No, I, um, just wanted you to know they're originals."

Brian tapped his watch, putting an end to their discussion. "She'll guard them with her life, Jack." The young man paled even more at that, but he looked at Maggie, then bobbed his head shyly and ran back up the stairs.

⁂

The drive to BART was a short one, and Bett went ahead to get tickets, saying that she'd meet Maggie at the entrance.

Brian stared after her. "Gorgeous skin," he said softly.

"What exactly are you up to?" Maggie demanded.

"And she has black eyes," he continued. "Did you notice? They say that's a Celtic trait, you know."

"Will you cut it out!" But Maggie knew he wouldn't. She only had one recourse. "You're a happily married man!"

"That's what Mary Jo keeps telling me. What about you?"

She chuckled. "None of those things, thanks. And I'll stay that way."

Brian tsked sadly, then changed tactics. "You're probably right. Too young for you. And her…"

"She's just fine, Brian." Maggie cut off his second effort. "Listen, I want to know what you find out about… the victim. If I go up to the cabin for a few days, will you let me know as soon as you find out anything?"

"Yeah, but it won't be soon. I called the morgue last night. They'll be backed up on that 13th Street drug bust until Sunday."

"I have to know, one way or another, Brian. I tried calling Scotty, but there wasn't any answer. He might be on the road, but I still want to hear what you find out. You can always leave a message for me at the Tavern. I'll stop there when I pick up supplies."

He considered that. "Is Hugh Miller still sheriff up there?"

"So far as I know."

"Okay. It's official business. I can get you word through him." Then he returned to their earlier conversation, asking if she was going alone. They both looked at Bett, who was reading headline news through the window of a vending machine.

Maggie answered slowly. "Hudson asked me that, too. I told him he was trespassing. I don't need to tell you that, do I?"

He scoffed. "Wouldn't do you any good! I'm *The Law!* We go anywhere we want." She smiled at his tough-cop act.

"Listen, I know you can take care of yourself," he said, "but some of your best features are caught in a sling now. Even if Bett doesn't help with the driving, she can ride shotgun and keep her eyes on your blind side."

"Makes sense," Maggie agreed cautiously. "But I know you. Yes, you!" She grinned at his innocent look. "Do I have to answer you now? Or are you going to threaten me first?"

He chuckled. "You never answer to me. Just keep yourself safe. You know, buckle your seatbelt, lock your doors, keep your legs crossed."

❖ ❖ ❖

Maggie's face was still red when she joined Bett and shrugged off her concern about fever. But as soon as they had settled into their seats, she dozed off. Bett nudged her awake when they arrived at their stop, and after only a short walk, they got to Dr. Holman's house.

Groggy from her brief nap, Maggie agreed to lie down. This time she fell into a deep sleep. Bett checked on her periodically as she inventoried what was available for dinner.

She liked fixing dinner for her father. It was as close as they could get to talking anymore. Her mother's death had severed their communication for months. Only recently could she come home and sit across from him without one of them starting to grieve. She had Ellen's comfort and support, but she knew he had no one to reach out to. Now they only saw each other once a month or so. Sometimes he'd call and stop for dinner on his way home. More often, they'd meet in the City.

As she paged through her mother's cookbooks, she wondered if he'd gotten her message. His answering service expected him to call from the 19th hole. She hoped she hadn't missed his callback. Then she heard the familiar hum and clatter of the garage door opening.

He came in, putting his black bag on the corner table where it always sat. "Hi, sweetheart! I was so surprised by your message, I had to ask them to read it twice!" He hugged her warmly.

She was equally surprised. He looked tanned and fresh. And he was joking. This couldn't be the same man she'd seen two months ago. He looked so old then, his face as gray as his hair. Today he was the children's doctor who'd raised her, the professional she wanted so much to emulate.

"You must have had a great day on the course!"

"No. Bob had an emergency call. I told him we'd make it up next week. So what's the occasion? You don't come to visit the old man on whim anymore. I hope you're not out of money again."

She followed him to the den. "No, I'm not out of money. I'll take one of your manhattans, though. I brought you a patient." Bett accepted the drink and told him what happened the night before, which took some time to tell, and she finished by explaining that she'd brought Maggie to see him. "She's asleep in my old room."

"How old is the patient?"

Bett sighed. "C'mon, Dad! I told you she's a friend of mine." Then she admitted, "I don't know exactly. I'd guess about 30 or 35."

"Oh," he translated. "Pretty old, huh?"

"Well, she's older than I am, but not as old as..." Bett caught herself.

"Just old, not ancient?" He smiled back at her. "I only ask out of habit. It makes a difference when treating children, but you know that."

They discussed Maggie's condition a little more, then Bett left to pick up a few things for dinner.

❖ ❖ ❖

Dr. Holman settled down to process the day's mail, but it didn't keep his mind from wandering. He found himself thinking about the promise he'd made to his wife, Sarah, shortly before she died.

"Let Bett live her own life," Sarah had said. *"Let her make her own mistakes."* Even as he gave his word on that, he knew it was the hardest promise he would ever make.

Recalling that exchange brought a whole series of events to mind, starting with finding out about Bett's first love affair. His initial reaction had been knee-jerk, but he consoled himself with the knowledge that at least he hadn't turned it into a profession like that charlatan counselor they'd seen.

Sarah had tried to explain her own view to him: This was Bett's life, a part that didn't have anything to do with either of them. It was Sarah's style to play a kind of gentle devil's advocate—never overtly challenging him, only suggesting that his view might not be perfect. And she'd been more subtle than usual after their first session at the Family Center.

"I know what you think of his general approach, Mark, but do you really think Bett can benefit from someone with his perspective?"

He'd had to consciously stop himself from endorsing the bastard. That was when he realized how much, how very desperately, he wanted to believe Bett was just going through a phase.

The idiot had begun the brief parental session—the one in which Bett was asked to step into the waiting room—by presenting a neatly canned speech: "What makes people gay? Well, *prima facie* reasoning would support the strong-woman/weak-man theory (e.g., parents)." He sprinkled inappropriate Latin phrases throughout and scratched the air with his hands, putting quote marks around his buzzwords.

"Since you two people don't fit that profile, we can safely assume this is just a 'phase' the child is going through. I think we'll find that she's experiencing the 'extended crush' phase. Most girls go through some version of it in their preteen years. And while examples of 'drift' appear at either end of the age spectrum, you shouldn't worry. She'll 'emerge' just fine. Indeed, one can still assume she is a 'sexual innocent' (i.e., a 'virgin'). From what you've told me, and clinically speaking…"

By the end of the counselor's first supercilious lecture, Dr. Holman utterly despised him. He turned off the rest of the little fact-fucker's monologue.

"No," he finally replied to Sarah, "Bett already knows enough Latin just from writing out prescriptions for me. What do you think?"

She had laughed softly, tucking her arm through his. "Thank you, Mark. You just saved me from killing the man outright!"

He smiled, too, some of his anger relieved by their shared perception. Then he asked, "Do you think there's any chance… that it might be something she'll get over?"

"You mean like the chicken pox? No, I don't think so."

She said it almost absently, yet it sounded like a death knell to him. This was their only child they were discussing. "We can't just give up on her!"

That startled Sarah. "No, of course not. But we can't just sit by ignorantly and note her symptoms, either. If Bett wants to keep on with these sessions, we should encourage her. We'll just have to find someone with a more balanced view."

"How much more balanced?" he asked suspiciously.

"I'm not saying we have to find a lesbian therapist. I don't even know if such people exist. But the man we just saw simply wasn't all there! God help him if he ever dropped by a hospitality suite at a medical convention!"

He had chuckled at that, but it still surprised him. Ordinarily Sarah didn't categorize people. She just let people be themselves, no matter how unusual that was. Then she surprised him again.

"It's a good thing Bett's okay with all this."

"Okay?" he said. "I thought we were doing this *for* Bett."

"We are. But she's doing it for us, too. She doesn't want to lose our love. And we do love her, but she's fine. We're the ones who have to think about things differently, or we'll end up rationalizing ourselves into a corner like that fool we saw tonight. We've both had great expectations for Bett. You wanted her to follow us in medicine."

"No," he protested. "She can do anything she wants to."

Sarah smiled. "You've bitten your tongue nobly, Mark, letting her choose that path herself. But it's still an expectation. I suppose it's like mine but on a grander scale. I've been waiting for some handsome prince charming to come by and ask her to the prom. I suppose one might, but she won't go. And it's the she-won't-go part that we don't understand. I'm not sure we ever will. I suppose for her it must be like having an extra sense or trying to translate a foreign language."

He never did understand, but he trusted Sarah's perspective. Her empathy made her a more than competent nurse, and her nonjudgmental views made her marvelously free-spirited, both as a wife and a mother. They all enjoyed so much more because of her. He had none of her gift for letting people be themselves. He couldn't give himself to others the way she did. No, she was the one to go to those sessions with Bett. He hadn't been able to face that again.

And he still couldn't meet Bett's friends without suspecting them all of being her lovers. He hadn't been able to do anything about that, either. Not without his wife's graceful warmth and casual openness. At least tonight he would have his profession to distance himself. It was an excuse for Bett's sake, too. She obviously wanted him to accept her friends. He'd read disappointment in her eyes so often. But he couldn't be like Sarah. No matter how much he wanted to be. That just wasn't how he was.

CHAPTER 6.

Willing to Go

A SOUND IN THE HALL bathroom brought Dr. Holman out of his reverie. He didn't know what he expected Bett's friend to look like, but it was nothing like the giant who padded toward him. In the light of his reading lamp, she seemed to fill the hallway. Then she entered the room, and he saw that she was really quite thin. A trick of light, he thought, standing to greet her face-to-face. But she still topped him by several inches.

"Good evening. Are you Dr. Holman?"

He liked her voice: a strong contralto with a slight lilt. "Yes. And you must be Maggie. Bett went to pick up something for dinner. She'll be back soon. Did you rest well?"

She nodded. "I'd shake your hand, but I guess I shouldn't do that yet."

He had noticed her eye and facial injuries immediately, of course, but his personal interests disappeared and pure medical concern took over when he saw her hands. The gauze wraps were stained, and despite the poor light, he could see that liquid had seeped through even the outer layers. He led her to the kitchen table, asking routine questions as he attached a device to her chair back and locked it in a reclining position.

"Lean back now. Let's take a look at that eye. Bett told me what happened. Do you remember anything yet?" He felt her tense to reply. "No, don't move your head. Just answer orally."

"Not yet." Then she smiled. "At least I can talk in this chair. Dentists are forever asking questions with two hands and a mirror in my mouth. They never ask yes or no questions, either. Have you noticed?"

"Uh-huh." He was trying to remove her patch without disturbing the scab.

"It got stuck before, too. Bett soaked it with a washcloth last night."

"Hard to believe Bett did this."

Maggie quickly came to her defense. "She just took the first patch off. If anything's wrong, it's my fault."

"What do you mean?"

She hemmed a little, then told him that she'd checked out of the hospital right after having her burns examined.

"Checked out?" he repeated. "You mean no doctor ever looked at this?"

"Uh, no. Just the medic at the scene, I guess."

"If you were mine, I'd tan you for being so thick-headed. What made you leave like that?"

"Hate hospitals," she said tightly. "Had to be in one when I was young. Not again."

"Here, don't tense up like that. Bett can help me with this later. Keep both your eyes closed for a minute now."

He rummaged in a drawer for a moment until he came up with a plastic lens and slipped it in place over her injured eye.

"There. How's that feel?"

He watched Maggie reach up cautiously to explore the lens and the thin elastic bands stretching from either side. "A pirate patch!"

He smiled and sent her to the mirror in the half-bath off the kitchen.

"Pink!" she said disgustedly.

"Flesh-tone," he corrected.

"I thought it would be black."

"To match your eye?"

She grinned at him in the mirror. "Sure is a shiner, isn't it?" Then she peered more closely at the bruises on her cheek and forehead. "Thanks. I'll put some shoe polish on it later."

He grunted at that, then rolled in a utility stool for her to sit on while they cleaned her hands at a sink that had been installed for use by children. He had finished cleaning her right hand and was taking the outer wraps off her left when Bett returned and crowded into the small room with them, casually draping an arm across Maggie's shoulders.

"How do they look?" Bett asked.

"Good so far," Dr. Holman replied. "We just finished cleaning one." He was pleased by his daughter's interest.

"How long before it'll start looking like skin?" Bett asked.

"Hard to say." He motioned to Maggie to put her left hand in the water. "But she should be able to go back to work in about two weeks."

Maggie gasped at that, then from sudden pain. She barely kept from jerking her hand out of the tepid water. Bett gripped her shoulder as Dr. Holman quickly un-wrapped the last layers of gauze.

He peered closely at the hand. "This burn is much more serious. See this?" He pointed to a tear in the healthy tissue. "Is that what hurt?"

Maggie nodded. "What do you mean? Two weeks?"

"You're badly hurt," Bett said. "I keep telling you!"

Dr. Holman nodded. "That's how long it will take the skin to re-form." He remembered Bett mentioning something about Maggie's boss. "I can give you a letter to keep you off work, but any fool can see you can't use your hands for heavy labor."

"Any fool," she echoed, closing her good eye.

"It's not the end of the world," Bett said gently.

"Do they have to stay wrapped?" Maggie asked.

"Yes!" Bett said. "And if you take care of them, they'll *heal!*"

"She's right," Dr. Holman said. "Burns like this are like open wounds, providing direct access to your system." He gestured at the torn skin. "That's going to be a problem to clean. Get me a local from my bag, Bett."

Bett returned with a syringe and a vial as Maggie was telling him about her fall on the hillside.

"Have you been having dizzy spells?" Bett asked.

"No." Then Maggie related the episode at the retaining wall in the hospital parking lot. "It hasn't happened since then, but why did it there?"

Bett had studied depth perception for a psychology course and shared what she'd learned: "It seems to work in adults even when only one eye is operative, so long as it developed normally in infancy. Perception has a lot to do with expectations, though. Last night you probably saw what you expected. When that turned out to be wrong, you subconsciously corrected your sight by adjusting your expectations as much as your vision."

"Does that mean I can drive with my eye covered?"

Bett didn't know about that. "What do you think, Dad?"

"You should check your field of vision first."

Maggie nodded. She watched Bett draw clear liquid from a vial into the syringe, then tap the side of the syringe sharply and slowly depress the plunger. When a drop of liquid grew at the end of the needle, Bett pressed it a fraction more, spurting a dash out. "Why do you do that with needles?" Maggie asked.

Bett handed it to her father and tore open an alcohol swab. "To keep from injecting any air under the skin. It's more important when you give a shot intravenously, since air in the blood stream can be fatal."

"Like a hydraulic system?"

Bett looked puzzled by the analogy, but Dr. Holman chuckled. "Exactly. But the human body came first, so hydraulics are like the blood system." He told Bett he would need help with Maggie's eye later, but she could start dinner now. He dressed the left hand and was wrapping it when Maggie asked if the bandages would last two weeks.

"You aren't thinking about going back to work, are you?"

"No, I'll take some time off. I just want to know if these will last, or if I'll have to come back to get them changed."

"You'll have to change them, or have them changed, at least twice a day. You can do it just once a day, but that'll be a lot more painful."

Maggie followed him to the kitchen table, resting her left hand gently. "How long will it be numb?"

"An hour or so. You'll have a little discomfort when the local wears off, but most of the pain from the cleaning should be gone by then."

Bett heard his reply. "Huh! That's doctor-talk for 'You won't be able to see straight!' Would you like a drink to ward that off?"

Maggie declined with a smile. "Coffee and a cigarette would taste pretty good, though. Mind if I smoke, Doctor?"

"Not me. The Surgeon General's in charge of minding that. Put a cup in the microwave from the pot, will you, Bett? Best little coffee-warmer in the world. I never got the hang of it for cooking meals, but it sure makes morning coffee drinkable again." He took out an ashtray and set it on the table. "Put myself on cigars about ten years ago, then quit those. I always thought it would be better if women could smoke cigars…"

"Oh, Dad!" Bett set a cup of coffee in front of Maggie. "Cigar smoke is even worse than cigarette smoke. As for disease rates, they just haven't studied cigar smokers the way they have cigarette smokers. And it's all numbers, anyway. The diseases are the same."

Dr. Holman asked Maggie how much she smoked.

"All things in moderation," she said easily. "Hardly at all when I'm working, or when I'm busy in general. Sometimes I don't even light up, except after meals or on break. Most days I suppose I smoke about a dozen." She looked at her hands. "Guess I'll have to keep an eye on the habit part, now that I can't work."

Dr. Holman nodded and went over to the chair he had treated her in, returning it to its upright position.

"That's a clever design," Maggie remarked. "Is it your own?"

He looked up in surprise. Most people—the ones who noticed the chair's modification at all—just said, "What will they think of next?" never dreaming he'd designed it himself. "Yes," he said with some pride, then added, "but I had to find somebody to build it."

She examined the adjustment mechanism. "That's usually how it goes. I only know one guy who invents his own stuff and has the savvy to build the prototypes, too." She pointed to the clamping device. "How'd you get this to hold? Oh, I see. The grip twists, right?"

He nodded, impressed by how quickly she'd grasped the feature that had given him the most trouble. "The guy who put it together for me wanted to use two sleeves with holes bored for a locking pin."

She operated the grip. "No, this style clamp is much better. Smooth, too. You don't fumble for a pin, either, and waste time taking it in and out."

Dr. Holman glanced at his daughter. Where did you find…? Then he turned back to Maggie. "Eh? What's that about a patent?"

"I just wondered if you'd applied for one. I know a guy who can do the drawings for you. He'll put you in touch with the right lawyer, too."

"You think it's that good?"

"Well, it might not make you rich, but I hear it can be pretty exciting to have a patent in your own name. What made you build a chair like this for your kitchen?"

He explained how he'd become the stand-in doctor for kids in the neighborhood when they'd outgrown his pediatric services and moved on to the hazards of high school sports. Many of them had stayed in touch through college. And though Bett was an only child, he and his wife often felt like they had a dozen. At Christmastime the house was filled day and night. "That is," he added somberly, "until these past two years. Bett's mother died the day after Thanksgiving, a year ago."

Just then Bett brought a platter to the table. "Chicken piccata is served! Help yourself. The salad's already dressed. I'll get the broccoli and wine."

They busied themselves fixing their plates, and conversation was halted as they started to eat. Dr. Holman saw that Maggie's appetite was good, and she seemed to be enjoying the meal.

But when she finished her plate, she pointed at the green, pellet-sized objects in the wine sauce. "What are these?"

"Capers," Bett answered.

"Are they hot?"

"No, but they have a strong taste. Try them with chicken."

Maggie's face revealed how much she liked the flavor. "Just one more question. Why do you call it *chicken* piccata? Where's the chicken?"

Bett was too surprised to laugh. "You just put a piece in your mouth!"

"But it's all flat! What happened to the bones?"

Dr. Holman laughed with Bett, then excused himself while they cleared the table and filled the dishwasher.

"More coffee?" Bett offered.

"Sure. Do you have any cream or half-and-half?"

"I'll check. But don't you take your coffee black?"

Maggie grinned. "Sometimes I treat myself. Haven't you ever heard of a 'poor man's dessert'?"

Bett's look turned sad so suddenly Maggie didn't know what to say. An awkward silence fell between them, then they both spoke at once: "I should get going..." "What would you like to..."

"Going?" Bett said. "I thought you'd stay?" Then she reminded her: "Dad has to look at your eye yet, you know."

Maggie studied her coffee. "Oh, yeah. I forgot."

Bett was still put off by her plan to leave. "He won't mind us staying. But I expected to spend the weekend with you. It doesn't matter where." She saw Maggie's surprise. "Am I being too forward?"

"No." Maggie spread her hands, a gesture of futility. "I just thought you'd..."

Dr. Holman returned at that point. "Is that decaf, or are you two staying up all night on a caffeine jag?"

"I'll make a fresh pot," Bett said. "Decaf?"

"I'd prefer that. Maggie?" He didn't expect her to jump so nervously and started to reach out to her, then withdrew to his professional posture, regretting again that he didn't have his wife's facility for putting a patient at ease. "I'll take a look at your eye now. I suppose you'll be taking off soon. Bett always says it's too quiet out here in the suburbs."

"I was just talking about heading back," Maggie said.

He interpreted that to include Bett. Sarah was still on his mind, as was the promise he'd made to her, and all the times he'd avoided talking with Bett. It was time to make some restitution. "It's no fun hanging around parents once you get past a certain age." He took Bett's look as a positive sign and led Maggie to the table. "So you're going back. What about work?"

"No, not to work. I'll just get my truck and head up to the mountains. Traffic should be light this time of night. There's a cabin up there I haven't been to for a while."

She closed her eye at Dr. Holman's direction. "Spring is wonderful up there. Everything is just beginning to turn green. You can even see wildflowers in the meadows if you time it... Yow!"

"Hold still now." He called Bett over and was pleased to see her instinctively soothe Maggie's face with a light touch.

"This'll sting a little," he told Maggie. "Bett, help her seal that lid while I... That's it. Try not to clench. Let Bett help you. It'll only take a minute."

Maggie's lid tightened in reflex.

"Relax your eye, Maggie." Bett said. "Just like last night. Roll it up, but keep the lid shut. That's it. Quick, Dad." Then: "Wait. I think I can see better from here."

Dr. Holman watched his daughter take over with sure, precise movements. "Very clean, Bett. Good, fast work. A thorough job."

Bett's genuine smile told him how much his praise meant to her.

"Can I look?" Maggie asked.

"Not yet," Bett said. "Should we dim the light, Dad?"

"Let's give Maggie a rest first."

When she assured him she was fine, Dr. Holman examined the eyelid carefully, making observations to Bett, who responded in kind. Then he told Maggie to open the eye slowly.

She told them she couldn't get it to focus. "That's bad, isn't it?"

"Not really. Much as I expected," Dr. Holman said. "Keep it covered for the next forty-eight hours. Wait until, let's see... Tuesday, I think. And don't run out and stare at the sun, either. You'll still be in the mountains then?"

"Probably."

He turned to Bett. "Make sure she gives it time to adjust to natural light. If her vision is still blurred, put the patch back on for another two days."

"But," Maggie started to object.

"No 'buts' now. Bett knows how to test your vision for this kind of thing. I don't want you second-guessing your sight and deciding it's okay. You might strain something."

He put the patch back over Maggie's eye and helped her sit up. "Besides, I sort of envy you your few days of spring in the mountains. Even after all these years, I still miss the change of seasons."

"Where are you from?" Maggie asked.

"Kansas originally, but we left there before Bett was born."

"I miss the seasons, too," Maggie said. "They only have two here: wet and dry."

❖ ❖ ❖

The two of them discussed Midwestern weather while Bett poured coffee. Then she joined them and listened quietly, reminded of all the times her mother and father had talked at this table. They would leap from one subject to another, as if it were all one. Occasionally they would slip back to something they'd touched on before, but to Bett it had always seemed like the most random of walks in and out of each other's minds.

She was brought back from those thoughts when her father started dictating instructions for treating Maggie's burns.

"There's always a risk of infection. I'll order a course of antibiotics for you. Another thing: You'll be in almost constant pain for the next week. Do you drink much?"

She shrugged. "Sort of like I smoke. None at all if I'm busy. Maybe a beer and a bump on the weekend."

He nodded. "I'll prescribe some pain pills for you, but you shouldn't take them more than every four hours. Codeine may seem strong at first, but it won't outlast burn pain. So act like you're on a long weekend and have a drink an hour or two after taking a pill. It'll help extend its efficacy. I want you to drink a lot of water and juice, too."

He reminded Bett to look for any signs of infection in the burn area, then explained that renal slowdown was another symptom to watch for. "If you see anything out of the ordinary, get to a hospital." He sent her to the den for a text on burns, then phoned in the prescriptions and ordered dressings for several changes. When he hung up, he reinforced the need for Maggie to take all the antibiotics. "I ordered you some sleeping pills, too."

She was shaking her head as Bett returned. "I don't need sleeping pills. Fact is, I don't sleep so much as I just crash. I don't even dream. Don't worry about me. I'm healthy as a horse!"

Bett tried to rebut her. "You're badly hurt, Maggie."

She shrugged. "I've been hurt before."

"This is a little different," Dr. Holman said. "The constant pain in your hands will make you edgy. Side effects of burns can manifest as physical nervousness or even mood swings. You don't have to take the sleeping pills. You *do* have to take the antibiotics."

"And the pain pills," Bett said.

Maggie said, "We'll see how it goes."

Dr. Holman drove to the pharmacy on the way to the BART station and waited with Bett while Maggie went in to pick up her prescriptions. "I didn't even get to ask how you're doing at school."

"Fine." Bett replied automatically. "I didn't ask how you got so tanned, either."

"Golf, mostly. And I've joined another club." He grew self-conscious then. He had news to share but didn't think now was the right time. Then he saw Maggie coming out of the store. "Your new friend... she's, ah, quite unusual, isn't she?" He didn't mean to sound like there was anything wrong with Maggie. "I mean, you like her a lot, don't you?"

Bett was too surprised to do more than nod.

"Good," he said simply. "I do, too."

Then Maggie got in, and it was too late to say anything until they got to the BART station. Maggie thanked Dr. Holman for everything. "Let me know what I owe you."

He made a face. "It'll cost you one name: the guy who'll do those patent drawings for me."

She grinned. "You've got it."

He turned to Bett. "Call when you get back. We'll have dinner. You can tell me all about the change of seasons."

There was so much Bett wanted to say, but now wasn't the time. "Love you," she said simply.

Maggie was waiting on the platform. "Do you really want to go with me to the mountains?" she asked.

Bett was astonished by her question, then hugged her. "Of course I do! But let's go for more than a few days. Let's go for a whole week."

Maggie smiled thinly. "Think you could stand me that long?"

No, Bett thought, but I could lay you down for a week and wonder where the time had gone.

"And what about school? Won't you miss classes?"

"About as much as you'll miss Hudson!"

Bett watched her smile broaden and drew her closer. The platform was empty, but she would have kissed her even if it had been filled with commuters. It was the first embrace they'd shared in twenty-four hours.

Finally Maggie leaned back. "You do, um, understand about my hands, don't you?"

Bett laughed. "Your hands aren't your only asset." She loved Maggie even more for her sudden blush of shyness.

"If we leave town by midnight, we'll miss the bar crowd."

"What about your eye?"

"We can check that out at the yard. If it doesn't fly, you can drive."

Bett shook her head. "I can't drive. I don't have a license."

"What happened? They yank it?"

"No." She smiled at the term. "They never gave it to me." She took a breath. "I don't know how. To drive, I mean."

When the silence between them grew, Bett was sure Maggie was hiding disappointment. Silence was so often that. Or anger. She didn't want her to be angry, either. "It isn't that hard to learn, is it?" It was one thing to have principles. Quite another to need a certain skill.

"Not that I remember." She grinned. "Been a long time since I learned. Didn't your folks have time to teach you?"

"No, that's not it." Bett extolled the advantages, and necessity, of mass transit. She continued in that vein for some time before realizing Maggie's smile hadn't diminished. "Are you laughing at me?"

"Nope!" she said easily. "At myself, really. I thought all native Californians had blond hair and blue eyes and knew how to drive from birth!"

Bett smiled wryly. "You have a lot to learn about California women!"

※ ※ ※

Tracy Ebert saw Sergeant Kessler check the time. They had an hour before their tour ended. Their last tour together after two weeks of observation. Then he would only have to write the report on her; the one the shrink had ordered. Ebert knew the drill. She also knew the Sarge didn't like Dr. Smalys much, but he always followed orders.

"Where'd you learn to drive, anyway?" he asked conversationally.

"Thought you knew."

"I know you drove the circuit, but who taught you first? Your mother or your father?"

"Neither. Uncles, mostly. Why?"

"My kids are getting close to that age. Time to think about teaching them. Driver's Ed. is worthless. And you're better than average."

"I thought for a minute you were going to say better than most men."

"Hey, I said average, didn't I?"

"Yeah. I guess that means most men."

"Sexist."

Ebert choked a short laugh and took out a cigarette for herself, then passed him the pack in invitation.

"And why do you buy such hard-ass cigarettes? If you smoked Silva Thins, I'd at least have an excuse for not taking every one you offered."

"Those cowboy commercials are just to get the macho market."

She saw him sort that out, then nod with a wry smile. They rode in silence for a while, each of them on alert, but it was a quiet night.

After a few minutes, he said, "Take us up the hill, will you? We'll do this last hour on the QT."

"Don't forget," she said, "you want to go by the morgue later."

"Yeah, we'll drop the prints off there on the way back."

Ebert picked side streets and quiet avenues to get to the area he'd suggested. Soon they were cruising a neighborhood that featured trim, grass-bordered strips in front of solid brick homes. The biggest crime in this part of town was when a resident drove over his own garbage can.

Kessler pointed out a 7-11 store up the street and nodded at it. "Pull in there. Get us a pack of Macho. I've bummed enough from you."

Ebert gave a start, then tried to quell the feeling of dread that rose in her stomach at the thought of entering the store ahead. Not trusting herself to speak, she spent her energy turning into the parking lot. A moped was chained to a pay phone near the door. Ebert guessed it was the clerk's. A late-model Olds slanted across the yellow parking lines, taking up two spaces.

She got out of the car and concentrated on making her legs work. The pain in her thigh felt real. She kept repeating what the doctors had told her: It doesn't hurt. It's phantom pain. She didn't know she was limping as she approached the door of the store. She didn't know she'd unsnapped the holster on her hip, either. All she could see was the door of the other store…

A slight black kid—he couldn't have been more than fifteen—was backing out, carrying a shopping bag. She pulled the door open to help him when a voice from inside the store shouted at her unintelligibly: "Get down!" or "Look out!"

She glanced in, taking her eyes off the kid. That's when the sound hit her; the pain followed. The jagged, tearing, shocking assault made her leg go out from under her, made her fall against him, knocking the beer-filled bag on top of his gun. She heard it skitter. Saw it lying a few feet from her face. Such a tiny gun: It looked like a toy. But the noise echoed eternally in the small space where she lay half-in, half-out of the doorway. She couldn't think. She could only feel the space shrink as the door closed on her leg. Then, from far away, she heard herself scream.

"Are you all right, Officer?"

The clerk's concerned voice broke her thoughts. She found herself at the counter in the store. Blinking in the bright light, she looked around. A woman in a pink pantsuit was reading a label on a can of cat food. The three of them were the store's only occupants.

"Fine," Ebert said distantly.

The clerk asked hesitantly, "Is it… very warm out?"

She couldn't think straight with all his questions. She put a hand to her brow. It was wet. Slick with… She checked her hand. It was only sweat. No blood. No armed robber. Only a 7-11 store in a sleepy Oakland neighborhood. She shivered, feeling her tension ebb magically. "No," she said. "Matter of fact, it's a beautiful evening."

The clerk filled her order. When she put her change away, the flap of her holster rattled. Her gun was exposed. "Have to get that fixed," she said, snapping the flap shut. "Seems to pop open at odd times."

She delivered Kessler's coffee, and he asked what had taken so long. She looked at the store as if seeing it for the first time, then shrugged. "Guy inside wanted a weather report!"

Brian seemed to relax, as though she'd reassured him in some way. "Let's head down to the morgue."

"Whose prints are you taking in?" Ebert tore an opening in her coffee lid and blew into the cup.

"I got a tentative ID from that freeway fire last night."

"Did Maggie remember something?"

"No, not yet. I stopped by the yard this morning. Told her to take some time off. She sure didn't look very good."

"She's going to be okay, isn't she?"

He looked up at the concern in Ebert's voice. "Sure. You know Maggie."

"Yeah. Tough nut."

"Her girlfriend described the guy they picked up." He shook his head. "Something funny about that fire."

"Like what?"

"The size of it. Two explosions, not one. A blown-up gas can with the wrong nozzle. And the victim—the body might stay a John Doe forever."

"Thought you said you had an ID on him."

"Yeah. That's another problem. It could be Scott Fenn."

"Friend of Maggie's?" Ebert recalled Maggie's atypical display of grief.

"Not so much a friend as a kind of adopted brother. They both came out of the same orphanage Back East."

"Orphanage?" Ebert couldn't hide her surprise.

Brian nodded. "Yeah. Seems he left headed straight for trouble, and she's been trying to turn him around ever since. She had to get him out of some county jail a while back. I thought it was Boys' Town, but she says he's her age. He sure doesn't look it. Bett even described him as being about twenty-five or so. I came across him when I was on a stakeout down on Telegraph a few years ago. He was the driver in that attempted Bank of America robbery."

"The one you and Janovich broke up when you went to cash a check?"

He chuckled. "Yeah. He was the only white-haired driver on the block. He sure picked the wrong guys to do that job with." He grew thoughtful. "I met him at Maggie's one time, so I called her after I booked him. Maybe that was a mistake. She made her case to the judge, and he let him go ROR."

"Was he that good a prospect for recognizance?"

"Guess he stayed pretty clean. Maggie fixed a place up for him, helped him get a job. That's not what's bugging me, though. It was something Bett said about the fire."

"At least she noticed there was one." She sensed his glance. "Got nothing against the girl personally, Sarge, but she doesn't even drive. What's she going to notice about a freeway incident?"

He tsked. "Ebert, you're going to have to get over your prejudice against pretty young innocents. You might turn into one yourself some day."

She ignored that. "Okay, I give. What did Bett say about it?"

"She said there were two explosions. But the victim didn't get blown up. He got burned up."

Ebert made a disparaging sound. "Burned up, blown up. Dead is dead. It wasn't you or me or Maggie. Just an ex-perp."

He was surprised at her callousness. "Tell me something. Why aren't you happier to be alive?"

"Wait a minute!" She took her eyes off the road. "I disguise my personal feelings on the job just like they tell us to." She focused on driving again. "In fact, I happen to be Thrilled to Death to be alive. If you can't tell that, then I must be doing my job right."

Brian shook his head, and Ebert thought she glimpsed disappointment in his look. Then she dismissed the thought. What would he be disappointed about?

CHAPTER 7.

The Road I Took to You

IT WAS JUST PAST MIDNIGHT when Maggie pulled away from her duplex and coasted to a stop at the end of the street. "Have we got everything now?"

"Everything you listed," Bett replied, "plus one stowaway puppy!"

They had found him at the M & M yard when they went to get the truck. Maggie tested her sight by driving around the yard, then adjusted the passenger-side mirror for Bett to use to help widen her field of vision on the right. When she unlocked the office to leave a note, the puppy dashed out and ran straight to Bett, who led him to a patch of weeds where he left a puppy-sized deposit. It seemed natural to bring him along, and Maggie picked up a box and an old towel at her place to make a bed for him. After that short stop, they were on their way.

"Ready on the right!" Bett called out.

Maggie looked left and saw a vehicle moving away from the curb on the cross street. At first she thought the driver would go past them, but the truck—she could see it was a pickup—slowed, indicating by its angle that it would turn onto her street.

"No signal," she remarked, idly diagnosing the cause: "Parking light's out." She turned right and glanced in the mirror. The other truck made a shallow turn onto Natchez and pulled out again, as if to make a U-turn. She forgot about it after that.

Soon they were on the freeway, and traffic was as light as she'd expected. That was good, since Bett couldn't share the driving. Then other events of the day fell into place. "Now I know why you didn't take the Buick. My note probably didn't make much sense, did it?"

"I don't think I took it the way you meant." Bett told her what had happened and endured her chuckle, then asked, "Are my legs too short to drive?"

"Oh, no. The seat's adjustable. Are you ready to try?"

"Maybe later. Unless you're tired."

She smiled. "We just started. I can drive all the way there and back again without blinking an eye. Don't worry, I love to drive. You can even nap after we get over the Straits. There won't be any traffic after that."

Bett seemed to consider that. "What happens when you *do* blink, Maggie?"

"Nothing very magical. Why?"

It was Bett's turn to smile. "I guess you can blink as well with only one eye, but what if you get something in it? Won't you be driving blind then?"

She hadn't thought of that. "I suppose. Want to learn how to steer now?"

"Can I?" Bett asked nervously.

"Sure. It's how I learned. Probably how everybody does."

"Should I sit in the middle, like I did last night?"

"Last night?" Maggie started to pursue that, but they were at the top of the incline above Carquinez Strait, and she needed a traffic check. The few cars around them were jockeying for position, anticipating the tollbooth across the bridge. When they rumbled over the caution strips, the chattering vibrations woke the puppy. He gave off a whimpering yowl before circling the bedding in his box and lying down again.

Maggie paid the toll and pulled off the road a few hundred feet beyond. They wouldn't attract attention there, and she knew the Highway Patrol would frown on one-eyed driving.

"Do you want me to drive now?" Bett asked.

"Not yet."

But now that they were stopped, Maggie had to cover her good eye just to keep from dwelling on how Bett looked in the moonlight. Her misgivings about the trip resurfaced. She wasn't at all sure she could spend a week with her and not want to make love again. That was impossible. She hoped Bett understood. Maybe she was only interested in nursing, and they could just be friends. Maggie rubbed her face to change thoughts.

"First things first. You get settled in the middle. Put the dog on the floor while I fix the outside mirror again."

When Maggie got back in the truck, she checked the driver-side mirror. A vehicle had stopped some distance behind them and was slowly pulling out. She felt safe preceding it.

Bett said, "Can I ask a dumb question?"

"Anything you want. But it probably won't be dumb."

She tapped Maggie's wrist, the one hanging over the gear stick. "How come you move this around so much when you first start up, and then just let it sit there?"

"Stick shift," she said shortly.

"Is this a very old truck, then?"

Maggie turned her head slightly. She could only see Bett in the mirror, now that she was sitting so close. "What makes you think it's old?"

"I don't, really. I mean, it can't be that old, with all those dials, right?"

Maggie chuckled. "For somebody who doesn't know much about cars, you sure spotted the speedometer fast."

Bett sighed.

"Figure out why it looks different yet?" Maggie asked.

"Huh-uh. Why does it?"

"Pre-'75 model. Goes up to 120."

Bett groaned at the technical reply.

Maggie read her response all wrong. "I knew you'd see it as soon as I said something. Does your dad's stop at 80?"

"My dad's… what?" Bett finally managed to ask.

Maggie paused, too. "Should we back up and try this again?"

"Well, maybe you could start by telling me what 'stick shift' means…?"

"This," Maggie tapped the gear lever, "is a stick. You shift gears with it. First, second, third?" she added hopefully. Bett didn't reply. "We're in third now. That's the highest gear on this truck. Usually the highest on any column stick. The Buick has a floor shift. Four gears. Some floor shifts have a fifth gear, but it works more like overdrive. Now, what else do you want to know about standard transmissions?"

"*Standard?* What's so standard about it?"

Maggie laughed, then squeezed Bett's knee to take the bite out of that. "Sorry, darlin'. It's a standard transmission whenever you shift for yourself. I suppose they started calling it that when automatics first came out. Had to call it something."

"Seems to me they call it a lot of things!" Bett twined her fingers with Maggie's unwrapped ones. "Will you explain all these dials to me so I won't ask any more dumb questions?"

"Not dumb." Maggie was much too conscious of Bett's touch. "Here, put your hand on the knob." She checked the side mirror. Only one set of lights appeared behind them, and they were at a safe distance. "Okay, we're going up to second now." She engaged the clutch and guided Bett's hand to push the gear lever up. "Second." She let go. "You put it in third. Straight down."

Bett tugged gingerly at the lever. It released easily, and she let it fall of its own accord. The engine roared again, but they continued losing speed.

"Keep going," Maggie urged. "That's neutral. Third's right below it."

Bett pulled the lever harder, all the way down to where they'd started. The engine noise quieted, and they stopped losing speed.

"What did we just do?" she asked.

"Shifted from third to second and back again."

"Why?"

"To show you two of the four gears." And, Maggie thought, to slow my heartbeat. Both of her hands were back on the wheel. Bett's hand was on the gearshift.

"You said third gear was as high as your truck went. What's this fourth-gear business?"

"Reverse." Maggie explained the H structure of the column shift, then told Bett to put a hand on the wheel to get the feel of the truck. "You steer for a few minutes now while I stretch, okay?"

"Are you sure?"

"I'm not going for a walk, darlin'." Maggie checked the mirror before releasing the wheel. The traffic behind them was still keeping its distance. It felt good to close her eye. She tossed her head to relieve a neck kink, then arched her back. Ordinarily she'd shift position as a matter of course, but driving with only one eye meant keeping tedious control of her movements. Bett's steering would help a lot.

"Maggie, am I doing all right?"

"You're doing great! Haven't so much as run over a truck turd."

"What's that?"

"Retread blowout. They're mostly on the side of the road."

"Is that why we're going so slow? You think I'll run into something?"

Maggie glanced at the speedometer, then hit the gas. Jeez, they were only doing 45! She quickly checked the mirror, wary of being rear-ended, but the headlights trailing them were as distant as before.

"No, darlin'. I just wasn't paying attention." She checked the mirror again. Why hadn't that vehicle passed them? They'd been traveling well below the speed limit. Then an old caution came over her. "Don't worry about speed now. Just keep your eyes on the road and steer, okay?"

Maggie pressed the accelerator smoothly, driving the needle beyond 60, letting it creep past 70, then watched as the headlights behind them diminished. She didn't want to scare Bett. And there might not be anything to worry about.

It was a vain hope. The lights behind them changed from pinpricks to high beams, coming on fast. A knot formed in Maggie's stomach as the vehicle began closing the gap she'd created. She tensed her leg, knowing she could keep this half-mile lead and more if she kept going. Then she turned to check the center mirror and saw Bett's silhouette. Her leg relaxed automatically, and she eased them back to 60, putting an arm around Bett instinctively. She couldn't risk it.

"Is this my reward for straight steering?"

Maggie hummed a reply, wondering who could be trailing them. Not a bored highway patrolman. He would've flipped on his red light as soon as she hit 65. Could be a drunk. Messy enough, depending on how drunk he was, how fast his wheels. That didn't fit, either. A drunk would be passing them, showboating all over the road.

Then Bett announced a freeway interchange ahead. "Do you want to take the wheel now?"

Maggie considered fleeing again, but she couldn't risk it with only one eye. "No, darlin'. You're doing fine."

She expected the interstate to be crowded with tractor-trailers. They owned the road at night, even on weekends. She wasn't disappointed. They joined a dozen eastbound eighteen-wheelers. There were almost no four-wheelers, which would make the follower easy to spot. She guided Bett through the rigs, keeping an eye on traffic behind. At the 505 bypass, they lost some of their protective cover. They also seemed to have lost the four-wheeler. She had Bett change lanes several times in an effort to spot it, but it was no longer in sight. Finally they settled in the middle lane, ahead of a Yellow Freightliner and pacing a P.I.E. Traffic was moving at 70. When they got east of Sacramento, she relaxed her vigil and reached for her cigarettes on the visor.

Bett was studying the dashboard. "What does rpm mean?"

"How fast the engine's going. Revolutions per minute."

For just those few seconds, neither of them was watching the road. The pickup wandered into the right lane of its own accord, rumbling across the Botts' Dotts in the lane dividers. Maggie looked up as an air horn blast sounded. She grabbed the wheel, speeding ahead of the semi that had warned them, then flashed her lights. The lights behind dimmed in response.

"I'm sorry, Maggie. I thought you were steering, too."

"It's okay, doll. I was, except for just then. Don't worry."

"But I'm supposed to be helping you, not causing…"

"Hey!" Maggie touched Bett's chin, tracing her jaw. "The only reason I wasn't steering was because you were doing such a good job. I completely forgot you were just learning!"

"Really?"

"Really!"

"Are you steering now?"

Maggie nodded, then heard the familiar metal 'snick' of a seatbelt being released. She opened her mouth to say it wasn't safe, when Bett kissed her. Kissed her in such a way that her line of vision wasn't obscured, but in such a way that made her want to close her good eye, even as the road ahead blurred and wavered. By the time Bett released her, she could scarcely breathe, and the speedometer needle had danced to 75 mph.

She consciously eased her foot off the gas. "You shouldn't do that," she whispered into Bett's hair, "when I'm driving."

Bett grinned. "You shouldn't compliment me," she kissed Maggie where her shirt was open at the neck, "when I don't deserve it."

Maggie pulled her away gently but firmly. "Are you hungry?"

"Mmm. You might say that!"

Maggie felt herself blush. "How about a traffic check?"

Bett looked in the side mirror, seeing two sets of headlights behind them, but when she looked out the back window, only one set was visible. "Just that truck that honked at us."

Maggie suggested they stop for a sandwich and coffee, and they pulled off at the next truck stop. After they settled into a booth and placed their order, she became aware of Bett's close scrutiny.

"I can't have food stuck between my teeth yet!"

Bett laughed. "No, but you look pretty tired. How's your head feel?"

"Empty as a beer keg on Sunday morning." She smiled wryly. "I still can't remember last night. It's driving me crazy."

"You shouldn't try." Bett reached out to comfort her, but Maggie slipped her hand away as the waitress arrived with their food.

"You don't understand," Maggie said. "What if it *was* Scotty?"

"We don't know who it was," Bett reminded her. "Tell me about Scotty. How did you meet him?"

She smiled a little. "I never really *met* him. We grew up together. Then I lost touch with him. With everybody…"

"Go ahead," Bett prompted when she looked away. "You shouldn't force your memory about last night, but it's all right to think about things that happened before then." When Maggie didn't say anything, Bett pursued the subject more directly. "So you lost touch for a while, then found him again. Where? Here in California?"

"No. Back home. We hung around together in high school."

"But you're not the same age, are you? I mean, the guy we picked up looked like he was my age."

"He's always looked young for his age. I used to get him out of trouble over that when we went out. We'd go over to the next state—the drinking age was only eighteen there." She grinned. "We go back quite a ways. Scotty taught me how to square dance and drink hooch and drive country roads in the middle of the night!"

"So he was an old flame," Bett teased.

"Not really. I was… seeing somebody else. Scotty knew I'd be in hot water if anybody knew. We sort of looked out for each other. He got a class ring for me to wear. Even had his picture taken for me to carry around. Sort of took the pressure off dating guys." Then she added, "Not much pressure."

"Who was the somebody else?"

Just then the waitress returned. Maggie asked for a coffee to go, then reached for the bill. "We should hit the road."

Bett took the check from her. "No arguing, now. My dad gave me some cash before we left. And you said you hadn't been able to get to the bank, didn't you?"

Maggie cocked her head. "I only meant…"

"Huh-uh. I'll get it." Bett quickly figured the tip and set it on the table. "We were just talking about taking care of you. Scotty did before. Now I will!" She closed her wallet. "I think I should drive for a while."

Maggie raised a burned eyebrow, then considered the idea. Freeway driving was fairly easy in the country, especially in the middle of the night. And although the meal had refreshed her, she was still tired. She nodded. "Okay. But when do you usually go to bed?"

Bett nearly dropped her cup in the saucer. "Ready when you are."

Maggie blushed instantly, furiously. "It's not safe to drive more than an hour or two after your bedtime. You might fall asleep at the wheel."

Bett laughed. "That's the *last* thing you have to worry about!"

Maggie drove around the parking lot, demonstrating low gear and how to downshift. "First has synchromesh," she explained. "So don't worry about grinding gears if you have to drop it in before coming to a stop."

Bett covered her face. "If you keep telling me about things I don't have to know and in such a foreign language, I swear I'll...!"

Maggie put a bandaged hand over Bett's. "Sorry, doll. None of that will matter once we're on the road. You'll be in third the whole time. You sure you want to do this?"

"Yes!" Bett seemed determined to help, but as soon as she got behind the wheel, she had trouble. The adjustable seat didn't work.

"What? Everything on my truck works!" Then Maggie apologized, knowing how new everything was to Bett. She handed her the puppy and went around to the driver's side. Bett slid out of the way.

Maggie sat down and released the lever, hearing the spring activate. But the seat still didn't advance. All she could do was roll it back slightly. "Well," she noted optimistically, "at least it's still on track." But even using the steering wheel for leverage only brought the seat forward an inch.

Bett reached underneath Maggie for the tool that she'd shoved there last night, but moving that didn't help, either. She slid the puppy box aside to check in front of the passenger area. "Aha!" She pulled a knapsack free just as Maggie rolled the seat back and, with an extra effort, hurled it forward with all her strength.

They shot forward, and one of Maggie's knees rammed the dashboard. She yowled with shock, then put her head on the wheel, closing her good eye.

Bett turned away to keep from laughing, then calmed the puppy, who was yipping excitedly, and tucked the knapsack in front of his box. She waited for Maggie to curse, but she didn't.

"Jeez," Maggie finally said, lifting her head from the wheel, "am I ever glad you volunteered to drive!"

They switched places again, and Maggie guided the gearshift into first, coaching Bett to release the clutch slowly and press the gas pedal smoothly. On the third try, she managed to do both, jerking them forward without killing the engine. It roared dramatically when Bett followed Maggie's instruction to give it more gas, and they raced toward the on-ramp. She needed some help finding second, but when they rounded the turn and she shifted into third gear by herself, Maggie praised her like she'd won a prize.

As they merged onto the freeway, Maggie reminded her to signal.

"Even when nobody's going to see it?"

"You never know," she warned. "There might be a drunk driver out there with no lights on. *He'll* see it!"

Bett checked the mirror and said, "Oh!" when she saw a vehicle on the side of the road with its headlights off and only one little light on in front.

As Maggie looked on, she wasn't surprised at the trouble Bett was having with her first driving experience. Like most first-timers, she kept too far to one side and couldn't seem to keep the truck heading straight ahead. It constantly rumbled over the lane dividers, keeping the puppy on edge. He'd yelp and jump into Maggie's lap, then onto her chest, licking her face. But she didn't say anything. So long as there wasn't any traffic, she'd let Bett learn by doing. The truck would be fine.

With her legs across the puppy's box, she got as comfortable as possible in the foreshortened cab, angling toward the middle of the cab and keeping an eye on the right-hand mirror. It wasn't perfectly aligned but gave her a pretty good view of the road. Passengering this way wasn't entirely restful, either, but holding the puppy gave her a physical comfort and calmed her as they noisily crossed Botts' Dotts.

She sensed Bett's growing frustration and reached over to steady the wheel. "What's wrong, darlin'? You didn't have any trouble before."

"I was sitting in the middle before," Bett retorted. "I could center the damn truck there!"

Maggie started to chide her for cursing but realized Bett didn't know garage rules. She was understandably tense, too. "I'll show you the secret for that. Let go a minute." Maggie adjusted the truck to the center of the lane. "Now, look down the hood. See that bump in the middle? It's not real easy at night, but…"

"I see it!" Bett took a breath to calm herself. "Now what?"

"Sight that bump and line it up with the edge of the road."

Bett moved left in her seat.

"No, *you* don't move. Steer the truck."

"Huh? What do you mean?"

"Keep your eye on the bump." Maggie adjusted the wheel fractionally. "Now, is it closer to being lined up with the edge of the road, or further away?"

Bett didn't say anything for a long moment. "How'd you do that?"

"Must've blinked." Maggie's smile grew when Bett laughed. "Think you can keep your eye on the road and check that sight once in a while?"

"Sure. But it looks like we're too close to the other side."

"Trust me. We're right in the middle."

"But how can looking at that put us in the middle of the lane?"

"I don't know. I think it has something to do with geometry. I know why some rules work; others I just follow because they do. Speaking of rules, stay at 60 or you'll over-drive your headlights."

"What's *that* mean?" Bett took her foot off the gas, and the truck's speed fell off quickly.

Maggie kept her eye on the speedometer as Bett tried again, but soon the needle passed 60 without pause and was heading toward 65. "It means you won't have time to stop if you see something in your headlights."

"I happen to have excellent vision! And you drove faster than 60. You were going at least 70 when we were behind that truck by Sacramento."

"Mmm. You're right." Maggie listened to the engine. "That's it. Ease up now. Good. Keep it right there." She glanced from the panel to the road ahead, then at the mirrors. "As for how fast I drive, I can read truck signals; the warnings they use. They have much better brakes than cars have, too. That's why they can speed on an empty load." She touched Bett's elbow lightly. "Slow up now, just a little."

Bett made a sound like a growl, and the puppy's ears perked up. "It goes too fast all by itself!"

"Yeah, she likes to go 65. But you're in charge now. Tell her she can't go that fast at night." She saw Bett shoot her a look, then press her lips together tightly, not voicing her thought. Maggie turned her attention back to the road, absently stroking the puppy to calm him. Within a few miles, Bett's driving smoothed out, and she seemed to relax a little as the truck responded to her more-moderate adjustments.

Soon the puppy was asleep in his box, and Maggie could reduce her vigilance as Bett developed a routine of checking her speed, using the bump-sight trick to keep them in their lane, then glancing at the mirrors. On one of her dashboard checks, Bett pointed at the fuel gauge.

"Will we need gas before we get to the cabin?"

Maggie leaned over to read the dial. "Shoot! I should've checked that when we stopped before. Yeah, we should get some."

"Okay! You relax. I'll look for gas signs."

"Sure you'll be all right?" Maggie stifled a yawn.

"I'm fine now," Bett said, quickly running through her checkpoints again. "And I haven't seen that drunk for a while."

Maggie looked up from her sprawled position. "What drunk?"

"The one you said wasn't using his lights."

Maggie remembered the lights-off drunk she'd invented to get Bett in the habit of using blinkers. She looked out the back window. The moon had set, but it was still a bright, starlit night, and the stretch of road behind them was empty. Repositioning her seatbelt connection so it wasn't digging into her, she opened the wing window, then lit a cigarette and pulled out a cup of coffee, ready to enjoy a spell of unfocused quiet. She felt her physical tension subside with those comforts.

The trip was too much for her. She knew that now. Her hands throbbed, sapping her ability to attend to the smaller movements of driving. And her face ached with the bruises around her eye. Almost like getting beat up, she thought wryly. Ten years ago taking a punch didn't slow you down like this. You're getting old, Maggie!

And speaking of age… She sighed quietly and made herself think about Bett. She'd put that off too long already. Thinking about her. Talking to her. Telling her… what? How do you tell someone not to fall in love with you? No, that was too presumptuous. But how could she warn her off? Could she say: "No one's looked at me with eyes so full of hope and promise in a hundred years. Don't do this!"?

She closed her eye to shut off her thoughts, but it wasn't enough. The scent of Bett's hair was on her fingers. She remembered her kiss, the feel of her, tucked beneath her chin. You can always tell her how she makes your knees weak and your heart pound. Maggie rolled that thought around in her head but couldn't imagine saying it out loud. It would sound like she was reading from a perfume ad.

She didn't know how to talk about her feelings. All she could ever talk about was engines and tools, how she made them work together. With her hands, of course. In some ways she'd really only learned to talk with her hands. She didn't think Bett would understand that. It would sound like she was talking about sex. But that…

"Maggie, look! There he is! Look quick!"

"Who?" She peered out the back window. The vacant road unwound behind them.

"The drunk driver."

She felt like she'd fallen for a child's trick and expected Bett to chant: "Made you look! Made you look! Made you buy a penny-book!"

Then a light appeared, glowing dimly before vanishing. It wasn't a headlight. She knew what it was. The knot in her stomach returned.

"How long's he been there?"

"Why? What's the matter?"

Too late, Maggie realized she'd revealed her tension. "Oh," she drawled, "you shouldn't let drunks get too close, is all."

"How do you know he's drunk?"

"Driving without lights in the country usually means there's a drunk or a car thief behind the wheel. In the city, it's usually high beams."

"Why?"

"High beams are illegal in town because they blind oncoming drivers. Drunks don't see the warning light, and car thieves can't always find the dimmer switch."

Bett didn't even know those things existed. "What about those little lights underneath the headlights?"

"Parking lights? They're illegal on moving vehicles. They're not much good in the country at night, either."

"Do they come on when you put a car in Park?"

Maggie smiled. "No. The first notch of the headlight switch. It's how you can spot a drunk at night. He thinks his lights are on because his dash is lit."

"Do they burn out a lot?"

Maggie glanced at the dashboard and pointed to the dark eye that flashed when the turn indicator was on. "We're okay. That bulb stays lit all the time if there's something wrong with the parking light or blinker. That's how a driver can tell without checking it from the outside."

"You're kidding! You mean if a blinker's broken, this light stays *on?*"

"That's how it works."

"Well, no wonder everybody's is out all the time! How backwards can you get?"

Maggie thought it was a clever device. "It doesn't happen that often."

Bett scoffed. "It's practically epidemic! What about that truck back in Oakland? Didn't you say his parking light was out? And now this drunk."

The knot in Maggie's stomach grew, but she refused the connection Bett offered. Nobody would follow us over a hundred miles. It had to be coincidence. One helluva lot of it!

"Maggie? Should I pass these guys?"

"Hmm?" She was watching for the dim light again, but the foothills had become steep slopes, and the curves limited her view, too. She turned to see two semis riding nose-to-tail a half mile ahead. Bett was gaining on them steadily, but Maggie didn't see any problem. She coached her into the left lane, warning her not to speed up to pass. "You'll be going fast enough as it is." Then she turned to the road behind again.

If Maggie had been driving, she would have felt the change in the road, would have noticed the increase in the grade and been warned. But she wasn't. And Bett didn't notice any difference. She kept the speedometer at 60, only knowing that it was okay to pass. She didn't say anything when one of the trucks signaled a lane change. Maggie had told her the left lane was the fast lane, only for passing. So when the rear truck moved into her lane to pass the front truck, she expected it to speed up. Sure enough, as soon as it got in the left lane, it started gaining on the slower truck. But not as fast as Bett was gaining on him.

Maggie turned from the back window. "Holy Jeez! Hit the brakes!" She tried to keep her voice even, but they were on a steep incline, only a hundred yards from the trailer ahead. The right lane was blocked by another semi, and they were going almost twice as fast as the one in their lane.

Bett took her foot off the gas just as a series of bright red flashes came from the taillights directly ahead.

"Brakes!!" Maggie shouted over the truck's air horn blast.

Bett hit the pedal hard, nearly cracking her head on the steering wheel when the pickup answered her jamming action. She tried to hold the wheel, but her balance was off. Maggie grabbed it, having already braced herself, and the emergency dissipated with their speed.

The semi crawled forward, finally clearing the slower truck and moving back into the right lane. Then everybody saluted everybody else with their lights.

When Bett accelerated, the truck chattered noisily. Maggie guided Bett's hand on the gear knob. "Clutch," she said softly, and they downshifted together, regaining speed and passing the rearranged trucks another half mile down the road.

Maggie pointed to a switch on the panel. "Push that in and out twice, then watch the mirror."

Bett did. The truck behind them flashed his lights, too. "How did you know he'd do that?" she asked.

"Truck-talk." Maggie was relieved that Bett wasn't hysterical over their near miss. "Are you okay now?"

She nodded. "But I still don't understand why it happened."

Maggie explained about the change in road grade, then fibbed a little. "You had good reactions."

Bett shook her head. "If you hadn't shouted, I would have hit him. We could have been killed!"

"Mmm." Maggie agreed lightly. "But we weren't. Fact is, you just passed your first driver-improvement lesson!"

"Which is…?"

"Always drive faster than the car behind you; slower than the one ahead!"

Bett smiled. "You're just trying to reassure me." She glanced at Maggie. "Your voice went up at least two octaves, and I've never heard you come so close to swearing before!"

"I'm fine." Maggie brushed Bett's dark hair back from her brow. How long had it been since anyone had picked up on such small things about her? A hundred years maybe.

Bett exited at a twenty-four-hour gas station and followed the posted ramp speeds, shifting into second by herself and turning right through a yield sign, then right again into a parking lot. She braked the truck to a jerking, fitful stop as the engine died.

"You forgot…"

"I know." Bett put her head on the steering wheel and closed her eyes. "I forgot to clutch."

Maggie laughed. "You get the puppy. I'll get the gas." She was glad to reclaim the driver's seat, where she pushed the clutch in, shifted into gear, and turned the key, all in one fluid motion. Stroking the accelerator, she listened to the engine, feeling some of her own energy return with those familiar acts. Then she eased the clutch out, drawing away slowly and pulling the door to. "Meet me at the pumps!"

✧ ✧ ✧

Bett ran with the puppy to a small woods at the edge of the parking lot. A fence kept anyone from going down the slope to the freeway, and she felt her way along the narrow path next to it. She looked down at the road, thinking: "I drove that!" The pride that came with that thought surprised her.

Just then a tractor-trailer topped the distant rise and signaled its exit. She recognized the chatter and clatter of gears and engine whine that meant downshifting, but when he flashed his lights and blew his horn, she had to guess what kind of warning he was giving.

Below her, a pickup truck was parked on the side of the exit ramp. Its lights came on in response to the air horn. Before that it had been nearly invisible and was again when its lights went off. Then a match flared. Bett was too far away to see the smoker's face, but she could see two people in the cab. She wondered why they had stopped there.

Just then the puppy jumped up on her, yowling for attention. She bent to pet him and, out of the corner of her eye, saw the smoker turn toward the sound. Taking refuge in the shadows, Bett stayed low, frightened without really knowing why. She moved away from the fence quietly, making sure the puppy was following her. When they emerged from the woods, she raced him across the tarmac to the truck and jumped into the cab just as Maggie climbed in the other door.

Bett told her about the other pickup. She was still a little panicked and glad to see Maggie take the news calmly.

"Did both parking lights come on?"

A tick sounded in the back of Bett's head. Maggie's tone set it off. It was the same tone she'd used to ask about the one-light drunk. "I couldn't see that. Just some-body smoking in the cab. You think it's the same guy?"

"Oh," Maggie shrugged, "it could be anybody."

"Don't..." Bett almost said "patronize me" but couldn't bring herself to use that harsh an epithet. "Don't treat me like a child!"

Maggie shook her head in silent apology. After a long minute, she said, "I think we're being followed. I don't know why."

And with that, several things fell in place for Bett. She didn't like the fact that Maggie had withheld her suspicions and said as much. "We're in this together, after all."

"After all," Maggie echoed.

"Don't mock me!" Bett's anger flared again. "Just because I don't have a driver's license..."

"Sorry," she said quickly. "But I feel responsible for you being here."

"Well, you're not! I'm here because I want to be. Don't you know that?"

Maggie nodded silently, then started the engine.

"What should we do?" Bett asked.

"I'm not sure. But I don't want to go to the CHP."

Bett agreed. She wanted to avoid the helpless-female syndrome, too. "Can the truckers help? You can talk with them on your radio, can't you?"

"I thought of that." Maggie drove to the edge of the lot and put the truck in neutral, then lit a cigarette. "But we'll be leaving the interstate soon. The rigs keep going east." She took a drag. "There's always a positive side, though. Think they know where we're going?"

"Probably not." Bett didn't know. How could they?

"Right. Maybe we can lose them before we get there."

"How?"

"I don't know yet." She put the truck in gear. "Let's see if they follow us." As she turned onto the freeway, Maggie warned Bett not to look out the back window. "Use the mirror instead. Don't let them know you're watching."

"Why?"

"I don't want to force their hand."

Bett heard Maggie swear under her breath and knew she was more upset than she'd let on. That was another oddity of hers: never swearing out loud. Bett kept watch in her mirror. "They've got their headlights on now, but it's the same truck: That little light is still out." A curve put the vehicle out of sight. "Why do you suppose they're following us?"

"I don't know. The last time…" Maggie waved a hand in dismissal.

"You mean this happened before?" Bett was incredulous.

"Not really. Different circumstances entirely."

Bett waited for her to go on, but she didn't. "What happened then? God, I have to drag every gram of information out of you!"

"Well, it's sort of embarrassing. And it happened a long time ago. I was young and dumb and drove a much slower car."

"And…?"

"How old are you, Bett?"

"What? You mean you're not going to tell me the story unless I'm old enough?"

"No, that *is* the story. I was out with somebody underage."

Bett still didn't understand. "I'm twenty-one."

Maggie nodded, still not saying more.

Bett persisted. "You were driving around with somebody underage, and you were followed?"

"Well, we were parked in this driveway. A cemetery entrance, actually."

"Was this a female-type somebody?" Bett teased.

"Mmm-hmm."

Bett rolled her eyes. "And what does underage mean? Surely she wasn't five or six years old."

"No, in that state the age of consent was eighteen. I would've really caught it, except for a glitch in the law."

"This could be fascinating! Why don't you tell me the whole story?" But Bett's sarcasm was lost on Maggie.

"You want to hear about somebody else I went out with?"

"Of course! And eventually I want to hear about everybody you ever went out with, but now I want to know why *that* story is like this one."

"Oh, yeah. Well, like I said, she was young. Only seventeen. She'd told her husband about me." Then she muttered, "How could I have done it twice?"

"Done what twice?"

"Nothing. Anyway, he… caught us. We were just making out, but he wanted me arrested for statutory rape. It wouldn't fly, though. She was married. That was the glitch."

Bett couldn't believe it. "You made that all up!"

"Truth!" Maggie raised a hand as if taking an oath.

"Did you get a lawyer or what?"

She snorted. "I got a broken nose and an invitation to go on stage. One was leaving in ten minutes. You know that old joke?"

Bett was weak with sudden anger. "He… hit you because he couldn't have you arrested? That's criminal! Did you go to the police?"

"Police were there." She tossed her head. "Like I said, it was a long time ago. I haven't been out with anybody that young since."

"Well, they're not following me," Bett said. "If anything, I'd guess it was your friend Ebert!" The ensuing silence lasted longer than she expected, and she was sure she'd stepped on precious toes.

"Tracy isn't that far gone," Maggie finally said. "Besides, she drives a 'Z. A blue Datsun. What made you mention her?"

Bett heard her studied indifference. "I think she's mad about something. Maybe I set her off somehow."

"You're right about her anger, but I don't think she's following us. And I don't think she's mad at anybody in particular, just the world at large."

"Will you tell me about her sometime?"

Maggie squeezed her hand. "As soon as I figure her out myself!"

They rode in silence after that. Bett looked up at the sky through the back window. Scattered clouds had rolled in, but the canopy of stars held steadily spectacular. And the headlights behind continued to trail them.

❖ ❖ ❖

As they turned off the interstate, they both checked the mirrors, hoping theirs would be the only vehicle taking that route. Moments later, the three-light pickup appeared behind them on the state highway. They traveled at a steady pace, only passing through a few small towns. Bett asked how far they had to go.

"About a half hour now. If it weren't dark, I'd be showing you the landmarks…" Then Maggie remembered the fire tower. It was accessible from two separate roads, about a hundred yards apart. They were both short, steep grades, but the second one was virtually hidden from this direction, unless you knew to look. She'd only found it by driving up the near road to where it topped out in a small parking lot. If they drove up the far road and waited on top, they could double-back after their pursuers went by. Timing would be critical, but it could work. She outlined the idea to Bett, who supported it enthusiastically.

"Where are we now?" she asked.

"About ten miles from Eagle Pass. The tower's a few miles beyond that. As soon as we get to Eagle, look for the red light on the top of the tower. Thank god it's clear. You can probably see all the way to the Mississippi tonight."

When they got to Eagle Pass, Bett checked the back window. "How far ahead will you need to be to get up to the tower without them seeing us?"

"I'm not sure. The road to the cabin is about a mile this side of the tower." She tried to remember the stretch of road beyond it. "We'll have to see what the highway is like between the cabin road and the tower."

"Okay," Bett said. "After we go around a curve, you drive like hell to the next one. As soon as I see their lights, I'll yell and you slow down so we don't look like we're running. Then do the next curve the same way. If they aren't too close when we get to the tower, we'll follow your plan. But if they are, we'll keep going. To the Mississippi if we have to!"

Maggie nodded. A contingency plan made sense. She felt keyed up now, as if she'd had a full night's sleep. Or made love in the late afternoon. She didn't wonder where that thought came from. She just dismissed it.

"I see the tower light!" Bett yelled.

Maggie had forgotten how broken the terrain was outside of Eagle Pass. "Maybe we don't have to drive like hell..." She glanced in the mirror, but the three-light truck was only a few hundred yards back. They needed more distance. Now. She picked up speed. Taking the downhills too fast, she squealed around the bends, crossing the double yellow lines like a slalom skier.

Bett watched through the back window as they drew further ahead. Soon she couldn't see the other truck's lights directly, only their silver reflection on the power lines overhead.

"Here's our turnoff," Maggie announced as they passed a sign.

"Let's take it," Bett said. "They're out of sight."

Maggie didn't even slow down. "North Slope Road is too straight. They might spot our taillights. Besides, I think it's the only turnoff on this stretch. If they stay on this road, they'll get to Triangle Points. I want them to think we kept going there."

Another mile past North Slope, the tower's red light disappeared when they got to the base of its hill. Maggie took her foot off the gas briefly, searching for the hidden drive, then braked hard and downshifted, accelerating up the gravel road, kicking rocks and dirt in their wake. The rise topped out suddenly, but the parking area was visible only for an instant as she switched off the lights and cut the engine. She applied the emergency brake, and the back of the truck slewed around before coming to a halt. Darkness enveloped them.

The puppy yowled and yelped twice. When no one got out of the truck, he quieted. Garrumphing sleepily, he settled back into his box.

The silence was as thick as the darkness. Bett moved in her seat, and Maggie hushed her. "Crack your window," she commanded softly.

Bett did, and sound drifted in the partially open window. The wind soughed through the trees, a comforting whisper.

"What are we doing?" Bett asked softly.

No reply.

Bett tapped her arm. Maggie raised a hand: Wait!

Then they heard an engine. The pickup seemed to take forever to come into view. Finally, from around a curve, lights shone on the road, pulling the sound behind.

The truck slowed to a stop almost directly below them, between the two roads to the tower, effectively blocking both exits. Maggie reached out instinctively to cover Bett's hand with her own bandaged one, calming her.

Voices drifted up to them, muted at first. Then they heard a familiar phrase: "...you shithead!" More words became understandable.

"Lights in the trees, huh? A flying truck, right?"

Another voice muttered a reply, then the louder one again: "Yeah? Well, whose fucking idea was this? Aw' right..."

The rest of the words were drowned out by engine noise as the truck pulled away, speeding up and disappearing around the next curve.

Maggie exhaled loudly and shook a cigarette out of her pack. "Friends of yours?" she asked blithely.

Bett took a breath, too. "*My* friends always call first!"

Maggie sat with her ear cocked to the open window. Smoke from her cigarette mingled with and fled in the pre-dawn breeze.

"Who do you suppose they were?" Bett finally asked.

"Oh, maybe a couple of drunk cowboys trying to find a date."

Bett ignored the thin joke and said, "That pickup seemed familiar somehow. Did you recognize it?"

Maggie started the engine. It sounded abnormally loud in the stillness of the forest. Shifting into gear, she rolled to the incline. "Sure. It looked just like the truck that followed us."

"No. I think I saw it somewhere else. Before tonight, I mean."

Maggie chuckled as she switched on the headlights and steered down the path, using first gear to check her speed. With a final glance to her left, she hit the gas and rolled out onto the highway.

"Darlin'," she drawled, "the day before yesterday you didn't know the difference between a pickup and a Travel-All. Now you think you've seen this chase truck before." She laughed again, but not meanly.

As they turned down the secondary road that led to Maggie's cabin, both of them watched the mirrors. No lights followed them this time.

CHAPTER 8.

Don't Lose Heart

BRIAN KESSLER WAS AT HIS desk early Sunday morning. It was his day off, but he wanted to finish his report on Tracy Ebert. He was reading through a draft when Arnie Weigert and Jim Harley came in.

"How's it going, Jim?" he said, greeting the rookie.

"Not bad, Sarge. You gotta work Sundays, too?"

"Once in a while, just to keep up with paperwork. But I didn't expect to see you this morning. Thought you were on second tour today."

Harley replied in his best navy-trained English: "Yes, sir." He thumbed at Weigert, who was studying the bulletin board. "He asked me to pick him up. Otherwise, I wouldn't be here a week early."

Brian smiled, then gestured for him to sit. "So, how's it going with Weigert? You're getting a chance at the wheel now, aren't you?"

"Yes, sir. I always drive… Well, I drive when I partner with Weigert."

Kessler ignored the difficulty he seemed to be having. "Do you prefer driving with Weigert to riding shotgun with Ebert?"

"No, sir."

Kessler leaned back. "I know Ebert always drives when you two partner, but it's important for you to work with other…"

"I'd rather ride with her," Harley said in a rush. He slowed then. "You asked what I preferred. And, well, I learn more from her. Sir."

"She's good with new officers," Brian mused aloud. "Why do you think you learn so much from her?"

Harley paused before responding, but then spoke with enthusiasm. His feedback was thorough, even listing a high-speed chase Ebert had taken him on, and the fact that they'd lost their suspect

When Kessler cocked his head, Harley quickly expanded. "She actually could have caught up with the guy—we were about a half block behind him—but she shut off the siren and pulled into a parking lot. Then she asked me if I knew why she'd quit the chase. I didn't, and she said, 'Look around.' That was when I saw all the kids. School had just let out, and they were everywhere.

"Ebert's always seeing things that other cops don't. And she always asks what I've seen, too, or what I'm looking at and why."

Kessler nodded thoughtfully. "Some say she's a hotdog."

"They're wrong!" Harley leaned back. "I know she's had problems…"

"What do you mean?"

"You hear things." The rookie downplayed his own remark. "Some of the guys think she's a hard-a… I mean, hard to work with. But she isn't."

Kessler shrugged. That wasn't what counted on the streets. Then the phone rang. It was the morgue.

"No match?… Either hand?… I know how bad he was burned… No, thanks. I saw the body… Yeah, send it over. I'll get it tomorrow?… Right. Would dental X-rays help?… Okay, I'll get back to you. Thanks." He hung up, grimacing. "Guy wanted to read me the path' report!"

Harley smiled at his exaggerated dismay. "You mean hearing that stuff gets worse the longer you stay on the job?"

"No, I just don't want to hear how 'burnt to a crisp' translates in medical terms!" Kessler gave him a brief report of the freeway incident.

"Something special about this John Doe?" Harley asked.

"The victim might be a friend of Maggie McIntyre's. You know, M & M?"

Harley looked blank.

"The garage over on Kenning…? Hasn't Ebert taken you down there?" He waved a hand. "Wouldn't have to be her. Half the force hangs out there. Ask her to take you over sometime."

"Any chance I could ride with Ebert today, sir?"

"I'll see if I can get the change in before roll call." He finished the note to Maggie. When he looked up, he smiled. "I don't want to burst your bubble, Jim, but you'll still have to rotate so long as you have different days off."

The light in Harley's eyes didn't fade entirely. "I just said I wanted to ride with her, Sarge. I didn't say I wanted to marry the woman!"

Kessler laughed, even though he couldn't picture them as a couple. He didn't know why, only that it had nothing to do with race.

❖ ❖ ❖

Bett woke to soft, wet kisses on her cheek. She knew she'd been dreaming, but those weren't the kisses she dreamed of.

Taking the still-nameless puppy by the scruff of the neck, she carried him, yipping and yowling, out the front door. The wind was already up, making the morning seem brisker than the temperature alone would have. She decided to warm up with a run, and a few minutes later trotted down the driveway with the puppy tagging along behind. This was new territory, and she was glad for his company.

She remembered Maggie saying she'd be up early to make a run to town for breakfast supplies. So much for being indefatigable, Maggie! Bett thought she looked so vulnerable in the gentle repose of sleep, with one hand extended from the covers, displaying worn bandages.

They had discussed changing them when they arrived and Maggie started building a fire. Concerned that the gauze might catch a spark, Bett pointed out: "I could start the fire, you know." When she agreed to be careful, Bett let her be and looked around the cabin.

Maggie had described it as "a little primitive," but once inside, Bett accused her of false advertising. "Well," Maggie elaborated, "there's no phone, no TV, no dishwasher, and no microwave oven."

In fact, the cabin was much better furnished than Maggie's apartment. The main room was the largest and centered the cabin. A flagstone fireplace, flanked by built-in bookcases and pine-paneled walls, made the atmosphere cozy despite the initial chill of vacancy.

There were two bedrooms, but only one was ready for use. The front bedroom was empty of furnishings, except for a double mattress leaning against the wall. Maggie called it the "Winter Room" and said something about not having been up to put things to rights. She led Bett to the back bedroom. It was simply but comfortably furnished with a double bed, covered by a bright yellow down comforter. A round claw-foot table held a reading lamp, and a wingback chair was tucked in a corner next to a chest of drawers. The bedrooms connected through a bath that offered complete indoor plumbing. There was no tub, but Bett couldn't complain, since there was a perfectly adequate shower.

Although fairly small, the cabin had two entrances. The front door opened on a western-style porch with smoothed log supports. The back door opened onto the steep upgrade of a hill. Bett loved it, especially when she saw the kitchen.

Parallel to the main room, it ran the length of the cabin. An oval, farmhouse kitchen table sat against the back wall, just inside the open-framed doorway. You could sit at the table and enjoy the warmth of the main room, or face the kitchen work area, which had plenty of counter space and a restaurant-size gas stove next to an unexpectedly ancient refrigerator.

Bett found Maggie clearing empty beer cans and liquor bottles from the counter and opened a plastic garbage bag to help.

"Some party you threw last time you were here," she teased.

"Somebody did." Maggie crossed to the refrigerator. "But I'm not going to grouse about it if the well isn't dry. Ah! Still a few left. Want a beer?"

Bett agreed to split one, and asked if it was okay for her to smoke a joint. Maggie nodded and tucked a bottle of schnapps under her arm, then brought the beer and glasses to the main room. Bett moved over to share the long couch, but Maggie settled in a recliner across the coffee table from her.

Neither of them spoke for a while, but it was a comfortable silence. Bett let her mind drift over the events of the last few hours. Then she remembered seeing that truck driver in his mirror. She giggled, and Maggie asked what was so funny.

Bett tried to tell her about the surprise on his face but couldn't seem to make it clear which truck driver she meant. She giggled again. Suddenly she seemed to know a *lot* of truck drivers. Then her thoughts took a jarring turn. "My mother had that same look on her face the day she died. I found her, you know. Do you suppose everyone is surprised by death?"

Without waiting for an answer, Bett started talking about her mother. How they'd discovered her cancer only a year before she died. How the oncologists had said there was nothing they could do. That was when Bett decided to quit pre-med. It shocked her father, but not her mother.

"She knew me so well," Bett said through tears she didn't realize she was shedding. "She reminded me of something I'd said about being gay—how hard it was being so different from everyone else, even though I knew I couldn't change who I was. She said medicine was like that for me. A fire that had to be tended. It was my spirit. If I didn't tend it, I'd die inside. Worse even than dying outside, she told me." Bett sniffed. "I didn't have any choice about that either, she said. I could leave pre-med, but I couldn't quit doctoring or nursing. I'd always do that kind of work, whether I had the degrees or not. Always tend the sick and dying." Bett was crying in earnest now.

"Like loving women. I didn't have any choice. I'd told her I couldn't suddenly decide to love men. She reminded me of that. I couldn't just decide to be a computer programmer, she said. It wouldn't compute, or it wouldn't fly." Bett started laughing through her sobs then. "She said it wouldn't heal right. And I forgot. Isn't that hysterical?"

Maggie went to her, wrapping her arms around her and calming her. She combed Bett's hair with her fingertips, tracing her face lightly, wiping her tears with a soft cloth she made appear out of nowhere, just like Brian's handkerchief. Bett wanted to tell her how funny that was: The whole world used disposable tissues except for Maggie and Brian. But she couldn't talk, she could only cry. And when her crying eased, she had the hiccups.

Maggie poured a shot of schnapps and told her to toss it down. "You won't taste it so much that way."

Bett tried to follow her advice but choked on the vapors. Her throat felt like it was on fire, and an overpowering peppermint taste filled her mouth. Then the liquor hit her stomach, and her whole body hiccupped. When she could breathe again, she said: "You *like* that stuff?"

Maggie grinned. "Glad you're feeling better!"

It was true. Her hiccups had disappeared. And she had none of the crushing depression that always came with talking about her mother, either.

Then Maggie led her to the bedroom, where she laid her down and drew the comforter over her, stroking her face lightly. "You've been up nearly twenty-four hours, darlin'. You're dead on your feet. I'm going to get some things from the truck. Will you keep the dog here? Out of my way?"

Bett nodded. "Promise you'll hurry?"

Maggie leaned over and kissed her forehead. Bett drew her closer, kissing her lips. When bandaged hands cupped her face, she moved to make room on the bed.

Maggie drew back. "Promise," she whispered, and then she was gone.

Bett never heard a thing after that. She woke up under the covers, wearing a nightgown that wasn't hers. All that was familiar was the comforter and the warmth of Maggie next to her. And the puppy, of course.

She finished her run feeling clear-headed and walked the last hundred feet to the driveway. She wasn't prepared for the thinner air here. Then she smiled. She didn't seem prepared for anything related to Maggie.

Looking up, she saw Maggie's truck parked next to the cabin. The M & M symbol stood out boldly, reminding her of Elise's help in remembering that emblem. Damn! Bett thought. I forgot to leave her a note. I'll have to call her when we go into town.

She loped up the drive and crossed a railroad tie, the first in a row of stepped ones that formed a retaining wall alongside the driveway, then followed a footpath across the yard and paused on the porch to look out on the landscape, breathing in the fresh air. It invigorated her as much as her run. It was a beautiful day. She smiled. It would be a wonderful week!

She repeated that thought when she found a note on the refrigerator door.

> *Fresh eggs, milk, and juice in here. I took a run to the store when I finished unloading the truck. Hope you slept well. I'll sleep 'til Tuesday unless you wake me at noon.*
>
> *Maggie*
> *P.S. The clutch is tight!*

At noon, Bett delivered a tray to the bedside table. But waking Maggie wasn't easy. She was about to give up, thinking it was the wrong point in her sleep cycle, when Maggie finally stirred.

"Is that coffee I smell?" she muttered.

Before Bett could reply, the puppy scrambled up and started pawing her shoulder, licking her neck and ears. Bett pulled him off, then piled pillows behind Maggie as she sat up.

"It's coffee, juice, milk, toast, and eggs. Did I forget anything?"

"Coffee first. Talk later."

The tray was on Maggie's blind side, and Bett handed her the mug, warning that it was hot. "It might be too strong, too. I wasn't sure how long to perk it. You forgot to mention there's no automatic coffeemaker!"

Bett saw her smile and sat back, enjoying these early waking moments as yet another facet of this new woman in her life. When Maggie finished eating, Bett asked, "Do you always wake up so sleepy?"

"Only on Sundays." Maggie started to put the plate down for the puppy, then asked, "Do you mind?"

Bett took the plate and set it on the floor. "Only if you'd hated my omelet."

"Some people have funny ideas about cleanliness and dogs."

"And some people just have funny ideas."

Maggie reached for her coffee again. "What do you mean?"

"Waking up sleepy just on Sundays. Or were you kidding?"

She smiled over the mug. "I always heard Sunday was a day of rest. It's the only day I sleep late, and the only time I wake up sleepy. Makes sense to me. What's so funny about that?"

Bett shook her head. "You're unbelievable. By the way, did you pick up dog food?"

"Mmm-hmm." Maggie nodded at the puppy. "He doesn't know how to stay yet. I was afraid he'd wake you, so I brought him with me. When we got in the store, he ran right over to the dog food and pointed at something called Chunky Kibbles. I showed him puppy food, but he wanted that stuff. I think he's after the Captain Fido offer on the back."

Bett laughed and watched Maggie take out a cigarette. She was tempted to take it away, wanting nothing more than to make love to her right then. Not knowing if Maggie liked making love first thing in the morning, she picked up the tray instead, promising herself she'd find out about that later in the week. She headed for the door. "How are you feeling this morning?"

Maggie squinted through a haze of smoke for a long moment before shaking off a silent thought. "Fine, thanks." Then she inhaled the coffee instead of her cigarette and choked. Coughing violently at first, she waved Bett away. "Went down... wrong pipe." Finally able to clear her throat, she took another sip. Successfully this time.

Bett put a cool hand to her face. "Are you running a fever?"

"I'm not running anything today. I'm on vacation, remember?"

Bett picked up the tray again and went to the door. "I've already been out exercising the dog. It's a gorgeous day. Are you going to get up now, or is this one of those eat-and-sleep vacations I hear old people talk about?"

"Old, huh?" Maggie threw a pillow, which hit the footboard, landing two feet short of her target.

"I rest my case!" Bett laughed, closing the door behind her.

⋄ ⋄ ⋄

Twenty minutes later they went out the back door and up the hill, with the dog scampering ahead and then back again to check on them. Maggie suggested the walk, saying there was a path on top of the ridge. "We'll get a view of the valley and go down to the pond. How's that sound?"

"You sure you're up to it?"

"I'm not an invalid!"

"Just checking," Bett said easily.

At the top of the ridge, Maggie pointed out a distant spot of fog as Eagle Pass and the ribbon of blacktop as North Slope Road. Smoke plumes marked a few isolated cabins on either side of the road.

The puppy amused them as they walked. He seemed to think all birds, chipmunks, squirrels, and swirling leaves were invaders of his private turf, and he charged one or another at every turn. After each sortie, he would return, panting and woofing to lope at their heels.

"We may end up carrying him back," Bett said.

"Yeah, he might be too young to go to the pond. It's a good mile."

"How young is too young?"

Maggie smiled. "Don't worry. You're old enough."

Bett persisted. "Was that married woman old enough?"

"Which… married woman would that be?"

"Maggie, stop! I want to know a million things about you, but you won't open up. Is there something you don't want me to know? Some deep, dark secret? Is somebody after you? The CIA? The KGB? Somebody's husband? Somebody's wife?"

"The ones who chased us last night?"

Bett could see she wasn't trying to be evasive. "No, not that. I mean, so far as I know, you flew in from outer space two weeks ago and wandered into the Fox Borough to test your English language skills. I hardly know anything about you!" She saw wariness in Maggie's eye. "Am I pressuring you somehow? I don't mean to."

"No," Maggie said. "A friend of mine once told me never to volunteer anything. He was talking about not giving bankers any information that wasn't on the balance sheet. Maybe I took his advice too much to heart."

Bett waited for her to go on, but that seemed to be it. She sighed. "That's a perfect example of what I mean. Now I know you have a friend who gave you some advice, but I don't know any more about *you!* What you thought about it. Whether it works for you in some ways but not others. Nothing."

Maggie absorbed that, then said, "Okay," and set off down the path again.

"Okay *what?*" Bett ran to catch up.

"I'll work on it."

Bett took her arm. "Is it really so hard to talk about yourself?"

Maggie shook her head, then grew thoughtful. "I don't actually talk about myself much, except for what goes on at M & M. But you're not asking about that, are you?"

"No." Bett smiled but didn't add more.

Maggie thought a moment longer, then took a different tack and reminded Bett of how she talked about herself. "You talk about your family and friends, even your teachers in college. Other people and…" She paused as if searching for a word.

"My relationship with them?" Bett suggested.

Maggie gave her a half-nod. "I suppose."

"Of course I do. All women do. That's a classic difference between men and…"

Maggie shook her head. "That's not how I think of myself."

"Are you sure?" Bett challenged. "What about work?"

She shrugged. "Maybe I used to feel like one of the guys, but not much anymore."

"Why not? No, wait! First tell me what you mean by 'one of the guys.'"

"Don't tell me that expression has faded with the years!"

Bett smiled. "I hardly ever hear women use it."

"There never have been many women in my line of work."

"Is that why you don't work with any?"

"No. Well, maybe. We had a bad experience a few years back. One worked in the office. Had to fire the little nympho!"

Bett was as shocked by her venom as by her description. "Little what?"

"Hey, she nearly cost Phil his marriage!" Maggie said hotly. "And that's another thing! When it happened, one of the guys had the balls to say, 'At least she wasn't screwing the boss!' But that wasn't the point…" She stopped then, disgusted at herself for getting so worked up. "Forget it. You weren't there." She strode off, beyond a stand of trees, leaving Bett to wonder what had happened.

Bett ran to catch up, then saw Maggie motioning her to come forward quietly. As she got closer, Bett followed her gaze across a pond—a hollow of sand-edged blue nearly surrounded by fir trees—except on the far side, where yellow and purple wildflowers danced in glory. Three deer stood poised to flee. Then one slowly lowered its head to drink, and a fawn emerged from hiding, prancing on uncertain legs to the water's edge.

Bett ducked under Maggie's outstretched arm and encircled her waist, touching bare skin where her flannel shirt had come untucked. Maggie tensed briefly, then settled her arm around Bett. They stood together that way, silently watching the deer for several minutes until a bird flew over, cawing loudly. The deer froze for an instant, then followed the leader in bounding leaps and disappeared one by one into the far forest.

The two women looked at each other, and before Maggie could flee the way the deer had, Bett reached up and kissed her. For a moment, she didn't respond. But only for a moment. Then she put both arms around Bett and returned her kiss.

It was all the encouragement Bett needed. Stroking Maggie's back with one hand, she slipped her other hand inside her shirtfront, gently counting her ribs by touch. Just enough, she thought, and covered Maggie's breast, feeling her response even as she heard her moan, deep in her throat.

Maggie broke their kiss, then hugged Bett so tightly she couldn't move her hand.

"Maggie," Bett said, as well as she could, nestled this close, "you've got a lot of explaining to do!"

"Girl," she sighed, "you take my breath away."

"Woman," Bett corrected. "I am a woman."

"Oh, yes," Maggie breathed into her hair. "Definitely."

They stepped apart then, agreeing wordlessly to go down to the pond. They held hands loosely as they walked to the meadow, settling on a slab of rock there among the wildflowers. They took off their jackets as the puppy splashed in and out of the water, then curled up between them and instantly fell asleep.

"Will you tell me what's going on?" Bett asked softly.

Maggie started to answer, then looked away.

"Come on," she urged gently.

"I don't want you to think it's your fault."

Bett shook her head.

"Well, I'm having a really hard time keeping my hands off you."

Bett waited for her to go on, but she didn't. "Uh, Maggie…? I know there's another, very clever way to say this, but I *want* you to touch me."

"Yeah." She nodded. "I know. I'm sorry."

Silence reigned.

"What's the problem then?" Bett asked hoarsely.

Maggie looked up in surprise. "I can't."

"Can't? Can't *what?*" Bett wished she didn't sound so close to hysteria.

"Touch you."

"But you *have* been!" Bett put her hands to her head. Her logic ticks and chittering mice were having a regular Mardi Gras over this conversation. She saw Maggie start to reply and held up a hand. "Wait! If you're going to say 'I know.' Don't. Don't say it. Because if you do, tiny little animals inside my head will blow the top off. I know I sound hysterical, but I'm not. Not yet!" She took a deep breath. "Let's start with Friday, before the accident. We'll pretend it's Friday. You take it from there."

"Well, I suppose in a way, if Friday night hadn't happened…" Maggie shook her head. "Let me think this through. I have to figure out some other way to put it." After a moment, she said, "This might not make much sense at first, but bear with me, okay?" At Bett's nod, she went on. "When I say I'll do something, I do it. People who know me expect that. It's how I've gotten where I am. Making promises and keeping them."

"Perfectly clear so far," Bett encouraged.

"That's why I wanted to be clear about our time together this weekend." She paused briefly. "I guess I wasn't, huh?"

Bett motioned for her to keep talking.

"In business, when you do a job for somebody and they come back for more, another job I mean, it's because you did okay the first time, or your price was right or whatever the deal was. They also come back because they have an expectation. It's a warranty or guarantee. I could never figure out the difference. Anyhow, I take that real seriously. And I didn't want you to have any, well, false expectations about me."

Bett paused before completing that thought. "Or what you could do this weekend? Is that it?"

Maggie nodded.

"You're serious, aren't you?"

"Absolutely! Why?"

"My god!" Bett gasped, "I don't know whether to laugh my head off or smack you in your bad eye."

Maggie's brow furrowed. "I understand why you're angry, but…"

Bett overrode her. "Let's see if I've got this right. You think I came to see you the other night because I'd gotten such a good deal two weeks ago? Because you'd done a good job. Is that it?"

When Maggie nodded, Bett was too shocked to be angry. "I've never heard such bizarre thinking in my entire life!"

"What do you…?"

"Maggie, did you…" Bett had to swallow to keep from laughing outright. "…enjoy making love with me two weeks ago?"

She blushed and turned away. "Of course."

Bett moved with her, taking care not to startle her. It was very hard not to think this was all an elaborate hoax, but the sounds in her head were silent. Bett consciously erased recent events from her mind and went back to Friday night. "When I showed up at M & M, did you think we could have that same kind of evening? Remember asking me if I wanted to go to dinner?"

"I remember that part."

"Did you expect, or hope, to make love that night?"

She nodded.

"If this was Friday night, would you make love to me?"

"Can't."

"You mean you couldn't?" Bett clarified.

"No, I can't now." Maggie raised her bandaged hands.

Bett shook her head. "I understand everything you've said except that. After all, there's more than one way to make love!"

Maggie's eye narrowed. "I thought you liked how we did it before." It was half a question, half a statement.

"That doesn't mean I wouldn't like it another way, too."

She nodded. "That's what I meant about your needing someone else."

Suddenly a new logic gate opened up for Bett, and she heard herself ask: "Would that someone else make love to me differently from how you did?"

"Probably."

Bett was almost afraid to ask her next question, and she didn't even know why. "Maggie, would you make love to me differently?"

"Can't."

Bett watched as she lay back, using her jacket as a pillow. "Why not?" She had to ask, even though she fully expected Maggie to say "Because of my hands." They were going to be here until dark.

"Don't know how." Maggie closed her eye.

"What?"

"I don't know how any other way," Maggie expanded.

"Wait a minute…" Bett was sure she'd misheard her.

Maggie sighed. "I mean, how I made love to you is how I make love. Period. Like the Kentucky Fried Chicken commercial: 'I do one thing and one thing only. And I do it really well.'"

Oh, Maggie! Bett closed her own eyes. Do you have any idea how many ways there are to fix chicken?

She put her head down to keep from laughing out loud. Their entire conversation had been so unbelievable she couldn't go on. A full minute went by before she could compose herself enough to look up.

Maggie was sound asleep.

Still lying back on the rock, with her jacket packed behind her head, she had dozed off in just those few moments. Twenty minutes elapsed before she stirred. Then she woke with a start and began apologizing.

Bett stopped her. "You slept because you were tired. On this planet, that's called being human. Come on. Time to change those bandages."

∴ ∴ ∴

It took them some time to walk back to the cabin. Maggie was moving slowly, feeling like she couldn't quite shake the aftereffects of her nap. But when they got to the path leading down to the cabin, her feeling of lassitude disappeared.

"We've got company," she said, nodding at the bottom of the path that led to the cabin. Two vehicles were parked behind her truck. The tail end of a car was just visible beyond the corner of the cabin, and next to it, another white pickup. As she watched, the pickup backed to the woodpile, turned, and drove away. Then a horn sounded, startling the puppy. He took off as if called, barking down the path, with Bett dashing after him.

"Bett, wait!" Maggie followed as fast as she could, not wanting Bett to face whoever was at the cabin. At least not alone.

Running downhill was easier than running up, but much more dangerous. She was almost at the bottom when a wave of dizziness overtook her. She wrapped an arm around a small birch to steady herself. Then the barking turned frantic, and she heard Bett's voice: "Stop! Don't shoot!"

Maggie tore around the corner of the cabin. She saw the squad car first, then the sheriff's deputy, his gun drawn. Bett was reaching for the puppy. Swerving to avoid them all, Maggie stopped her dead run by grabbing the doorframe of the car. Pain shot up both arms; white light filled her head.

The deputy put his gun away, and Bett picked up the dog, who finally stopped barking. Maggie sat down in the shadow of the car. Everything seemed abnormally quiet for a moment.

"What happened to you?" the deputy asked. "You look like hell!"

She didn't reply. The emergency was over, and she felt like she was going to pass out. She wasn't ready for questions yet. Helluva run, she thought. It was all so familiar: out of breath, dry throat, hands hurt like hell. Just like... but memory fled, ran out of her head with the wind.

"Maggie? Are you all right?"

Memory flashed again. A firefly in the darkness. She tried to reply but could only nod. Uniformed legs came into view. Oh, no! Bett's joined the police department. Then, alongside the khaki, Bett's jeans and running shoes appeared. Maggie's head cleared a bit more.

She greeted the deputy without looking up. "What's going on, Berger?"

He snorted. "You girls playing king on the mountain or what?"

Maggie saw Bett's feet shift toward him and sensed her anger.

"Bett, would you get me a beer?" She knew she'd succeeded in distracting her when Bett crouched down. "And could you bring me one of those white pills, too?"

"Sure." She headed for the cabin at a run, still holding the puppy.

"Hey, slow down!" the deputy called to her.

"Can't keep her from running," Maggie said. "Hobby, you know." She still felt dizzy but knew she had to deal with Berger. She put a hand to the ground to rise. Pain lunged at her. Clenching her teeth, she crossed her arms on her knees and stayed put, leaning back against the squad car.

"I always knew you flatlanders were crazy." Berger pointed a piece of paper at her. "Here!" He shook the flimsy slip. "This came in for you. *It* doesn't make any sense, either."

Maggie took it and tried to read it. The print was faint, and the first line seemed to be in code. She followed the letters and numbers across the page, but he was right about it not making sense. Then her eye dropped to the middle of the sheet.

```
OPD. Doe still Doe. Fingers burned. Do you know
dentist? Girlfriend?
Should we go to Kansas. BSK—OPD.
```

"Here, Maggie." Bett returned with a can of beer and handed her a pill.

The deputy stepped between them. "What's that?"

Maggie held the pill up between her thumb and forefinger. "You know what sulfur smells like, right? This anti-burn pill has sulfur in it. Smells awful. Tastes worse. Take a whiff."

He sniffed. "Phew!" The stench from her burns made him step back.

Bett started to correct her. "That's not…"

Maggie gave her a quick look. "It's okay. The deputy's just doing his job. Right, Berger?"

"Yeah." He was looking at Bett intently and moved alongside her, resting a hand on the butt of his gun and lounging against the fender. "We haven't been properly introduced. My name's Berger."

Bett barely glanced at him as she gave Maggie the beer and watched her swallow the pill.

"Some people say *rare,*" he added, turning Bett his way. "That is, until they get to know me."

She glanced at him, astonished at his blatant leer, then looked him over in frank appraisal and saw him shift one leg intentionally.

"And what do they say then?"

Berger's voice dropped a notch. "They say, 'well done!'"

She couldn't check her sarcasm. "My, you are witty, aren't you?"

He accepted the compliment with a shrug. "Guess I am."

"Then you'll get it when I tell you to *bugger off!*" She saw him working out how she'd slurred his name. Then his face darkened to the shade of old meat. She turned her back on him in dismissal and helped Maggie up.

They both heard his obscenity as he yanked the car door open. "If I see your friends again, I'll tell 'em you're too busy to drink their beer."

Maggie turned to him. "What friends?"

"The ones waiting for you when I got here. Said they saw you come in last night." He started the engine and turned to back out.

"Berger!" It was a command. "Who were they?"

He faced her again. "How the hell should I know?"

"Locals?"

"Flatlanders. Probably looking for Captain Graf." Mentioning the cabin's owner seemed to distract him. "Where is he? Haven't seen him around."

"Dead," she replied in a flat tone.

He processed that news, then another look crossed his face. "Old man Graf didn't know about you, did he? You made out like a bandit, didn't you? Left this place to his Candy Girl. What a fool."

"Miller on duty today?" Maggie's tone was even, as if she hadn't heard his insults at all.

"After three." He waited for her next question, but she strode to the cabin. He shifted into drive and left, spinning his wheels in the gravel.

CHAPTER 9.

You Are Not My First Love

INSIDE THE CABIN Bett found the puppy jumping all over Maggie as she rummaged through a corner cabinet in the main room. She was clearly upset and either ignoring the pain in her hands or oblivious to it. She banged them more than once, pulling things from the cabinet. Bett shooed the puppy away and ran a hand over her back.

Maggie stopped then and turned to her. "Good thing you're here, darlin'. I feel awful funny." Her voice was thick, and she shuffled a foot forward. "Think I better sit down before I fall down."

Bett guided her to the couch. Only then did she see the tears on her cheeks. Maggie seemed unaware of them, and her eye was distant, unseeing.

"Does it hurt that much?" Bett knelt between her legs and held her face.

"Nope! Funny, huh?" She tried to focus on Bett, but her gaze kept slipping off. "Can't hurt me." She rubbed at her open eye awkwardly, even as a tear escaped the patch and followed an erratic path down her bruised cheek.

"Have you ever taken codeine before?" Bett asked.

Maggie pondered that a moment. "Huh-uh. Is that why I feel like this?"

"How do you feel?"

Another pause. "You mean the pain? It's very far away. Almost gone. Berger's gone, too." She leaned back. "I'd kiss you now, but I don't think I'd feel it. I like feeling that." Her head fell to one side, at rest on the back of the couch. "You make me feel so good."

Bett smiled. "You're higher than a kite!" It occurred to her that now was a perfect time to ask all sorts of questions. "Do you want to lie down?"

Maggie murmured a negative. "Like being drunk. I don't want to get sick. Thirsty, though. See my beer anywhere?"

"No more beer." Bett patted her knee as she got up. "I'll get you water. Or would you prefer juice?"

"Water. Please. Does everybody get like this from codeine?"

"Mostly. But it'll wear off. Should we dress your hands now?"

At her nod, Bett went to fix a saline bath. When she reentered the room, she thought Maggie was asleep. Then her eye opened.

"You are so beautiful."

The unexpected compliment made her slop water from the bowl. "Tell me that sometime when you're straight."

Maggie closed her eye again. "Oh, no. Tried that. Tried most everything. It didn't work, though."

Bett brought the kit of dressings her father had ordered and knelt in front of Maggie to snip the bandage across her palm. The outer wrappings fell away, leaving only saturated gauze patches between her fingers.

"How long did it take to figure out you weren't straight?" Bett set her hand in the water, warning, "This might sting."

Maggie held still, wincing slightly, then relaxed. "A long time. Terrible long. I didn't know then." She paused. "I tell all my guys the same thing: You are who you are. You can't run away from yourself. You can't suddenly be short!" She exhaled. "I was very old. Except when I started. Then I was just a pip-squeak. But, I was a *tall* pip-squeak."

Bett hid her smile. No, now wouldn't be a good time to ask questions. As she pulled the last of the gauze from the wound, Maggie flexed her hand and picked up a towel, gripping it to take the water off her palm. She didn't dry the back, but held it up to the light to examine it.

"Ugly, huh?"

Bett took her wrist, turning her wound out of sight. "It's healing just fine. Don't look at the burn."

She twisted easily from Bett's light grasp and smoothed her cheek with those freed fingers. "See how beautiful you are?"

Bett smiled. "Even when you're high, you're a charmer!"

"I wasn't high 'til I met you," Maggie said softly. "And I haven't come down since."

Bett warmed all over with those words and kissed her palm before putting it back in the bowl. "We have to soap that first, then do your other hand."

When Maggie turned away, Bett realized that she'd taken the change of subjects all wrong. She took her face in her hands again. "I want you. And I mean to have you. But not when you're high. I want you to feel me! Not remember as if I were a dream."

Maggie nodded. "Don't worry. I never dream."

Bett began working on her hand. "Never is a long time," she said lightly. "Didn't you have nightmares when you were little?"

"Never little; always tall. I can't remember. Not then. Not now."

"Don't force your memory," Bett said. "The amnesia will fade."

"No, I meant a long time ago. Forgot everything then, too."

Bett mulled that over. "You mean you've had amnesia before?"

"Yeah. Lange called it something else. But," she smiled tiredly, "I can't remember what."

Bett set the treated hand on the towel and went to get fresh water. "Who's Lange?" she asked on return.

"Oh, no!" Maggie balked, then giggled, a wholly uncharacteristic sound. "I don't kiss and tell."

Bett asked the obvious: "Did you kiss her?"

She nodded solemnly. "But I didn't tell."

"Who did?" Bett snipped the bandages off her other hand.

"I don't know. Maybe he figured it out by himself. I don't think she told him. I kissed him, too," she admitted.

"Oh, a *ménage à trois!*" Bett teased, slipping Maggie's right hand into the bowl.

"No, she was a social worker, and he was a salesman."

It was Bett's turn to giggle.

"Not funny," Maggie said. "I never could remember. Then I didn't want to." She sat forward. "What a mess, huh?" She pulled her hand from the water and studied it intently. "This one looks better, doesn't it?"

Bett viewed it with her father's eyes and agreed. "Back in the water now." She didn't want Maggie to focus on that. "Tell me about Lange."

"It's really all one story: Lange and forgetting. She thought the doctors were wrong. They said it was some kind of amnesia-with-puberty, but Lange said that wasn't it."

"What did she think it was?"

"I don't know. She wrote a paper on it. She called it a thesis. The paper, I mean, not the forgetting. But this isn't anything like before. You don't think I'm stupid. They did. They didn't even think I knew how to talk. They put me in speech class at the hospital." She sighed. "I talked to Lange, though. Right from the start. She was easy to talk to. Like you."

Bett smiled at her for that. "Why were you in the hospital?"

"They didn't know what else to do when they found me."

"Found you where?"

"At the orphanage where I used to live. It had been torn down the week before. Somebody took a picture of me sitting on the steps. It doesn't look much like me, but I guess it was a long shot from the street. I looked real small."

"And you were always tall," Bett said for her. She wrapped Maggie's left hand carefully. "How old were you then?"

"Oh, twelve or thirteen. Lange said I'd been in two or three hospitals before they brought me to the one at the university. That's how she got me. She was a student there. She used that picture when she got her paper published. Not for a picture of me, but because of what the orphanage looked like. There's a mound of bricks and rubble behind me, and I'm sitting in front. The newspaper headline was *Refugee Orphan*, but all the wars had been over with for years. What would I be a refugee from? Lange's paper had a different title. Something about a transfer…" She paused. "That's not it exactly. It was called 'Trans-something or Fiasco.' She was writing about the change in the orphan system."

"Transition, maybe?" Bett guessed the word from what Maggie was saying. She was utterly appalled by her story.

"I think that's it: 'Transition or Fiasco.'"

"Where were your parents?" Bett asked quietly.

"Oh, they died years before." She said it matter-of-factly, as if it was a common reality. "My gram died then, too, but that was a long time before they put me in the hospital."

Bett was even more appalled. "Who was taking care of you?"

"Foster parents. Lange told me they put all the kids in temporary homes when they closed the orphanages. That was the transition part. I used to say, 'Foster homes were the transition; I was the fiasco.'" Maggie saw Bett's look. "Lange never thought that was funny, either. She said I was a state ward, but my losing my memory really threw a monkey-wrench into how well they thought the change worked."

Bett tried to take all of that in as she rose to get fresh water. "It's hard to believe people can be so cruel."

"They weren't. They just didn't know what to do with me. And I didn't help much by not talking for a year or more, either."

"Still," Bett called from the kitchen, "it sounds like they didn't know what they were doing." She reentered the room. "And what are *you* doing?"

Maggie was at the cabinet where Bett had found her earlier. "Looking for my gun. It's not here. I have to find it."

Bett knew the edge in her voice was more than worry over misplacing something. The thought of a gun in this peaceful cabin made Bett angry, and seeing Maggie looking for it in her condition made her uneasy. She set the bowl down and went to her.

"I'll help you find it later." Bett hated lying like that. "We have to wrap your right hand now. You didn't use it to search, did you?"

"Huh-uh." Then she gestured at the objects she'd taken out. "Have to put this stuff away."

"I'll do that later, too." Bett led her back to the couch.

Maggie sighed. "I'm tired. Are you?"

Bett nodded and rinsed her right hand, then quickly dried it and began applying Silvadene. "When we finish this, you can lie down for a while. Are you still dizzy?"

"No. Just tired from the pain. How long before the pill wears off?"

Bett estimated another hour or so.

"Good. Then we'll go to town and get something to eat. Stock up on food for the next couple days."

"Tell me more about Lange," Bett suggested as she taped the outer wraps and helped Maggie to her feet.

"It's not much of a story," she said. "If I had a daisy, I'd show you how it went real fast."

Bett looked up quizzically.

"You know: 'She loves me. She loves me not. She loves me.'" Maggie smiled faintly. "People still do that in the springtime, don't they?"

Bett's smile was slow but certain. "I've been meaning to tell you: I love you, Maggie McIntyre. Forget about daisies. I know I always will."

She was glad she had chosen that moment to first say those precious words. Glad they weren't in the middle of a passionate embrace. She didn't want her feeling dismissed as merely fleeting passion. It might have started there, but it had only grown more certain and more powerful since.

"Isn't *always* kind of a long time?" Maggie asked lightly.

Bett noticed that her smile didn't quite extend to her eye. Didn't quite match her tone. "Neck and neck with forever!"

❖ ❖ ❖

An hour later, Bett covered Maggie with the comforter, knowing she would sleep for a while yet. She put some water on to boil, reflecting on her story. It was sad. Most coming out stories were. It fit another pattern, too. Maggie had fallen in love with an older woman, a caregiver. Bett's friends had fallen for camp counselors, teachers, coaches, even a school bus driver.

Bett had tried to empathize, the way she did when other women told their stories. "I suppose somebody moralized about how you'd been exploited!" But instead of making Maggie feel better, she nearly made her cry again. "Sorry," Bett said. "Maybe that wasn't your experience."

Maggie shook her head. "I never thought of it as wrong. Lange once said it was her fault. Maybe I didn't know what she meant. I didn't always. I only knew she loved me." She smiled faintly. "And you know the rest of the daisy story, don't you?"

Bett listened, thinking Maggie's description of herself as a teenager fit her fairly well now, too. Some traits had changed. Her long red hair, for example. She'd cut it short years ago. Said she never regretted it.

The shyness Bett sensed in her was once a terrible timidity, connected to her memory loss. She had emerged from that with Lange's help and with her discovery of a mechanical world. She had Lange to thank for that, too, since she was the one who had found the Iversons.

Bud and Libby Iverson were a middle-aged couple who lived in a small town fifty miles north of the university where Lange worked. Maggie wasn't happy about moving so far away, but Lange promised to visit. And the Iversons welcomed Maggie warmly, giving her the first real home she'd had since she was orphaned. Bud taught her everything she could absorb about cars and engines.

Maggie's face lit up as she talked about learning how things fit together. "It's almost magic," she said. "Like a socket wrench fitting a hex nut."

"What's so magical?" Bett asked. "Aren't they supposed to?"

"Sure, but a hex nut only has six sides. A socket might have six notches or a dozen. They don't mirror each other, but they still fit. And the right size socket even fits a square head: only four sides, but they fit right together!" She smiled at her own enthusiasm. "It made sense to me, anyhow. I suppose I never got over things finally making sense. It seemed like a magic time."

"Didn't Lange have something to do with that?" Bett asked.

"Maybe." She shrugged. "Anyway, Bud let me work in the garage with him. He thought he'd have to close it when the freeway opened up a few miles east, but we went and talked to the pump jockeys."

"Who?"

"You know, the Fill-'er-up? Wash-yer-winders? Check-yer-oil-ma'am? guys." She grinned when Bett laughed. "I did that, too, but mostly I worked on cars. The guys at the exit stations promised to send us jobs they couldn't do. Then business started to take off. Bud bought a tow and taught me how to bid salvage." She paused. "This can't be very interesting to you."

Bett smiled. "I had to guess what kind of *toe* Bud bought, but everything about you interests me." She let Maggie register the pun, then asked: "Was Lange the 'someone else' you were seeing when you and Scotty went out?"

Maggie gave her a long look before nodding. Then she went on.

It was through Lange that she found Scotty again. In her research, Lange treated Maggie's experience as a case study: *The Orphan M.* Refusing the medical theory that her amnesia was physically based, Lange made a list of children who had been in the orphanage with her, then interviewed them.

"I told her what I knew," Maggie explained. "It wasn't as much as the other kids could have told her, but Scotty said they didn't trust anybody."

"He was an orphan, too?"

"Yeah. He kept getting sent back to the orphanage. He told me how to get sent back, but…"

"Why? Didn't you want to be adopted?"

"It's not always up to the kids. Besides, I had to get back. I was supposed to be taking care of the others. Getting sent back wasn't hard." Her voice got tight again. "When I told him how I'd found him, he wanted to meet Lange and ask her to find his real parents. He knew he'd been abandoned. It made him crazy when he was a teenager, but he seemed to calm down as he got older."

"How did you find him? Weren't all those records sealed?"

"I don't know about that. I just kept a copy of the list of kids Lange interviewed. I used to help her out with stuff like that when I stayed with her on weekends."

"You do tend to skim over the more interesting parts," Bett said dryly.

"Like what?"

"Like how you started staying with Lange on weekends."

"Guess I did skip that part, didn't I?"

Bett only smiled, not wanting to push. Obviously, little of Maggie's story was easy. She made an internal promise not to interrupt again.

"Lange visited me every month. She got her paper published a few years after I left the hospital. Then the university offered her a teaching job. She took to that like it was what she was supposed to be doing." Maggie grew thoughtful. "I guess we both found out what we were supposed to do at the same time. Anyhow, when some of her students asked what had happened to the *Orphan M*, she invited me to come to her class.

"Bud and Libby weren't keen on the idea. They thought I'd get upset and maybe lose my memory again. I told them that was all kids' stuff. I'd be fine. Lange said we could make a weekend of it, since her husband was out of town."

"Her husband?" Bett couldn't help herself. "When did she get married?"

Maggie shrugged. "I don't know. She always was. When we met at the hospital, she was wearing a wedding ring, so I called her 'Mrs. Lange.' She smiled and said I should just call her Lange; we'd be first-name friends."

Maggie explained that they'd gone to the glass-walled visitors' room overlooking the street, where she told Lange about a game the kids from the orphanage had played: guessing the make, model, and year of passing cars. Even though Maggie wasn't very good at guessing the year, Lange didn't challenge her the way the kids did. Instead, she seemed impressed.

"Funny how things work out," she said. "Maybe that game is what made her think of Bud and Libby as foster parents. Anyhow, Lange met me at the bus depot. I wanted to drive down, but Bud said city traffic took some getting used to, and maybe I should wait on that." She shook her head. "Everybody was being so careful. Just of the wrong things.

"Lange had about a dozen students in her class, and they were real nice, but I didn't know what they were talking about most of the time. They used words I'd never even heard before. I memorized some of them to remind me why not to go to college."

Bett smiled at that.

"They talked about 'regression.' The doctors thought that was it. But Lange didn't. And she said it wasn't connected to puberty because the 'onset of menses' hadn't occurred until I was nearly fifteen." She lit a cigarette. "Of course, I had to pick *that* phrase to ask about. I thought they'd never stop laughing." She tossed her head. "I really got mad at Lange. Acted like a twelve year old."

"Like a pip-squeak?" Bett said lightly.

Maggie gave her a long look. "You listen to everything I say, don't you?"

"Every word."

She took a drag. "That weekend... I guess that was when I changed. Or learned how I really felt about Lange. We... I slept with her that night."

Bett's eyebrows rose. "You slept with her? She didn't sleep with you?"

Maggie shrugged. "It wasn't the same for her. She was married. Maybe if I'd known more about marriage..."

"What didn't you know?"

She lifted a hand and let it fall. "Anything. Why people got married in the first place. I guess I thought it was some kind of protection. I understood that much about people. I figured that's what marriage was about, too, if I thought about it at all. It wasn't on my mind much. Seemed to me people got married when they got to a certain age. I didn't know why exactly."

"What about sex? Didn't you have sex education?"

"No. I might've known more about her and Tom if I had, but I didn't. And it wouldn't have changed how I felt about her."

"Did you make love?" Bett asked softly.

"No. That's another thing. I don't remember the first time we made love. Not as clearly as I do that night. I never forgot the perfume she wore. And she brought a glass of amaretto to bed." Maggie's voice grew low. "I've never ordered it myself, but sometimes I can still taste it. I kissed her." She glanced at Bett. "I guess she kissed me, too."

Bett didn't say anything.

Maggie continued. "Funny how you have to learn everything for the first time. I didn't know how to kiss."

"Some things come naturally," Bett assured her.

She shrugged. "Maybe. I sure didn't know what I wanted to do. Just that I had to do something with my feelings. I didn't sleep much that weekend."

Bett did smile at that. "Eventually you became lovers?"

She closed her eye tiredly. "Yeah. Thanks to Scotty."

"Why him?"

"He taught me about sex."

"What do you mean?"

"He told me some of what I needed to know." She opened her eye. "Some of it wasn't very clear in the books I read. He was good about answering my questions, until I asked him what an orgasm was. He kind of looked at me sideways and said, 'You'll know it when it happens.'"

"And did you?" Bett thought it was safe to tease a little.

"Not the first time." She smiled thinly. "I'll tell you about that another time." She looked away. "I guess things would've worked out the same even if Scotty hadn't met Lange."

Bett couldn't bear the sorrow in her voice. "Did he... take her from you?"

"No, not Scotty. Tom, her husband, sort of took her back, I guess." She closed her eye. "You really want to hear all this?"

"Only if you want to tell it," Bett replied gently.

Maggie opened her eye. "Don't feel sorry for me, Bett." Then her tone softened. "It was a long time ago. None of it matters anymore."

Bett reached out to her, but she shifted to put out her cigarette. Bett tried an innocuous tangent instead: "How old were you then?"

"Old enough to know better. If Ebert had been there, she would've said things were going too well. I should've known I was riding for a fall." She sighed. "I turned eighteen that year. Scotty tried to warn me, too. He took me to the library and showed me a bunch of books that said homosexuality was a treatable illness. Asked me if I wanted to be *treated.*" She saw Bett's look. "Scotty never put me down for how I felt about Lange. He just wanted me to be careful. He thought I might outgrow it like the books said. Or maybe I'd have to live with it all my life. 'But don't kill yourself over it,' he said. 'It's only sex.'

"I knew what he meant about being treated, but he was wrong about the other part. It wasn't just sex. Not then, anyhow. Scotty said I was too dependent on Lange. He was probably right, but I don't think she knew that. After he showed me those books, I asked Lange if she knew anybody like us. 'Like us?' she asked. I said, 'Yeah, lesbians.' She said: 'I know *about* them, but I don't know any personally.'"

"Oh, Maggie." Bett reached for her again. "That's so sad!"

"She was just saying there wasn't anything wrong with me."

"And there wasn't!"

Maggie nodded easily. "I know that."

Scotty finally wore her down about meeting Lange. Maggie relented on the condition that he promise not to mention the orphanage. She didn't think Lange would connect his name to the old list, since she'd interviewed most of the kids by phone. When Maggie mentioned "this fellow Scott" and suggested a double date, Lange thought it was real cute.

They'd gone to a movie, and everything was fine at the start. Scotty and Lange seemed to hit it off. He could talk to anybody about anything. He told her he was thinking about going to college and asked her opinion of the business school at the university. She ate it right up.

"I knew Tom, of course. He was kind of a loud guy. Not at all like Lange. I should've known something was up when he paid so much attention to me that night." She looked at Bett. "You never would have swallowed his line like I did. You've got those kinds of smarts."

"What happened?"

"I drove back with Tom. I forget why exactly. Maybe we stopped for cigarettes. Anyway, Scotty's car was parked in front of Lange's apartment, and Tom pulled around back, but we didn't go in right away. He said he wanted to talk to me about Scott. Tom said Scott had told him how happy I made him. And would I make him happy, too?"

She saw the alarm in Bett's eyes. "He didn't rape me. I have to give him credit: He was too smart for that. He said he'd grown fond of me, through Lange, and felt like a brother or a father. Told me I shouldn't let Scott get away. He was 'my man.' He covered all the bases: how he used to worry about Lange being alone while he was out of town, how glad he was I'd been around to keep her company. Now he was getting promoted and wouldn't have to be gone on weekends anymore. Good news, huh?" She snorted. "I never even saw that one coming.

"There was more, but it was just dressing. What a snow job! It took him a while to say it all. Meantime he held me close and kissed me, just on the cheek, you know, but he had whiskers that scratched my face every time he moved. And my dress rode up, but I didn't pay any attention. He never put his hands where it made me uncomfortable. He was just clumsy. I'd gone out with a guy from school like that. Part of what you do is push away a little at a time. I thought the guy at school was worse, but I didn't know what Tom was up to yet.

"Then he looked at his watch. 'My god!' he says. 'It's one in the morning!' He gave me a huge kiss on the lips, pulled me out of the car, and raced us upstairs to the apartment. He threw the door open and started apologizing about being so late. Lange and Scotty were just sitting and drinking coffee.

"Tom had really set the scene, though: tucking his shirt in and checking his fly. Then he pulled me into the room. I was straightening my dress and wiping my lips and trying to get my shoe back on. My face must've been bright red from running and from whisker burn. Hairpins falling out—I was a real mess. I laughed with Tom, like it was the funniest thing ever.

"Then I saw Lange's face: She was furious. I'd never seen her like that. She wouldn't listen to either of us. Tom tried to explain." She shook her head. "Balls and brains. Never underestimate men. It's a hard lesson."

"You couldn't explain?" Bett asked.

"No. Lange wouldn't listen. I told Scotty all about it on the way home. I was still trying to figure out the joke, but Scotty saw right through it. When I finished telling him about Tom and stopped crying about Lange, he gave me two pieces of advice. 'Never trust anybody whose motives aren't clear.' I didn't know what he meant. I thought Tom's motives were plenty clear."

Bett knew Scotty wasn't talking about Tom. "What was his other advice?"

"He wanted me to go away with him. I said I was going back to Lange. Scotty didn't think she'd have me. And if I did go back, he said, Tom would probably kill me. I wouldn't believe him about Lange, but I knew he was right about Tom. I finally figured out it was a setup." She crushed out her cigarette and lay back on the pillows.

"Scotty was always right about everything then," she told Bett sleepily. "Except about leaving with him. I still don't think that would've worked. Everything else, though, I could've taken to the bank." She closed her eye.

A few minutes later, Bett let herself out of the room.

CHAPTER 10.

Something About the Women

BETT'S TEA GREW COLD as she absently stroked the puppy. Maggie's story had given her a lot to think about. She didn't understand all she'd learned, but that didn't bother her. They had the rest of their lives to spend on that.

She put things from the corner cabinet away, then went to the kitchen to clean up the breakfast dishes. Under the sink, she found an upturned dishpan and pulled it out. Something heavy slithered onto the floor. She looked down and gasped. It was a gun.

She stepped back, directly into the refrigerator, and stared at the small black object. It was faintly shiny, as if it exuded oil. She didn't pick it up immediately. She didn't even try. Instead she looked out the window and thought again of the deer by the pond. The small noises the puppy made as he chased along the ridge. And Berger, drawing his gun.

Berger was a bona fide asshole, no doubt of that. But even the way he came on to her didn't make her want to shoot him. Maggie's overreaction was probably from the codeine. It not only made her tearful and loquacious—it changed her from sanguine to paranoid. Then Bett realized she couldn't tell her she'd found the gun. If anything, she had to hide it again. She reached to pick it up. And couldn't.

She put a hand to her head to calm the ticks and chitters, wondering how she was going to hide it when she couldn't even touch it. She tried to reason through her fear, knowing she had to act. She couldn't very well be walking around the gun doing dishes when Maggie got up. No, she had to deal with it somehow. So far she'd only been able to handle it by dropping it. Maybe she could drop it all the way… She stopped beating herself up and let her idea form. Throwing it away wasn't the answer, but she could treat it like trash; sweep it up and put it someplace. Maybe in the wastebasket, under the bag. Taking broom and dustpan from the closet, she handily swept it up. A sound from the other room made her freeze.

"Bett…?"

There wasn't time to put it under the trash. She looked around the kitchen. Over the refrigerator? No, Maggie would see it right away. Every place was too visible. Then she saw the chair against the wall on the other side of the table. She remembered a hiding place from years ago when her mother had hidden an Easter basket in the kitchen.

Bett was crouched down, practically under the kitchen table, broom in hand, when Maggie emerged from the bedroom.

"You don't have to do that."

"Hi!" Bett took a quick breath. "It's no bother. How did you sleep?"

"Fine, thanks. You ready to go to town?"

"Yeah, sure."

"Okay. I'll be right out."

Bett put the broom away, then went to the front door and looked back at the kitchen table. The oilcloth hung low enough to make her hiding place undetectable, even from across the main room. With a sigh of relief, she put on a jacket and went out on the porch to wait.

A few minutes later Maggie came out, snugging on a Stetson. Bett looked her over in surprise. Her hat wasn't all she had changed. She'd traded in her work shoes for cowboy boots and wore a soft leather jacket over a gingham shirt, closed with pearl snaps.

"You look like you've lived here all your life," she said with a smile.

Maggie shrugged. "I do what I can to blend in."

Bett saw what she meant when they got to Eagle Pass. It had a look of the Old West, with wooden walkways and hitching posts lining the main street. The locals seemed to favor the same clothing style Maggie wore, but Bett saw others wearing running shoes and T-shirts. She wouldn't stand out.

Maggie parked in a diagonal space at the Eagle Tavern & Food Club. A connecting storefront advertised "Ammo 'N Bait," and she headed that way, whistling for the dog to follow. As he blessed a post and scrambled up to join her, Bett asked if it was okay to bring him along.

"This is love-me-love-my-dog country," Maggie replied. "Besides, we aren't going anyplace where dogs don't already live."

For proof, she opened the bait shop door. The puppy scurried in ahead, then came to a leg-braced halt in front of a sleeping Labrador lying just inside. The big dog opened one eye but didn't give the intruder more effort. Even so, the puppy stayed between Maggie's booted feet after that.

She went to the ammunition counter and pulled a paper from her jacket pocket. The bulky hand wraps gave her a little trouble, but she managed. Then a stocky young man with a handlebar mustache emerged from the next room, wiping his hands on an apron. He nodded to Bett, who was looking at the cases of fishing tackle, but he seemed to know who his real customer was.

"Yes, sir!" he greeted Maggie as he went around the end of the counter. "What can I do for you today?"

Bett expected a strong reaction, but Maggie merely nodded hello and handed him the papers. "You got a gun in for repair that matches this one?"

The clerk looked up at the sound of her voice, then cleared his throat and examined the paper. "Nope," he said, handing it back. "I'd know if anyone brought this in. We don't get many German…" He looked at Maggie more closely. "Say, aren't you Matt Graf's, er, friend?"

She nodded. "It's his gun that's missing. I'll give you a number where you can reach me if it shows up, but let Sheriff Miller know, too."

"Sure, sure." He pulled out a pad of paper and pen.

Bett joined them, concerned that Maggie might buy a replacement. "I have to talk to you," she said urgently.

"This'll only take a few minutes. Why don't you go in and order us some lunch?" She nodded at the door the clerk had come through, then turned to him. "Or are you by yourself?"

"No, the wife'll take care of you in there."

Bett gave up. She couldn't very well admit to hiding a gun just reported missing. Not in front of a gun salesman. If Maggie did buy one, she'd tell her about finding the black one. They could return the new one before leaving town and discuss her behavior change then, too.

Maggie watched her go through the door with the puppy and turned to the clerk. "Have you got any .22s in stock?"

"Sure do. One I think you'll like in particular. It's not the quality gun the Captain had, but…"

✧ ✧ ✧

Ten minutes later Maggie entered the restaurant. The unmistakable sound of a wildly thumping tail led her to Bett's booth. Sliding in across from her, she took off her hat.

"What did you want to talk to me about?"

Bett was relieved to see her empty-handed. Now she wouldn't have to tell her about finding the black gun.

"Bett?"

"Oh, I, uh, was admiring your hat, but they didn't have any next door. Is there someplace in town where I can buy one?"

"Be cheaper if I just called you *sir* once in a while!"

Bett laughed. "You handled that perfectly, you know."

Maggie shrugged. "You learn. When you're tall and flat-chested and…"

"You are *not* flat-chested!"

"Well, somebody once told me I was lucky: I'd never have to deal with 'blouse gap'!" She gave Bett the same split-second wink that she'd given her the first night they met. "And I never did learn how to act very feminine, even in frilly square-dance outfits." She poured some beer into a glass. "Besides, people generally react in my favor when they see their mistake."

"Who's this Graf fellow everybody keeps mentioning?" Bett changed subjects to lessen Maggie's embarrassment, but her face closed tightly as she pulled a fly-specked menu from behind the napkin holder.

"Old friend," she mumbled, studying the tattered cardboard. "I'm starved. Did you order yet?"

Bett took her unwrapped fingers, stroking them lightly until she was certain she had her attention, one way or another. "Yes," she said softly. "I ordered an open face for you, with a side order of continuing saga."

Maggie's smile came slowly. "And what are you going to have? Not more of that boring old drivel?"

Bett tightened her hold. "I'm hopelessly in love with you, Maggie. I wish you'd let me without so much resistance."

Maggie arched what used to be her eyebrows, then her focus changed, and she pushed the menu into Bett's hands, disengaging their fingers. "Here you go!"

Startled, Bett sat back just as the waitress arrived with their food. She set a steak sandwich with home fries in front of Maggie and gave Bett a salad, promising steak sauce on return.

"And two waters," Bett called after her. "You have to drink more water, Maggie. Alcohol dehydrates you. Even beer."

"Yes'm," she said meekly, cutting into her steak. Then she looked up. "How'd you know this was what I wanted?"

Bett smiled at Maggie's pleasure. "Read your palm. And an old grocery list at the cabin. But I guessed about the medium-rare part."

"It's perfect."

Maggie ate hungrily and fed fat scraps to the puppy under the table while they discussed what errands they had to run.

"I have to stop by the sheriff's office."

"About the gun?" Bett had hoped to avoid that topic entirely.

Then the waitress returned. "Brought you coffee," she announced. "How was that steak?"

Maggie complimented the food, then asked about the weather.

"Heard there's a storm coming up the valley," the cheerful woman replied. "Due in tomorrow night, they say."

"Snow?"

"Ice at least. It's still getting down at night. Sure hope Jimmy piled more wood by the door. Nearly broke my hip last spring when we got the same kinda' storm."

Maggie reached to pay for the meal, but the waitress stopped her.

"Your friend paid for all but the coffee. Gave me enough tip to cover that, too." She winked at Bett, then addressed Maggie again. "You bring her back, now. We like being spoiled!" She walked away, cackling to herself.

Maggie leaned forward. "What am I going to do with you?"

Bett shook her head. "We can work that out. You just worry about what you're going to do with*out* me!"

Maggie finished her coffee before reaching for her pocket again. "Now listen, Bett. You can't take me to such nice places and not let me pay my fair share! *I'm* buying the groceries!"

"Okay, but I guessed about the steak. What else do you like to eat?"

"Whatever you're willing to fix. If you don't mind cooking, that is. I'll do the dishes... Rats!" She looked at her hands. "I can't."

"I don't mind," Bett said quickly. "And I'll get you rubber gloves. You're going to have to help out somehow or other!" Bett knew then that she would do anything for the shy smile Maggie wore. Her head was slightly turned, and while the dim light was kind to the lines in her face, it was her smile that gave her warmth. Her gray eye focused on Bett gently, like a touch.

Maggie looked down at the money she'd taken from her pocket and saw a flimsy piece of paper stuck in the bills. She handed Bett the money and the note. "I have to see the sheriff about this message from Brian. The victim's fingers were too burned for prints." She paused briefly. "A dental match won't work, though. Scotty has perfect teeth. No cavities, anyway. I doubt if he's been to a dentist since grade school."

"Can't you tell Brian that? It's something."

"No, they need an exact physical match. A tattoo or something."

Bett reread the note. "Does he have a girlfriend in Kansas?"

"No, Lois lives in Fremont. Brian's got his 'square states' mixed up. Scotty was in jail in Nebraska for a few days once."

Bett thought about Friday night again. "Too bad they don't take footprints. I don't think the body..." She stopped then, suddenly realizing what she was about to describe.

But Maggie was smiling. "They do! Or they did—on old birth certificates. And I've got a copy of Scotty's. What a great idea!"

Bett felt like she'd won another prize and grinned back at Maggie idiotically. "Here," she said, taking out a pen. "Let's work on a reply."

Maggie dictated a response to equal Brian's obscure message.

```
Perfect teeth. See Lois Delano Fremont. Try foot-
prints. My file. Second apt. You mean Nebraska.
    MMc - M & M
```

"Apartment?" Bett challenged. "Don't you mean second floor?"

"No, the one across the hall from mine. I divvied it up a while ago. Kept some files and stuff in the other half."

She said it so matter-of-factly that Bett could only stare.

"I told you I could be stranger still," Maggie added softly.

Bett fought a sudden temptation to kiss her. "I love you," she whispered.

106

Maggie sat back in the booth. "I, uh, think I'd better give you directions to the grocery store."

Bett laughed at her ongoing shyness. Then, after setting a meeting time, they went their separate ways.

❖ ❖ ❖

Maggie kept the puppy with her, but before crossing to the sheriff's office, she stopped in the Tavern to check for messages from the garage. Dan the bartender hadn't heard from M & M, but somebody had stopped in that morning asking about her.

That surprised Maggie. "Who was it?"

"Never saw 'em before. They didn't exactly ask for you. Just described you and your truck. I thought it was kind of funny. Asked about somebody else, too. You got a gal-friend with you?"

Maggie gestured with what could have been taken for a nod. "What did you tell them?"

"Nothing. You know me. They bought a couple six-packs and headed out. Then the big guy stopped at the topo' map. Asked if there's any cabins for rent in the area."

"Any particular area?"

"Nope. Said he'd been to Triangle Points but wanted something closer. Then the skinny guy pointed to North Slope. I said those were all private. They just looked at each other and split."

Maggie saw on the wall-mounted map why the strangers had spotted North Slope Road. It was the only one leading off the main highway for five miles in either direction. That explained how the other pickup had found her cabin, but not why.

She considered mentioning it to Sheriff Miller, but their conversation went another way, and that incident was lost. After explaining her injuries, she reported the missing gun and asked him to send a message to Brian, adding that she'd be at the cabin for a week or so. "If you get the chance, stop up and have a beer with us."

"Us? Oh, yeah! I hear your friend's a real hellcat."

Maggie looked at him closely. "Berger?"

"Ah-huh." Miller smiled. "Think I oughta run her in for maltreatin' an officer of the law?"

She matched his tone. "You wouldn't want to embarrass the poor guy, would you? Be a mark against his record to get sued for false arrest, eh?"

Miller chuckled, then said, "Berger never would've bothered you if Matt was still alive. I'm sorry. I mean, my condolences and all."

She nodded. "He was your friend, too, Hugh. I know you miss him. We all do. And I appreciate your keeping an eye on the place, like always."

He acknowledged that with a nod. "You got everything straightened out...? Sorry. None of my business."

Maggie never understood why Matt let people think they were lovers. They'd always been friends. And business partners. She owed Matt a lot. Much of it could still be seen, totaled on the M & M books. But that was only the tangible part. The intangible could never be measured.

"He left me the cabin," she said. "And all its contents. The will was pretty specific. It had a part I memorized to remind me to avoid lawyers. It said '…and all contents of each building thereon and all structures appurtenant thereto.'"

"That'd keep you away from lawyers, aw' right."

"I think Matt put that in there so I could have all the buried treasure he left!"

They both laughed. They both knew Matt Graf.

"His two daughters tried to fight the part about the cabin's contents, but the will stood. And they couldn't complain about money. He believed in insurance and left them well off." She shrugged. "Still, I felt kind of sorry for them. Took them up to the cabin and cleaned out his… the Winter Room. The bedroom set was an old family heirloom." She thought about Matt's daughters. The brats had refused the mattress, but had taken the box spring. People were funny about things. She remembered the look one of them gave her as they loaded the U-Haul. She wanted to spit on Maggie, but she was too well-bred.

"Matt and I were always friends first. It might've seemed like we fought about M & M, but that was just business. The last time I saw him, he told me he was thinking about retiring, spending more time up here. I don't think he had any regrets, except maybe that he was deadheading instead of flying that plane when it went down. He was probably on his way to the cockpit, cussing and swearing at that little mosquito that hit them. That's what he called those little twin-engine jobs. He said mostly rich gnat-heads flew them." She'd gotten a smile out of Hugh, using his friend's tone. She whistled up the puppy.

"What do you call him?" Miller nodded at the dog.

"Haven't named him yet. With us talking about Matt, maybe I'll call him Gyp. That's what he called me when we first met."

"Short for gypsy?"

"That's what Matt said. I told him I'd settle down some day, when I found the right place."

She said good night to the sheriff and left, pulling her jacket close against the wind. The sun was starting to set, taking its warmth beyond the mountains. She was grateful for the closed space of the truck cab and glad to see Bett just rolling a cart out the door. She hadn't had to wait in the cold. Maggie helped load the bags into the back and secure them with bungee cords from a Servis compartment. Bett settled the puppy in his box with a chew strip and asked Maggie about her visit with the sheriff.

"We had a nice chat. Turns out you're already a celebrity in town."

Maggie related their exchange about Berger, and they laughed together. When they got to the North Slope turnoff, Bett suggested they keep going to the ranger tower to watch the sunset.

"But go slower up the hill," she pleaded. "The way you did it last night, I couldn't see the ground. I thought we were going to drive off a cliff!"

"You've got a lot to learn about this truck." But Maggie took the steep hill slowly. She had to shout to be heard over the straining engine. "Some things don't work very well slow. Fast might seem scary, but that's how it has to be sometimes." They leveled out, and she wheeled the truck to face west, then cut the engine.

"You're right." Bett slid over, releasing Maggie's seatbelt. "I've got a lot to learn about this truck."

Maggie forgot all her promises when Bett's lips met hers. She drew her close, free-falling in the world of her touch.

She thought her muscles ached from the accident, and she'd chalked up her physical tension to that. But those muscles weren't what felt strained today. And she thought she was stiff from being careful of her hands. She still couldn't use them, but her rigidity melted, and she felt herself relaxing, unable to stop. She didn't want to stop.

It seemed as if Bett's hands were never still. Maggie felt them inside her shirt, as if snaps didn't exist. She gasped as Bett cupped her breast, stroking her nipple to proud awareness. She couldn't stop her this time. And when Bett released her mouth, coursing down her neck to find her breasts again, Maggie felt an inner glow. She knew she had to return her caresses, but when she tried, Bett stopped her.

"No, darling," she breathed softly. "Not yet."

Then Maggie lost what remained of her balance as Bett's mouth covered her ear completely, and she felt the delicate probe of her tongue. She might have moaned, but she couldn't hear anything. And she couldn't make a sound: She hadn't breathed for hours.

Suddenly she was lying on the seat of the truck, not knowing how she'd gotten there. Bett's mouth came back to hers hungrily. Maggie tasted her again. Each time a different taste. Each move a new sensation.

She never heard Bett unzip her. Her orgasm shocked them both with its suddenness. And still Bett didn't stop. Her tongue parted Maggie's lips, teasing her with air and moisture—deliberate, incredible strokes. Her fingers matched that movement, lightly at first. Then more firmly. They probed, then withdrew, crossing her still-sensitive point.

Maggie felt herself responding. From deep inside, pleasure grew. She would explode with feeling. She knew she couldn't come again, yet she was helpless to stop her. And the eerie, deep-throated sound that escaped her didn't begin to tell the story Bett's hand created. Maggie arched impossibly in the too small space.

And then she knew nothing of space. Nothing of time. Only sensation, rising, ever rising. And color. Brilliant color that became whiteness. Pure and absolute. She thought she'd died.

Maggie opened her eye and stared at the cab's dome light, barely visible in the growing darkness. She was relieved to see that they had both those things in heaven: truck cab dome lights and darkness.

She could feel every cell in her body. The moment she thought about it, the knowledge faded, and she could only feel each muscle and tendon. Then she could only feel her skin. It felt delicious. Every inch of it.

"I didn't explode!" She spoke wonderingly to the plastic disc overhead, as part of herself seemed to float up from her chest. It was Bett's head. No longer part of her.

"I sort of thought you did." Bett moved closer, kissing her lips lightly. Then again, more deeply.

Maggie moaned. "I'm all used up, darlin'."

"Mmm, should I believe you?" Bett's voice was throaty and full of joy. Her lips brushed across Maggie's eye, down to her mouth again.

Maggie tried to reply. "Ymmf." To her surprise, she found that she could lift one arm. She pried Bett away, knowing, with the distant marvel of the dreamer, that she didn't have the vaguest idea where her other arm was.

"Yes." She could speak after all. God, she felt weak.

"No energy, hmm?"

Bett could talk. Maggie marveled at that, too. "Cigarette," she muttered, wondering if she was about to be thrown out of heaven. She was.

Bett bit her nose gently, then followed that with feathery touches across her ribs. But Maggie couldn't stand tickling. She found her other arm and used the steering wheel to pull herself upright, slumping over it when the blood rushed from her head. Bett sat on the drivetrain hump, grinning.

"How did you do that?" Maggie asked generally. *That* could mean so many things at the moment.

"Short legs is the secret," Bett replied impishly. "I was afraid you wouldn't let me. But I'm a brave schemer."

Maggie could see how pleased she was with herself. She groped for her cigarettes as Bett continued.

"You wouldn't have let me if I'd suggested it, would you?"

Maggie lit up before answering. "How'd you know?"

"Oh, little things. Big things. The way you talk about your hands, as if they'd been cut off instead of just hurt. They're not your only asset, you know. And why *not?*"

"Darlin', it doesn't work that way." The words were out of her mouth before she knew it. "Really it doesn't! I can't just come..." she tried to snap her fingers, "like that! And I never come twice in a row. Never. Besides, I always have to make love to the other person first, or I can't come at all. It won't work with my hands like this. We'll both end up frustrated."

Bett rested an elbow on the seat and cupped her chin. "Fascinating. Absolutely fascinating." She nodded as if concurring. "Perfectly clear. Crystal. Pristine. If there was another word for clarity, I'd use it." Then she cocked her head. "Maggie, do you ever hear little sounds in the back of your head sometimes? Sort of like clock ticks or mice squeaks?"

She shook her head, wondering what Bett was getting at.

"Mmm, I didn't think so. Too bad." Extricating herself, she began putting Maggie back together.

Maggie cautiously broached the topic again. "Is that okay with you? I know it means we can't make love for at least two weeks, but…"

"You're not serious! What's this magic two-weeks number?"

"Well, you know, my…"

"Tell me something." Bett took Maggie's face in her hands and looked her in the eye. "What did we just do here? Didn't I just make love to you?"

She nodded a little, shyly.

"And did you enjoy it?" Bett smiled. "Didn't you *like* it?"

"Of course I did." Maggie moved her hands to make her own point. "But it was just a freak thing. An accident. It never works that way."

"You're sure about that?"

She nodded again.

"Is this part of your theory about how to cook chicken?"

Maggie's brow furrowed. Then she recognized her reference. "Exactly!"

Bett nodded. "I see. This was just some kind of chemical anomaly then?"

Maggie eyed her suspiciously. "Is that like chicken piccata?"

Bett laughed all the way back to North Slope Road.

❖ ❖ ❖

Tracy Ebert hated Sundays. Sunny Sundays in particular. Add spring to that, and she was ready to crawl out of her skin.

A cool April morning had turned to eighty degrees by noon. It brought them out like flies to a rodeo. All the troubled ones, looking for some peace to drift down from the blue sky. All the troublemakers, too. And everybody's brother, cousin, aunt, and baby sister came along. Squalling infants. She'd forgotten how loud they yelled in the clear air.

They moved their lives out to stoops and driveways and street corners. Bringing their music and jump ropes and basketballs and handballs and cigarettes and beer cans and bottles with them. And some, the ones with change in their pockets, moved into the corner bars.

Ebert knew them. That wasn't the problem. Every cop knew them. The problem was she understood them. Too well. Learning that, on a sunny Sunday afternoon in spring, just about put her over the edge.

She and Harley were only three blocks from the Lucky Spot when the call came. She squealed onto the concrete apron behind the bar as Bull Jason finished with

Abel Gant, beating him senseless with the broomstick they were using to bat bottle caps up against the wall. Bull swore to them he hadn't meant to hurt Abel, but he'd been driven to it. That Abel, why he hadn't brushed him back from the plate, he'd throw'd right at him! And what Reggie Jackson wouldn't take, Bull wouldn't either. Just thinking about Reggie set Bull off, and before they could stop him, he'd grabbed the broomstick again. It took both cops to get him cuffed and in the backseat.

Ebert limped to the front of the car and leaned against it to massage her bad leg. One of Bull's swings had come close to her scarred wound. She left Harley the job of dispersing the crowd.

Kids of every age milled around the alley of the Lucky Spot—the young ones fascinated by blood drops on the cracked concrete; the older ones, not quite old enough to be inside the bar, eyed the interior of the squad car before wandering off.

Harley went to get the bartender's statement while she kept an eye on the car's occupant. No one came near Bull. He seemed to be sleeping with his eyes open. Then a paramedic came over to tell her the victim was conscious, and they were taking him in for X-rays. Did she want to talk to him?

She spoke with Gant. He didn't want to press battery. Bull was his friend. He'd just as soon forget it. "If it's all the same to you, ma'am."

She left, wanting a cigarette. Sure. It's all the same to me. Tomorrow you'll both have a dozen beers and a couple of bumps. One of you'll take out a switchblade or your wife's carving knife. Couldn't bring it today, she was using it… Shit, Ebert. Cut it out. She hated that grinding-down thought spiral. She headed back to the squad car, getting there just in time to haul a youngster out of the passenger window.

"I only touched it. Is it really a sawed-off…?"

He babbled, even as she pulled him out and shook him with just one hand. She still had the grip to do that. She held him up by the back of his shirt and bellowed: "Whose kid is this?" Her jaw clenched, so hard it made her teeth ache. Her ears filled with a rushing sound as a familiar surge went through her. She felt herself growing stronger. She could handle this one. He'd be the scared one; he'd be the one to pee in his pants this time.

She reached for her club. Her free hand slapped an empty hip. Once. Twice. It still wasn't there. Sweat on her palm made her tighten her grip.

He yipped, high pitched, "Lem'me down!"

She turned toward the squad car. His flailing foot struck the fender. Hard. She shook him again, straining the seams of his worn cotton shirt. Twisting her hand, she felt the bones of her fingers tightening into the cloth.

Then another hand covered hers, releasing her death grip just by touch. "He's mine, Officer. I'm sorry. Did he hurt anything?"

She barely heard him. Only when the weight left her arm did the rushing sound recede. Only later would she recall hearing him smack the boy's backside. She couldn't then. She could scarcely breathe. Then Harley was there. She started breathing again;

woke from the waking nightmare. She looked around. They would've killed her. Uniform or no.

She managed to drive after that. She could always drive. Ebert thought of Maggie then. "You'll probably drive into heaven!" Maggie would kid her in that corny way only she could get away with.

God help me, Maggie. The perps are getting younger, and the guns are getting bigger. She was sure the kid was bringing the shotgun out. That was where the fear came from. But what triggered the rage? Was that what it was? Anger run wild? It didn't feel like anger. It didn't feel like anything she knew. Maybe it was madness. She glanced in the mirror. Bull was motionless. Now she knew why. Now she understood.

"*Tracy!*" Harley's voice finally penetrated her fog.

"Yeah, just a side trip," she said, turning onto Natchez and circling the end of the cul-de-sac. There was no pickup in Maggie's driveway. "A little moonlighting," she added.

He grunted noncommittally. "Anybody pressing charges?"

"Not unless it's the bar owner." She gave him Gant's story. "I figure we'll run him in on a D.C. You got another idea?"

Harley turned to Bull. Yes, sir. He had a wife. Home fixin' dinner. Roast pork tonight. Didn't know how she did it, but she'd promised.

"What do you say we take him home?" Harley suggested. "Think a judge would believe disorderly conduct on him now?"

Ebert's look alone asked if he really meant that.

"Well," he hedged. "We can try it on for size." When she didn't challenge him further, he cranked his window down a notch. "And it's too nice a day to be locked up indoors. That's one reason I wanted to be a cop."

She glanced over to make sure he wasn't setting her up. "Join the team. Work in the great outdoors. Meet interesting people. Like that?"

"Yeah. Like that." He paused briefly. "That's not why you joined, is it?"

She shook her head, not saying more. A few minutes later they pulled up to Bull's address, immediately drawing another crowd. Ebert went to get Mrs. Jason, trailing her by a dozen steps on the way back to the car. Harley got out to give the Jasons some privacy. He sat on the fender having a cigarette while neighbors waited at a distance. Finally Ebert nodded, and he got back in to talk to Bull.

She let Harley do the cautioning and issue all the warnings. It went down better when he told them. Not because he was male, but because he was black. They'd listen if she said it, but they'd resent it. Not because she was female, but because she was white. They wouldn't resent it out loud or even consciously. They just would. Too bad. She knew resentment as well as any of them. She was a spittin' authority on it. It made her comfortable being a cop in Oakland: a city seething with resentment.

Maggie would chuckle at that, then remind her that it was "a real working-class town." That's why she'd settled there instead of 'Frisco.

Ebert thought she was nuts. "Don't call it *Frisco*," she'd told her a hundred times.

113

"And listen, I work in this sewer of a town. I know what it's like!"

"So do I, Hot Shot!" Maggie's easy smile always soothed her.

Tracy wondered how she'd been doing since Friday night. Maybe she'd call her mid-tour, see if she wanted to get out for a while. They could go to that bar in the City. The one they'd gone to once before. That night seemed like a long time ago. Ebert divided her life into two eras now: Before Shooting and After Shooting. *BS* and *AS*. It was nearly six months AS now. She hadn't seen Maggie, except for that foggy hospital visit after the shooting, for six months before then. Tracy hadn't even seen her when she asked to use the cabin last month.

Maggie had laughed over the phone when she offered to pay rent. "Use it in good health, doll. Nobody's been up there most of the winter. Might be a little cold, but there should be plenty of wood. Enjoy yourself."

Had it really been a year? It seemed like ten. Friday night it seemed like a minute. Seeing her lying on the ground, Tracy was sure she was dead. But then Maggie wise-cracked her, just like always. "Laying on the hands now, Trace? They teach you cops everything these days, huh?"

She'd forgotten Maggie. She was just another BS memory: vague, distant, unreal. Nothing mattered in AS time. Suddenly Maggie mattered. A lot. She wouldn't call. She'd just drive by. Maybe they could talk. Like old times.

"More moonlighting?" Harley asked mildly as she headed down Broadway, away from their usual area.

She turned off the avenue to cruise the side streets. She'd forgotten about Harley. He was that quiet. She really sort of liked the guy. No matter. They could do a drive-by of the M & M yard later. That wouldn't make Harley suspicious. And it would let her ease back into checking on Maggie again. Ebert had missed that, too.

"Yeah," she finally said. "We'll go by a place you should know about. Run by there just before end of tour." She relaxed a little, tossing her head to relieve a neck kink. It was a gesture she'd picked up from Maggie years before. "I'll let you buy me a beer." She looked over in time to catch his soft smile.

"Great," he said dryly. "I haven't had an offer like that since the last time I paid rent!"

Ebert laughed. A little stiff sounding even to her own ears, but she'd work on that.

CHAPTER 11.

Strange Paradise

Maggie was downshifting to make the turn in the driveway when she remembered to tell Bett the puppy's name.

Bett waited for her to stop alongside the cabin before asking, "Why would you name a dog after a brand of peanut butter?"

"Not Jif, Gyp. G-Y-P. Short for gypsy."

Bett asked the dog how he liked it as she opened her door, but he leapt out of the truck and raced to the front of the cabin, barking and yowling.

"Think he hates it that…?"

Maggie touched her arm, silencing her, then switched off the engine. Gyp had stopped barking. There was no sound at all now. Just the relative stillness of dark woods. Bett got out and headed for the steps, then looked back and saw Maggie reach for the glove compartment. Something metallic glinted in the faint cab light. Trust you to have a flashlight handy, she thought. She heard Maggie's door close softly. Total darkness descended.

"Stay there, Bett."

"Why?"

"Something's wrong. I have to check it out."

"That'd be a lot easier if you'd turn on your flashlight."

Bett's eyes adjusted slowly in the country dark. Feeling her way along the side of the truck, she expected to run into Maggie, but she got to the driver's door without finding her. Then she knew it wasn't a flashlight. Maggie had bought a gun after all. She was angry with herself for not preventing the purchase. Then her fear for Maggie returned.

She headed up the driveway, angling left to find the steps with her hands. The stink of creosote reached her before she got to the railroad ties. She felt her way along the perpetually damp wood, then ran up the steps. It was even darker in the cabin's shadow. She was about to call to Maggie when she sensed movement near her head. Reacting instinctively, she grabbed the assailant's elbow and wrist, then registered the gauze on the hand she held. She hugged Maggie's arm in relief, wholly unprepared for her anger.

"I told you to stay at the truck!" Maggie hissed.

It was all Bett could do to keep from elbow-jabbing her, or finishing the body slam she'd started. Instead, she strode to the front of the cabin where Gyp was standing stiff-legged at the foot of the porch steps. The cabin door was ajar. She started up the steps. Gyp's growl stopped her. Maggie drew her to the side of the steps and pulled her down to a crouch.

"Stay here!" she whispered. "And stay down!" Then she rose and put a booted foot on the porch soundlessly. Keeping low, she moved to the wall between the window and the door. Bett could barely see her.

Suddenly lights came on inside the cabin. Bett's heart jumped. She saw that Maggie had reached in to flip the switch, then shoved the door open. Gyp barked sharply and ran in. Silence descended again. Bett waited. So did Maggie. No one responded to the lights or to the dog.

Maggie peered around the doorframe, then stepped to the other side, still not entering. Bett saw her holding the gun up, not like cops on TV, but ready to shoot. Bett started to warn her.

Too late: Maggie went in.

Bett froze, gripping a support post, fearing a sudden noise. Then she heard boots on the bare floorboards. Maggie and Gyp came out the door. She could breathe again.

Maggie pulled the door to. "Come on. We have to go get the sheriff."

Bett looked up at her tone. Maggie was a stranger now. A stranger in a cowboy hat with a gun. A stranger who told her so little; scared her so much. She closed her eyes. "This can't be happening."

Then she felt Maggie's arms around her. She let go and turned to hug her. One cheek touched the cool metal circle of a shirt snap. She inhaled the warmth of Maggie's skin, still fragrant from their lovemaking, and started crying.

"It's okay," Maggie soothed. "You don't want to stay here, doll. We'll go get Sheriff Miller and come back together, okay?"

Bett nodded, still hugging her, so close she could feel her heartbeat. Maggie was alive. That was all that mattered. Then she thought of death, and her anger returned in full measure. She pushed her away.

"You scared the shit out of me, Maggie. What were you going to do with that gun? Shoot somebody?" She tried to keep her voice steady, but tears warmed her cheeks again, even as she saw Maggie's open eye turn cold.

"I'm sorry you were scared," she said evenly.

"No!" Bett shouted. "You're not listening. I said *you* scared me. What if somebody had been there? Were you going to say 'Hey! This is my cabin.' *Blam!*" She watched her turn away. "Damn it, Maggie! Why didn't you go get the sheriff *before*?" But she couldn't go on talking to herself. She took a measured breath. "Please put the gun away."

Maggie nodded coolly and slipped it into her pocket.

Twenty minutes later they were in the sheriff's office.

"Look, Maggie, I'm not saying he's Boy Scout of the Year, but Berger wouldn't do that. Not to Matt Graf's place."

Maggie replied heatedly. "Of course he wouldn't do it to Graf's cabin. But he'd do it to mine. And today he found out it was mine! Where's he been all night?" At Miller's look, she backed off. "Look, I don't want to tell you your job, but would you at least call and see if he's home?" When the sheriff nodded, she pushed through the swinging gate to join Bett, who sat on the waiting room side of the spindle-railing divide.

Bett's anger had cooled on their way to town, and with it her fear. It was all one. She knew that now. Fear caused her to blow up at Maggie. She wanted to apologize and didn't know if she should.

"You okay?" Maggie asked gingerly.

She nodded. "Do you really think it was Berger?"

"I don't know. He's a ten-year-old kid with a gun on his hip so he can get his other gun up." She dragged on a cigarette. "If it wasn't him…" She rose as Sheriff Miller approached.

"His wife hasn't seen him since lunch. He called about seven and told her he was playing poker at the Tavern. Says he sounded a little pie-eyed."

"Let's go get him." Maggie ground out her cigarette.

"No!" Bett objected.

The sheriff agreed with Bett. "You can stay here or go back to the cabin. Whoever did it is long gone. I'll check on Berger, then join you up there."

Maggie nodded, then turned to Bett. "Unless you'd rather wait here?"

She shook her head.

On the drive back, Bett raised the issue of what had happened between them. "I wish you understood how I felt when you rushed off with that gun."

Maggie chose her words carefully. "I asked you to stay at the truck. Maybe I was wrong about that. I'm sorry."

Bett could tell how difficult her admission was. "Would you ever use a gun? On a person, I mean."

"I don't know."

"Well, I wouldn't!" Bett said emphatically. "I mean, if somebody *had* been there, and you shot him, who do you suppose they'd haul off to jail?"

Maggie didn't reply. As they pulled up the driveway, both of them were relieved to see the dog stayed curled up in his box.

"Can we just wait here for the sheriff?"

"Sure." Maggie lit a cigarette, taking care to exhale out the window. "I'm sorry I scared you," she said quietly.

"I know you are." Bett sighed. "And I'm sorry I yelled, but I just don't understand you sometimes. Not at all."

Maggie smiled. "Here, doll, lie down." She patted the seat in invitation.

Bett put her head in her lap. "I have to tell you something, though. I hate it when you call me *doll.*" There. She'd said it. She hoped she hadn't hurt her feelings too much.

Maggie chuckled and stroked Bett's cheek, then ran a hand along the length of her, resting it on her hip. "Are there other pet names you hate?"

"Well, don't tell anybody, but I love it when you call me *darlin'.* It sort of rolls off your tongue like it comes from deep inside you." She waited for a reply, but Maggie just kept stroking her gently; soothing her with her wonderful broad hand. "At first I thought it was kind of corny."

"Guess I am." Maggie's voice held a smile. "I've been told that before."

"No!" Bett objected to anyone else being brought into their discussion. "You just have some funny ideas."

"Do I?"

She nodded. "Like the idea of taking care of me. You don't have to, you know. I can take care of myself."

"I used to be better at that. Been taking care of people all my life. Seems like I've lost my touch." She lifted a bandaged hand. "Bad joke, huh?"

Bett kissed her fingertips. "Terrible." Then she changed her mind about her earlier protest. "Who else have you been taking care of lately?"

"You mean people like you?"

Bett nodded, looking up and touching her face lightly.

"Nobody."

"You mean you haven't been taking care of anyone lately, or there hasn't been anyone like me lately?"

"Yes." Maggie grinned fully.

"You're impossible! And you haven't been taking care of people *all* your life. What about when you were a little kid?"

"I was never a little kid."

"But when you lost your memory before, you had to be too young to be taking care of anybody then."

Maggie looked out the window. "Maybe. I thought I was supposed to be. It didn't matter in the end. I guess it was meant to happen that way. That's just... how it works."

Bett heard her melancholy. "Why are you so sad sometimes?"

"Am I?" Her voice was bright again. "I don't mean to be."

Bett reached up to hold her face in both hands. "Don't hide from me, Maggie. Whenever you do, I want to take you apart and find out what's wrong and fix it." Bett felt her smile across her palm; felt her lips move.

"You are so inviting..." Maggie tensed as headlights flashed in the mirror. Then she relaxed. "It's the sheriff. Let's go clean up the mess."

Mess was an understatement. Everything from the bookcases had been dumped on the floor. The couch and recliner were slashed and their contents disgorged. The glass-front secretary was broken open and papers were scattered on the lapboard. The drawers beneath were pulled out, giving the desk a stair-step configuration.

The bedroom was a similar ruin. Stuffing spilled out of the mattress that lay half off the bed. The closet had been emptied along with their luggage. Clothing and personal effects were strewn throughout the room. The front bedroom showed little disarray, but there wasn't much to harm in there, and that mattress wasn't cut as badly as theirs.

The kitchen canisters had all been delidded, spilling or displaying their contents. The cupboards were open, and all the drawers were pulled out like those in the secretary: stair-step fashion. At the far end of the counter, Bett saw a pair of cassette tapes lying next to a thermos bottle. A knapsack lay crumpled on the floor below. It was the one she'd taken from under the seat of the truck so long ago. Last night.

"Sheriff?" Maggie asked after they'd gone through the cabin, "is it okay to use the stove? Set up some coffee?" With his nod, she emptied the glass percolator of morning coffee and filled it with cold water, then put it on a lit burner and asked Bett to let her know when it came to a boil.

Bett sat at the table, keeping an eye on the water, and listened as Maggie told the sheriff about being followed up to the cabin, giving him her couple-of-drunks theory. They discussed that for some time until Bett told them the water was starting to boil. She went to the bedroom to try to restore some order to their clothing.

When she returned, they were in the kitchen. He was measuring coffee into a plastic bowl while Maggie added a raw egg. Then he stirred the concoction with a fork.

"It just doesn't figure, Hugh," Maggie said. "Get down in the corner there, now. You left a dry spot... Okay, you got it."

"Key-riste, girl! I was making egg coffee before your daddy's twinkle."

As she backed off, Bett moved in to watch. Miller gave her an abrasive look. "Maggie says you cook. You probably never even heard of egg coffee!" She shook her head, and he gave Maggie an I-told-you-so look. Then he set the pot on a cold burner, removed the lid, and dumped in the egg-soaked coffee. When he put it back on the flame, it boiled up, the grounds coagulating on the surface. A puff of steam pierced through, and he turned off the gas, stirred it once, and set it on a cold burner again. As he replaced the lid, he looked at his watch, then at Maggie. "You wanna' bet?"

"Seven minutes," she replied.

"I give it thirteen." Then he got down to business. "See this?" He pointed at the kitchen drawers, then crooked his finger, leading them to the secretary. "And these drawers here. Vandals would've busted the place up. It's messy, but nothing's broken, not so much as a lamp bulb." He shook his head. "No, they were thieves—burglars, technically. But only the gun is missing, and that was gone before they broke in."

Bett stifled a gasp. *"That's* what they were after?"

"Doesn't fit," the sheriff said. "Nobody hides a gun inside a mattress or a cushion. Under it, sure, but not in it."

Bett turned to look at the table. When they'd first come in, it had been tilted back, nearly upright against the wall, its underside exposed. The oilcloth was rucked up on the floor. There was no point in checking the chair seat now. Either Maggie or the sheriff had righted the table, re-covering it while she was elsewhere in the cabin. If the gun had been there, they would have said something. If not then, now. She followed them room to room as they examined the damage with a different focus.

"Burglars," Miller repeated. "Looking for something not too big. You saw the canisters, huh?"

"About that size?" Maggie asked.

He nodded and looked at his watch. "Let's see who's buying tonight."

Bett wondered what he meant as they returned to the kitchen. Half the grounds had settled to the bottom of the coffeepot. As they watched, the remainder lost its surface tension and sank.

"Well, I'll be," Miller sighed, checking the time again. "You've got a calculating mind, Maggie."

"That's why they pay me the really big bucks, Hugh!" She turned to Bett. "Mugs all around and free shots on the side. Compliments of the sheriff."

It didn't make any sense to Bett, but she got the mugs out. Maggie poured the rich dark brew through a strainer, then brought shot glasses and a bottle of whiskey to the table. The sheriff turned his glass upside down. "I'll have to pass up Matt's tradition, Maggie. Still on duty," he explained.

The coffee looked funny but had none of the bitterness Bett had come to expect. In fact, it tasted delicious. Bett remembered her experience with the schnapps from the night before and put her glass aside.

"What's so important about the drawers sitting like that?" Maggie asked.

"No prints," he said briefly. Too briefly for them. "Say you want a pair of socks or a scarf from a dresser and don't know what drawer it's in. You open the top one, look around, then close it and go down to the next, leaving a nice fat thumbprint behind. A burglar just slips a finger around the knob, pulls the drawer out and leaves it. Now, you can't start at the top, or the whole thing'll topple over as soon as you get half of 'em open. And you can't see what's in the next drawer when the top one's open. So a burglar starts at the bottom and graduates the rest going up.

"That's why the secretary's like it is." He nodded at the counter drawers. "That there's just habit." He took a sip of coffee. "Make a list of damages and bring it by. I'll sign it as an official witness. Insurance ought to cover the soft damage. And get an estimate from Axel for repairs on the desk and doorjamb. Matt would've…"

He stopped and glanced at the open door to Matt's old room. His gaze grew distant briefly, then he looked at the two women with a glimmer of new awareness. He cleared his throat. "The mattress in the Winter Room ought to work as a replacement for the cut up one in your room, Maggie."

She nodded slowly, returning his direct look. "I was thinking the same thing, Hugh."

He seemed to relax with that exchange, then confirmed: "You got another gun?"

Bett tensed at that, but Maggie nodded, then reached over to pat Bett's hand and rose. "More coffee?" she offered, heading for the stove.

"No, thanks, Maggie. I, uh, have to get going." He stood, adopting an official stance. "I'll check the cabins up the road, see if they're working a line." He tipped his hat to Bett and reached for Maggie's hand, then touched her shoulder instead. "You're okay."

She smiled. "Sure."

Maggie saw him out, then poured herself another cup of coffee and sat down, gesturing at Bett's shot glass. "Try it. You might like it." She grinned at the face Bett made and ruffled her hair. "It's not hiccup juice."

Bett took a sip. It was as smooth as the coffee was non-bitter. She sipped it again. "I think I'm losing my taste buds hanging around you!"

They divided the cleanup, and within the hour, all they had left was bagging the cushion debris and switching mattresses. Bett started putting the bulky pieces in a trash bag while Maggie went to the kitchen for a broom.

Then she called out, "Have you seen the dustpan anywhere?"

Bett felt her stomach drop. She couldn't admit what she'd done with the gun now. She couldn't face Maggie's derision. She closed her eyes. The thieves were out there now, *armed!* All because of her.

"Heck of a mess to make just to steal a dust… Bett? Are you okay?"

She opened her eyes. "Sure. Just tired."

Maggie looked at her more closely, then suggested that they fix the bed. "I hate making one up when I'm too tired to appreciate it. Let's get it ready."

Bett decided not to read anything into that. As they dragged the spare mattress to the back room, she wondered aloud why it was barely cut. They finally agreed they didn't have minds criminal enough to figure it out. It only took a minute to replace the cut sheets and tuck in the blanket and comforter, which hadn't been harmed. They were grateful for that respite from destruction, too.

Maggie tore a lid off a cardboard box to use as a dustpan, then had to deal with Gyp, who was having great fun with all the commotion. He chased the broom, and Bett laughed at his antics as she held the bags and tied them off. They were almost finished when he began attacking the cardboard pan, and Maggie gave up, sitting back on the cushionless couch with a sigh.

"Just two more things," she said.

"What two?" Bett was lying supine on the floor where she'd been trying to distract the puppy.

"One of us has to get the groceries from the truck, and the other has to get the dog in afterwards. Choose your detail!"

"How about three bags in one trip and let the dog fend for himself?"

"Done!" Maggie rose. "Uh, there *is* one other thing."

"What's that?" Bett got to her feet, not noticing her too-calm tone.

Maggie put her arms around her. "I have to bring the gun in." She felt Bett's reaction. "Do you want to wait here?"

"No. It's okay."

Surprised, Maggie stepped back. "It is?"

Bett nodded. "I just don't want you charging off like Teddy Roosevelt going up San Juan Hill. It isn't like the movies. You could've been killed!" She saw Maggie start to smile but was determined to make her listen. "And where would I be then? I'll tell you where: sitting in a truck I can't drive with a dog named *Gyp*, of all things." She hugged Maggie close to hide sudden tears, hearing her chuckle echo in her chest.

They stood that way, neither of them speaking, until the dog broke them up with a short woof. His tail slapped the cabin door noisily with every wag. When they turned, he lowered his front half in a back-breaking stretch and whined softly. His tail never stopped moving, and he seemed to know he'd gotten their attention without declaring an emergency.

They went out to the truck then. The sky had cleared, and they talked about the weather prediction, agreeing it was exaggerated. Neither of them mentioned the gun while they were outside. Gyp followed them back without any problem.

As they were putting away the food, Bett asked, "Is it as hard to learn how to shoot as it is to drive?"

"I don't know. Why?"

"Maybe I should learn something about that, too, if you're going to have a gun around."

When Maggie didn't reply, Bett asked: "Don't you think I can learn?"

"Oh, no. Anybody can if they want to. I was just thinking about the way you asked about guns and cars." Then she shrugged. "It's the same in some ways. You have to be careful and pay attention all the time. I guess they are alike. We'll start tomorrow. Maybe take it all apart and clean it first. That way you can see how it works."

"It's a good thing you don't teach driving like that!"

Maggie cocked her head. "That's not a bad idea."

"Incorrigible!" Bett muttered.

It was nearly midnight before they got to bed. The day had been so strange that Bett didn't know what to expect when they finally turned out the lights. She was delighted when Maggie reached for her. She didn't ask for anything more than to lie in her arms, tucked under chin.

Just before dropping off to sleep, she drew back a little. "You know, Maggie, I've lived almost twenty-two years now, and in all that time I've never had three days like this, let alone three days in a row. I'm not built for this kind of excitement."

Maggie smiled. "Stick with me, kid. You ain't seen nothin' yet."

And it was nearly midnight when Ebert and Harley turned onto Kenning Lane. As they approached the yard, Ebert sped up, acting like something was wrong . "Gate's open," she said tersely. "Use the spotlight."

Harley did as he was told but didn't understand her alarm. Lots of garages leave their gates open for easy access. They cruised the yard, and at the back of the building, he shined it on the M & M tow truck.

"Well, at least that's here," she said, pulling around to the office. "Keep the spotlight on the window." She got out and slipped her baton into its holder, softly patting that hip twice. Then she drew her gun.

Harley's anxiety spiked. There hadn't been any sign of trouble. So what if the gate was open. It wasn't like the door was off its hinges! And Ebert hadn't told him why she was taking out her piece. It was one of the reasons he liked riding with her. She always told him why she did something. And it always made sense. She'd told him early on that if he wanted to learn instinct without getting shot first, he should pay attention to her.

Until now, that had been sound advice. But now Harley's own gut was telling him something was wrong. He watched her approach the building; saw her limping slightly. She tested the doorknob, then wiped her hand on her pants and tried again. It didn't turn either time. She inched toward the office window, back to the wall, and peered in. Finally, she put her gun away.

Harley let out his breath. He hadn't even considered what he was supposed to be doing. That was bad. Real bad. He couldn't shake the feeling that something was going on. With Ebert.

"No disturbance in the office, but we better call it in anyhow."

Harley stopped her. "Call in what? We're a ways off our beat."

"So?" She pulled out her cigarettes.

"There's not much to report, is there?"

She lit one. "You think it might look funny?"

Harley tried to figure out what she wasn't telling him. He liked working with her. Like he'd told Kessler: She was smart, savvy without being cocky. He didn't mind her solid silences. It was a better way to patrol than how the guys did, jabbering all the time. But he was completely lost whenever that dark mood came over her. He'd seen it in her eyes behind the Lucky Spot earlier today, and it had continued through most of their watch. He expected that kind of malevolence from outside the car, but he couldn't deal with it from her, his partner and backup.

Finally he said, "Unless something's wrong at the gate, I'd say somebody just forgot to close the barn door when he went home."

"What if there is something wrong there?" She drove toward the gate.

"If there is, I'll buy you two beers."

"And if there isn't?"

"Then you have to tell me what you've been thinking about all shift." He turned to her, but she hit the brakes sharply, and he missed her expression.

Moments later, he found the chain and padlock still hanging on the movable section of the gate. He called her over, ready to tease her again. His smile broadened when she tested the lock. It was securely holding the two ends of chain together.

Then she yanked the chain through the gate and held the free end under her flashlight, displaying the unmistakable marks of heavy-duty cutters.

He radioed the local unit to report the situation. It had been worth it, he thought. Not the two beers. That was cheap at twice the price. No, what had made it worthwhile was seeing her smile, genuinely. Her look of relief kept puzzling him, though. And he never did find out what she'd been thinking all through that tour.

CHAPTER 12.

From the Beginning

GYP WOKE MAGGIE EARLY. She stirred, and he was at her, licking her every bare space. When he managed to get her teeth, she decided that 6 a.m. was a fine time to get up.

She watched from the porch as he wandered the edge of the open space in front of the cabin, marking his territory. She'd have to put him with another male dog soon if he was going to learn to lift his leg. It didn't come naturally. Bett said that yesterday... about what? Oh, yeah—kissing.

Maggie turned, mentally, at the thought of Lange, then put that thought aside the way she always had, by getting to work. She had to prepare for the predicted storm: see about the wood supply and haul the generator up from the shed. She didn't want to have to deal with that slope if it was an ice storm.

She dressed quickly, then checked the cache of wood under the porch. It wasn't enough for the two days of steady heat she considered safe. Down at the toolshed, she loaded an ax and maul into the wheelbarrow and brought them up to the turn in the driveway. Anticipating Bett's concerns, she brought a pair of Matt's work gloves along, too. They were only slightly too big, and her bandages made up for that now. She pulled on a glove and tightened the wrist cinch, smiling at the thought of rubber gloves for dishes, leather ones for outdoor work. Bett would be pleased.

She tried to put the left glove on but found that the wraps on her fingers made them too bulky to fit in the holes. She stuffed that glove in a back pocket and set the first log on the cutting stump. Then she realized, even without swinging the ax, that she couldn't split logs today. The glove she could wear was too snug to give her flexibility, and the bandages on her left hand kept her from gripping the handle safely. It was frustrating. She longed for the physical release that wood-splitting would provide, but she finally had to content herself with rooting around in the log pile to separate right-sized logs from those that needed splitting.

Within the hour, the wheelbarrow was stacked to its limits with oak logs and dozens of pine sticks for kindling. She rolled the barrow up to the porch and went in to heat some coffee, then took her cup out to the porch, savoring the morning quiet with a sense of having done a job right.

She'd always been able to work until she was too tired to think, too tired to dream. These days she worked less with her hands, and they'd gotten soft, their calloused texture lost. For years they'd been creviced with grease and dirt that no amount of scrubbing could clean entirely. The cracks and lines kept the dirt, reminding her of what they were made for: taking apart, repairing, rebuilding. Nothing softer.

"You got to *feel* the oil on the dipstick," Bud had told her so many years ago. "Those fancy stations 'oot on the Interstate use paper towels. Caugh! You can't feel engine grit like that. A paper towel can't tell if it's water or oil. But *you* can. Those amazin' fingers. All those nervous systems they teach you abo'ot in school. You got to use 'em, Maggie."

She could still hear his voice, with all its Canadian influence. Bud's enthusiasm had become hers. He told her things in ways she could understand. Right from the start, he taught her all he knew, then fought teachers and administrators, all the way to the district board, to get her into shop. "Why she'll show ya' what she knows!" he told them. "She can pull an engine faster 'n anybody!"

They finally let her into shop. At first it didn't matter that she was two years behind the other kids. But when Scotty left, she turned inward. Libby noticed. Maggie heard her talking with Bud one night.

"She doesn't go out anymore. She doesn't even go to see Lange on weekends. She just sits and stares out the window at the street, like she did when she first came."

"Shush. If anything was wrong, would she work like she does? Like there's no tomorrow? She misses Scotty is all. Don't you see her waitin' for his letters?"

And Scotty *had* written: "Interstate's almost finished. Pretty soon I'll be able to go from Chi-town to the Coast without a single light to slow me down. Wait'll you see the world from the cab of a rig! You always said you wanted to drive truck. Think about what I told you, okay?"

Maggie smiled at that memory. What kind of life would she have led if...?

"If it isn't Sunday, do you always wake up smiling?" Bett stood in the doorway in her nightgown.

"Good morning, dol... darlin'! Guess I do. How 'bout some tea? I put water on to boil."

"Found it, thanks, and my tea is steeping." Bett shivered. "Are you coming in, or is it customary to drink the first cup outdoors, no matter what the temperature?"

"Be right in. Soon as I unload this wood."

A few minutes later, Maggie brought in a load of wood, trying ineffectively to kick the door shut. Bett jumped up to close it and help stack the logs.

"What have you been doing with your hands?" she asked.

Maggie glanced at them. They did look funny, with one encased in leather, the other covered with bark chips and needles glued on with pine resin. She smiled. "Don't worry. They're fine. Really."

"Don't they hurt?"

She tried to reassure her. "No. It's the bandages that make them look so bad. Here, I'll take the glove off, and you can see for yourself."

But the glove wouldn't just slip off. It was part of the bandages now and had to be cut off. Bett wanted her to take a pain pill, but Maggie refused. "I don't need a pill," she said, continuing to try to remove the glove.

Bett shook her head. "I think you will." She went to get the scissors and a pan of saline solution.

As soon as the glove was cut, Maggie's hand began to throb. She lost all the color she'd earned gathering wood, then nearly lost consciousness when her hand entered the tepid salt water.

She heard Bett get out the whiskey and was vaguely aware of the sounds of water running. When Maggie looked up, Bett was standing over her.

"I want you to drink this and take this pill."

Maggie shook her head. "No pill."

"I'm not giving you a choice," Bett said flatly. "I can't treat you if you're reacting to pain."

Maggie nodded, then sat forward and took the pill, swallowing most of the drink with it. She lost track of Bett for a moment as she focused on the cold water and soothing heat of the alcohol. Anything to take her mind from the waves of pain emanating from the end of her arm.

Then she felt Bett's presence again in the form of a warm washcloth wiping her face and neck free of clammy shock-sweat. Time seemed suspended as she felt herself breathing more deeply, relaxing her jaw and searching with her tongue for a taste of the whiskey, still pushing away the pain, keeping it at bay.

Then she heard Bett call to her: "Ready?"

Maggie opened her eye and saw Bett watching her closely, even as she managed the pan of water that held the wounded hand. It was next to her on the couch, not on the table where it had been when they'd started. Maggie nodded and sat forward, with Bett guiding the pan back to the table.

Bett looked up from removing the last pieces of gauze stuck to the hand. "Don't watch, honey."

Maggie glanced beyond her and concentrated on the fire.

After a while, Bett asked, "Where do you go from the pain?"

"The wall." Maggie's voice was hoarse, and she cleared her throat.

Bett helped her sip some water. "Where's the wall?"

"Don't know. Can't get there. Just keep… running. In my head. Can't get away this time. The pain's all around. Tripping me up. Have to get behind the wall." She paused. "Now it's like fog. Not the pain, the pill. Pain can't get me in the fog. But I can't get to the wall. Can't find it. The pain can't find me, either. Just sits out there. Barking like Gyp."

She was relieved when Bett began drying the cleaned hand and applying the cream. Then Bett got a fresh pan of salt water.

"I want to fix your other hand," she said. "Now, while the fog is the thickest.

127

Ready?" Maggie closed her eye. She heard scissors scraping. Then, from far away, she sensed something like thunder on a still summer night. It was her hand, throbbing. When Bett put it in the water, sheet lightning flashed in the dark sky of her mind, and the air filled with cold, gray light. She heard herself breathing hoarsely. Then Bett was holding her. She let go. Safe at last.

The noise was gone. And the gray light. The terrible cold feeling had left, too. She opened her eye but couldn't see anything. She rolled her head to the right and a dog barked. Bett's face hovered over her.

"Hi, doll!" Too late, she remembered she shouldn't have said that. Bett was smiling, though. It was wonderful to see her so happy. Maggie closed her eye and slept.

❖ ❖ ❖

Brian deciphered the message from Maggie and sent a standard request to Douglas County, Nebraska, then called the Alameda County Morgue to ask about his copy of the autopsy on the John Doe from Friday night.

"We only got one John Doe," the clerk replied.

"Right. The guy I'm checking on doesn't have any dental records. What's the report say about identifying marks on the body?"

"All the skin features—scars, birthmarks, tattoos—are marked N/A. Guess his brother couldn't give us any details on that, either."

Brian grimaced at how badly burned… "Wait a minute. Whose brother?"

"The John Doe's."

Brian knew about the morgue's sense of humor. "Ralph Doe, right?"

"Nope. Request for personal effects came from somebody named Ross. Not sure if that's a first name or last. The note just says 'brother.'"

Brian sighed. "So where's my copy?"

"You should have gotten it in this morning's delivery, but interdepartmental might be delayed by the rain."

Rain was putting it mildly. A monsoon had struck the Bay Area, creating traffic foul-ups everywhere and giving everyone Brian encountered an extra load of Monday Morning Syndrome. He called Towing next, where his request was greeted by laughter.

"What's so funny?" Brian asked.

"You mean this vehicle isn't blocking traffic on both sides of the Nimitz, hasn't shut down the Bay Bridge, and isn't lying on top of three VIPs from Yugoslavia, visiting the Oakland Zoo on their only day in the U.S.?"

Brian admitted the wreck wasn't doing any of those things.

"Then you won't mind waiting 'til my trucks get back from those calls?"

Kessler was tired of being everybody's straight man this morning. "Just put it on your list of things to do *above* the line about going home."

Shortly after that, he ran into someone who made up for all the others. Tracy Ebert was standing in the hallway reading her official notice. She looked almost radiant.

"Hey, soldier!" he greeted. "You're out of uniform."

"Shit, yes! Sarge, I could just kiss you for this report."

Brian grinned. "Glad you're pleased with it. You earned it." Then he added: "It's not a hundred percent, you know. One more session…"

"I know. One more with Dr. Small Eyes, then six months with my choice of counselors. Thanks, Sarge. You won't regret it. I promise."

"Well, since I've been waiting for that smile of yours for so long, I guess it was worth it. Who knows," he added, walking her to the main door. "You keep smiling like that, you might turn into an innocent young thing yet!" She was a very pretty woman out of blue, he thought. Both kinds of blue.

Brian worked on routine duties until lunch, then called Probation. Fenn had once reported to Joe Hawkins, who was out until four. Brian knew Joe, a P.O. with a reputation for detail. He left a message for him, then found a number in the Newark-Fremont-Union City directory for L. Delano, Fenn's girlfriend. But there was no answer when he called.

He picked up his slicker and signed out.

☙ ☙ ☙

Bett knew Maggie was awake when a hand capped her crown heavily. "Is this my punishment then?" Bett turned, "To be beaten on the head until you wake up and realize who I am."

"Jeez, you're beautiful."

"Don't change subjects," she said lightly. "If you can trot out those Irish compliments, you're well enough to get up and take nourishment."

Maggie made her way to the table where she found soup and a whole-wheat sandwich packed with thin slices of ham, cheese, and what looked like new grass. Bett called them alfalfa sprouts.

Then Bett poured her a mug of coffee and set her cigarettes and matches on a plate as a kind of dessert.

Maggie smiled at the plate and looked in the mug. "That's egg coffee! I thought I drank the last of it."

"The sheriff made it when he came by. There weren't any other robberies, by the way. And he showed me how, so I can make more later if you like."

"Did you bet?" Maggie asked.

"Yeah, but I lost. Why does it take so much longer sometimes?"

"I have no idea," Maggie admitted. "I'm sorry I missed Hugh. How long did I, uh, sleep?"

"Not long. And he said he'd stop by later."

Maggie smoked silently for a few minutes. "I fainted, didn't I?"

Bett nodded. "But only for a minute or two. Then you fell asleep. I don't think you're getting enough rest. With your body trying to recover, you need more sleep. What time did you get up today?"

"Around six."

"Why so early?"

"That's late for me. I have to be at the yard by 6:30. I usually go to bed earlier, though."

"How early?" Bett replied skeptically.

"Around 9 or 9:30. Later on Friday or Saturday if I'm out. But I don't go out that often."

"You were out a lot later than that the night I met you."

Some color came back into Maggie's face. "That was a special occasion. I don't do that very often, either."

"Is that why you didn't show up the next week?"

"No. I didn't want to be disappointed."

Bett was stunned. "With me?"

"No! That's not what I meant." She paused. "I... didn't think... I mean, I was afraid... you wouldn't be there."

Bett was sure there was more to this. She went to the stove, thinking physical distance might free Maggie to say more.

"How long will my hands keep watering?"

Bett sighed to herself. Damn. She'd lost, for the moment at least. "That's the two weeks my father told you about."

"Is there anything we can do to help them heal?"

"Yes, but it'll still take time. We can soak them in saline more often."

"Can we get saline up here?"

She had to smile at that. "Of course. It's just salt water. It's the salt in the water that makes your hands sting. The same chemical reaction makes your skin heal faster. It toughens it."

Maggie considered that. "So I need tough skin to keep the liquid inside?"

"That's about it."

"If we soak them every hour, would they heal a lot faster?"

"Every hour is probably too often, but every three or four hours would be all right."

Maggie nodded thoughtfully. "Okay. Is it time yet?"

Bett was incredulous. "Are you a masochist?"

"Huh-uh. Used to be Catholic, but..." She stopped at Bett's laugh.

"You're unbelievable!" She looked at the clock. "We can do them again at one, but only if you promise to take a pain pill before we start."

"Every time?"

Bett nodded firmly.

"I won't get addicted, will I?"

"Of course not!" A tick went off in the back of her head. "I mean, you won't be taking them for long. And since you fight it now, when you're in real pain, you won't need it after a few days, physically or psychologically."

"Okay." Maggie rose. "I'll take a look at that blueprint Jack gave me." Then she stopped. "Or do you want help with the dishes? I can dry."

Bett smiled a little. "No, you go ahead and look at your blueprint." She turned back to the sink, wondering if they were ever going to get past the beginning of this relationship.

∴ ∴ ∴

Brian got the key to Maggie's other apartment from Mrs. Dhu, the downstairs tenant. The apartment conversion had created an L-shaped, studio-style unit. A couch separated the living room from the kitchen at the back. A single bed sat perpendicular to the couch, with an end table between.

Behind the door, the short leg of the room's L created an alcove containing a desk and a tall filing cabinet. Brian opened the top one and found a dozen or more folders, each one labeled with a name. He wondered why Maggie kept such personal files separate from her own living space. That wasn't all that baffled him. He didn't know why she continued to search for the kids from the orphanage. After all, she had the Dhu kids downstairs, and she'd always been fond of his children, Mark and Jenny. Not to mention that rag-tag bunch at the garage.

He said as much to his wife once, but Mary Jo disagreed. "Those orphans weren't just any kids. They were probably like brothers and sisters to Maggie." That made sense, and he knew Maggie never interfered with anyone she found. Fenn was the only one Brian knew she saw regularly. All the others seemed to lead normal lives. She thought Scotty was doing all right, too, until Brian told her about the bank holdup.

She wasn't surprised. Brian gave her credit for seeing Fenn in that much true light. All she said was, "He's too smart for his own good."

Brian agreed. Fenn was no typical petty- or grand-theft operator. He was a planner. Somebody who got beyond, "Then we take the money and go!" Most criminals didn't think past the first fifteen minutes of a crime.

After arresting Fenn outside that bank, he'd inventoried his personal effects. They included four tickets to a Saturday A's game. They were for cheap seats, not the box seats he expected of a guy who knew he'd be flush soon. No, he was planning on staying in town to pick up his laundry—the receipt was marked for Friday—and going to the ballgame the next day. He hadn't planned on spending big soon.

Even so, Brian was sure Fenn had masterminded that holdup. The two clowns they'd nabbed inside the bank could never have planned it. Maybe Fenn hadn't even let them know he'd put it together, maybe even offered to take a smaller cut, since he was just the driver, and laid the biggest risks on them.

Brian resumed his search and found a file marked Fenn, which contained several bills of lading. Brian wondered why they were in there, but then he found the birth certificate—a pre-Xerox photostat of the original. He hadn't seen one like it in years. The details were extraordinarily clear, right down to the footprints Maggie had promised. But no toe prints—none of the whorls and loops that fingerprint cards showed. Just tiny marks of life from long ago. Maybe they could read them like palm prints.

He looked for an empty envelope and saw one wedged in the back of the drawer. But it wasn't empty. Inside were two unframed photographs. One was an informal wedding picture of a couple running hand-in-hand up a set of flagstone steps. Brian did a double take of the bride. It wasn't Maggie, though. The eyes were wrong. He found her eyes in the groom's face. The broad forehead and distinctive brow line had passed unmistakably from father to daughter. The second picture was of the groom alone, in Marine Corps dress blues. The patent leather of his brim had caught the flash, enhancing the man's permanently laughing eyes. Lines like arrows drew the on-looker to that part of the face, just like Maggie's did. There were the straight brows, ridges over wide-set, gray eyes. The caption identified him as Cpl. James F. McIntyre.

There were letters in the envelope, too; postmarked Camp Pendleton and addressed to Eileen McIntyre. Brian didn't read them. Instead he removed a newspaper clipping and a telegram that were bound up with the letters.

The clipping was brief:

> *Mrs. James (Eileen) McIntyre was pronounced dead on arrival at St. Francis Hospital yesterday after being struck by a hit-and-run driver in the 200 block of Crescent Ave. She is survived by her husband, now serving in Korea; daughter, Margaret; and mother, Mrs. Henry (Agnes) Dugan.*

The official telegram was even more brief: "We regret to inform you…"

The dates of the two fatalities were only days apart. Brian looked at the wedding picture again and wondered if either could have survived the other's death. It was that kind of picture.

He refiled the envelope, feeling like he'd solved a mystery, and a bit like an intruder. Maggie never mentioned her natural parents. She often talked about Bud Iverson, and she'd mention Libby Iverson, her foster mother, but never her parents. Brian guessed she barely remembered them.

He rolled up Fenn's birth certificate and tucked it inside his slicker. Twenty minutes later he was back at his desk, checking the afternoon mail—still no ME report. But a Sergeant Williams had called from Homicide. "Re: the Friday night shooting." Brian returned the call, puzzling over the message, but Williams was out.

He called M & M and asked Hudson if the wreck had been towed yet.

"Wreck? Oh, yeah. Guess so. It wasn't still hooked on the tow when I took it this morning."

"You mean this afternoon?"

"No. This morning. Don't tell me what time of day I did something."

"Okay, relax. It's just that I didn't call for the pickup until nearly noon."

"That ain't my fault, is it?"

Brian tried again. "What time did you take the tow this morning?"

"About seven when we got the first call to drag somebody out of a puddle. Everybody ran into 'em. Couldn't run out again." He laughed phlegmatically. "Didn't get back until almost one.

"Well, where'd it go then?" Brian asked.

"Where'd what go?"

"The wreck."

"Search me. Wasn't here when I got in."

"Would anybody have moved it?"

"Could've. Stony was showing a little billy something about the blocks, but he's up in Richmond now."

"Well, see what he says about it. I'll check back later."

Brian hung up thinking the day was turning into a real joke: An orphan turns up with a brother; a report lost in the mails; a missing wreck he'd have to pay somebody to take. Maybe, if he was lucky, somebody would steal the body, and the whole thing would turn out to be a bad dream.

He made one more call. A woman answered. Brian identified himself, but before he could ask if she was Lois Delano, she shouted at him.

"I just *called* the cops! What is this? Cut-rate service from Proposition 13? Now you call the cops, and they call you *back*? Send the flatfoots out here, would ya? This place is a mess. And what are you calling *back* for?"

"Is this Lois Delano?" Brian finally asked.

"Of course it is. What happened? Did you lose the address or what?"

"Uh, Ms. Delano, just a minute, please. I think we've got a little mix-up here. I'm calling about Scott Fenn."

"Sure! And where's he when my place gets broke into? On the road, I suppose— forgot to tell me he had another run to Lost Wages. He's never here when I…" Then she seemed to realize something was out of sync. "Hey, wait a minute! How'd you know Scott lives here?"

She answered Brian's questions freely then. Yes, Scott lived with her and her two kids. He went to work Friday morning, as usual. Said he might be late coming home; had an errand to run. Sometimes he had to take a load without much notice. She bowled Friday nights anyhow, but no, it wasn't unusual for him to leave town without telling her. He was tight about himself, what he did and where he went. But that was all he was tight about. He treated her good, and the kids like they were his own.

"Ho! Wait a minute," she interrupted herself. "Doorbell. Maybe it's the cops." She returned a moment later. The Fremont police had arrived. "They want me to list what's missing. Anything else you…? Hey! Why *did* you call?"

Brian knew this was no time to hint that Fenn might be dead. "Put one of the patrolmen on, would you? I don't have any more questions for you now, Ms. Delano. Thanks very much."

He heard her hail one of the policemen. "He calls me *Ms!* Pretty classy, huh? Wants to talk to you guys. Didn't say which one."

There was a note of confusion in Officer Wright's voice as he identified himself. Brian quickly explained the reason for his call and warned: "Don't say anything to her about it. Just call me and let me know what's missing."

Brian avoided using the phone for the rest of the day. It only seemed to produce more trouble than it solved.

 CHAPTER 13.

Shooting Star

MAGGIE'S GOOD EYE WAS CLOSED when Bett finished wrapping her hands, and Bett felt she could relax a little, too. She'd taken her time with this cleaning, checking for any signs of infection or tears in the healthy tissue. But Maggie's hands didn't show lasting effects from their morning exercise, and they looked almost normal in clean wraps.

Bett rubbed her face. Half past one, and she was already exhausted. When she looked up, Maggie was watching her.

"This sure has been a barrel of laughs for you, hasn't it?"

Bett gestured at the bowls of dirty water. "I suppose we're about even on how much fun it is."

Maggie shrugged. "It's real nice outside. Want to take a walk? We can go downhill this time."

Bett nodded and got a jacket from the closet where she found a belted canteen that she filled to take along. As she stepped out on the porch, she thought *nice* didn't quite describe the day. Grand, billowy white clouds sailed across an azure sky. Fir trees on the ridge bent in the wind, and she zipped her jacket and turned her collar up against the breeze that rushed down the hillsides. She promised herself a run later. The weather was perfect, with still no sign of the predicted storm. But more than exercise, she needed a run to re-center herself. Too much had been happening.

Maggie came out and plopped a worn felt cowboy hat on Bett's head. "Found it when I was cleaning up the Winter Room."

Bett loved it, but they both laughed at the fit. It was too big by any measure. Maggie got a sheet of newspaper and told her to fold it into the brim liner. Bett did, then snugged it down, hearing the paper crackle in her ears. But now it fit as if it had been made for her.

They stopped at the woodpile to pick up the ax and maul and bring them back to the shed. "I thought this was an outhouse when I saw it yesterday," Bett said. "Maybe that's why the thieves didn't break into it."

Maggie snapped the padlock closed. "That's why it's down here instead of next to the woodpile. Matt didn't want it to look like a toolshed." She glanced at Bett. "I suppose you figured out he left this place to me, eh?"

"Mmm-hmm." Bett heard the tightness in Maggie's voice and didn't want to close her off. She was rewarded when Maggie continued.

"He built it before I met him. He was an airline pilot—a captain, based out of SFO. San Francisco International, I mean. He'd come up here whenever he had a long layover. He and Hugh Miller were great friends. They'd play cribbage for hours on end. Quarter a game. Fifty cents a skunk. Sometimes when I was up, we'd play cut-throat. Jeez, I sure lost a lot of quarters." She smiled wistfully.

"Would you teach me how to play cribbage?" Bett loved seeing Maggie's face light up.

"Sure! It has three parts to it. The first..."

"No, not now. When we get back to the cabin."

"I guess it would be easier with cards and a board." Maggie smiled at her. "You really are a hands-on kind of person, aren't you?"

Bett cocked her head. "I'd like to be, but we don't have to talk about that now." She saw Maggie's relief and linked arms to lead her along the path. "So, did you meet him up here often?"

"Often enough for most of Eagle Pass to know about us."

"What did they know?"

"Nothing!" Then she tossed her head. "Sorry, darlin'. I don't mean to take it out on you. It's people like Berger who think they know. Matt used to tell me to let people think what they pleased. Said he took the looks he got from the other old-timers as a compliment. Claimed he had to fight them off between reels just to keep me to himself."

"Old-timers? How old was he?"

"His late forties, I guess. He kidded a lot." She smiled, then added: "But that's something I never quite figured out."

"What?"

"Why older men are..." Color rose in her cheeks.

"What? Why they're attracted to you?" Bett laughed at her sheepish nod. "You're awfully silly. Why wouldn't they be?"

"No, not that." Maggie stopped her rapid walk. Gyp plopped down to listen, too. "Why *only* older men find me attractive."

Bett took advantage of their break to lift the canteen from her belt and take a drink before handing it to Maggie. "You know, if you look around just now, you might find some tiny particle of dissent on that theory." She wanted to kiss Maggie very much as she stood in the sun-dappled path, her face upturned to capture water from the canteen. A small dribble escaped, trickling down her neck to disappear inside her collar. The thin water trail caught the sun, sparkling for an instant until she moved again. Bett wanted to kiss the look of surprise in her eye as it grew to understanding, then to the glint of a shared joke.

Maggie's eye twinkled. "I was talking about men."

"You mean young men aren't attracted to you?"

"Right. None of the guys in my shop give me any trouble."

Trouble, she calls it. Bett sighed. "Are the men you work with mostly Hudson's age, or closer to Jack and Stony's?"

"Hudson's the oldest of the crew, but yeah, guys like Jack and Stony." She recapped the canteen and handed it to Bett. "I'm impressed. You only met them once, and you know their names."

Bett remembered how shy Jack had been. Stony was more relaxed, but he was deferential to Maggie, too. "I think you intimidate younger men." She voiced the thought as it came to her, surprising Maggie.

"But not younger women?" Her twinkle returned.

"Not a chance! We're a new breed entirely."

Maggie drew her close, carefully ducking around the brims of their hats, then stopped. Bett didn't hesitate. She put her arms around Maggie's neck, removed her hat, and held her there. Maggie leaned forward the remaining few inches and kissed her lips lightly.

Bett knew if she pressed, she could have more. Then, remembering her therapist's advice about getting to know Maggie outside of the bedroom, she let go and checked to see that the canteen was secure. When she handed Maggie her hat, she saw faint surprise in her eye.

Neither of them said anything, but their moods stayed light, and they laughed as Gyp discovered all the strange noises he could make running through piles of leaves. They wound their way through the woods, finally arriving at a clearing another slope below the toolshed.

Maggie crossed the open space and began pulling old tin cans and still-shiny beer cans from behind a split log, setting up a series of targets.

"Are you a good shot?" Bett asked when Maggie returned.

She grinned. "Matt used to say that if I'd been practicing, I could hit the sky on a day like this. But I keep trying."

Bett's smile faded as she saw Maggie take the gun from her jacket pocket and turn toward the log. "You aren't planning on using your hands, are you?"

"How else could I... Oh!"

"How can you forget like that?" Bett went to her then. "You can still teach me, can't you?"

"If you still want to learn."

Bett nodded, yet even as Maggie handed her the gun, butt-end first, she couldn't take it.

Maggie withdrew the gun and took Bett's hand. "Have you ever handled a gun before, darlin'?"

"No," she admitted in a small voice. "Only with a broom and dustpan."

"Huh?"

Bett told her about finding the black gun, and before Maggie could ask where, went on to say that she'd hidden it again, under the kitchen table. "Don't laugh," she pleaded. "I don't know why it scared me so much. But you were so upset when you were looking for it. I was sure you were going to shoot Berger." She hugged Maggie tightly. She knew her reasons for hiding the gun sounded silly, but she didn't want to be laughed at.

Maggie returned her embrace, then drew back, puzzled. "I remember seeing you sweeping the floor under the table yesterday. And last night, the table was flipped up on the far chair seat. I righted it and put the cloth back on. The thieves must've found it, then split." She focused on Bett. "Is that why you were so upset last night?"

Bett nodded. "They're armed now, and it's all my fault!"

"No, darlin'. Whoever didn't put the gun away last gets the blame for that. If I show you how this one works, will you promise not to hide it?"

Bett stepped back to look up at her. "I promise."

Maggie started with the safety catch. It would keep the gun from going off, even if she dropped it or tripped over something when she had her finger on the trigger. "Matt's gun didn't have a safety, so you were smart to be careful with it.

"Now, I don't usually start with the 'nevers' of something, but guns are a special category." She listed all the things that shouldn't be done with a gun. Never look down the barrel to see if it's loaded. Never twirl it by the trigger guard like TV cowboys. Never point it up or down a river or road; across it, okay, but never up or down. And never, *ever*, play with a gun. "Berger plays with his," she added derisively.

"Which one?" Bett asked.

Maggie snickered at that, then whistled for Gyp. "I'll hold him 'til we see how he reacts to the noise."

Bett still wasn't entirely comfortable, but to her surprise, she found that shooting was easy. The gun barely kicked at all, and the noise it made was no more than the sharp pop of a firecracker. Still, she didn't hit anything. She asked what she was doing wrong.

Maggie smiled. "Let's start with what you did right. You didn't jerk when you fired, and your aim was only a little high. I saw the ground spit just above the can. And shooting high is natural when the target's low."

Bett followed Maggie's additional suggestions about her stance and hit three cans with her next five shots. As they headed to the log to reset the cans, she saw Maggie reaching for the back of her jacket and went to help her.

"Funny place for a pocket."

"It's got a funny name, too. They call it a duck pocket. You're supposed to carry what you shoot in it, but I just use it for ammo. Get six bullets out, will you?"

Bett grabbed a handful and counted them out. They were so tiny! To think that such small things could cause… She stopped, finally registering the ticking sound in her head that she'd been ignoring for the last twenty minutes. This was wrong. All wrong. Now she knew why.

"Maggie, I can't do this."

"Can't do what?" Maggie was focused on reloading the gun.

"I can't believe I let you talk me into this."

"What...?" It was plain that Maggie had no idea what she was talking about.

"Shooting a gun. Don't you know how deadly..." Bett turned away, unable to finish her sentence, unable to even finish her thought. She tried to cope with a sudden rush of fear but couldn't.

"What exactly did I talk you into?" Maggie asked evenly.

Then Bett's fear turned to anger. "This is some kind of game to you, isn't it? Well, it's deadly. And death is *never* a game!"

She stalked off to get some space on her feelings, then realized she had no place to go. She was on foreign ground again. She saw Maggie's utter bewilderment and had to look away, knowing she was the cause of it. When she faced her again, Maggie was shaking her head slightly. Bett saw how worn she looked. Not just tired—weary with sadness.

"Let's go up to the cabin," Maggie said.

Bett noticed again how still the hollow was. Birds twittered distantly. She heard Gyp exploring a nearby section of woods. No other noises invaded. "No," she said. She spoke softly, surprising herself. She was still so angry. So frightened. "No," she repeated. "I need some time to myself. Go ahead. I'll be... I'll come up in a little while."

Maggie called to Gyp. "Or do you want to keep him with you?"

Bett shook her head, but Gyp didn't know why they weren't together. He ran to Maggie, then back to Bett. Any other time she would have laughed, but she was in too much turmoil to find his anxious race amusing. She shooed him toward Maggie, who waited on the hillside.

Then Bett turned away, still struggling with her emotions. Why hadn't she stood her ground? Refused to even touch the gun? She had principles. Good, sound, reasonable ones. Why had she compromised them? Was she so eager to please this woman that she'd become a different person for her? Would Maggie change solely for her sake? Wasn't that the sort of setup that only created problems for the future? What future?

"Oh, Ellen," she groaned. "Where are you when I need you?" Oh, shit! She'd forgotten to cancel her Wednesday appointment.

Bett reconsidered her headlong rush into Maggie's life. Maybe it wasn't the greatest idea she'd ever had. Maybe she should just go back... Then she remembered Maggie's hands. She couldn't leave her now. Maggie would forget they were even hurt!

Tears stung her eyes. No, damn it. You can't *feel* your way through this. She sat down on a dry stump, crossed her legs, and tried to meditate.

❖ ❖ ❖

Tracy Ebert was determined to enjoy her day off, despite the rain. She drove to a women's bar in Hayward where she wouldn't have to worry about being seen. It wasn't likely to be rousted, either. Not on a Monday. She ordered an Oly and shot a few games of pool with the bartender. Regulars began drifting in, and the bartender called it quits. "I owe you one!" she said, setting a cold bottle down without dragging change from Tracy's pile.

Tracy glanced down the bar to a trio of young women. One wore a hard hat and looked about sixteen. She had half a mind to card her, then remembered the last time she'd used her rank out of uniform. She didn't want to think about that, but the memory came to her anyway.

She thought Maggie's workers were all such losers. Hiring dirt-poor people was asking for trouble. When she offered to do background checks on them, Maggie only smiled.

"I don't even credit-check my customers. I'd never do it on my guys."

"What about Hudson? Didn't he lose his business? What if he's an embezzler or something? He could ruin you!"

"He isn't. And I don't run my place like that."

Despite Maggie's tone, Tracy did check on Hudson. He had owned an automotive battery shop in Albany with his wife. He also did dope. Not much. Just enough to get caught. He did two years and sold the business when he got out. What was left of it. Tracy guessed it couldn't have been much. But she didn't wait for the written report. If she had, she wouldn't have said anything to Maggie at all. Not the way she did, anyway.

They'd gone for a beer that night. Even in the dark bar, Tracy could see Maggie's eyes turn stone cold on hearing the gist of what she had learned.

"Is that all?" Maggie's voice grated, as if she'd strained it.

"Isn't it enough?" Tracy pictured Maggie crushed by the news, then grateful to have somebody with connections looking out for her.

But Maggie came at her from a different angle entirely. "Remember when you joined the force and thought people would make you a token? Or a trophy? Woman-cop on our team. Woman-cop slept here."

Tracy wanted to laugh at her old naiveté, but Maggie's eyes stopped her.

"How you worried about people seeing you in uniform and razzing you? How you'd have to take in a change of clothes every day? Make yourself into a civilian after every shift? Well, you don't have to worry. You're all cop now. They'll probably start saluting you from a distance. That blue's getting under your skin. Pretty soon you won't be able to take it off. You won't even be able to wash it off."

"You're crazy," Tracy protested. "Nobody knows I'm a cop. Not here."

"Only because you haven't offered to *help.*" Maggie's voice had risen, but still grated. "They'll figure it out soon enough. The question is, will you? You can't run away from yourself, Tracy. So be careful what kind of cop you turn into. Be the kind that takes the badge off at night. Not this kind." Then she turned and left.

Tracy threw some money on the bar and followed, but there was no sign of

Maggie when she got to the street. Two days later, she got the written report; all the details she hadn't been interested in before. When she read it, she was furious with Maggie for not telling her what she already knew, for letting her make such a fool of herself. But after a while, even she saw the flaw in that. She apologized, but it wasn't a solid effort. Maggie accepted her stumbling I-didn't-mean-it with a characteristic shrug, but Tracy quit hanging out at M & M, and she stopped seeing Maggie altogether.

She felt she had to do something about that now. It wasn't right for them to be so distant. She finished her beer. Time to make amends. She called the yard, but Maggie wasn't there. Then, thinking Maggie might still be recovering from Friday, Tracy drove to her duplex. The Buick was out back, but there was no familiar white pickup in the driveway.

She saw kids playing in the park across the street and remembered the college kid with the weird name from Friday night. Maybe Maggie wasn't dating her. Maybe she was somebody's sister. Then she remembered seeing them on the bench in the hospital parking lot. She didn't sit like anybody's kid sister. What the hell was her name, anyway?

Tracy flipped through her notebook, searching for the page from that night, but she'd given it to Kessler. Now she'd have to figure a way to get it from him. She thought a minute longer. The kid's name was Bett. No 'e.' She remembered "taking a stab" at her last name, too. Holman. That was it. She didn't have to call Kessler. She could use the phone book.

Ebert didn't want the Sarge to know she was keeping tabs on Maggie. He didn't even know they were friends. No sense letting him, either. He'd start thinking about her then. She didn't want that. Nobody on the force knew she was gay, and she meant to keep it that way.

CHAPTER 14.

Second Chance

BETT FOUND A NOTE from Maggie asking her to wake her at four. There was no mention of a clutch. No P.S. at all.

The chill in the cabin was noticeable. She stirred the fireplace coals, added kindling and a log, then fanned the embers until flames sprang up. When she went to the bedroom, she found Maggie asleep, covered only with her jacket. She had managed to get one boot off, but not the other, and had put a fold of newspaper under it to protect the comforter.

"You're a bloody fool," Bett said softly.

Gyp was lying on the bed, too. He whapped his tail happily. Bett set him on the floor, then pulled Maggie's boot off and covered her with the comforter. She never stirred.

Bett returned to the fireplace then, her feelings as chaotic as they had been at the foot of the hill. Her meditation hadn't helped much. Though she did manage to get beneath her anger, enough to realize that shooting a gun hadn't caused her reaction. No, it was the realization that she could so easily ignore her own principles. All for the sake of pleasing someone else.

She had made her decision as she climbed the hill. In the morning she would check Maggie's eye, then take a bus home. Just say good-bye to Eagle Pass and guns and burglars. Say good-bye to the woman who would rather faint than take a pain pill. By the time she crested the hill, Bett's mind was made up. And the moment she found Maggie with a boot on top of a newspaper, she changed it again. She knew she could never leave her.

Then she went to the kitchen to start supper. She'd bought ingredients for chili, anticipating cold weather, and she looked forward to making it, too. Cooking would be familiar, even if nothing else was. She danced a pat of butter in the skillet, then chopped an onion and scraped it in. As she watched it turn translucent, she sensed something missing from her routine. Each kitchen was different, but food preparation always felt good. She enjoyed the process of taking such disparate raw materials and making them edible.

Still, something was missing. Usually she would come home from class, turn on a record… That was it: music! She hadn't heard a note since meeting up with Maggie last Friday. That was a long time to be without it, and now she regretted not bringing her Walkman.

She stirred the beef in, then turned the heat down and went on a music hunt. She'd seen cassettes somewhere, and where there were tapes, there had to be a player. Today she would have even settled for Maggie's AM radio, but she couldn't even find that lowly a machine. She returned to the kitchen even more aware of the lack of sound.

After sprinkling on the chili powder she'd thought to buy, she added the meat and onions to the beans and tomatoes in the pot, then looked for other spices. Some cumin would be perfect.

Maggie found her standing on a chair, checking the cabinet above the refrigerator. "Don't believe I've had the pleasure of looking you up before."

"Not that you weren't invited!" Bett looked down at her and knew again why she'd come to the mountains, and why she would stay. Maggie's easy smile gave the lines in her face meaning as well as beauty.

"I wasn't sure the invitation was still open."

"Bull shit." Bett said it without malice. "Dinner's almost ready. Where do you keep the spices?"

Maggie opened another cabinet and took out a kind of spice holder Bett had never seen before. It was a carousel, with tube-shaped jars clamped two high on an outer frame. Maggie spun each rack in turn, then twisted the handle to pull up a sleeve of tinned spices stored inside. "This might have what you need."

Bett loved the design of the unit and made a mental note to look for one the next time she was in the City. It was just the sort of gadget her father would love. Then she looked around. This kitchen had a hundred times the supplies and accessories of Maggie's apartment. "Who keeps the cabin stocked like this?"

"Matt set it up to start. He liked to cook. Said it was his hobby before it became such a man's sport. Everybody contributes what they use, though. One of the rules is that you replace whatever you use up or bring low."

"Who else uses the cabin?"

"Mostly the guys from work, but outsiders, too."

Bett would have asked who qualified as an outsider, but Maggie had taken a pill and gone to the other room. Bett followed a few minutes later with the bowls of saline.

The more frequently they changed the wraps, the less painful it was to remove them, since there was less chance of them healing into the wounds. But the cleansing itself was still painful, and by the time both hands were wrapped, Maggie showed the strain. Bett had her lie down, then wiped her face with a warm washcloth.

"Two more weeks of this'll kill me," Maggie said with her eye closed.

"Not if you quit hurting yourself," Bett admonished. "Don't use your hands for anything strenuous."

Maggie nodded. "I guess I just forget. I never had to think about my hands being hurt before."

Bett stroked her forehead, feeling her relax under her touch. "I've done some thinking, too. I'm sorry I blew up at you earlier. I don't know why I thought learning to shoot would be okay." She shook her head. "I mean, I've always thought guns are morally wrong, but today I found out how easy they are to use. That just made it worse. Easy to use *and* deadly. It was really frightening."

"Is that how you feel about driving?"

Bett considered that. "I guess it's not so much morally wrong as excessive, especially in cities where mass transit…" She stopped, then admitted: "Maybe fear is the real reason I never learned to drive. But I suppose we all have fears we're not willing to face."

Maggie opened her eye. "Some more than others?"

Bett turned that around on her. "Sure. But you'll work through them. With a little help."

Maggie smiled tiredly. "If you're trying to pick a fight, you'll have to wait 'til the drug wears off. Besides, I'm not afraid of anything."

"Hah! Except for the past and me!"

"Pfft. Not afraid of either one. The past is gone. As for you…" Maggie paused briefly. "I'm not afraid of you, darlin'. I just don't want you to get hurt."

"Are you the love-em-and-leave-em sort?" Bett teased, more lightly than she thought possible.

"Nah, I just bore them out the door."

"Have you shown many the door?"

"Not really. Most found the way by themselves."

"And you didn't stop them?"

Maggie nodded, closing her eye again.

"Did anybody want to stay longer?"

Maggie was silent so long that Bett thought she'd fallen asleep.

"Only one," she finally said. "Maybe two."

Bett heard the emotion in her reply, and the ambivalence of her count. She wondered if Tracy Ebert was being counted.

"Bett…?" Maggie still had her eye closed. "Why didn't you kiss me again in the woods today?"

She smiled. "Not because I'm bored with you."

"That's good." Her brow unfurrowed.

"Did you think I was?"

"Not really. I just didn't know… why you stopped. Like it didn't matter."

"You don't really think it didn't matter, do you?" Bett drew her finger along Maggie's jaw, back up into her thick red hair.

"I didn't know…" she said softly.

Bett answered honestly. "I wondered what you would do. The first night we met, you were very sure of yourself."

"I was whole then. Not drugged and handicapped. I could please you."

"And now you can't?"

Maggie shook her head.

"Are you sure?" Bett saw color rise in her face. "How many lovers have you had since Lange?" She grinned when Maggie's eye sprang open. "Hey, if you're going to be uncomfortable, I might as well get my money's worth."

"You just want a count?"

"No names, no addresses. They can be totally anonymous."

"Why would you want to know something like that?"

"Let's just say I collect numbers."

"Mmm." Maggie closed her eye, not sounding convinced.

Bett waited through long, silent minutes. Finally she said: "Maggie…?"

"Shoot!" She opened her eye. "Now I lost count."

Bett was wholly unprepared for that. "How high did you get?"

"I don't know. I was still subtracting."

"Subtracting…? Subtracting what?"

"Cities. Want me to start over?"

"What cities?"

"Where I've been."

"You've had lovers in every city you've ever been in?"

"Huh-uh. I told you: I was subtracting."

But that only made the noises in Bett's head louder. Ticks and chitters went off simultaneously, and she raised her hands in surrender. "I give up. I'm going back to cooking!" She stood and looked down at Maggie, who was laughing openly now. "Hungry yet?"

"Starved. Anything I can do?"

"Nope. I'm just going to grate some cheese. What do you want to drink with dinner?"

"Beer is best with chili."

"Water first." Bett reverted to her nursing role. "You can have as much beer as you want, so long as you drink at least as much water."

Bett went to the kitchen and unwrapped a block of sharp cheddar. Then she shook her head, thinking she was hearing things. Soft strains of horn and flute music filled the air. Knowing she wouldn't subconsciously hum "Appalachian Spring," she went to the main room. The music was definitely emanating from there.

Maggie was putting another log on the fire. "I thought you might like some music with dinner. Is this okay?"

"It's wonderful! But I looked all over and couldn't even find a radio."

Maggie led her to the corner of the room near the secretary and showed her a stereo hidden behind a panel. The speakers she pointed out were more visible. Set in the soffit above the built-in bookshelves, they were obvious, but Bett hadn't been looking for speakers before. Then Maggie sprang the catch on another panel, revealing three shelves filled with record albums.

"Remarkable craftsmanship!" Bett was even more impressed by the cabin's interior now.

"Yeah, Matt was really proud of it. He and Axel—the guy Hugh mentioned about fixing the secretary—worked on getting this section just right. Matt was kind of a secretive guy. He liked little hiding places for things. Liked to bring me boxes he'd find in bazaars overseas, for hiding jewelry in or money."

"Do you think he hid something? And the burglars were looking for it?"

Maggie considered that. "Could be. But I know this cabin pretty well. I don't think anything's missing. Anyhow, I'm glad you like the system. Matt always raved about the great sound."

Bett agreed and headed to the kitchen. "What kind of music do you like?"

Maggie followed, stealing a bite of cheese. "Mostly country-western. I listen to other kinds, too, but I don't have much musical taste."

"Aaron Copland isn't exactly the natural choice of someone who doesn't have taste."

"I suppose not. It was one of Matt's favorites, though. And except for his jazz and German operas, I liked what he played. That collection is almost all his. I've got a few Larry Gatlin and Johnny Cash records. He'd listen to the Gatlin Brothers, but he only liked the ones they sang without music."

"*A cappella?*" Bett confirmed.

Maggie grinned. "I always called it Acapulco, just to make Matt laugh."

Bett asked gently: "Were you lovers?"

"No. Would it matter if we had been?"

The question took Bett by surprise. "Why would it?"

Maggie shrugged. "I went out with somebody once who told me never to admit that I'd slept with a man."

"Who would say such a thing?"

Maggie chuckled and reached for the dishes. "Feed me some of that chili, and I'll tell you anything you want to know!"

They ate silently, and hungrily, for several minutes. Bett was please by how much Maggie seemed to enjoy her cooking. She offered seconds, but Maggie declined, then set her plate down for Gyp and fixed him a bowl of dog food and fresh water.

When she sat back down, Bett brought up the earlier subject again. "So why shouldn't you admit to sleeping with a man?"

"A woman I knew a few years ago. She filled me in on PC stuff. PC means politically correct," Maggie explained. "Sleeping with men wasn't. Probably still isn't. She had a name for that, too, but I can't remember it."

Bett was tickled by her show of knowledge. "PI, maybe?"

Maggie studied that as she lit a cigarette. "Maybe. What's PI mean?"

"Politically *in*correct."

"Yeah, that's it. I thought it was dumb, but I didn't tell her that."

"Why not?"

Maggie shrugged. "She was so serious. I couldn't even laugh. It'd be like laughing at somebody with an accent or a speech problem." She paused. "What she said *is* a kind of speech problem. Saying things can't be talked about. And with people you'd most like to, too."

"I'm not sure she meant it quite like that. You could talk to me…" Bett thought she might be being too direct again, but Maggie missed her lead.

"Not if she was here. She'd be on my case, every time I mentioned Matt." Maggie tossed her head, dismissing the subject. "Never mind. She's not here. Now it's time to work off all that chili. Want to help stack the rest of the wood?"

∴ ∴ ∴

Officer Wright called Brian from the Delano/Fenn apartment and reported that the only thing missing was Fenn's knapsack. Mrs. Delano said he always took it when he went on the road.

Brian asked for a copy of the official report, then signed out for the day. Across the street at the Last Tour, he found Probation Officer Joe Hawkins in a corner booth, making notes on a pad of paper and sipping a draft. Brian brought two more over and slid in across from him.

Hawkins spoke without looking up. "In the next evolution, we'll have permanent ink sacks under our fingernails. When the ink runs out, we get to retire. No matter what else needs to be reported." Twisting his pen closed, he offered his hand. "How you been, Kessler?"

They chatted briefly before Brian asked him about Scott Fenn.

"Don't tell me you're after him, too?"

"Why? Who else is?"

"Homicide." Joe shook his head. "I'd never peg Fenn as a murder suspect. I could hardly believe he was up on attempted robbery." He glanced at Brian. "Sorry, hey. That was your collar, right?"

Brian waved off his gaffe. "It'd be too easy to just pick up the ones who *look* guilty."

Hawkins laughed. "Christ, yes. I'd be in jail forever!"

"Who'd you talk to in Homicide?" Brian was sure Bett had described Fenn, but maybe somebody else had gotten caught in the explosion.

"Never talked to anybody," Hawkins replied. "Just got a standard request and sent a copy of his file."

"Did you look it over first?"

"Yeah. I wondered if he was getting tagged on that warehouse fire."

Brian's ears perked up. "What fire?"

"One in Vegas about a year ago. Fenn's kind of a special case. Not like anybody else on my rolls. He was prompt, clean, even employed. Oddball, start to finish. Somebody helped him get a job at a computer company down in San Leandro. Seemed pretty sweet to me, but he only stayed there a few months, then up and quit. Before I could even get on him for that, he got his Class 1 and went to work for a trucking company in Hayward, a subbing outfit that takes overloads from other carriers. It's small, but Fenn said he'd have a chance to learn different jobs. He drove truck years ago; now he'd do some dispatching and maybe get into the sales end."

Joe sipped his beer. "Fenn never caused me any trouble until I found him living with some chick south of Hayward. I gave him hell for moving out of Oakland without telling me. It didn't faze him. 'No big deal,' he said. 'I'm still in the county.' He was about a half mile from breaking parole. But that's how he was. He'd check the limits on something, then pull right up next to it. Weird guy."

"Tell me more about the Vegas incident," Brian said.

"I never got anything official on it. Just Fenn's story. One day he came in all wild-eyed. If it'd been anybody else, I'd say scared. He gave me a folder with some log sheets in it, a news clipping, and a motel receipt from Albuquerque. The clip was about a fire on the warehouse strip that the Vegas PD was investigating for arson. His log showed he'd been there the day before the fire. He knew they'd check on everybody who'd been near there, and he'd be a suspect just because he was on probation. A night guard died at the scene from a heart attack or stroke. Fenn knew that meant a capital offense. His log showed he left Vegas about two that afternoon. The fire broke out after midnight, and his motel bill put him in New Mexico by then. All I could do was offer to keep the 'proof.' He looked at my office and snorted. Said he'd pay the freight on a safe deposit box. Thanks anyhow."

Brian grinned. The disarray of Hawkins's office was legendary.

"That's all I know. Nothing ever came of it while he was on my rolls. Fact is, once his probation was up, I never heard of him again until today. How come you and Homicide are both looking for him?"

Brian told him about Friday night. "But there's still no firm ID on the victim. And I have *no* idea why Homicide's after him."

Joe smiled wryly. "As usual, Fenn's either in a whole lot of trouble or he's out of it completely!" He checked his watch. "I'd have another beer, but I promised Jeanne I'd come by early."

He and Brian left together. It had stopped raining late that afternoon, and a milky sun was emerging, just in time to be swallowed up by the evening fog. They parted, and Brian stood at the curb, considering what to do next. He could go down to the morgue and get his copy of the path' report, look up Detective Williams from

Homicide, or call Towing and see about the wreck. He was a little logy from the beer, though, and decided all that could wait until tomorrow. Now it was time for dinner.

✧ ✧ ✧

Ebert parked behind a Berkeley squad car at Bett's address. A BPD cop was talking to a student on the front walk. It made her curious, but she didn't stop. In the entryway, she checked the mailboxes, then went down the hall where she found another officer examining the door she was headed toward.

Ebert showed her ID. "What's going on?"

"You the resident here?" he asked.

"No, but I know her. What happened?"

"One of the tenants reported prowlers on the premises."

"Prowlers?"

The patrolman grinned. "We got a kick out of that, too. Call came in about seventeen hundred. The perps split when the caller hollered 'police.'"

"Ever helpful," Ebert sympathized. "What'd they get?"

"Nothing. They didn't get in. My partner's getting the property manager now. The tenant's a student and hasn't been around since Friday. She might've gone home for the weekend. Could just be somewhere on campus now."

His partner came down the hall then with an elderly man who identified himself as Mr. Winkler, the manager. Ebert nodded to the policemen, went out the front door and lit a cigarette, wondering what to do next.

Someone called out: "Are you a cop, too?"

Ebert searched for the owner of the voice, then saw a girl who looked about eighteen years old hanging out the first floor window. She had pushed the screen away to see more clearly, and Ebert hadn't felt so fully scrutinized since her prelim interviews for the Academy. She gazed into a pair of blue eyes. Paul Newman blue. She smiled without realizing it. Finally she said, "What makes you think I'm a cop?"

"I saw you talking to the BPD in there. They wouldn't tell *me* anything, and I know Bett. You don't know her, or you wouldn't have checked her mailbox for the number. I saw you."

"Are you a cop?" Tracy asked. "The way you watch strangers sure makes you sound like one."

"You think so? Really?" The girl was evidently thrilled at the idea.

"I don't know," Tracy said solemnly. "What else did you see?"

"Well, two guys pulled up in front. One of them kept looking at a paper, checking the numbers on the buildings like they were looking for a place to rent. But they didn't look gay."

"Huh!" Tracy wasn't sure what her involuntary grunt conveyed, but a non sequitur like that must have been intentional. She appraised the girl from a different perspective.

"The way I figure it, the only reason two guys go looking at apartments is if they're going to live together. In this neighborhood, it's all students or starving gay artists. These guys definitely weren't students. And we already covered the other subject."

"Which are you?" Tracy realized she'd been given a perfect lead when the girl put a hand to her throat melodramatically.

"I? Which am I?" She even tittered a little. "I'm starving!" Then her voice returned to normal. "Want to have dinner? There's a great restaurant up the street. Oh, come on up! You look silly down there with your mouth hanging open. It'll just take me a minute to get ready."

Tracy watched the screen close, then looked around, suddenly conscious of where she was and the kind of conversation she'd been having in public. She put the cigarette to her lips, only to find herself grinning idiotically. She flipped the butt toward the curb and reentered the building.

CHAPTER 15.

I Know You Know

Darkness fell as Maggie and Bett unloaded the wheelbarrow. Bett reflected on everything she'd learned about Matt and Lange and wondered aloud why it all seemed so strange. "Not weird-strange," she added when Maggie chuckled. "But when other people tell me about their experiences, I can usually figure out how they think about things. What they believe."

"And you can't with me?"

"Well, your experiences have been a lot different from mine."

"The problem might not be your experiences. I've met all kinds of people, but I've never met anybody who thinks like I do."

"Don't you feel terribly... alone... believing that?"

"Nope." Maggie lifted the wheelbarrow handles. "But then I don't think about it much. C'mon. One more load to get."

Bett followed the bumping noises down the slope, nearly running into the wood-pile at the bottom. "Should I go get a flashlight?"

"Nah, this won't take long. Look up at the sky a minute."

Clouds had moved in, and the moon was no more than a hazy patch of white. Yet when Bett looked down again, she could see logs that had been invisible before. "How did you know my eyes hadn't adjusted?"

"From the way you followed me down the path. Like you didn't know there was one. That's another difference between us. Your first instinct is to go get help. Mine is to figure out how to do with what I've got. But your instinct was right to get help when we found the cabin broken into." She unloaded an armful of logs. "And speaking of broken, that's what you nearly did to my arm!"

Bett had forgotten all about that. "I was just going to throw you."

"You mean over your head?" Her voice was bright with laughter.

"Yes! And I will, too, if you ever leave me behind again!"

Bandages flagged the darkness as Maggie raised her hands in surrender. Bett hugged her and was delighted when those flags settled easily on her back. "We have this in common," she said lightly.

"Beat me to it again, darlin'. You're too fast for me."

Then Maggie surprised her again by leaning down and kissing her—right there in the great outdoors, without any hesitation. Bett responded eagerly. Perhaps too eagerly. Maggie broke their kiss and hugged her close.

They stood together in the darkness, just holding each other. Finally Maggie said, "Ready for some coffee and a lesson in cribbage?"

Bett leaned back in her arms. "This cribbage business. Pretty exciting game, is it?"

Maggie laughed, and they headed up the hill.

Just as they got to the porch, a vehicle pulled into the driveway. It was Sheriff Miller. Maggie waited for him, and when they came in a few minutes later, Bett had already turned the burner on low under the coffee. Maggie poured a cup for the sheriff and brought it to the table. She considered telling him that the gun had been stolen during the break-in after all, then decided that Bett's reasons for hiding it might sound silly. And it had already been reported missing. There wasn't much point.

"I can't stay long," Hugh said. "It's raining pretty bad down in the valley. Expect we'll get that storm before morning."

They discussed the weather briefly. He hoped for snow but didn't think it was cold enough. "We'll get ice, and I'll end up driving point for the sand trucks. You'll see."

Bett had gone to the main room, and Maggie offered her coffee.

"None for me," she said. "I'm on a music hunt. Anything you'd like to hear, Sheriff?"

He shook his head and turned to Maggie. "I just came by to tell you about Berger. He's so hung over, he barely knows his own name. Fact is, I couldn't get back to you until now because I had to nail down his alibi, then work his shift."

The poker game hadn't been hard to find. Berger was gone, but Dan confirmed that the game had started in the back room when Berger came in at four. "I don't think he did this."

Maggie nodded. "What you said last night about the kind of damage made sense. Did you tell him I accused him of it?"

"Nope."

"Good! I'd have a hard time apologizing." She saw Hugh's wry smile and realized the position he was in. "I don't mean…"

He waved her off. "I have to work with him. Not like you, getting to pick the boys in your shop." His brow knit then. "You fire anybody lately?"

She saw where he was headed. "No, I haven't had to do that in quite a while. They're not always happy with me, but I'd know if somebody was that torqued. And, like you say, somebody with a grudge would've done different kinds of damage." She reconsidered the problem, with Berger out of the picture. "Did you get a chance to ask Dan about those two guys?"

Hugh nodded. "He gave me a description but didn't see their vehicle, so no plate number. No way to identify them at this point." He rose, then saw the extra wood on the hearth. "You all set for the storm?"

"Almost. Mind giving me a hand with the generator?"

Bett looked up from her search. "Want me to help, too?"

"No, that's okay." Maggie grabbed her jacket and a flashlight, resisting the impulse to reach out to her. "Check the Winter Room closet, though. I saw some albums in there."

The wind had picked up considerably. She shivered and switched the flashlight on to read the thermometer at the edge of the porch. "Still mid-thirties," she announced, turning to Hugh. He wore an odd look. "Something wrong?"

"No. Just thinking about Matt again. How he used to always bet on the temperature, too."

They headed down the path. Maggie aimed the light a few feet ahead. "He was a good man," she said quietly.

"Did you...?" Hugh cleared his throat. "Do you miss him?"

She looked at him. "Of course I do. I couldn't even come up here after he died. I thought you... Sorry. I just thought you'd understand." They got to the shed, and she unlocked it and swung the door open. Hugh's hand on her shoulder surprised her.

"I do understand," he said quietly. "Or I thought I did. I asked Berger why he was so ticked. He told me..." The sheriff paused.

"Told you about the queers up at Graf's place, didn't he?" Maggie said tightly. She trained the flashlight inside the shed, but it cast enough light for them to see each other.

"Something like that."

"What'd you say?"

"I told him he was crazy and to keep his yap shut until he learned some manners."

"And what do you think now?" Maggie softened her tone, remembering how he had watched her calming Bett last night.

He shook his head. "I thought..." He stopped again.

"You thought I loved Matt? You weren't wrong, Hugh." She heard him sigh. "But Berger's not crazy."

"Guess I know that, too." His look was direct, even in the diffuse light. "But he still doesn't have any manners!"

She laughed. "Right again!" Then she said: "You're one of the few people whose opinion of me matters, Hugh. I don't want that to change."

"You don't have to worry."

They exchanged a look of understanding, borne of years of comfort with one another, then turned to the generator and dragged it from the shed together. She put the padlock back on, then faced him again.

"Did Matt know... about you?" he asked.

"Yeah, he knew." Maggie smiled wryly. "He used to razz me a lot about who I went out with."

They started up the hill, neither of them speaking until they made it to the porch and set the generator down. Hugh settled against a support post.

"So Matt used to tease you, huh? What would you have told him about Bett?"

"Not much. I'd scuff my feet in the dirt. Turn red, like I am now." She tossed her head. "I'd tell him she's smart about things I'm not." Maggie went on with some pride about Bett's medical knowledge, then told him about her judo hold.

"Sounds like she's got common sense, anyhow," Hugh said.

Maggie bristled. "And I don't?"

"That's not what I meant. But I told Matt when he bought that damn gun: Don't go looking for trouble just because you've got one in your hand. You'll find it. And I'll have to pick up the pieces." He stood. "That's it for the lectures. Say g'night to Bett for me. I'll drop by later this week, and we'll play some cut-throat. You *did* bring quarters, didn't you?"

Maggie watched him drive away, feeling more lighthearted about being at the cabin than she'd ever hoped to again. She sat on the porch, enjoying the very presence of the mountains. The night didn't seem cold at all anymore.

❖ ❖ ❖

"So what were you before you were a cop?"

Tracy choked on a sip of cognac and had to hold her breath to keep from coughing it out again.

"I figure you weren't born with a gun and badge in your…"

"Not so loud!" Tracy looked around the restaurant, newly irritated that the subject had come up again.

"God! Are you always so uptight? Or did it just hit when you turned thirty? Want to go to the City later? I can always study tomorrow."

Tracy had been dodging those kinds of impertinent and rhetorical questions since they'd met in the girl's apartment. Her name was Elise Trinos, and Tracy found herself shaking her head every few minutes at the way Elise talked about whatever came to mind. Dr. Smalys would have a field day with all her free associations.

As they left the restaurant, Elise put an arm around her. Tracy moved off and told her to behave.

"You sound like we'd get arrested for walking arm in arm! I don't believe it. Besides, you could tell them you're a cop."

"I never said that. Why do you keep insisting I am?"

"You've got wary eyes. Either you're dying of heartbreak, or you're a cop. My money's on the badge, but I've got both covered. We'll see what your eyes look like later." Then Elise took her by the hand and ran her up Telegraph Avenue.

Tracy was breathless when they turned the corner. Not just from the run. She'd never been so blatantly propositioned before. She didn't know what to make of Elise. She was nothing like Carole, Tracy's ex. Carole was a long time ago. BS time. They hadn't really split until AS time… No. She wasn't going to start thinking about Carole now.

But her mood had dimmed. As they turned down Elise's street, she anticipated some awkwardness, even when first encounters started off with a roar the way this one had. Then she realized she'd let her hopes climb. She pulled out her car keys. "Listen, Elise, it's been real…"

"Don't be silly! You've been drinking. You can't drive."

Elise took her arm again, and they went up to her apartment. Opening the door, she waved Tracy in and closed it behind them. Then, in the darkness, Elise grabbed her from behind.

Ebert's instincts took over, and before she knew it, she'd twisted Elise to the floor and pinned her. Releasing her throat press and moving a knee off her arm, she started to apologize.

Elise put a hand over her mouth to shush her, then cupped her breast with the other, stroking it until she felt Tracy gasp.

"I was sure you were a cop," she said huskily. "Are you going to lie about being gay, too?"

They didn't get more than five feet from the door until much later that night.

⋄ ⋄ ⋄

Bett only found one female vocalist in the shelved albums: Judy Henske. Then she remembered Maggie's comment and checked the Winter Room. Capital *W!* Capital *M! Women's Music!* She dragged the box of albums she found there to the main room, put on *The Changer and the Changed*, and turned up the volume. Then she sat in front of the fire, eyes closed, and let herself drift with the sensuality of the music. She didn't realize Maggie had come in until the sound was lowered.

"Sorry if it's too loud. Isn't it beautiful?"

"Mmm-hmm." Maggie put the flashlight on the mantle and hung up her jacket, then headed for the kitchen. "Time to do my hands?"

"Sure." Bett followed. "Why do you keep them in the closet?"

"I always keep jackets in the closet. That way…"

"The records!" Bett said impatiently.

"Oh, those. I don't know why they were in there." She took a codeine from the bottle. "Tracy must have left them."

"Tracy? Ebert? You mean they're not yours?"

"Nope. I never buy albums." She drew a glass of water and took her pill, then pointed at her ear. "No musical taste, remember? I don't think Tracy will mind if you play them, though."

"How do you know they're hers?"

"What's wrong? I thought you'd like that music."

"I do. I just wanted them to be yours. You do like Women's Music, don't you?"

"Not particularly." Maggie drank the rest of her water and got out a beer.

"Why not? What don't you like about it?"

"Hey, wait a minute. You didn't ask that about German opera. Is this a loaded question?"

Bett knew she was being too eager, but music written and played and produced and sung by women was such a fundamental joy that she couldn't imagine anyone disliking it. At least not any woman. "It's not the same thing!" She followed Maggie to the main room. "Women's Music is our banner. It speaks for us. It shouts for us. It's our poetry. It gives us emotion in sound and words. It tells our story." Bett ran out of breath.

Maggie paused briefly before drawling, "And German opera doesn't?"

"Oh, Maggie! This is really important!"

"Okay," she said easily. "Play what you like. I don't care."

Bett couldn't fathom her stolid indifference. "Have you ever listened to it? The lyrics and the sound? It's unique. Really it is. Even the critics say so."

Maggie smiled patiently. "You're like the new sales reps they send to the yard. You'll sell more if you don't force it down the customer's throat."

"Be serious! Everything isn't about the garage or engines. Women's…"

"I am being serious." Maggie retorted. "I've heard a lot of music, but maybe I don't hear what other people do."

Bett saw she was upset by the high color in her face, but that quickly faded as leaned back on the couch. It looked like the codeine was having some effect, and she took Maggie's hand, surreptitiously checking her pulse. It fit the rest of her symptoms. What didn't fit was why she was so upset. Bett stroked the inside of her forearm, not knowing what to say. But it was Maggie who spoke in the silence between musical cuts.

"I'm sorry, Bett."

"What for?"

She spread her hands and let them fall.

"Huh-uh. I don't accept blank apologies. Comes from hanging out with someone who said I'm sorry all the time: when she was late, when she was early, when she called, when she didn't, when we got stuck in traffic, when we didn't make love."

Maggie couldn't resist: "What about when you did?"

"No. The only time she should have, too!" Bett laughed at her look. "What? Surely in all those cities you must have been sexually disappointed sometime?"

Maggie smiled. "How do you know she apologized if she didn't call?"

"She told me. She'd say, 'I know I didn't call, but I was sorry. You weren't there, but I said I was sorry. Sorry.' Drove me absolutely crazy." Bett enjoyed Maggie's laughter but hadn't missed her feint. "You didn't answer my question."

She shrugged. "Guess it depends on what disappointed means, but I don't think so."

"Ever?"

"Well, there were times when I haven't… connected. But not when I have."

"What does 'connected' mean?"

"Oh, you know…" Maggie's color rose again, and she could barely get the words out. "Met. Someone."

Bett sighed. Plainly, "What does that mean?" wasn't going to work. She still preferred the direct approach, though. "Does meeting someone mean going to bed with them?"

Maggie took her time answering. "Not necessarily." Another long minute passed, then she opened her eye and struggled a bit to sit up. "I'm okay," she said as Bett reached to help her. Then she nodded at the stereo. "How about playing some more of your music?"

"Sure!" Bett was delighted. "But first tell me what you *don't* like."

Maggie cocked her head. "Most people don't ask it that way."

"Pretty soon you'll figure out I'm not like most people."

Maggie smiled and asked for something not too loud.

Bett selected a record, then saw Maggie unwrap the outer bandages on one hand and slip it into the saline solution, stretching her fingers and grimacing at the healing sting.

Rejoining her, Bett removed the rest of the wrappings and cleaned and rinsed the wound. She examined the hand before drying it lightly and dressing it with salve. She could see Maggie watching her, wearing a soft, almost dreamy look in her eye.

"How's it feel?" Bett asked in a low voice, not wanting to disturb Maggie's distant gaze.

When Maggie closed her eye suddenly, Bett monitored her pulse, then smiled to herself as she waited patiently for a reply. At the end of a minute the pulse was nearing normal again.

"Fine," Maggie said. "It hardly hurts at all." She opened her eye. "What's wrong?"

"Nothing." Bett set clean 4 x 4's in place to wrap the first layers of gauze. "What were you thinking about before when I asked how it felt?"

"I don't suppose you'd believe me if I said I didn't remember."

Bett shook her head, stifling a sigh. "No. But you don't have to tell me if you don't want to."

Maggie paused, holding her breath a moment, then she let it out slowly. "I was thinking… how much I like it when you… touch my hand."

Bett watched her face turn crimson with that admission but didn't tease her. Instead she said, "I'm glad."

It saddened her to realize how difficult this was for Maggie. And she wondered why, remembering the light banter they had shared the first night they met. As she cleaned the other hand, she thought about everything that had happened since Friday night. Maybe Maggie was finally registering how seriously she'd been injured. Add to that how unsettling it was for her to take drugs, and Bett began to see Maggie's discomfort as part of a larger picture.

Those thoughts relieved her, and she looked at Maggie with new awareness, see-

157

ing again how pale she was, how tired she looked with her eye closed. "How does your right hand feel?" she asked carefully.

"I want you so..." Maggie's eye sprang open at her own admission. "I mean, it's... I... It feels fine."

Bett cocked her head, drawing back slightly. "Which is it?"

Maggie started to answer quickly, then stopped. Tilting her head to match Bett's pose, she said softly, "Would you mind if I meant both?"

Bett felt relief, then amusement. She replied deliberately: "No. I. Would. Not. Mind." Then she sighed. "Maggie, I want you to want me. I want you to have me, any way you want. Any way you *can!*" Then she pointed to the bowls. "But I can't heal your hands any faster than this."

As Maggie's eye closed again, Bett wondered if they were ever going to get past this... whatever it was. It wasn't as if the only way women made love was with their hands. No. They'd already had that conversation at the pond. Maybe they were doing too much talking, face-to-face across bowls of saline. Maybe she'd taken her therapist's advice too literally. She knew it was easier to discuss intimate things in the dark. It didn't have to be in the bedroom, though. They didn't have to make love, either. They could just lie together in front of the fire. Turn the lights off. Play soft music. She would let Maggie know there was nothing to fear from talking together. She could say anything. Everything.

Bett wrapped the final layer of gauze and reminded herself to be patient. They had all the time in the world.

CHAPTER 16.

Imagine My Surprise

TRACY STRETCHED LUXURIOUSLY and reached for her cigarettes, then stopped. She didn't want anything just yet. She was that sated. How long had it been since she'd felt like this? She turned to Elise at her side, wondering how she could know so much at her age. Not that there was that much difference in their ages. And a lot had happened in the ten years since she'd been twenty-one, but nothing quite like this.

Then she did take out a cigarette. She was squinting against the flare of the match when Elise blew it out.

"How can I kiss you with one of those things in the way?"

"Have to kiss me someplace else, I guess."

She tore another match free as Elise began exploring her, then gasped involuntarily. "No, don't!" Tracy barely controlled her voice, then reminded herself: *It doesn't hurt! Phantom pain isn't real!*

"No, Elise. Don't look, either. It's just a scar."

"What happened? How did you get a scar there? Does it hurt?"

"No!" Tracy fought for self-control, then forced herself to speak in a normal tone. "I didn't mean to yell."

Elise stopped her apology with a kiss, and Tracy felt a hand traveling up her leg, sweeping past the puckered scar of bunched muscles. Higher yet.

"Does it hurt here?" Elise whispered.

"No, lover. Nothing can hurt me tonight." Tracy kissed her lightly and rolled off the bed. She was tempted to stay but knew she had to leave. She had to get some distance on tonight, or she'd be too vulnerable on the job. She looked down on Elise. Oh, yes. Far too vulnerable.

She dressed quickly, then leaned down and kissed Elise, who opened her eyes and plucked at her sleeve.

"You've got all your clothes on." Elise puzzled over that briefly, then asked: "Want to go on a picnic later this week? We can go to the park and see if the merry-go-round is running." She noticed again that Tracy was dressed. "You're not really leaving, are you? That's just what happened to Bett. What did you come to see her about, anyway?"

Elise went on, not giving Tracy time to answer. "I'm really starting to worry about Bett. She's never gone this long without telling me. I threw her cards today after those guys showed up. They didn't look good. Her cards, I mean. Please stay, Tracy. I'll throw your cards for you and study another time." Then she hugged her. "You know how I came on to you? So strong, I mean? I never do that. I've never even picked anybody up before. Not ever. Not like you!"

Tracy smiled, happy to hear that. Happier still that Elise had chosen tonight to change.

"And I have to tell you something else, too. I'm not sure I can explain, but I'm... fey about some things, and... you're in danger. Don't laugh. I'm serious. Really."

Tracy kissed her. "I'm a little like that myself. But your imagination's working overtime. I won't be in any danger, even on patrol tomorrow. But that *is* why I can't stay."

Elise kissed her deeply, almost convincing her to stay.

Tracy drew back. "You know what you can get for trying to bribe a cop in this state? I won't walk out of your life quite as fast as you invited me in." She kissed her lightly. "Thursday's my next day off, and I start late on Friday. We could do the park then. Now, did I forget anything?"

"Turn on the light. I want to see something." Elise took her face in her hands and studied her eyes. "That's what I thought! You *are* a cop, and you're no longer broken-hearted! Now you better get out of here so I can study, or I'll read your immediate future without any tarot cards!"

⋄ ⋄ ⋄

When Bett returned from emptying the saline pans, Maggie had spread an old quilt in front of the hearth and was getting something from the secretary. "Ready for a game of cribbage?"

Bett joined her on the quilt and picked up a polished rectangle of wood that had been uniformly drilled with dozens of holes. "What's this?"

"A cribbage board. It's how you keep score."

"Oh, do we have to keep score right away?"

"Sure." Maggie smiled. "But I won't let you beat me too badly. Turn it over, and get the pegs out of that little slot." She went on to explain the game's leap-frog counting method. "Any questions yet?"

Bett picked up the cards, shuffling them absently. "Mmm-hmm. What do you usually do after work?"

"Go home. Eat. Go to bed."

"Don't you have any social life?" Bett didn't want to offend her, but it seemed like a pretty narrow existence.

"Sure. I met you, didn't I?"

"I know, but the bouncer at the Fox said you didn't come in that often. Where else do you go?"

"Nowhere. Just the Fox." Maggie reached for her cigarettes.

"But she and the bartender said you don't come in often." Bett expected sounds from the back of her head. There were none.

"Nope. Every two or three months." Maggie's pack was empty, and she asked Bett to get another one from her jacket.

"That's all?" Bett asked, tossing her the pack.

"Yeah, just my cigarettes."

Bett sighed. "I mean, you only go to the Fox every two or three months? Or you only go out that often?"

"Same-same." Maggie lit up.

"You mean you only go to the Fox when you go out, and you only…"

"Go out every two or three months," Maggie finished. Her eye twinkled in the firelight as she leaned against the couch. "I think I've got the hang of this now. Should we run through it a few more times, just to be sure?"

Bett didn't know which was worse: Maggie's laughter or the sudden mice chitters in her head. She tried another tack. "But when do you see people?"

"I see people all day long. Evenings, too, with meetings and the like."

"Women's meetings?"

"No, work stuff. We try to meet as a group at least once a month. The managers are too busy during the day." She took the cards from Bett. "But I thought you were talking about going out socially."

"I was." Bett was distracted by a memory of something the sheriff had said, but it wouldn't gel. Then another thought occurred to her. "Maggie, do you have another lover?"

Maggie almost riffled the cards into the fire. She smiled wryly. "No, no other lovers."

"Then how…? I mean, what did you do before you met me?"

Maggie laughed. "You're very clever, darlin'. Is this another way of asking how many lovers I've had since Lange?"

"No, er, yes!" Bett closed her eyes briefly. "I've never met anyone like you! I'd love to know what kind of women you go out with. And do they *all* have this much trouble talking to you?"

She chuckled. "I've gone out with all kinds of women. And not one of them has as much trouble as you seem to. Or didn't say so if they did. Of course, I never talked this much before. Maybe that's…"

"Never talked this much?" Bett couldn't believe her ears.

"Nope. I figure it's the codeine. I don't know that for a fact, but it does sort of stand out as what's different." Then she added softly, "Of course, it could just be you."

"That's not possible! You've hardly said anything! Give me one example, just one, of something you've told me and nobody else."

"Oh, that's easy. Lange, for one. And Scotty. The part about knowing him from before. Only Brian knew that we…"

Bett overrode her: "You never told *anyone* about Lange?"

She shrugged. "Not much to say, is there?"

Bett was appalled. No wonder Maggie's story had been so painful. All those years of never airing her feelings…

But Maggie was focused on Scotty. "Are you sure it was Scotty we picked up Friday night?"

"Pretty sure. Why? Did you remember something?"

"No, but I will one of these days. Or I'll ask him about it. He remembered for me before." She looked at Bett directly. "I know you and Brian both think he's dead, but we're close in a funny way. Sometimes I know he's in trouble even before he does. I would've known if it had been him in that fire." She shuffled the cards and dealt automatically. "And Brian's probably checked those footprints by now. He'd let me know right away if they matched."

"That's okay as far as it goes," Bett cautioned. "But if Scotty wasn't the victim in that fire, who was it? And where did Scotty go?"

"He would've split as soon as he saw the first CHP unit."

Bett shook her head slightly, knowing that the Oakland Police had arrived first, not the Highway Patrol.

"He might not have seen me," Maggie went on. "Brian said it was Scotty's car, but something might've happened we don't know about. Maybe he got jumped. Somebody could've been trying to hot-wire his car when he got there, pulled a weapon on him. I still can't figure out what caused the fire." She paused. "It's not supposed to work that way."

"Do things always work the way they're supposed to?"

"Mostly they do, yeah."

Bett didn't want her to dwell on that. She picked up the six cards in front of her. "Okay, give me all your fives!"

Maggie smiled at her demand from the children's game of Go Fish. "Not on your life! The first thing you do in this game is give away, not ask for. Next you'll want to know what to give away and what to keep. Pretty soon you'll be learning the rules, and who knows who'll win?"

Bett laughed, glad to see Maggie's familiar grin, then listened as she explained the rules. Within the hour they were headed down "third street." Bett was slightly ahead.

"Okay, my count first. I've got a pair for two, and fifteens for two and four and six, and a triple run times two. Sixteen!"

"Almost." Maggie smiled. "Come on, now. Count it right, or the sheriff will run you out of town when we play cut-throat."

Bett rearranged her cards on the quilt, pointing to them as she counted. "Fifteen-two, fifteen-four, fifteen-six, and a double run of three for eight is fourteen. Right? Hey, did I get credit for the pair?"

"Right! You got it with the double run, remember?" Maggie counted her own hand and moved her peg ahead before displaying the cards in her crib. "Another nineteen-point crib! How can you keep doing that to me?"

"Where?" Bett looked closely at the cards. "You don't have any points at all. Not even with the turn-up card."

"I know. In cribbage a bust hand is called nineteen points because you can't get that count with any combination of cards."

"Why not?"

"It won't add up. You can get eighteen points, and other hands add up to twenty or more, but never nineteen. It's impossible, given the value of the cards."

Bett found that mathematical quirk fascinating, and though she'd quickly caught on to the card combinations and values, she didn't understand why the counting was so formal. She dealt, looked at her cards, and threw two in the crib.

"What about a triple run of three and two pair?" she asked, mentally adding those values of fifteen plus four.

"Tough to do with just five cards!" Maggie cut the deck, and Bett turned up the jack of spades. "Take two for talking!"

Bett moved her peg. "This game has the oddest expressions! Why do you say that when a jack is turned up?"

"Automatic two points for the dealer. You didn't do much to earn it, did you?" Maggie smiled. "Not much value in talk. Or talk is cheap. However that saying goes."

"Not with you! You'd think words were gold fillings in your teeth. Got to pull them out. One by one."

"Pfft. Not true!"

Bett lay down on the quilt, imitating Maggie's position on the couch an hour earlier, and barely moved her lips: "Met... Someone..." She kept her eyes closed as part of her mimicry, waiting to hear laughter. But there was only silence. When she opened her eyes, Maggie was looking down at her, wearing a mixed expression.

"Didn't I though." Maggie leaned down slowly, as if drawn by a force. Bett reached up. They both closed their eyes to kiss.

Bett held her to keep her from falling. Then just to keep her. When Maggie started to draw back, Bett levered her forward, catching her as she tumbled off balance.

"I've got you!" she declared in triumph.

"Oh, Bett." It was all Maggie could say in that moment. Finally she added, "If I promise not to run away, will you let go a minute?"

"A minute is too long," Bett protested. But she loosened her hold. "Where will you go if I let you?"

Maggie resettled alongside her, facing the fire. "Not far. How's this?"

"Not bad," Bett replied. "But how did you know I wanted the lights out, too?" She could see beyond Maggie. The room was dark except for the light cast by the fire.

Maggie would have turned to see what she meant, but Bett stopped her. "You promised you'd stay."

"So I did."

They kissed again. Longer this time. Bett's heart raced as she drew Maggie close. She heard her breathing slow. Heard her sigh deeply as their kiss ended. Felt her head settle easily on her shoulder. Bett caressed her and whispered, "I love you," as she began unbuttoning her shirt.

"Please don't." Maggie's voice was muffled against Bett's neck, but her discomfort was plain.

Bett maneuvered to be able to see her face. "Don't make love to you? All right. I don't mind waiting." She knew that wasn't the exact truth. "Don't tell me not to love you, though. It's too late to change that."

When Maggie started to speak, Bett kissed her again, unable to risk her reply. Not wanting to know which kind of loving she was refusing. She rolled Maggie over on her back and looked down at her, seeing the firelight reflected in her unpatched eye.

"But does it hurt so much to be loved?"

Maggie smiled. A tiny smile. "No. I forgot how much it hurts not to be able to."

Bett brought Maggie's right hand to her lips, kissing those unwrapped fingers, drawing them into her mouth one by one, nibbling sensuously.

"What are you doing?" Maggie seemed to be holding her breath again.

"Seeing if you've lost your sense of touch."

"No." Maggie lay back, closing her eye. "Not at all."

Bett risked another question. "Don't you want to make love with me?"

"More than anything in the world," Maggie said sadly.

"But...?"

She raised her left hand, the one that bandages covered to the tips of her fingers, and waggled it. "Can't. Out of order. Closed for repairs."

Bett sighed at her description. "I'm going to tell you something. Pay attention. You have..." she trilled a drumroll, "*bilateral symmetry!*"

Maggie raised an eyebrow. "Is there a cure for that?"

Bett giggled. "It means you have two of nearly everything! Now it's Test Time! Ms. McIntyre, can you give me just one example of something you have *two* of?"

Maggie smiled even as she shook her head. "I know I've got two hands."

"And...?"

"I use one of them for almost everything." She waved her right hand.

Bett cocked her head. "*Almost* everything?"

"I make love left-handed, darlin'. I never... Well, I don't know how any other way."

Bett stared at her. That was too incredible. "Do you mean you don't know *how* to make love right-handed?" Astonishment raised her voice.

Maggie shushed her, then nodded again.

"It's practically the same as doing it left-handed, Maggie! All you have to do is get in on the other side of the bed!"

❖ ❖ ❖

Tracy was glad for the rain now. It kept traffic down, even as it made the road hard to see. Then she realized it wasn't the rain that was causing that. She pulled over and got out, turning her face up into the downpour and letting it wash away her tears.

She didn't know why she was crying. Only that it didn't hurt. She felt like laughing. Maybe she was drunk. Still? Finally? She'd never felt like this before. Maybe she needed that therapy the Sarge ordered. But not with Small Eyes. With somebody who'd felt like this once.

She got back into the car and lit a cigarette. It tasted salty, reminding her of the last time she'd cried. She hadn't thought about her week in the mountains in a long time. She didn't want to think about it now, but flashes of memory came to her anyway.

She was holding a black gun, knowing she had to find a way out of her terror, a way out of the crippling fear she'd been living with for so long. She'd tried holding it down with pills and drink, but it stayed, deep inside her. She had to get rid of it. Smash it. Blast it. Tear it out of herself. She couldn't live with fear. One of them had to go. One of them had to die.

She remembered putting a single bullet in the gun, spinning the cylinder, aiming it at the center of her pain. The hammer fell on an empty chamber, and she'd cried again. In relief this time. She'd finally scared the fear away.

Her memory of the rest of that night wasn't very clear. The next thing she knew, she was at a rest stop on I-80. It was just light enough for her to see the trashcan she was throwing up in.

Tracy blew her nose. Christ, she must've left the cabin an absolute wreck. And Maggie had been so good about letting her use it, too. No questions asked. Maggie never got on her case, but Tracy knew she deserved it at times. She made a U-turn, away from home. She'd started out right that afternoon; started out to find Maggie and make her apology. Now she would follow through.

Tracy circled the end of the cul-de-sac, then let out a whoop: Maggie's kitchen light was on. The tailgate of a white pickup was just visible at the end of the driveway.

She climbed the stairs, savoring the thought of seeing Maggie again, the same way she savored her inner sense of peace. It had been so long since she'd felt good about herself. She thought of Elise then and started to smile, rubbing her face self-consciously as she approached the door. It was open a crack. Warm light spilled into the hallway. She could almost hear the laughter she and Maggie would share. Like old times. Tracy pushed the door open, not knowing what to say. Maybe just, "Hello, old friend."

She stopped inside the door. The room was a mess. Maggie's few books were on the floor. Her dresser drawers were all pulled out, too, like steps leading up to the ceiling. Sensing movement on her right, Tracy turned, expecting to see Maggie's sidelong grin over the disarray. She'd tell her Bett was cleaning or something. What a joke!

Tracy tossed her head left. That odd gesture saved her life, as the blow caught the side of her head instead of splitting her crown. She hit the floor soundlessly, still wearing the smile that she'd brought for Maggie.

⬩ ⬩ ⬩

"Maggie, do you mind if I ask you a question?"

"Will you ever stop asking me questions, Bett?"

"Am I so tiresome?"

"That's another question."

"I know, but am I?"

"That's three."

"Two and a half."

"Three. Repeats are still questions."

"Maggie!"

"All right, what's your question?"

"What's the best hand you can get in cribbage?"

Maggie opened her eye in surprise, then sighed at what she saw in the firelight. Bett was tucked close under her arm, their legs intertwined. Such a beautiful body. She could easily reach Bett's knees, and did, giving her a slow, intimate massage. She paused briefly at the top of her legs, then stroked a hip, only brushing her mound lightly. She couldn't bypass her breasts. She had to stop there, en route to her face, and cup each one in turn. When she moved to kiss a nipple, Bett touched her face.

"There's a question hanging in the air. Have you forgotten?"

Maggie grinned down on her, then lifted Bett's chin slightly to make sure their lips met fully. They kissed the dessert of kisses: slow, timeless, easy. The rich aftertaste of loving.

"Is your arm tired?" Bett stroked Maggie's shoulder.

She started to shake her head, then pried Bett's mouth open instead and peered in. "It's a bottomless well of questions!"

Bett pushed her off balance and rolled over on top of her, tickling her ribs, then rested her head on Maggie's chest, listening as her heartbeat slowed.

"The answers to your questions are: No. No. No. Twenty-nine. No. And no. And you won't believe this, but I hate saying no to you."

Maggie reached overhead to the coffee table, finding her cigarettes by touch, and extracted one from the pack. She set the pack on Bett's back. Bett shivered involuntarily, and Maggie rolled her closer to the fire, then sat back and lit up, never quite taking her eye off Bett. "You're an odd duck," she said, exhaling.

Bett smiled. "That's a nice way of putting it. In high school they called me a 'queer duck' as if they'd invented the phrase."

Maggie felt her jaw tighten at that, but Bett shrugged.

"Don't worry," Bett continued. "I had a much easier time of it than you. I had a support group. The treatment I got from my peers was like a saline bath for my soul." She deepened her voice. "Made me tough on the inside."

They both laughed.

"But why do you so politely think I'm an odd duck?"

"Well, for two days now, while I've been doing all I can to keep from wanting you, you've asked me about lovers or making love or women I go out with. And finally, when we do…"

"Finally!" Bett echoed with a delicious sigh.

"You ask me about cribbage!" Maggie grinned. "You get twenty-nine points when you hold three fives and a jack in your hand, and the fourth five is turned up in the same suit as the jack."

Bett shook her head slowly, deliberately.

"You don't believe me?"

She kept shaking her head. A small, knowing smile played at the corners of her mouth.

Maggie picked up the cards. "I'll show you! I'll even count it for you."

"You already have." Bett drew her down. "I'm going to deal you an even better hand."

They kissed, then Maggie felt Bett's touch everywhere. She thought they couldn't possibly make love anymore. That she was safe from that. But she wasn't. And she knew she shouldn't let her. Then she decided that breaking a rule now and again wasn't so bad after all.

A long time later, Maggie rested her head on Bett's shoulder, then felt fingernails skating lightly over her back. She moaned in response to the sensation.

Bett laughed softly. "You're getting more articulate all the time. I didn't even ask a question. You volunteered something!"

Maggie blew noisily on Bett's neck, then asked, "Did you learn how to deal that kind of hand in sex education?"

Bett giggled. "They don't teach you how to make love in sex ed."

"They don't?"

"Of course not. Are you serious?"

"I never thought about it much. I just figured that's why people objected to it being taught to their kids."

"You're serious!"

"So, what do they teach then?"

Bett gave her a brief synopsis.

"You mean they just talk about parts and how they work?"

Bett nodded.

"Then why do people object? It's just personal biology, isn't it?"

"Of course. But that's the politics of knowledge."

"Politics? How'd we get from sex to politics?"

"It's all related. It's all about power."

"Power? Knowledge I understand. Politics I don't."

"Next you'll tell me you don't vote."

"You mean like for president?" Maggie grinned. "I won't tell you that. You can talk politics with Hudson, though. He doesn't vote, either, but he'll give you his opinion on it all day long."

"You really don't vote?"

"I told you I wouldn't tell you that. Aren't you tired? Don't you want to go to bed?"

"Ah! I thought you'd never ask!"

Maggie smiled through a yawn. "I thought it'd be a while before I could." She pitched her cigarette into the fireplace.

Bett caught her hand. "You really never made love any other way?"

Maggie shook her head for what seemed like the hundredth time.

"I still don't understand why."

Smiling, she stroked Bett's cheek. "Never had to. My left hand… Well, I guess I just started out that way. Never saw the need to learn any other. You were very patient."

"Hell, after two, three days, I'd hardly call me patient! But how did you learn to begin with?"

"To make love? From Lange, I guess."

"Nobody else?"

"She taught me well enough. Except for emergencies."

The dog jumped up then and headed for the door.

"I forgot all about you, Gyp." Maggie rose to her knees and turned to help Bett up, but they couldn't seem to let go of each other. They kissed even as Gyp yelped impatiently.

"Whose dog is that?" Maggie mumbled against Bett's lips.

"I don't know. Seems to me there was a tall redhead around here a while ago. But that can't be you. You're not that tall now."

"Mmm. If you're really good, I'll show you how we're almost exactly the same height when Gyp and I get back."

Bett kissed her neck and went to the bedroom. A few minutes later, Maggie came into the room, slipped a nightgown on, and got in bed only to find Bett shivering. Holding her close, Maggie rubbed her skin firmly, but nothing seemed to stop her shaking for more than a few moments.

"Bett, relax your shoulders. You'll warm up in a minute." Maggie felt her shivering stop briefly, then it started again.

"Relax your shoulders, darlin'," Maggie repeated softly.

"My shoulders aren't cold! I'm cold on the inside."

Maggie pulled Bett on top of her and massaged her neck and shoulders. Bett's shivering finally faded, to be replaced by quiet, even breathing.

"Warm yet?" Maggie whispered.

"In a week or two," she answered sleepily. "Do you know how wonderful you feel?"

Maggie chuckled softly in the dark, then sighed contentedly.

They slept until long past dawn on Tuesday.

CHAPTER 17.

The Best Woman Money Can Buy

MAGGIE KNEW SOMETHING was wrong as soon as she woke up. She opened one eye, but that wasn't what felt strange. She was almost used to limited sight by now. Bett lay sleeping in her arms. Maggie smiled. That certainly didn't feel wrong.

The light from the high bedroom windows was bright, matching her inner clock. It was definitely late, yet much too quiet. She put on a robe and wool socks. The floor was shockingly cold. The fireplace was dead cold, too.

When she opened the front door, Gyp bounded out with a loud yelp. It took a moment for her eye to adjust, then she saw why everything was so silent. A final stab of winter had come in the middle of the night, making the landscape look like spring had never happened. Here and there, dark spots of tree trunks appeared, but everything else was shrouded in snow.

Gyp plowed into it, full tilt. He didn't know whether to bark at it, roll in it, or eat it. Maggie closed the door on his uproar, knowing he'd be back when his paws got cold. She started a fire and went to make coffee, then opted for a cup of instant instead. She let Gyp in, and they settled in front of the fire where she wrapped herself in the quilt and tried to figure out why she felt so disoriented.

The quilt reminded her of last night. Seeing snow shocked her. Snow. Cold. The scent of loving. She closed her eye against memory, but images came to her anyway. Events she hadn't thought about in years.

"If I promise not to run away," she'd said last night. But she had run away. It was all she could do after seeing Lange for the last time.

It was winter when she left. Her only plan was to go south, away from snow— the deadly cold of winter. Her heart never felt the cold. It was already frozen. As empty as the dark windows of the shops and houses she passed. She couldn't stay another day. Not another minute.

Before she knew it, she'd crossed the steel-span, open-grid bridge and was headed south. She drove without stopping, except for gas and occasional rests. She'd pull off the highway into a dead cornfield or unmarked side road, dozing fitfully until the cold seeped through to her again. She could drive without thinking—focus on counting telephone poles or notches on the speedometer. But she kept remembering Lange's last visit.

She'd recognized the car first, then seen Lange struggling with the door against the bank of snow plowed up in front of Bud and Libby's. She ran to help her. Who cared if it was ten below? She laughed all the way to the car, her breath a white fog in the air. Lange had come back. Finally.

Maggie hugged her like a child, still not noticing. Not until they were in the kitchen and she'd called to Libby to see who was here, the way she had a hundred times before. Libby noticed right away. She had a mother's eyes.

"Oh, my dear," she greeted Lange. "I'm so happy for you. When...?"

"Not until May. I feel so big already."

Maggie barely heard their conversation. Lange was so beautiful. Her eyes were dark with shadow, yet Maggie read love there. She couldn't seem to let go of Lange's hand. She just sat staring, oblivious to their talk. Gripping Lange's hand too tightly. Loosening her hold, but only a little.

She heard Libby laugh. A teasing sound. Unusual for her. "Well, Maggie hasn't missed you at all, as you can see." The two of them laughed lovingly.

Lange smiled. "I hope she won't have to miss me anymore."

Maggie's heart stopped for a long moment. When it started again, she was sure they could hear it, too. Had Lange really said she wanted her to come live with her? Only for the rest of my life! I do. I will. I promise. I love you. Life was so wonderful in that moment. "Yes! Of course!"

"Well, not this minute, Maggie." Libby turned to Lange. "Probably not until when? Early June? After the baby comes?"

Maggie felt her face turn as red as her hair. The room dimmed as she let go of Lange's hand—her warm, wonderfully soft hand. In that instant she became aware of the difference between them. Aware of her own hand: so coarse, so rude, as it gripped the oilcloth. Aware of her own womanhood. So foreign to Lange's. Then she knew Lange's breasts weren't just smaller in her memory; the softness she sensed wasn't her imagination come to life. Lange was pregnant. Of course.

"We can work something out," Lange was saying. "She won't have to miss any final exams." She smiled at Maggie but kept talking to Libby. "And she can sign up for a class at the university this summer. She'll do fine in college. A taste of summer school is all she needs to get started."

Then Libby left to do her shopping. It was just the two of them. Maggie could still hear the whirr of the second hand on the kitchen clock: the tick it made passing the six. She fixed on those sounds, trying to understand. Then Lange touched her hand gently, easily.

"I missed you," was all Maggie could say. Her voice sounded dead. But she had to say that, even if she was dead.

"I know." Lange's voice was like honey. "I missed you..., too."

Was she going to add something there? Call her *dear heart* as she once had? Maggie's heart flickered briefly. "Do you really want me to come and live with you? Like old times?" She had to be sure.

"Yes!" Lange laughed softly. Then: "Not entirely like old times. Do you understand…?"

She shook her head. "I never understood, Lange." Her heart tore completely then, just saying her name.

Lange tried to explain. "I got all your letters, but I couldn't answer them. You love me too much, Maggie. It's just not right." She took her hand, holding it loosely. "I've thought about you a lot since… well, since the last time I saw you. I never really believed that you and Tom…"

Hope rose in Maggie again. It was all Lange's stupid husband's fault. Why hadn't he explained that night? It didn't matter now. That pain was finished. "You're not angry with me?" she pleaded.

Lange smiled. "Of course not. I felt bad about how we parted. I've always cared for you, Maggie. I'll always love you. You know that."

She only had to say it once. Fire glowed in Maggie; her heart beat again.

Lange continued: "But you have to understand. I made a mistake with you. It was a natural mistake. You're very attractive, you know. Becoming a beautiful woman." She smiled her most heart-stopping smile, and Maggie felt herself melting away.

"But we… I let you need me the wrong way. Things just went too far. It's time to think about the future." Lange paused. "I have… responsibilities now. I came to tell you all that. And to make sure you were all right. I know how much you love children, Maggie."

She kept talking as if it were all one subject. I love you. You love children. I can't love you. I'm having a child. You can help me raise this child.

"You'd make such a good teacher, Maggie. You have too good a mind to waste it fixing cars and pumping gas. What can you do with that? Remember how I helped you study at the hospital? We can do that again. Take the baby to the park and watch the kids play. Read to each other. Talk about what you're learning. Bud and Libby have been so good to you. They'd be pleased if you went to school. Will you let me help you again?"

Maggie just kept nodding. Knowing it didn't matter what she said. That nothing would ever matter again. Of course. It was just a stage we went through. You're a mother now. I'll be a mother later. These things happen. We get over them. We go on. I'm young. I'll marry. Perhaps Scotty. Yes. Scott. He's fine. Driving truck now. But maybe not him. Maybe I'll meet someone on campus. I'm fine. Just surprised. I didn't know you were pregnant. How wonderful for you. And Tom, too.

She could feel the last seam of her wall closing with those lighthearted words. It had been easy after that. She just wouldn't care. She'd just change her mind. What did it matter how she felt? What could ever matter again?

Even now the wall supports me. Thick enough to let me stand tall, unflinching. High enough to hide behind. Such a grand, strong wall.

See this spot? Someone tried to break in; bashing through the outside of me, only to find the cold stone inside. See these scars? Faded and old, they barely mar the surface. See this new wound? Only a fracture, really. Barely wide enough to see. It travels, unhurried, across old futile efforts, fissures long since sealed.

But the crack widens. Warm air issues from the stone. It can't breathe. A wall can't feel. That's why it's a wall. It can't support life. Yet something green is planted there. You can't grow here. "No! Go away." She pulled at the fragile growth, and the wall shuddered. Flecks of stone fell to the ground. "No! It isn't safe!" You'll die. This is a wall! She stroked the tiny plant, trying to dislodge it gently. But it held fast, embedded deep within the ancient stone. She could feel it growing. Stretching its roots. Undoing all her work. "No!"

Then someone was cradling her. "Maggie, shhh. What is it? A dream? Are you okay? Wake up, honey. Do you want to tell me about it?"

She felt Bett kiss her eye. Her mouth. Felt her drawing her away from the wall, away from the terrifying sensation that it was falling in on her. She returned Bett's embrace. Feeling her softness. Tasting her still. Wanting her. Not wanting to bring her into the dream. Nothing grows here. Nothing can.

"It doesn't matter, Bett. It was… just a dream."

⋄ ⋄ ⋄

Brian got to work Tuesday, knowing it wasn't going to be his day. For starters, he hadn't had enough sleep. He'd gotten the phone call about Ebert after midnight and was up half the night trying to find out more. When he learned Jim Harley had caught the call, he tracked him down. As expected, he was still reeling from finding Ebert lying in a pool of blood. Brian tried to distract him from that. "I thought Ebert was off. Did she get called in?"

"No. She wasn't in uniform. We got a call to an address on Natchez."

"A duplex on Natchez?" Brian interrupted.

Harley confirmed that, explaining that a Vietnamese woman had met him at the front door and taken him to an upstairs apartment. He didn't know it was Ebert at first, with all the blood on her face, and she was still out cold. "She came to when the paramedics were doing their thing, saying things like 'find Maggie' and something about a 'lease.' It didn't make sense. But she said 'Brian knows,' so I thought I'd mention it. And we did a drive-by on that duplex Sunday, but she didn't say why."

Brian heard the question in Harley's voice. He didn't know how to answer it. He could only reassure him that they would find out more as soon as the hospital let them visit. Then he told him to go home and get some sleep.

He was still trying to sort it out the next morning. Of course Ebert knew Maggie. He'd introduced them himself. He saw her at M & M just like he'd seen other cops there. They went to M & M with their cars like they went to Denny's for their coffee. But why was she at Maggie's house? Then he remembered how they'd snapped at each other Friday night. He didn't want to think about what any of it meant in terms of their relationship.

He was grateful when his phone rang, however briefly.

The dispatcher in Towing was beside himself. "I don't know who you're pulling a fast one on," he yelled, "but leave us out of it from now on. I sent a truck to M & M, and they don't know what you're talking about. My driver didn't think it was funny, and neither do I!"

"Who'd he see down there?" Brian asked.

"A guy named Steve... Jaguar or something."

"Jaeger." Brian corrected him automatically. "Spelled *J*, pronounced *Y*—Jaeger. Stony Jaeger."

"Well, he didn't have no wreck for us. Spelled *W*, pronounced *R*. Wreck. My order says, 'Pick up wreck.' Only there ain't none!"

Brian hung up, needing a cup of coffee, even if it was machine-grade. In the hall, he waited as a black man in a brown suit looked at the dispenser sourly, then dropped his coins in, slammed its side, and selected coffee with X-tra Creme in it.

"That make it taste any better?" Brian asked.

"Dun'no," the man replied. "I never drink it any other way."

Brian saw the corner of his lip move, indicating intentional humor.

"Williams. Homicide." He stuck out his hand. "Kessler, right?"

Then Brian recalled the odd message from yesterday and led the detective to his desk, explaining that he'd returned his call.

"Yeah, I got the word late. A Lake Merritt jogger called about a body. Turned out to be cats. Little ones. Want one? Got a whole bagful up at my desk. They might still be there, so I thought I'd come see you instead. Wish it'd been a body. I can handle that. Just can't stand that squalling."

Brian tried to imagine confusing a bag of cats with a body.

The detective continued: "Add-on to the ME report says you gave them a footprint match on the John Doe." He thumbed through a notebook. "Here it is. The Doe's real name is Scott Fenn. What can you tell me?"

Brian shook his head. "This has to be some kind of paperwork snafu. I heard Homicide was looking for Fenn as a suspect. How you got involved in this freeway incident is beyond me." He gave Williams the file he'd started, having added a *Tribune* article that compared the Friday night traffic snarl to a similar jam-up that had occurred a couple of years before when a newspaper truck overturned on the Bay Bridge at rush hour. Brian kept it for a detail that he and Ebert had missed: the name of the trucker with the fire extinguisher.

Williams agreed that it didn't sound like a shooting. "But the report lists the cause of death as gunshot."

"What else does it say?"

Williams looked up from his notes, then lowered his voice. "I hate reading those path' reports. I check the cause-of-death box, then talk with the reporting officer. I'm good at slug work. You know: follow up, witness questioning, like that. But I lose weight reading that blood and guts stuff."

Brian couldn't believe what he was hearing. He offered to stop by the morgue and straighten out the confusion. "A body with a bullet hole in it can't look the same as one that's been burned up, right?"

Williams rose. "I'll just put a hold on this report from your man Tebert."

"Ebert." Brian closed his eyes briefly, wondering if the whole day was going to be like this. When he looked again, Williams was gone.

He picked up the phone. He had to let Maggie know about her apartment break-in, but if he called now before going to the morgue, he wouldn't have to confirm even worse news. He was still sure it was Fenn who'd died in the fire, but he didn't know how they could match footprints to the wrong body.

"Sheriff's Office. Deputy Berger."

Brian identified himself and asked for Sheriff Miller.

"He's not on duty yet. Anything I can do?"

"I need to notify somebody about an apartment break-in. The name's McIntyre. She's got a cabin up on North Slope Road."

"Yeah? So?"

Brian shook the phone, certain the connection had gone bad.

"…us to do about it? Hold her hand?"

"No, I just want to get word to her."

"Well, we're a little busy for that, Sarge. We had an ice storm last night, with snow on top of it. No power for twenty miles around. And we don't have any female uniforms who can do that sort of thing to her liking."

Brian suddenly knew, first hand, what apoplectic meant. And just as suddenly, knew he was overreacting to his own feelings. He took a measured breath, left his phone number, and slammed the phone down, wanting to wipe the smirk out of the deputy's voice. He promised himself that Miller would hear about his deputy's attitude before the day was out.

❖ ❖ ❖

Maggie responded well to the coffee Bett made for her and brightened even more after eating soft-boiled eggs and toast. Bett couldn't help feeling that some kind of barrier had come between them, though. And given how wonderful last night had been, it stymied her. She had been sure Maggie would leave her defenses behind now, but there she sat at the table, staring at the fire. Bett asked what she was thinking.

"Oh, a hundred different things. What to do with myself today. What to do with…" She turned away.

Bett knew exactly what she could do with her, but they'd never get anywhere if she kept filling in the blanks.

Then Maggie smiled a little. "I guess we are alike. You don't know what to say sometimes, either."

Bett knew she was no closer to understanding Maggie now than she had been their first day at the cabin. "This time I think it's our differences that matter more. There are times when we don't know how to talk to each other, but where I blunder through and say something, you won't. You stop, look both ways, then leave the country. And you don't come back until the subject's been changed. I may be laughable, but at least I'm still here. Why do you keep running away from me?"

Maggie didn't say anything for a long minute. "I suppose I have been. Thought I'd finished all that when I left Lange."

"You left her? But you said…"

"We split. It doesn't matter who stood on the doorstep and waved."

Bett wanted to assuage Maggie's anger, yet knew instinctively she couldn't.

"Actually," Maggie smiled ruefully, "I thought I'd turned all my running into travel and adventure. I did travel, but it was before I had any money, so even having a meal could be an adventure in those days."

Bett was sure she was exaggerating but wanted her to keep talking. "So, where were you going?"

"Just to the next job, I guess. Most times I could get work in junkyards. They all knew each other in that business. But I missed working on running cars. That's how I started cruising at night, helping out breakdowns."

"That's dangerous! You don't do that anymore, do you?"

She smiled. "Now you sound like Tracy. She calls it 'looking for trouble.' Matt always laughed at that. That's how I met him. He was on his way to DFW in a rental car when it broke down. I gave him a lift."

"What's DFW?"

"Dallas-Fort Worth Airport. He was piloting a night flight, but he made me promise to meet him the next day. You know, like that old movie line: 'He made me an offer I couldn't refuse'?"

Bett nodded. She knew the line.

"When we got to the terminal, he reached into his pocket. I wasn't going to take anything, except maybe the two bits they charge to go through the airport down there. I never took anything for helping folks out. But he pulled out a wad of bills bigger than I'd ever seen. The inside sheaf was all hundreds. He must've had ten or twelve C-notes. I'd never seen a hundred-dollar bill before. Seeing a bunch like that… Well, he tore one of those bills in two and gave me half. 'I land at 3:30 tomorrow. Meet me here at 5, and you can have the other half.' Then he got out of the truck; never looked back. I guess he thought he had me."

Bett couldn't stand it. She went to the fireplace to stir the coals instead of venting her anger on Maggie, who clearly didn't understand the forces in her life. She didn't even know when she was being bought. A trinket in a bazaar. A slave worker to

That-Jerk-Hudson. Bett was too angry to hear the tick in the back of her head. Even too angry to hear Maggie approach. But she felt Maggie's hands on her shoulders and reached to cover them gently.

"Relax your shoulders, darlin'." Maggie kissed the top of her head.

"But I'm not cold." Bett leaned back anyway.

"It's an exercise you can use for more than one thing." Maggie crossed her arms around her. "In my business, they call that a multi-purpose tool. Now tell me: Do you walk out in the middle of movies, too?"

"What do you mean, 'too'?"

"Well, you don't ever want to hear the end of my stories. I figure it's either the way I tell 'em or something else. So, do you leave in the middle?"

"Oh, it's not the way you tell your stories…"

"Huh-uh. I'm asking about movies."

"No, I don't walk out of movies. But I only go to ones with happy endings. I'm a hopeless romantic, you know."

Maggie laughed and drew her up. "You'll be glad to hear something I've learned. Everything has a happy ending. All you have to do is live long enough to see it."

"You're sure about that?" Bett tried to shrug off Maggie's story about Matt, but they were in the man's cabin. It didn't matter that he was dead. He'd played such an important part in her past. It made Bett sick to think it all started with money. Maggie didn't know how pathetic her life was. What would it take to make her realize that it didn't have to be male-run? That she didn't have to live under their rules?

"So far," Maggie was saying, "that's been true for me. How about it? You ready to try another day?"

Bett smiled then. "Sure. I even have a good idea of how to start this one."

Maggie grinned. "Oh? You remembered my patch, too?"

Bett started to correct her, then realized she was being teased again. Some day they'd both be thinking about the same thing. Some day.

They went to the kitchen together. Maggie took a pill while Bett prepared the salt water. A few moments later she brought the pans to the main room, just as Maggie came from the bedroom wearing corduroys and a plaid shirt.

"Well, there goes my idea for our next activity, " Bett said.

"Because I got dressed?" She smiled. "Not what I'd call an obstacle for you! Besides, I feel stronger about pain when I'm dressed."

Bett cocked her head "Sometimes you make a lot of sense."

"Sometimes? I have to make sense all the time, or it all quits working"

"You're funny!" Bett laid her on the couch with her head by the lamp and slipped the patch off. "Don't open your eye yet. I want to see it first. In fact, keep both of your eyes closed. That's it." She twisted the lamp switch, but nothing happened. Then she remembered last night's power loss and looked around for the flashlight, seeing it on the mantle.

"Why am I funny?"

Bett fetched it and flicked it on. "Because you can say things like that and not sound arrogant or dumb but just plain innocent. Now we all know that's not true, so how do you get away with it?"

Maggie smiled. "Tracy says it's because I'm corny."

"Tracy again, huh." Bett shined the light on her injured eye, gently lifting the lid. The scab would make it stiff to open. "Roll your eye up. Where did you meet her? No, don't tighten up. Sorry. Did I hurt you?"

"Huh-uh. Just surprised me, is all."

Bett put Maggie's hand over her good eye and told her to open the injured one. "How's it feel?"

"Sore." She was considering Bett's interest in Tracy. "Why do you want to know?"

Bett ignored the mouse chitters that question caused. "Okay, close again. No, keep that one covered. Open and close the sore one to loosen it up."

Maggie concentrated on that, then shrugged. "In a track pit."

Bett drew back a little. "Well, it's not pretty! It's still a black eye."

Maggie laughed. "I said 'in a track pit.'"

"Is that English?"

"Mmm-hmm. Hey, which one of us took that pill, anyway?"

"You did, obviously! Okay, open now. Can you see me yet?"

"Yup. I just can't understand you sometimes."

"Now you're stealing my lines. How many fingers am I holding up?"

Maggie couldn't quite focus yet and guessed four.

"Huh-uh." Bett moved her hand, watching her eye follow the motion. "Close now. Rest a minute. Still feeling the pill?"

"Just starting to. Think we ought to try this later, after it wears off?"

"Once more." Bett held up two fingers. Maggie answered correctly this time, then closed her eye.

"Good. I hate being wrong. Or so she says."

"She who?"

"Tracy, of course. Weren't you the one who asked about her?"

"Mmm. Seems like hours ago, now."

Maggie sat up. "They say drugs do strange things to people. I didn't think this was what they meant."

"I asked where you met her!"

"Watch my lips, darlin': In. A. Track. Pit."

She stared at her. "It's a new language, right?"

Maggie chuckled. "Tracy was a racecar driver before she was a cop. We met when I was on the race circuit, working the pits. I'm the mechanic, remember?"

Bett unwrapped the bandages thoughtfully. It *was* a new language. She decided to start with what she knew. "Didn't you work in junkyards?"

"Yeah, but I found out how to make more money at a track in Oklahoma. They had a demolition derby before the main race; had to scratch their best junker. Threw a rod, right through the wall."

Bett was amazed. "They pay you for that in Oklahoma?"

"For what?"

"Throwing a rod...?" She stopped at Maggie's laugh.

"Sorry, darlin'. I forget you don't know engines. I'll explain if you want."

Bett slipped Maggie's hands into the pans of water. "Just tell me how you met Tracy."

"I started pulling engines on demolition cars at fairs. Eventually, a team picked me up for pit work on regular races. That was a lot of fun. And that's how I met Tracy."

"In a track pit." Bett repeated the phrase.

"Right!" Maggie beamed at her.

It was just like learning a foreign language. It didn't actually make sense, but if you said the right phrase at the right time to the right person, you got rewarded for it. She watched as Maggie flexed her hands in the water, eyes closed. When she opened them, they were bright with pleasure.

"Now you got it!"

Bett knew that wasn't true, but it wouldn't matter for her next question. "Was it love at first sight?"

Confusion crossed Maggie's face.

"You and Tracy!"

"Lord, no!" She laughed.

"Well, it's not impossible. Tracy is gay, isn't she?"

"Yeah," Maggie said slowly. "But we're too much alike for that."

"*Alike!*" Bett was staggered. "You couldn't be more different if you were the sun and the moon!"

Maggie sighed. "How are we different?"

"Tracy's so cold and distant. She's all uniform and stiff."

"She hasn't always been like that. And she has to be disciplined on duty. It's part of her job."

Bett rinsed the hand she'd been cleaning. "How else are you alike?"

Maggie thought a minute. "Well, we're both Catholic. From the Midwest. Gay." She paused thoughtfully. "I wanted her to come into the business with me, but she'd already joined the force by then."

"Why did she do that?" Bett began rinsing Maggie's other hand.

"I don't know. On the circuit, she always talked about wanting to be like Janet Guthrie. You know her?"

"I've read about her in women's magazines. She wants to be in some big race in Chicago."

Maggie rolled her eyes. "Not Chi-town, Indianapolis! The Indy 500. The main event on Memorial Day?"

Bett shrugged.

"Well, Tracy wanted to do that, too, only she started getting superstitious about tracks and what day races were running. One day she just missed a bad smash-up. Drove right through six cars blowing up and ramming each other. She got turned around on the track, then got spun again. When she finally pulled into the pit, we yelled at her to get out. There was fire all over the track. We were afraid her car would blow, too. But she couldn't even let go of the steering wheel. We had to pop it off and take her to the hospital with her hands still gripping it."

"Didn't anybody know how to make her release it?"

"No, we couldn't get at her fingers. She was wearing gloves, and her fingertips were wrapped into the palms." Maggie closed her fist to show how they'd tried to free her from the wheel.

"Not like that." Bett pressed her wrist tendons. "Pressure points."

"That might work on regular people, but Tracy's got forearms like a blacksmith from driving. They said she was in some kind of shock and gave her a shot to relax her hands. She finally let go of the wheel, but she couldn't even hold a fork for days. I had to feed her. Jeez, did she ever hate that!"

Bett smiled. "That's the first thing you've said that makes you two sound at all alike. Lie down now." She finished wrapping Maggie's hands. "Isn't that how you've been about your burns?"

"I suppose."

"Did you come to California together?" Bett asked.

"No. We sort of went our separate ways after that. She showed up at the garage one day with Brian. She was in uniform and acted like we were just being introduced. I didn't like doing that to Brian, but I figured she'd tell him what the story was after she got to know him better." Maggie closed her eyes. "She's kind of weird about being a cop, but it makes sense to her."

Bett wondered about this new Maggie, who had talked so easily all the way through the cleaning without seeming to notice the pain or the personal information she revealed. And she'd told Tracy's story without hesitation. Why couldn't she be like that about herself?

"How is she weird?" She stroked Maggie's forehead, careful to avoid the bruised ridge over her eye.

"Oh, secretive. I think she got helping people mixed up with something else. Then she got shot and started getting superstitious again."

"How did she get shot?"

Maggie told what she knew.

Bett felt more sympathetic toward Ebert after that. "I can see why she'd be superstitious, but what made her go from racing to being a cop?"

"I think she got used to the edge."

"What edge?"

"I'm not sure. It's just something I hear people talk about. The edge of life. The edge of death. Maybe it's the risk itself. I suppose that's what skydivers and other kinds of adventurers are after."

Bett kissed her lightly. "Like you."

That amused Maggie. "You keep guessing wrong about me, darlin'. I'm as cautious as they come. I don't take risks."

"Then how did this happen?" Bett outlined her black eye.

She smiled. "I'll tell you when I remember. But it wasn't because I thought there was any risk."

Bett shook her head. "I think you *are* from another planet. You just don't know what all the words mean yet."

"We'll see." Maggie closed her eyes then and slept.

Brian got sidetracked on his way to the morgue. He was still fuming over his conversation with Berger when he glanced up, directly into the eyes of the Marlboro Man. The billboard reminded him of what Ebert had said about her brand of smokes, and he decided to take a run up Pill Hill to see her before going to the morgue. As he drove, he reviewed his motives. He had a responsibility to visit an injured officer, but the real reason was to find out about her and Maggie. That mattered to him, even after he and his wife, Mary Jo, had talked it over last night.

"You aren't assuming things about Maggie again, are you?"

"I'm not even talking about Maggie," he snapped. "And what do you mean *again?*"

"Oh," Mary Jo replied neutrally, "you mean you'd be just as upset if Ebert had come to you and said, 'Don't worry about me riding with the rookies, Sarge. I'm gay.'" She smiled at his chagrin. "And I mean again because you overreacted like this when Maggie told me she was gay."

"I wasn't mad because she's gay. Just that she hadn't told me herself."

"And you should have been as relieved as I was! Did it ever occur to you that I was worried about you?"

"You mean me and Maggie? That's ridiculous. There's nothing between us. Never has been."

"Of course there is. It just isn't sexual. It took me a while to figure that out, but I know something about jealousy, myself."

"There was never anything for you to be jealous about!"

"Brian, all you said was that you'd met the most remarkable girl who was helping somebody fix a flat in the middle of Broad Street at rush hour. And you'd run into her again at a diner two weeks later. Then you said: 'I invited her to Sunday dinner!'"

"But you liked her right away," he protested.

"Yes, I did. But I spent three very anxious days wondering what was wrong between us. And I was glad when she talked about Matt. Not just because it meant there was a man in her life who wasn't…"

"I never liked him," Brian interrupted.

"No kidding! I just hope you got all of *that* out of your system before Jennifer starts bringing any boyfriends home."

"Was I that obvious?"

"You were so protective it's no wonder Maggie told me about being gay instead of you. She was pretty scared to tell either of us, you know."

"She was?"

Mary Jo gave him a look. "She couldn't very well come to you after knowing us for two years and say, 'Don't get so upset about Matt, Brian. I much prefer women.'"

"Why not? Isn't that what she said to you?"

"Of course not!" Mary Jo laughed. "She was very careful not to sound like she was 'preferring' either of us."

"Oh." That hadn't occurred to him. "Should I have worried?"

"Not about my attraction to her. And I don't think Maggie felt that way toward me. She said I was lucky to be able to have women friends. She doesn't think gay women can. I think she's lonely that way."

"Why? Aren't you two friends?"

"Yes and no. Friends as in 'Brian and Mary Jo.' But not me alone. She rarely just sits and talks with me the way she does with you. Sometimes I think friendships are more complicated than marriages."

"Only for women," he replied. "Men don't have any trouble."

"Right. The same way men don't have any trouble with the question of whether a falling tree makes noise in a forest if nobody's there to hear it."

Brian sighed. "Now you've lost me completely. Who cares? So long as it doesn't fall on me?"

"My point exactly. Men don't have any trouble with any kind of relationship until it falls on top of them. They just go through life on a kind of fixed path. Maggie's like that about some things. I wonder if it's a lesbian trait or one she picked up from hanging around men all the time."

"Why do I feel like one of us has just been insulted?" Brian turned out his light.

"Oh, I suppose because you're just an insensitive cop." She snuggled into his arms. "Mmm, what's this?"

He smiled. "Just little old me, trying to be sensitive."

"Not little," she whispered between kisses. "Or old. As for trying…"

Later, as they lay together at rest, Mary Jo said, "I don't know how you could ever object to Maggie enjoying pleasure like this with a man."

"Not just any man. Matt treated her like he owned her. He always had a hand on her."

"Yes, and she always brushed it off. But I don't suppose you saw that. Poor Jenny."

"Matt never seemed to notice, either!"

"Oh, he noticed all right. He just never gave up. I suppose it's just how he was with women. He was absolutely taken with Maggie. And he was a good influence on her."

"So you say."

"You know he was. He smoothed her rough edges. She doesn't just wear steel-toed work boots anymore. And he took her places."

"He took her to San Francisco," Brian sneered.

"He widened her horizons in other ways, too. If it weren't for him, the fanciest restaurant she'd go to is Marie Callendar's."

"Maybe you're right," Brian conceded. "I just didn't like how he was always after her."

"It wasn't just sex."

"What else?"

"Maybe her spirit. She's so alive, so full of energy. She gives something of herself to everyone. Especially kids." She paused. "Maybe there was some kind of father-daughter routine between them, but I think she appealed to the little kid in him. You know how she affects Mark and Jenny. They follow her all over." Mary Jo nestled closer. "And don't feel bad about not knowing about Ebert. Maggie says men hardly ever suspect women of being gay. Other women seem to know much sooner."

"Did you?"

"Not really, but I was curious after seeing her with Matt. She sure wasn't buying his package. I might've known something if I'd ever seen her with a lover. You've met some of them. Does she act differently with her lovers?"

"Not that I could tell." He thought a minute. "She never has before. Did I tell you about the girl she was with Friday?"

"Woman," she said automatically. "And how do you know they're lovers?"

He sighed at her correction. "When you meet Bett, you can tell me if she's a woman or a girl."

"I can tell you now. She's post-adolescent, isn't she?"

"Oh, yes! Definitely!"

She jabbed him. "A simple yes or no will do."

"Okay, she's a woman. As for them being lovers, it's just a guess. Maggie's stiff as a board when Bett's anywhere near."

"You're turning into a regular detective!"

⋄ ⋄ ⋄

Brian yawned noisily in the hospital elevator. Reflecting on his talk with Mary Jo helped to sort out his feelings, and he felt more ready to deal with Ebert. Until he saw her. The nurse let him have ten minutes, but he wasn't sure Ebert would even stay awake that long. After giving him a weak salute of thanks for the cigarettes, she managed to smoke one with him.

Brian kept his approach general. "How're they treating you?"

She gestured at her cheek bandage and the support collar around her neck. "Roke jaw; wrap neck. Doc'ers dumber 'n cops!"

He smiled and stubbed out his cigarette. She couldn't talk today. "Is there anybody you want me to call? Anybody who'd want to know you're here?" He asked casually, the way he would have asked anyone. But her response was vehement.

"No!" Her eyes widened, then closed against pain.

He patted her hand. "Okay. Relax. No problem."

She looked up then. "Where they fin' me?"

"Don't worry about that now. Just get well." He saw her eyes narrow and watched her fumble with the bed controls, raising herself to a sitting position. Then, to his surprise, she took his baton from his holder and rested it across her thighs, gripping the ends with both hands.

"Where?" she repeated firmly.

He replied vaguely: "An apartment. You must've interrupted a burglary."

She shook her head. "They din' ge' in."

Brian was confused. Had they broken into Maggie's *after* hitting Tracy? That couldn't be. "Didn't get in where?"

"A' Be'z," she said feebly.

"Where?"

She gripped the baton more tightly. "Be...TT," she grunted. "Ho'man."

"Bett Holman?" he echoed.

Tracy nodded, then relaxed against the pillows.

Brian was concerned by her mix-up. "Do you know who found you?"

"Par'ner," she said, eyes closed.

"Right. Harley found you at Maggie's place. In Oakland, not Berkeley."

Her eyes opened in disbelief. "Nuh-uh. Her TV doan e'en work."

Brian breathed a sigh of relief. She was starting to make sense again. "You and I know that, but burglars don't. Maybe..."

"She's cop-frien'!" Tracy cut him off. "Won' go near place li'e tha.'"

As she gripped the baton tightly, he could see the tendons and veins on her hands, reminding him of Maggie's hands. Distracted, he only heard part of what she said. "What lease?"

She shook her head. "Guys in truck. Rip off Be'z 'par'men.'"

"Wait a minute. Are you saying Bett's apartment got robbed, too?"

She nodded. "See 'Lise. Same thing. Yes'erday."

"Somebody broke into Bett's apartment yesterday?"

But Tracy couldn't answer.

Brian watched in frozen horror as her face turned the color of putty and her eyes rolled back. The baton clattered to the floor, and he nearly tripped over it as he ran to the door, yelling for the nurse.

CHAPTER 18.

Face the Music

Maggie didn't sleep long, but she didn't dream, either. She woke to find Bett studying a medical text at the kitchen table.

"Got enough light?" She flipped the switch as she came into the room, and it took her a moment to register that nothing had happened.

"All there is," Bett replied.

Maggie flipped it again. "When do you suppose we lost power?"

"Last night while we were playing cards."

"No! I would've noticed."

"You were noticing something else." Bett grinned impishly. "Besides, what do we need lights for?"

"We don't just need lights. Did you put anything in the freezer?"

They checked. It had defrosted itself nicely during the night, and the drip pan was filled with water. They emptied it, and Bett asked what to do with the thawed chicken.

"Not my department," Maggie said. "I'll get the generator going, though. We can put the main feed on the fridge and run extension cords from there. Then let's go to town and see about replacing the cushions and mattress. How's that sound?"

"Fine. Want some help bringing the generator in?"

She smiled. "Not unless you want a serious carbon monoxide headache. It's gas-powered. And kind of noisy, too." Maggie considered all engine noise a form of music, but she didn't think Bett would agree. Then there was Gyp's reaction.

He went out on the porch with Maggie, staying close by until she pulled the starter cord and the engine sputtered to life. He crouched low, barking loudly. She was unwinding electrical cord from the side mounts when Bett came out and called to her. Unable to hear over the generator and the dog, Maggie cupped one ear. Bett picked up Gyp, reducing some of the din.

"Can you turn the volume down?" Bett yelled.

Maggie adjusted the throttle, then motioned her in and drew the power cord through a space at the inside corner of the door. When she closed it, the noise was muted. "How's that?"

"Okay," Bett conceded. "But how long will the floor keep vibrating?" Maggie gave her a double-take. "Just kidding! But it *is* noisy. Can't we just put the food in a box on the porch and wait until they fix whatever's wrong? It must be below freezing out there."

She shrugged. "Power could be out for a few hours or a few days. You never know. Why don't you put some of your music on and drown out the generator that way?"

"But you don't like it too loud!"

"I'll be warming up the truck. And I'm pretty good at tuning out loud noise. I have to at the garage."

Maggie took some extension cords from a cabinet. "I'll plug in the stereo anyway. That and the fridge and a couple of lamps ought to do it."

A few minutes later, Bett tested the stereo sound level and adjusted the volume slightly higher than the generator noise. "Is that okay?"

Maggie nodded and headed for the door.

"It's too bright for your eye," Bett warned. "Put your patch back on or get some sunglasses."

Maggie reached for her patch. "Can't stand shades. You can't see a person's eyes if they've got them on."

They went out together with Gyp at their heels. But once they stepped off the porch, Bett put both hands up to shade her eyes. "How can you see in snow-sun like this?"

"No problem. Just squint a little. Your eyes will adjust." Maggie demonstrated what she meant.

Bett copied the motion. "So *that's* how you got all those wrinkles!"

"Nah, got 'em on sale at a truck stop outside Kansas City. Big discount if you bought 'em by the pair."

They headed toward the truck, laughing easily together.

"Beautiful, isn't it?" Bett said, looking out on the steep, sloping valley. The snow gave everything a pristine brilliance, and the hills were dotted with patches of color as firs shed the melting snow from their boughs. The sky was clear, an ocean blue.

"Great day for a drive," Maggie replied. "The roads should be cleared soon. We can take a ride over the ridge before we go to town if you like."

"Do you really like to drive that much?"

"My favorite thing," she replied honestly.

Bett caught her reaching for the door handle and turned her around, backing her up against the side of the truck. "*Most* favorite?"

Maggie felt Bett's hands cup her face and tossed her head shyly. "Well, of the things I do daily."

"Oh? You don't like making love daily? Or even more often?"

"I hear people say they do that, but mostly it's just guys talking." She felt herself responding to Bett's stroking fingertips; her whole body hummed. "I figure they're exaggerating. Don't you?"

Bett chuckled, deep in her throat. "I hardly ever talk to guys about making love. I was asking what *you* like!"

"You are persistent, aren't you?" Maggie laughed and kissed her before climbing into the cab. She turned the key, and the engine cranked noisily. When it caught, its normal sound was drowned out by a horrendous high-pitched squealing. She cut the engine and got out. Sweeping as much snow off the hood as she could reach, she raised the hood and pulled on a fan blade, grunting with the effort when it failed to move. She spewed a string of foreign-sounding words.

"What was that?" Bett had never heard Maggie talk like that before.

"I think it's a curse." Maggie squeezed the water hoses, then dropped to the ground and pulled herself under the truck. "But I don't know what language." She muttered it again, and Bett crouched to see what she was doing.

Maggie pointed to an icicle that had formed. "Look! Would you say something appropriately cussed about a blankety-blank frozen stopcock?"

Bett smiled. "Actually, that sounds bad enough by itself!"

"And this." She slapped a fan blade. "Can you say something equally bad about a frozen radiator? Jeez, why didn't I check the antifreeze before we left?" She wriggled back further.

"Where are you going now?"

Bett heard her say something about "freezing plugs." Then, more clearly: "Bett, look underneath over there and see if there are any of those icicles like on the stopcock."

She went to where Maggie was pointing but couldn't see any ice drips.

Maggie extricated herself. "Well, that's something, I suppose."

"What's wrong?"

"She's froze up. Shoot!"

"Maggie, it's okay for you to say 'shit,' but please stop calling your truck 'she.' It's so PI!"

She grinned. "Seems to me it's a lot less offensive than cursing."

"Swearing has its place. Calling an inanimate object 'she' doesn't."

"She... My truck is more than an inanimate object. Except when it's not working."

"Won't it thaw? The refrigerator did."

"Being indoors with a fire going helped with that. But maybe we can help the truck, too." She got in again and used the driveway's incline to back it down to the woodpile, wheeling as she braked to slant the engine for maximum sun exposure. "We'll let it sit like that a while, then start it again." They headed up to the cabin. "We need to get the engine to warm the water jackets without overheating the cylinders. That's why I asked you to check the freeze plugs. If they'd popped..."

"Maggie," Bett stopped her, "I don't understand a word of this!"

"I know. That's why I'm explaining it to you."

Bett put an arm around her waist as they continued up the hill. "Funny. That wasn't your response when I asked you to tell me about yourself."

"Oh, that's different. People and machines: very different!"

She said it so matter-of-factly Bett had to laugh. "Score one for the tall, perceptive contestant!"

Maggie tripped her in retaliation and reached out to help her up. Instead, she felt herself being upended as Bett flipped her, pulled her bandaged hands together, and rolled her. The steep hill took charge then, and they tumbled over and over each other, down the hill in a flurry of snow and giggling screeches. Gyp thought it was the best game ever and jumped over and around them as they rolled. Finally, they all ended up together in a heap at the foot of the hill.

"You are awful!" Maggie said when she'd caught her breath.

"Mmm." Bett propped herself up, brushing Maggie's hair back and leaning over her. "But look where it's gotten me."

Maggie returned her kiss, then felt Bett's hand sneaking toward a shirt snap. Maggie rolled them over again and sat up, shaking her head. "Worse even than I first thought! Don't you have any respect for winter? Do you know how cold it is out here?"

"Sure!" Bett grinned. "I was just trying to stay warm."

Maggie stood, brushing snow off. "C'mon. I've got a better idea."

⋄ ⋄ ⋄

Brian paced the room, never quite taking his eyes off Tracy and the nurse who had come on the run at his yell. After turning the bed flat, she checked Tracy's eyes and took her blood pressure. When she'd taken it for the third time, Brian couldn't restrain himself.

"Can't you do something to wake her up?"

"Why?" she snapped. "So you can ask her more questions? You know you can't interrogate a head injury! You can't stress a concussion like that. I don't care if she is one of yours!" She turned to Tracy again, muttering about cops not having any mental capacity to strain.

Brian tried to explain but knew he wouldn't get a fair hearing. When the nurse reluctantly admitted that she'd probably be all right, he left. In the lobby, he called in to find there was a message from the ME's office.

"Tebert signed report," it read. "Sorry for the mix-up."

He puzzled over it briefly, then silently thanked Detective Williams for checking his copy and contacting the morgue. With that cleared up, he decided to go to Berkeley and solve another mystery.

The modest complex of brick apartment buildings near the campus was reminiscent of where he and Mary Jo had lived when they were first married. It looked like the same used-VW owners still lived there, too. If Bett hadn't gone to the mountains with Maggie, she might be in class. He planned to leave her a note and was checking the mailboxes in the entryway when the door opened behind him.

"Oh, boy!" a female voice crowed. "More cops!"

Brian turned to face a young, curly-haired blond. She had the bluest eyes he'd ever seen. And her smile was so engaging he had to grin back at her.

"Looks like just one to me."

"Are you looking for Bett, too? She must know every cop in the East Bay. But she's still not back, and I'm getting kind of worried. You think those guys came to kidnap her? Her dad's a doctor, but I don't think he's rich. And that doesn't make sense, either. They couldn't kidnap her if she wasn't here, and she wasn't!"

Brian was staggered. "Wait! What kidnapping? I know where Bett is."

"Oh, yeah?" the girl challenged. "So where is she? She always tells me when she's going to be gone more than a couple of days, even if she just goes to her dad's. Besides, I threw her cards last night, and it looks like she's in a lot of trouble."

"You threw her what?"

"Her cards. Tarot cards. You can do that, even if the person isn't there. I was worried after those guys showed up. I called the cops first," she added proudly.

"What guys?"

"The two I told the cops about yesterday. Hey, you're not from Berkeley. Are you from Oakland?" She tilted her head a notch. "I have a friend with the OPD."

Brian wasn't sure whether she was reappraising him or daring him to top her contacts. "Yeah, I'm with the OPD. Who are you? Do you live here?" He felt better firing questions back at her, even as he rued his technique.

"Trinos." Shifting her books, she stuck out a hand. "Elise. I live upstairs. Bett lives down at the end of the hall. Bottom floor. I always told her she should move. The ground floor's the least safe. Crime prevention and all. But if that was true, wouldn't they build apartments on stilts?"

"Um, Ms. Trinos, I haven't talked to the BPD yet." He felt comfortable using abbreviations with her. "Can you tell me what happened yesterday?"

"Sure. It was weird. These two guys pulled up in a pickup truck. Real scuzzos, you know? They didn't look like students. Not your usual Berkeley types anyway. One of them had a paper and was checking addresses on the buildings, like they were looking for a place to rent. Surprised me!"

"What did?"

"That either of them could read, first of all! And I thought it was kind of funny. We always hear about vacancies. You know, if somebody gets the boot. Anyhow, I watched from my window, and when they came in, I went to the hall." She nodded at the second floor landing, which gave a perfect angle to view someone at the entryway. "They pointed to Bett's mailbox, and I figured if they were looking for her, I'd find out why." She led Brian down the hallway and pointed up to another landing at the back stairs. "I was about to tell them she wasn't home, but they never even knocked! The big guy just twisted the knob, found it locked, and threw his shoulder up against it. I heard the frame start to go and hollered 'Police' at the top of my lungs, then ran back to my place and called it in. Somebody else must've called, too, though. I'd never say they were prowlers like Tracy said."

"Tracy?" Then Brian put the pieces together. "And you're 'a lease.'" It was starting to make sense. The newspaper article listed Maggie and Bett as passersby who'd tried to help the victim. Ebert must have gone to Maggie's to make sure that her place hadn't been burgled. But if she knew about Bett's place, why hadn't she been more careful? It stopped making sense. "Have you known Tracy long? Did she know Bett lived here?"

"Not very long," she said honestly. "And I don't know how long she's known Bett. But I've got her number if you want to call her."

"Tracy's not in any shape to talk now." The words were out of Brian's mouth before he knew it. He was usually better at delivering bad news. Elise looked like she'd been punched in the stomach.

"No," she breathed softly. "I knew something was wrong. I threw her cards, too. The seven of swords and the two of cups... I didn't stop her. Worse yet, I ignored the goddess. You can't do that. You have to go on listening. Even if it's bad news."

Brian touched her shoulder. "She'll be all right."

She looked up then. "If you know where Bett is, you have to warn her. She's in danger! I saw it in the cards. That's why I was thinking about kidnapping. I even called her dad. I didn't want to scare him, but..."

Brian realized his skepticism was showing.

"You have to believe me! Some people throw cards for fun. I have to listen. Don't you see? It's a matter of life and death!"

"Okay, relax. I'll get a message to her. I have to call later this after..."

"Now!" Elise demanded. "Please! Use my phone. Or give me the number. I'll call. There's danger all around her!"

It took Brian several minutes to calm her and more than the simple assurance that he believed her. He kept reminding himself that hysteria came in all forms. This was just one manifestation of it. But she was frighteningly sincere. She obviously believed what she was saying.

But who, he wondered, was going to believe him?

❖ ❖ ❖

Bett didn't expect Maggie's idea to be anything like hers, but she was right about respecting winter. It had taken mere seconds to roll down the hill. Reclimbing it would take nearly half an hour. The ice beneath the wet snow made the climb a challenge. Bett fell several times, and by the time they reached the woodpile, she was soaked to the skin.

Maggie stopped at the truck, telling her to keep going to the back door. "Key's under the shingle, about head high. I'm just going to start the truck."

Bett only found the key after adjusting to Maggie's version of head high. Once she was inside, the heat of the cabin felt suffocating, then she couldn't get close enough to the fire. She added pine logs and a large oak split, shivering as much as she had the night before. She sneezed twice and headed for the shower, swearing she wouldn't catch cold because of their roll in the snow.

"It's just not fair!" she complained as soon as Maggie came in. "There's no hot water!"

"And won't be 'til the power comes back on." Maggie removed her eye patch and jacket, then hugged Bett, feeling the dampness of her clothes despite the quilt she was wrapped in. "You should get changed. Bring some dry clothes and dress by the fire. Get a towel, too. I'll fix us a hot drink."

A few minutes later, Bett was sitting at the hearth, struggling to remove her wet jeans. Maggie brought in two steaming mugs and set them down, then tugged on Bett's cuffs, slipping her pants off to reveal legs nearly the color of Maggie's hair.

"No respect for the elements," she chided, turning the pockets out to hang the pants from the mantle. "Where's that towel?"

Bett handed it over and unbuttoned her blouse as Maggie rubbed her legs vigorously. "I'll never be warm again!" Her words chattered from the cold and the massage.

"Sure you will! You haven't tasted my cure-all concoction yet." Maggie turned her toward the fire and draped the towel over her shoulders to rub her arms. "Besides, now that you've learned winter's lesson, don't you want to stay for spring? It ought to be here in another week or two!"

"Spare me!" Bett was feeling warmer but only slightly. Then something else occurred to her. "You *did* get the truck started, didn't you?"

"Yup! I got her… I mean, I got the fan moving. Might cost me a pump gasket, but I think the block's okay. I'll check the pressure in a bit."

"What about the blankety-blank stopcock?"

"Oh, I knocked the icicle off and cracked it opened a notch. Got a little dribble and…" She looked up at Bett's chuckle.

"You use the strangest combination of words, without so much as batting an eyelash. Don't you hear yourself?"

"If you knew anything about engines…" Maggie stopped herself and handed Bett a mug. "Careful. It's hot." There was no warmth in her voice.

Bett touched her face, asking softly: "What is it, honey?"

Maggie tossed her head, and with it her resentment. "Hot buttered rum."

Bett groaned. "I meant: Why are you so upset?"

She only smiled. "We'll talk after you get warm."

The drink smelled heady. Bett sipped it before taking a larger swallow. It melted her mouth with sweet heat, then her throat and stomach. She sighed.

"Like it?"

"Mmm, I think my tongue is having orgasms. What is it?"

"I told you: hot buttered rum."

"Huh-uh. I've had that before. It never changed my life like this!"

Maggie grinned. "It never tastes this good in Oakland, either."

"Is it your own recipe?"

"Sort of. I built it from other people's. It's about all I can cook, except for hard-boiled eggs and rice. I've got those pretty well knocked, too."

"I can hardly wait!" Bett's chattering had stopped, and she was beginning to feel the fire. "What I want to know is how you've survived this long!"

"On my wits and diner food. Oh! And clean living. I always forget to mention that part."

Bett put her mug on the hearth and set Maggie's next to it, then drew her into her arms and kissed her.

Would there always be that hesitation, Bett wondered. That slight pause before Maggie responded? What was she thinking? What was she feeling?

But then she did respond, and Bett wanted to stand time on its side to take each sensation and follow it. The way her fingertips trailed along the underside of her chin, casually changing direction, deliberately tracing the shape of her ear. Cupping her head to draw her closer...

The texture of her lips, so soft, so mobile, reshaping to match hers. The inviting thrill that came with the tip of her tongue, teasing her lips, parting them, then drawing back slowly...

The sudden taste of her: flavors that were of Maggie alone, mixed with pungent spiced rum and tobacco...

The scent of her: worn leather, damp wool, a breath of pine...

But time wouldn't stand still. Bett couldn't follow any of those sensations individually. They all rushed in on her at once, and she felt more than the heat of the fire as Maggie pulled her across her lap into her arms, then paused. Bett opened her eyes, and Maggie kissed them closed, then slowly drew her tongue down the side of her neck, kissing her exposed throat. Bett's breasts blossomed in waiting, and she heard Maggie sigh. So quietly, it was barely a sound at all.

Then she felt her hand moving down, sliding her panties off, slipping to the inside of her leg, crooking it to soothe the back of her thigh. Her fingertips brushed lightly as they went, teasing their way to the top of her legs. Slowly, a bandaged palm moved over her, pressing lightly at first, then more firmly. Bett rose in invitation, wanting her to be more direct. She nearly spoke, then couldn't—her breath taken away as Maggie's fingers delicately searched, then encircled her most sensitive part. With that, her movement slowed even more; became the tiniest of motions. Bett moaned when she entered her. So carefully. So slowly.

"Oh, Maggie," she breathed softly. Do I have to tell you I need more? Where is your confidence, woman? Where is your sure, certain...Then her thoughts fled, driven out by the feelings mounting deep inside her. The most exquisite sensation flowed through her. She marveled at the little baby org... "Oh, god!" She arched against Maggie's palm, but it didn't yield. The sensation kept growing. Bett couldn't wait, then knew she had to.

She had always envisioned coming as a form of flight. But this wasn't like flying. There was no up or down. No sense of movement at all. Only sudden light. Pure. Soundless. White.

She might have moaned, for the light changed as Maggie's fingers withdrew as slowly as they had entered. Bett felt them encircle her again. Even more gently than before. She felt them being drawn back, until only one remained. And that one stayed. Pale light came over her, limned in blue. Then she did cry out. Slowly, the room came back to her. She realized she was still breathing; the fire still burned.

She heard Maggie whisper: "I've never loved like this."

"Missed your calling!" Bett was too spent to say more but felt Maggie's smile and knew she'd been heard.

Maggie laid her down and drew the quilt over her. "I hate covering you up," she said softly. "You are so very beautiful."

She said the last in such a tone of awe that Bett opened her eyes. She couldn't believe Maggie was putting on her jacket. "Where are you going?"

"Out, uh, to the truck."

Bett laughed as she slipped her patch over the wrong eye.

Maggie smiled a little, too. "I won't be gone long," she added, moving the patch to her right eye. "Just have to... Well, it won't take long."

She opened the door, then paused and let her eye travel the length of Bett. Maggie shivered, not from the cold, and left. Gyp was right behind her.

Bett didn't move for a long minute. Had she let Maggie go because she was too dazed or too satisfied? Sighing at the sudden disquiet her leaving created, she reached for her rum mug. Her hand touched a cigarette pack on the hearth first, and she made up her mind to go after her.

∴ ∴ ∴

Maggie searched for her cigarettes, absently patting each pocket in turn, out of habit, then as a distraction. Part of her mind focused on that while she tried to keep from thinking about what had just happened. She strode to the truck and was nearly running by the time she got to it.

"It's not supposed to work like this!" She didn't realize she'd spoken aloud. Yeah, sure it's supposed to feel good. She could admit that much. But not this good! What the hell happened? Bett hadn't even touched her.

She cut off her thoughts and went to work on the truck, twisting the frozen radiator cap. It gave a little but wouldn't release entirely. Then she let go, giving in to her emotions and letting herself relive the last few minutes. As she leaned over the engine, her left hand moved dangerously close to the whirring fan blades. She yanked it out of the way.

Pay attention! Follow the rules! She gripped the grill with that hand and rested the other on the fender, hanging her head, knowing she'd broken another, much more basic rule. The one that said: Don't take too much.

There were all kinds of rules. The very first one was: Don't need too much. If you don't need too much, you won't want too much. You won't take too much, not even accidentally. It was so basic. If you followed the rules, you never wanted or needed more than you could afford. And that law was as absolute as gravity, only simpler: The most you can have is limited to the most you can afford to lose!

Such a basic, bottom-line formula. It had worked for so long. Now that didn't work, either. Nothing worked right anymore. She'd let go with Bett. She'd gone too far. So far that even making love was all turned upside-down. Maggie closed her eye against her next thought. No! Love cost too much. So much more than she could ever afford.

She was so occupied by the conflict between what she felt and what she'd lived by for so many years that she never heard the sudden gurgle in the radiator. The ice plug in its neck broke free, and the loosened cap exploded in a roar of steam.

Maggie opened her eye, ducking instinctively. But it was too late.

⋄ ⋄ ⋄

It was after two when Brian finally got back to his desk and sorted through his mail. The pathology report he'd been waiting for had finally arrived. Clearing space for his sandwich and coffee, he sat down to read.

His appetite disappeared by the time he got through the first paragraph. It was as gruesome as Williams had warned. The condition of the body could have been described in two words: "Nearly incinerated." Instead, the report went into details about the degree of burns and their extent: over 60 percent of the body. Lungs showed no signs of smoke damage. X-rays revealed several old breaks in the left leg: femur, hairline fracture; fibula and tibia, one serious break each. All fully healed.

Two paragraphs later, Brian discovered what had caused the "mix-up." A small-caliber bullet had been found in the victim's skull. Its entry point could only be assumed because of excessive burn damage, but Brian knew enough anatomy to picture the position of a gun when the larynx was involved: Fenn had been shot in the neck with an upward trajectory. The head wound was tagged as the "primary and instantaneous" cause of death.

Brian folded the report and shook his head. He was so sure they'd been talking about two different victims. What happened that night? Damn. If only Maggie could remember!

⋄ ⋄ ⋄

She came to, gasping for air. Dry-mouthed. Panting. Dizzy. She could smell the fire. Feel the flames. Her head hurt, and she reached up to hold it.

"No, Maggie. Just lie still."

It was a familiar voice, a familiar command. She kept her eyes closed.

Everything seemed far away, but she had to hurry. Something was wrong!

"Slow down," the voice said. "Breathe deeply."

Then she remembered running down the ramp. Damn her last two zillion cigarettes. She swore she'd quit, but it was Scotty who should have. She was sure that was what had caused the inferno. She remembered thinking all that as she ran down the exit ramp. Scanning the green ground cover as she searched for him to the left of the car. She ignored the fire, knowing the car was beyond saving. The stink of burning rubber filled the air. The inside of the car was blazing now. What a waste!

Smoke drifted by her. She quickly crossed to the shoulder of the road, wary of more traffic. A pickup racing up the exit had nearly hit her as she rounded the corner. The driver was watching the blaze in his mirror. He must've been practically next to Scotty's car when it exploded.

She was still a hundred feet from the fiery wreck when she remembered that his Chevy took fuel behind the license plate, not the rear quarter-panel. She looked fifty feet down the shoulder of the freeway. No sign of him. She shortened her search to thirty feet. Hope rose in her for a moment. Maybe he hadn't been standing there taking a drag as he poured gas down the neck of the fuel tank. She slowed her run. Maybe he'd stepped back, and something else had worked its violent chemistry. She looked around, hoping to find him standing aside, open-mouthed and bug-eyed as a kid. Then she zeroed in on the space at the back of the car. The flaming figure lay nearly beneath the ruptured tank. Black smoke and flames engulfed him.

Skidding to a stop, she unfurled the blanket, using it as a shield first, then smothering the flames with it. She didn't think about her own safety. She only knew she had to get Scotty away from the car. She shifted her weight, hearing metal scrape in the gravel. Out of the corner of her eye, she saw a gas can slide off the edge of the road; liquid dribbled from the spout.

She straightened, not seeing the trickle of fuel flash as it connected with the larger flames. The nozzle fired instantly, superheating the fumes inside. The second explosion caught the blanket like a wind sail, nearly knocking her legs from under her. Then the can's metal spout ricocheted off the fender into her face, knocking her back. She hung on, stunned, but intent on bringing Scotty to safety. Staggering, she stumbled on the road edge, wrenching her ankle. She tightened her hold as she felt herself falling back, into the fire. Suddenly she was rocked from behind, flung free of danger. She lost her grip.

"Scotty!!" She opened her eyes. Bett was there. Maggie barely knew her, but she wasn't surprised to see her. "We've got to save him!" She started to rise, but Bett stopped her.

Maggie looked left and quit her struggle. She looked right. Where was the freeway? The burning car? Scotty?

She closed her eyes again, in shock and confusion. Then wept with an overwhelming sense of loss.

CHAPTER 19.

Undone

BETT HELD MAGGIE, SOOTHING her and wiping away her tears. When her crying eased, she led her to the bedroom and suggested she try to sleep. The fewer contradictory sensations she experienced the better.

"Don't think about anything now," she urged. "Just sleep a bit. Everything will make sense when you wake up, I promise."

Bett went back to the main room where her own delayed reaction set in. She felt cold all over, and her hands were trembling. She mixed the rest of their drinks together and heated it on the stove, then brought a mug to the hearth and drank half of it down. The alcohol was probably all cooked off, but it soothed her anyway.

She stared into the fire, mentally replaying what had happened. How had she gotten to the truck so fast? She'd been tucking in her blouse, wondering what to do about her soaked Adidas, when a muffled boom sent her to the window. White smoke was billowing from under the truck's hood. Maggie was backing away, holding her head in her hands. Bett watched in horror as she stumbled, then fell in the snow and lay still.

The next few minutes were a blur of cold and fear. Bett flew out the door in stocking feet and hit the ground running. Maggie was semiconscious, and they staggered together to the back door. Some part of her mind told her she was breaking every first-aid rule in the book, but she didn't care about rules. All she cared about was seeing Maggie fully conscious again.

Bett witnessed her disorientation helplessly. She knew all she could do now was monitor Maggie's more normal rest and hope it would help reset her memory. She checked on her again, then closed the bedroom door. She turned to the hearth and saw Gyp at the front door, growling low in his throat. She looked out the window, but all she saw was the truck, still emitting wisps of steam.

"Don't worry, Gyp. It's all over now." She picked him up to show him the empty yard, but instead of quieting, he started barking in earnest. She put him in the Winter Room, and his bark returned to a growl when she closed the door. Then she turned the stereo on and stretched out in front of the fire, letting the music and the throb of the generator lull her to sleep.

The next thing she knew, she was in a grandstand: front row, center. Cars roared by on an oval track. It wasn't a race, though. It was a contest of some kind, and she was part of it. Deep trenches had been dug in the center of the track. Maggie and Tracy were standing in the one across from her. They were on some kind of team, passing a long rod from one end of the trench to the other where a lead man looked to Bett for a signal before hurling it skyward. Rods were being thrown from all the trenches, landing on the track in the path of the racecars. Several cars had been hit, but some rods had fallen in the grandstand, too. It was a violent, dangerous game. Bett didn't know why she'd agreed to play.

It was time to signal another throw, but Maggie and Tracy were laughing together. When they ducked into the trench, she stood to see where they'd gone. Suddenly Gyp appeared out of nowhere, barking loudly and knocking her down. She opened her eyes. A rod was falling directly on top of her.

She shut her eyes, telling herself it was just a dream, then opened them again. It *was* a dream. Nothing was falling on her. Someone was pointing a gun at her. Maggie told her never to look down the barrel of a gun to see if it was loaded. This one was fully loaded.

❖ ❖ ❖

Brian glanced dourly at his ringing phone. He'd put in a call to Williams after reading the PM on Fenn. Oh well, he thought resignedly, my turn in the barrel!

"Hello, Brian. This is Hugh Miller. Summit County."

Brian got right to the point and explained the details of Fenn's death.

"Maggie told me about the fire," Miller said, "but I doubt she'll take his being shot any better than being burned to death. Got any suspects?"

"Not a one. Homicide's working on it, but I managed to slow them down by insisting Fenn's death was accidental."

"Sort of a natural mistake," Miller offered.

"Maybe, but I've got a feeling it's not the only one. Maggie's apartment was burglarized last night. Nothing's missing that I know of, but a friend of hers walked in on it and got pistol-whipped."

"And you think it's connected with Friday night?"

"Yes and no. Fact is, Maggie has cops for friends. That sort of thing tends to keep local thugs off her street."

"So it wasn't locals."

"That's what I said. But the fanciest thing Maggie owns is her truck. She never spent money the way Matt Graf did."

"He had his hobbies. I guess she has hers."

Brian sensed coolness in the sheriff's reply. "Sorry. I didn't mean anything. I know you two were good friends."

Miller grunted acceptance. "I still don't see a connection. Next you'll be telling me her cabin break-in was connected."

"What's this?"

"It must've happened Sunday afternoon. But we get a fair number of off-season burglaries. From what you've said, the only similarity is that nothing was taken here, either. Not because they were interrupted, though. She'd reported a missing gun earlier. I figure it was stolen, and whoever took it went back, thinking they could get more."

Brian agreed. "Tell me, is Maggie alone?"

"No, she's got a young gal named Bett with her."

"I thought so, but that only adds to the mystery." He explained about the attempted break-in at Bett's. "I met a friend of hers; some kind of psychic. She said she'd thrown Bett's cards and…"

The sheriff snorted. "She *will* be in trouble if I catch her throwing cards!"

Brian knew about the cribbage battle between Hugh and Matt. "Well, it's weird how everything's happening at once. It's either all connected to Friday night, or it's the wildest bunch of coincidences I've seen in a while."

"I'm willing to go along with you on coincidence, Brian. When you start talking psychics, I'll take random chance any day. Look, if you didn't know Maggie personally, would anybody connect these break-ins?"

"I hadn't considered that."

"Okay. Start with Fenn. He gets shot, but it looks like he died in a fire. Maggie gets hurt trying to save him. Later her house gets robbed, then her friend gets robbed. You might as well chalk it up to biorhythms or star alignment. You think she'll see it as anything more than a string of bad luck? She doesn't strike me as the paranoid type."

"She isn't," Brian agreed. "And maybe I have let the week get to me. But I want things to make sense. It can't all be random chance. If I thought that, I wouldn't make a very good cop, except maybe in Nevada!"

Miller chuckled. "Look, I'll take a run up to the cabin and give Maggie the news. She'll probably want to call you back."

Brian felt better about things after getting that long-distance perspective. It still wasn't pretty, and he didn't envy Miller's task, but maybe it wasn't connected in any sinister way. Maybe it was just a run of bad luck.

❖ ❖ ❖

How do you surrender when you're already flat on your back?

Bett raised her hands over her head, forcing herself to look past the gun to the grotesque face of the man holding it. At least she assumed it was a man. It was just like in the movies. He was wearing a red ski mask with dark holes where his eyes and mouth should have been. Was she still dreaming?

No. Gyp's bark was too real. She had to think. Was Maggie all right? The gunman interrupted her thoughts with a terse wave of the gun, motioning her to get up. She heard him demand money and papers, then he muttered what sounded like somebody's name: Bill Zalading.

Bett nodded dumbly. Money she understood. She didn't know anybody named Bill, or where his papers might be. She scooted to a sitting position against the couch and thumbed at her purse on the kitchen counter. "Over there." She was surprised to find that she had any voice at all.

"Get it!"

Bett never took her eyes off the gun. She rose slowly and backed her way to the kitchen, bumping into the table. Until then, she was sure this was happening to someone else. She was merely the camera's eye.

She put out a hand, feeling her way around the table, past the center chair, guiding herself by touch. The counter was only a few feet away. She reached for her purse, holding on to the table. The table was real. Everything else was unreal. She touched her purse. It was real, too. Some things had to be real: the table, her purse. The gun wasn't real. The gunman wasn't, either. He couldn't be. She brought her purse around slowly and held it out, her arm stiff with fear.

He had followed her, step-by-step from the fireplace. "On the table."

She set it down, taking her eyes off him for an instant.

He shoved her into the chair at the end of the table, so forcefully that she rocked back, hitting her head on the wall and rebounding into the table.

"Stay there!" he warned.

Bett was too stunned to move. She watched him dump the contents of her purse on the table. It's not going to be enough, she thought. Bizarrely, she considered offering to write a check.

Suddenly the bedroom door opened. Maggie came out, looking around the main room, seeing the open front door.

That was when time started to move at different speeds for Bett. At the sound of the door opening, she saw Red Mask's mouth widen in surprise. Watched him swing the gun toward the main room. Saw his gloved finger pull the trigger. She pushed the table into him, just as he fired.

She saw Maggie duck the wild shot. Then Bett was looking down the barrel of the gun again. She had all the time in the world to realize that he meant to kill her. Meant to kill them both.

"I told you to stay put!" His voice strained with rage.

Maggie's voice boomed: "No!" It wasn't a protest. It was a command. "You want money? Come here. I'll give it to you."

Her voice was strong. Steady. Even her question was a statement. Bett knew it didn't matter. He would kill them anyway.

Then the gunman trained his gun on Maggie. She was starting to reach for her pocket. "Hold it!" He faced Bett again. "Put your head on the table."

She did, but she'd shoved it so far forward she had to extend herself to reach it. Her chair was still up against the wall, but the table was well away from it. She put her head down, keeping her eyes on the main room. Her left hand slipped off the edge of the table, striking something distinctly un-chair-like. Something like a plastic dustpan.

Red Mask moved into the main room where Maggie was pulling out her wallet. "Put it down." He waved his gun at the coffee table.

Bett moved her left hand and touched cold metal. They stole this! It can't possibly…! But she cut off that thought. She couldn't have mice chittering at her, too.

She had to act, but she couldn't move. She imagined aiming the gun at him. Shouting a warning. It would come out all wrong. Only a whisper. She'd pull the trigger. Shoot Maggie. Bett shut her eyes at the image, even as she picked up the gun. Nothing felt real. It was all a horrible dream.

"Wait!" Maggie said. "There's more."

When Bett opened her eyes, she knew it was a dream.

Maggie was taking folded money from one shirt pocket, then the other. Awkwardly reaching around herself, she pulled still more money out of her other back pocket, then slipped two fingers into a front pocket, drawing out another collection of bills, dropping it all on the table with her wallet. The different denominations piled up like the pot from a poker game.

Bett was spellbound. Maggie was poor. She couldn't have money in all her pockets. And who would carry it like that? No. Either it was all a dream or Maggie was, absolutely, the strangest person in the world.

The gunman looked at the coffee table, then back at Maggie. "What the hell do you take me for? A fuckin' idiot?"

Then everything began happening in slow motion again. Bett saw him lift the gun over his head. Heard him say: "I. Want. The. Money. And. The…"

"Noooo!" Bett wailed as Maggie raised her hands to ward off the blow. Then Bett stood, holding the black gun in both hands, forgetting everything Maggie had taught her. She pulled the trigger. Nothing happened. A dead click echoed in the cabin. She felt like she was doing everything underwater. His gun hand was coming down.

Aim carefully. Squeeze. Don't jerk. Maggie's words came back to her. Bett held her breath and pulled the trigger. The gun kicked so hard she felt it in the back of her neck, and suddenly she was facing the back door. Then she knew the gun hadn't kicked that hard. She'd been hit, turned around. She was facing another gunman. This one wore a blue ski mask. Good thing they wore different colors, she thought. Now we can tell them apart.

She heard Maggie say: "Put your gun down! We've got you covered!" That was when Bett realized she was now sitting on the dustpan chair, still gripping the gun, pointing it at Blue Mask.

"Huh-uh." He waved his gun between the two women. "You both got guns, but I'll take one of you with me."

Then a new voice sounded, a voice in pain. "Just get me outta here!" It was Red Mask, lying on the floor at Maggie's feet. "Don't fuck around. That one's a dead shot!"

Blue Mask wet his lips and looked at Bett, then at Maggie. "Aw' right. Here's the deal. We're going out the front. You stay here. I'm keeping my gun on one of you all the time. You're gonna give us five minutes after I get out the door. Got it?"

Maggie must have nodded. Bett was concentrating on keeping her gun trained on him. She watched him go to the main room quickly; heard Red Mask breathing heavily. Red Mask left first, holding his right arm tightly at his side. She couldn't see Maggie. All she could see was Blue Mask standing in the doorway. Then he was gone, too.

"Put the gun down, Bett."

Maggie was speaking from a long way away.

"Darlin'...?"

Bett felt a bandaged hand cover hers. The black gun clattered on the table. There was nothing like the feel of Maggie's arms around her. Even if one of her hands held a gun.

❖ ❖ ❖

Brian saw Williams come through the door. "I owe you a cup of coffee."

"Yeah?" the detective eyed him suspiciously. "What for?"

"The bum steer I gave you on Fenn." Brian took out the postmortem. "He was shot first, then his car exploded. I don't know much more than that, but I slowed up your investigation."

Williams shrugged. "The earliest we could've done anything was still seventy-two hours after the fact. You didn't cool any red-hot leads that I know of."

They discussed the case over coffee. Williams quizzed Brian, who didn't think there was much order to the questions. Finally he volunteered: "I know Fenn. Knew him, I mean."

Williams nodded. "That's why I came by. Got the report from Probation. You collared him on that attempted bank robbery."

"You mean *you* ordered the file from Hawkins? I thought Homicide had Fenn down as a suspect! Now I really feel stupid!"

"No need," Williams said easily. "I didn't read the whole autopsy 'til this morning, either. Why don't you tell me about him? The P.O. report's kind of thin. And his sheet's mostly arrests and releases."

"That's Fenn, all right. He was pretty much a loner. Whenever he did a job with somebody else, his luck would sour. That's what he told Maggie."

"His girlfriend?"

"No. That'd be Lois Delano." Brian turned over the notes on his conversation with her as he explained Maggie and Scotty's friendship.

Williams listened, making his own notes, then read Brian's. "What's this about a burglary?" he asked.

"Which one? Looks like we've got a dozen to choose from."

"Oh? Who besides the Delano woman?"

"I forgot all about that!" Brian told him about the burglary at Maggie's and the attempt at Bett's. "I'm not sure any of it's related to Friday night. It might just be a run of bad luck. You know: coincidence."

Williams lifted one corner of his mouth. "In the detective business, we call that a pattern."

Then Brian told him about the cabin burglary and added, "I'll give you pattern: Nothing was missing in any of these break-ins!"

The detective said: "That explains why there's been so many."

"Huh?"

"Yeah. It means they haven't found what they're looking for yet."

∴ ∴ ∴

Maggie watched from the front window as the blue-masked gunman took the keys from her truck. She waited to see where he'd throw them, but he stuffed them in his pocket instead.

When he followed the wounded one out of sight down the driveway, she returned to Bett, who seemed to be in a kind of trance. Maggie slipped Matt's gun into her back pocket. She meant to stay armed until she was sure they were gone for good.

Both doors were still wide open, and while that helped rid the rooms of the smell of gunfire, it turned the cabin into a virtual breezeway. Maggie took Bett with her as she secured the doors before opening the Winter Room. Gyp came flying out, jumping all over them, then investigated each room, sniffing and growling as he went. When Maggie led Bett over to the fireplace, he ran to them and licked their faces.

Bett reached out to him. "I'm sorry, Gyp. I just didn't know." She started to pet him, then froze. "Oh, Maggie. I shot that man!" She burst into tears.

"I know you did, darlin'." She lit a cigarette, not knowing what else to say. She could only hold Bett, letting her tears relieve her shock.

Finally Bett's crying eased. "I can't believe it. All my life I've *honored* life. Treasured it. It's all we have! It's all that matters. Nothing matters more. Oh, Maggie! How could I shoot somebody?"

Maggie felt her shudder with a new wave of tears and held her close. "You did what you had to. Survival is an instinct. The strongest one we have. And you didn't kill anybody. In fact, you probably saved my life—both our lives. That's a pretty good trade-off in my book."

Bett drew back to look at Maggie directly. Then she closed her eyes, took a deep breath, and hugged her tightly. Several minutes passed in quiet.

"Feeling better?" Maggie asked softly.

Bett stirred then. "I feel like everything is stopped. But I don't trust that. I want to do something, and I don't know what." New tears welled in her eyes. She gritted her teeth. "And I want to stop crying!"

Maggie brushed her tears away and kissed her forehead. "You should help me make some egg coffee then. Nobody ever cries when they do that, have you noticed?" Bett's smile was encouraging. And doing something routine would help. It always did.

They went to the kitchen, where Maggie put the pot on to boil and began filling Gyp's food bowl as Bett mixed the grounds.

"Do you know anybody around here named Zalading?" Bett asked.

"No. Why?"

"Maybe Red Mask had the wrong cabin. He asked for somebody. Said he wanted his papers."

"What papers?"

"I don't know. I'd fallen asleep. I woke up, and he was standing over me with a gun saying, 'Get me the money and the papers and Bill Somebody. I thought he said Zalading.'" She scowled at the dry coffee grains that were trying to evade the egg and charged them with her fork.

"Weird name. You sure it was Zalading?"

"I don't know. Maybe it was Slater. I didn't ask him to spell it!"

Maggie heard her testiness and knew it wasn't the time to pursue that. She leaned against the counter, feeling Matt's gun in her back pocket, and pulled it out. "Looks like you hid this pretty well after all."

She opened the cylinder, and her heart jumped: The gun held a solitary bullet, not a full load. She ran a fingertip over the spent shell, feeling the slight indentation from the firing pin, and wondered if Bett had known. She asked her about finding it.

Bett looked up at her change in tone. "Don't be angry, Maggie. I didn't know anything about guns then. And I was sure whoever broke in Sunday took it." She put her hands to her face.

Maggie crossed the small space between them to hug her. "I'm not mad. I just can't figure out how they missed it."

Bett nodded, then told her about finding it under the dishpan and hiding it on the chair seat. "Don't laugh," she pleaded. "I know it was dumb…"

"I'm not laughing, darlin'." She tightened her hold for emphasis. In fact, she was relieved. Bett hadn't checked the load. She didn't know she'd been holding a nearly empty gun. Maggie picked up the bowl of grounds, dumping them in the pot. "You just proved my point about happy endings!"

Bett smiled and wiped away an errant tear.

"Now, just to make sure this story stays that way," Maggie said, "I'm going to the truck to radio the sheriff, okay?"

"Wait! I'll go with you." Bett's shoes had dried, but her socks were still wet. She got a dry pair from the bedroom. When she returned, Maggie was at the coffee table, putting her money away.

"Where did you get all that money?"

"It's Friday's take. I didn't get to the bank, remember?"

"Won't Hudson be mad?" Bett sat on the hearth to tie her shoes. "Not that I care about him, but I don't want you to get in trouble." When Maggie didn't answer, Bett looked up to see her watching Gyp. He was growling at the door, the way he had earlier that day.

Maggie picked up the captured gun.

"No!" Bett grabbed her arm, afraid to let her go. Then a shrill whistle pierced the air.

"It's the sheriff."

"You're sure?" Bett asked, still not letting go.

Maggie nodded and led her to the window. "Thieves don't whistle first. See?" Hugh Miller was at the woodpile, examining the truck. "I'll get him."

Bett tightened her hold. "Please don't leave," she whispered.

"How about if I just go to the porch and holler?"

Bett finally released her and looked up into her smile. "You can do that much," she said, "and maybe later today, I'll even be brave enough to let you go to the bathroom by yourself!"

Maggie kissed her. "You are brave, darlin'. You just don't know it for yourself, yet."

Bett responded with a small smile. "I love you, Maggie. You won't let anything else happen today, will you? Please?"

"Talk about giving people power!"

They kissed again, even as a horn sounded, reminding them they couldn't stand there kissing all afternoon. They both considered it, though.

❖ ❖ ❖

Sitting at the kitchen table, Maggie disassembled the black gun and cleaned it as she told the sheriff what had happened.

"It misfired?" The sheriff was incredulous.

"I don't know what you call it!" Bett nearly shouted. "It didn't work the first time I pulled the trigger!"

Maggie gave him a brief look, then stroked Bett's hand lightly and went on. "Anyhow, she hit him the second time she fired. I saw the other guy come in the back door. Bett must've heard him, too. She had him covered practically before I got this gun out of the first guy's hand." Maggie pointed at the captured gun, lying on the table amid the cleaning rags and coffee mugs. She reached for it, but the sheriff stopped her.

"There won't be any prints, Hugh. They both wore gloves."

"I'll send it to the lab anyway. You got a plastic bag?"

Out of habit, Maggie flipped the light switch as she went to the other end of the kitchen. Bett was the first to notice.

"Lights! Oh, Maggie, can we turn the generator off now? Can I shower?"

"Sure. But hurry. We have to go to town, and I want to get back before dark." Maggie shut off the generator and plugged the appliances back into their standard sockets before sitting down with the sheriff again. He hadn't stirred from where he sat.

"What's the matter, Hugh?"

"Hmm?" He came out of his study of the gun.

"You've barely touched your coffee. What's wrong?"

He sat back muttering, "I don't like it a bit." Nodding to her offer of a fresh cup, he added, "Maybe you two ought to think about putting up at the Tavern tonight."

"Hugh! You're not leveling with me. What's going on?"

"I don't know, and that makes me cautious." He looked at her directly. "Brian Kessler called. I'm afraid I have some bad news for you."

"It was Scotty, wasn't it?"

Her anticipation surprised him, but he expressed his sympathy. "Kessler said he was like a brother to you."

She acknowledged that with a nod. "I finally got my memory back. He was nearly under the car when I got to him. I still don't understand that part. That explosion should've knocked him a good fifty feet away."

"Probably, but he didn't die in the fire. He was shot. The fire covered that up. Apparently everybody assumed he'd been killed in the explosion."

"Well, they shouldn't have! Anybody who saw him…" Then she remembered who *had* seen him. Bett didn't know anything about cars or gasoline fires. And Scotty wasn't under the car when Brian and Tracy got there. They hadn't seen how big the explosion was, either.

"Well," Hugh said, "I told Brian about the break-in here. I didn't think there was any connection. Now I'm not so sure."

Maggie shook her head. "I don't get it, either. They were after something besides money. You ever heard of a robber turning down a grand?"

"A grand? You been over to State Line or what?"

"Huh-uh. Cash from Friday's jobs. I didn't want to leave it at the yard. No sweat. Matt taught me how to carry money."

Miller sighed. "You keep a C-note in each boot now, too?"

She chuckled. "I only took up some of his habits. I've always carried cash, though. We mostly do cash jobs. I told Matt it made me feel rich to have money in all my pockets. Otherwise, it was just numbers on paper." She reassembled Matt's gun and loaded it, explaining as she did why it had "misfired" on Bett.

"Sounds like Russian Roulette to me," the sheriff replied.

"What does?" Bett emerged from the bedroom. "That shower was great! I'm a new person! Ready for anything!"

Maggie turned to Hugh with a grin. "Still think we need to run away to the Tavern? Sounds like Bett can handle anything that might happen up here!" She reached for her instinctively.

Bett took Maggie's hand in both of hers and sat close. "Catch me up on what you've been talking about." She looked at the sheriff expectantly.

He cleared his throat, then told Bett who had died Friday night and how, adding, "Yesterday, somebody broke into your apartments."

"My place?" That was the last thing Bett expected to hear.

Maggie was equally surprised.

He nodded. "Attempted break-in at Bett's. But they succeeded at your place, Maggie. Brian doesn't think anything's missing. Apparently a friend of yours walked in on it and ended up in the hospital, pistol-whipped."

"Who was it?"

"He didn't say. Started telling me about a friend of Bett's. Some fortune teller who wanted to warn her…"

"Elise!" Bett gasped. "She must have thrown my cards. I know she's good, but…" She saw the two of them staring at her. "Never mind. If we're still going to town, I can call her." She turned to Maggie. "Who do you…" She paled suddenly. "Red Mask was going to do that to you!"

Maggie put a hand to Bett's face, barely touching fingertips to cheek. "He couldn't, darlin'. Not with you around." She turned to the sheriff then. "What are the roads like, Hugh?"

"Main roads are clear. Cal-Trans took down the chains-only signs around noon. But it might ice up again tonight."

"Where's your car?"

"Left it halfway up the first leg of the driveway. With your truck at the turn, I couldn't tell if I could get by. You going back tonight?"

"Depends. I have to get my truck together first. I don't suppose you saw a radiator cap out there?"

He shook his head.

"Well then, we'll have to get to town for a replacement cap and a gallon of antifreeze before the parts store closes."

She detailed their tasks: Call Brian, the garage, Bett's friend Elise. They could discuss where they would spend the night after getting more information from Brian. If they didn't stay at the cabin tonight, they'd come back to get what they needed. They just had to get it all done before dark, before the temperature dropped.

"Got your shoes on?" she asked Bett.

"I may never take them off again!" She lifted both feet to show her.

Maggie called to Gyp, but he was already at the front door.

Hugh was the last one up from the table. "You and Matt make decisions faster 'n anybody I ever knew."

Maggie grinned. "Did he tell you about when we bought insurance? Made that salesman's head spin. He said, 'I always heard pilots made split-second decisions.' He asked me if I was a pilot, too. Matt called me copilot for a year!"

Although Bett joined their laughter, there was something that made her head tick in a too-familiar way, but she couldn't capture the cause.

At the truck, Maggie wrenched a small tin from its hiding place. "Spare keys," she explained. "They took the others from the ignition. Making sure I didn't come after them, I guess."

"Would you have?"

Maggie slammed the hood closed. "Nope. I don't take risks. Remember?"

They got in, and Gyp curled up in his box without any prompting. Maggie adjusted her visor against the lowering sun and rolled the truck down the incline, then honked to let the sheriff know they were ready to go. They rode to town in silence, each lost in her own thoughts.

CHAPTER 20.

The Changer and the Changed

BETT SMILED INTO THE PHONE. She'd forgotten about Elise's talking style. It was a shock to hear her verbal outpouring after being with Maggie so long. But she couldn't focus on all her friend was saying.

"Elise, you can tell me when we get home. I'm at the sheriff's office..."

"You haven't been arrested, have you? I called your dad last night. I was so worried after reading your cards."

"No, I haven't been arrested." Bett told her what happened at the cabin.

"You really shot him? Is he dead?"

"No. I'm not even sure where I hit him. I got hit and..."

"You've been *shot?*"

Bett couldn't tell if Elise was alarmed or excited. "No, it was more like a karate chop." Then she saw Maggie coming across the street. "I'll tell you all about it when we get back, okay? I have to go now."

But Elise had to tell her how she'd kept her apartment from being robbed. Bett lost track when Maggie came through the door. She felt safe now. She hadn't even been aware of feeling ill at ease before.

"Bett, are you listening?"

"Sorry. Maggie just came back. I was, though. You said the burglars disappeared without a trace."

Elise's exasperation came through the phone loud and clear. "Guess I'll wait until you get here to tell you about everything *else* that happened!"

Bett agreed to call her father, then hung up and joined Maggie.

"What's the report on his car say?... What do you mean, you can't find it?" She was silent for a long minute. "No, check with Stony. Hey, can you set up a drive-by on Kenning tonight? They stole my keys and I..."

Bett saw Maggie's face change dramatically and was shocked to hear her say tightly, "That's none of your business!" Then her voice changed again. "Is she okay?... You're sure?... Look, I have to get going. The roads... What?... Scotty's leg? Yeah. I forgot about that; broke it in three places. Said he did it walking the logs." She listened again. "Probably. If they keep them more than a few years... Uh, Grants Pass General or Memorial."

When she hung up, she passed the phone to Bett, who dialed her father's office. He came on the line after only a minute, and she assured him she was fine. "I know Elise called you. I forgot to leave her a note.... Yes, fine. We'll be back tomorrow, I'm sure. You better go take care of that squalling baby." She laughed. "Hear him? Hell, all of Summit County can hear him!... Love you, too, Dad."

The sheriff joined them then. "Going back to Oakland tonight?"

"Afraid I don't feel up to the drive," Maggie said, pushing her chair back. Gyp ran to the door. "Shoot! I forgot all about him. The Tavern doesn't allow dogs in the rooms. You want to stay in town, Bett? It'll be safer here."

"No!" Bett was shocked at the thought of being shuffled off to some hotel while Maggie and Gyp stayed at the cabin. She turned to the sheriff. "We'll be fine with Gyp on guard. And we've got two guns now, counting Matt's and the new one." God help me, she thought. I can't believe these words are coming out of my mouth!

The sheriff nodded. "If you'll wait until I get that report typed up, I can follow you to the cabin."

Maggie shook her head. "I don't want to get there after dark." She promised to radio in when they got there, and he finally agreed. "Maybe we can play some cutthroat," she added. "Bett's picked up the two-handed game pretty quick. You could probably clean us out of quarters with one arm tied behind you!"

He smiled. "Another time."

As they left, Maggie asked him to put on his siren when he arrived. "If my truck isn't in its usual place, call out the National Guard!"

He raised an eyebrow at that. "Just don't go looking for trouble!"

On the drive back, Bett asked how safe Maggie thought they would be at the cabin.

"We'll be okay if they aren't waiting for us. I don't think they'll stick around, though. Hugh figures they're the same two that tailed us here, and Berger thought our Sunday visitors were flatlanders, remember?"

"Do you think it's connected with what's happening at home then?"

Maggie shrugged. "Could be. My point is, they don't know the mountains. If the roads freeze up, they probably won't be back. But even so, we'll have the advantage of being inside, and they won't have the element of surprise. How safe do you feel?"

"I'm not worried as long as I'm with you, but why did you try to leave me at the Tavern?"

"You're only here because of me. I'm responsible for you."

"I've told you before, you take that responsibility stuff too seriously."

Maggie didn't reply. They were nearly at the cabin.

The sun dipped behind a bank of clouds as she pulled up the first leg of the driveway and slowly drove into her regular space, looking for any signs of recent visitors. But the afternoon sun had melted much of the snow. Even the marks of their hillside tumble had been erased. Footprints in the snow weren't going to tell them anything.

Maggie switched off the engine. "Let Gyp out, will you?"

He leapt out, and they watched him sniff the snow clods indifferently before looking back and yelping at them. Maggie radioed the sheriff then, reporting "all quiet" at their end. She nodded at Gyp as they got out of the truck. "I was afraid he'd be a nuisance on this trip."

"Aren't you glad we brought him now?" asked Bett.

"Well, I do feel a little like a coal miner with a canary."

"I never understood that. If I can smell gas, why couldn't they? Why did they have to kill all those poor birds?"

Maggie chuckled as they headed up the yard steps. "Natural gas doesn't have any odor, darlin'. The gas company puts something in it so you *can* smell it. Like carbon monoxide, it's tasteless, odorless, colorless. People think the blue smoke they see coming out of a car exhaust is dangerous, but that isn't the stuff that'll kill you."

"Oh, Maggie!" Bett hugged her. "Isn't there something we can talk about besides death? I even dreamt about it!"

Maggie returned her embrace, eyeing the cabin as she did. Everything looked the same as when they'd left. "Sure," she said. "We can talk about what to have for dinner. Seems to me I had some soft-boiled eggs about a hundred years ago. I could probably eat a dozen now."

"Food! I forgot all about it! I'm starved, too!" Bett faced the cabin. "If anybody's in there, get out! And don't come back until after dinner!"

They were both smiling as they went up the steps to the cabin together.

❖ ❖ ❖

Brian leaned on the counter at the Medical Examiner's office and decided he'd rather have migraine headaches than another two days like these.

"Let me get this straight. You say somebody named Tebert—some *guy* named Tebert—came in, flashed his badge, and said he was here to claim the personal effects of a John Doe identified as Scott Fenn. Is that right?"

"Yeah." The clerk nodded at a carton containing a partially burned blanket. "Asked me what we'd done with his wallet and papers. I said if we'd found anything like that, the victim never would've been listed as a John Doe. Then he asked if we'd sent anything to a next-of-kin. I told him Homicide would have to clear that. It's SOP. I expected him to give me hell for telling him what standard procedure was, but he just took off."

The clerk pulled the accident report from a file. "I send out the PMs. On weird cases like this one, I send a copy to the reporting officer. If I can read the name or they remember to put in their badge number."

Brian saw that Tracy had signed it in her usual way: *TEbert*. He could see how easy it was to misread. Then he explained that Ebert was a female.

The clerk raised an eyebrow at that. "Well, this Tebert was a guy. He's white;

211

mid-forties; no facial hair; a thin scar, about two inches long from the corner of his lip alongside his nose. Medium-brown eyes; no lenses; thinning brown hair." He shrugged. "He looked just like an off-duty cop."

"What about height and weight?"

The clerk stepped back and eyed Brian. "Not as tall as you. Maybe five-ten. About as big, though. 185?"

Brian grinned. "Thanks, but I haven't seen 185 since college. How come you're so good at some details and not those?"

"I read these reports and then look at the bodies to see what kind of traits I can see in them. But we don't guess height and weight. We use tapes and scales. And we do it on people lying down, not standing up!"

Brian nodded. "When you called about a mix-up, I thought you meant the victim, but then I got the report."

The clerk looked puzzled. "I left a message saying I'd *messed up*. I called you as soon as I saw the signatures. The badge numbers matched, but..."

"This guy had a badge?"

"Yeah, and the numbers are the same. It's the signatures that aren't. I had him sign the log before I asked whose personals he wanted."

He spun the clipboard around. The signature on the log sheet was nothing like Ebert's sign-off on the accident report. Then Brian remembered what Elise had said: The guy was reading a *paper*, not a newspaper. Only an accident report would list addresses. And anybody who knew how could get a copy of that. But what about the badge number?

He called the hospital and asked the nurse on Ebert's floor to check her belongings. After a few minutes, she came back on the line. The patient's personal effects bag contained a badge/ID holder but no badge.

Brian called in the theft, explaining the names the holder might use if he ever tried to pass himself off as a cop to an official, then requested an identity artist to work with the clerk to create a visual of the imposter.

Some of the pieces of this puzzle were finally falling together.

❖ ❖ ❖

Bett had intended to make a special sauce for the chicken, but they were both so hungry she broiled it instead. They ate crisp-skin chicken with a tossed salad. And they ate every bit of it.

After dinner she suggested cleaning Maggie's hands.

"Okay, but I don't want to take any codeine."

"You'll need it," Bett countered. "It's been so long since we've done it." She reminded her that the sheriff would be coming. "You said you didn't feel up to driving back tonight, so you're probably vulnerable to pain in a way you might not be ordinarily."

"Vulnerable, huh?"

"Are you so used to thinking of yourself as *in*vulnerable?"

Maggie smiled. "No, darlin'. Just careful." But she finally took a pill, and by the time one hand was completely cleaned and wrapped, she was glad of it. She said as much to Bett, who chided her lightly.

"You have to learn to trust me."

"I suppose. But the last time you made a prediction, it didn't come true."

"When was that?" Bett started cleaning the other hand.

"You said everything would make sense when I woke up."

"I only meant your memory would sort itself out. I never expected what did happen, god knows! But then, I haven't expected anything that's happened since Friday."

"That's when it started for you, huh?"

Bett looked up. "Why? When did it start for you?"

"About two weeks before that," Maggie said softly.

"You mean when we first met?"

"Mmm-hmm."

Bett chose her next question carefully. "Remember when I asked why you hadn't come to the bar the weekend after we'd met?"

Maggie nodded.

"You told me you didn't want to be disappointed, but then you said you weren't disappointed in me. Can you tell me what you meant?"

"No," she said sadly. "I'm not very good with words."

Bett reflected on her own talk-therapy. "I don't think words are the problem. I think you have trouble with feelings. Talking about them especially."

"What's the difference? If I can't, I can't." Maggie shrugged, helplessly, not indifferently.

Bett continued her cleaning. "My therapist once told me that whenever we talk about feelings—a lot of other things, too, but feelings most of all—she says I have all the answers. That anyone else is just guessing."

"Nice idea," Maggie said. "Imagine having all the answers." Then she cocked her head. "Why do you go to a therapist?"

It didn't sound like she was trying to change subjects, but Bett didn't want to lose the direction of their conversation. "I don't mind telling you, but why do you ask?"

"You seem pretty sane." Maggie waggled a hand to indicate the jury was still out on that. "I thought only sick people went to therapy."

"Don't you know? Therapy is California's second-favorite indoor sport!"

"Yeah? That doesn't change my opinion much."

Bett's smile faded. "I started seeing Ellen when we knew my mother didn't have long to live. I was trying to head off my grief."

"Did it work?"

"No, not the way I hoped." She finished drying Maggie's hand and began applying Silvadene. "You can't exactly store up what you need to ease that kind of pain. But Ellen knew me pretty well by the time Mom died. She had sort of a before-and-after picture and knew what all the pieces looked like— where they might fit when we tried to put me back together. I don't know if that makes any sense. I do know I never could've gotten through it without Ellen's help."

"You mean it didn't hurt as much?"

"There's really no way to tell that. But talking with her helps me heal. Like this helps your hands heal."

"Do you just talk about your feelings?"

"No. Sometimes I tell her what I've been doing. Especially if I've been acting out. Once I was going to take a boat to China to work in a women's clinic I'd read about." She laughed at herself, then sobered. "When I quit pre-med, we had to deal with how much that hurt my dad."

"Isn't medicine what you're supposed to do?"

Bett looked at her intently. "You put a lot of faith in that, don't you? That people are good at one thing, and it's just a matter of finding that thing."

"It's usually true," Maggie said. "What will you do without medicine in your life?"

"Oh, I don't know. Maybe I'll learn how to fix cars. Or be a cop. There are all kinds of different ways to earn a living."

Maggie scoffed. "You don't know the first thing about cars, and you'd make a lousy cop. Besides, I'm not talking about earning a living."

"I don't know what I'll do," Bett said softly. Then she made her voice bright again. "Did you always know you wanted to be a mechanic?"

"No. At first all I wanted to do was drive truck."

"But you do. Drive a truck, I mean."

"Anybody can drive *a* truck. Somebody who drives truck, well, that's what they do—long-haul mostly. It's more a way of life. I was going to do that with Scotty, but they wouldn't let us."

"Who wouldn't?"

"The company he drove for. Said we had to be married."

"I don't believe it!" Bett was too astonished to temper her reaction.

"That's how it was," Maggie said simply.

"But we're not talking about the Dark Ages!"

"I hope not. Think how old I'd be then!"

Bett sighed. "Have things really changed so much just in your lifetime?"

"I'm thirty-four, Bett. Not a hundred and thirty-four."

Bett was relieved somehow to finally learn Maggie's age. "And what's your sign?"

Maggie groaned. "I knew it. You are a native Californian, aren't you?" But her eyes were twinkling. "I was born on Memorial Day."

It was Bett's turn to groan. "Your birth *date*, Maggie. Your birthday can't be the last Monday in May every year!"

"Huh-uh. Years ago, before they changed all the holidays, Memorial Day was always the thirtieth of May. The day off used to wander around the calendar just like Christmas. You never knew when it would show up."

Bett laughed at that image, then wondered if it typified Maggie's view of things beyond her control. But that would be impossible to ask about. "Well, that makes you a Gemini and makes us compatible."

Maggie's eyes never dimmed. "Good thing you asked about my sign then, isn't it? Otherwise we'd never know, would we?"

Bett set the pans down and took Maggie's face in her hands, kissing her deeply. She wanted more, but Maggie stopped her.

"I thought you weren't going to do that to me when I was like this?"

"Only if you can't feel it," Bett replied.

When Maggie returned her kiss, Bett felt a stirring deep inside. She sighed. "I wish the sheriff would hurry up and get here."

Maggie drew back. "Why?"

"So I could throw him out and ravish your body." She helped Maggie sit up and picked up the pans again. "Guess I'll keep busy in the meantime."

Maggie was still blushing, but her next question surprised them both. "Would you like to go out with me sometime, Bett? When we get back?"

Bett nearly spilled the water. "Go out? Like on a date? Maggie, I want to marry you!" She laughed at the look that produced. "Of course I'll go out with you. When?"

"Oh, um, how about Saturday?"

"It's a date! Now, how would you like to go out with *me*? Say Friday? And Thursday? And Wednesday? Oh! And Sunday—all day Sunday!"

Maggie chuckled. "Sunday's fine. But I have to stay at the garage the next few days. Get the locks changed and prep for that meeting Friday."

"Stay at the garage?" Bett echoed on her way to the kitchen. "You can't work with your hands bandaged. And why would *you* have to stay? Let Hudson do it. I know your keys got stolen, but it's his garage. Let him worry about it." She heard a snort of laughter, then ticks and chitters sounded madly in her head. She stood with the pans poised over the sink and asked more directly: "You don't mean sleep at the garage, do you?"

"Sure," Maggie spoke up so that Bett could hear her. "When we first bought the place, I lived in the room upstairs where Jack…" The crash of pans in the sink made Maggie jump and rush for the kitchen. "Are you okay? What…?"

Bett's face was white with anger. "We who?" she demanded loudly.

"Me and Matt. The yard was our first joint venture."

"You and Matt…" All the bits and pieces of conversation from the last several days suddenly fell into place: the way Maggie talked to Hudson; the things the sheriff said; her relationship to Matt. She wanted Tracy to go into business with her. Maggie's business. All those men—Hudson, Stony, Jack—worked for *her!* Maggie's mechanics. Each and every one.

"Why?" Bett's eyes blazed with challenge. "Why did you lie to me? You think it's funny that I thought Hudson was your boss? It isn't funny. It's fucking hysterical!"

"I never lied to you." Maggie said firmly.

"You told me you were a mechanic who worked in a garage. That's not the truth. Not when everything's run by you. How many M & M...?" But she already knew the answer to that. She'd counted them herself. There were eight in the East Bay directory alone. She had called nearly all of them. They all knew Maggie. Knew *what* she was. Only Bett hadn't seen the obvious.

Maggie was shaking her head. "That wasn't a lie."

Bett controlled her voice with an effort. "You as much as lied to me! Why didn't you tell me you owned that garage? All those garages?"

"Would it have mattered so much if I had?"

"Of course!" she retorted.

Maggie's eyebrows rose. "Why?"

"Because you're a different person. You're in charge. You're not just some flunky mechanic working for That-Jerk-Hudson!"

Maggie tossed her head in an effort at indifference, but it was still an angry gesture. "Seems to me you're not too pleased either way." She lit a cigarette, shaking the match out with a snap of her wrist. "And by the way, I'm *not* a different person."

Bett started to reply when Gyp scrambled to the door yowling.

Maggie dropped her cigarette in the ashtray and took out her gun as she left the kitchen. Bett followed, but before they got any further, the wail of a siren sounded close by. Sheriff Miller had arrived.

"Don't go, Maggie. We have to talk." Bett watched her flip on the porch light and unbolt the door the same way she'd shaken out the match, with quick, angry motions.

Maggie reached for the doorknob, not turning around. "Don't worry. We will." She went out without another word, closing the door on Bett.

CHAPTER 21.

Consequences

HUGH MILLER COULDN'T FIGURE IT. That afternoon, nothing could keep these two apart. Tonight, it felt colder inside the cabin than out.

Maggie had left him fixing coffee while she went to the main room to get Bett. As he scraped the grounds into the pot, he could hear the tone of their exchange if not their actual words. Just as well he was on duty, he thought. Cribbage tonight would give a whole new meaning to the term cut-throat. He was settling in at the table when Bett entered and put water on to boil. Maggie followed, getting out mugs, then sat across from the sheriff. She asked Bett if she wanted any coffee, but she shook her head, not looking up from her tea preparation.

"The roads iced up again." Miller said. "Looks like you'll be safe enough here tonight."

"*If* they got off the mountain," Maggie said.

"Seems likely," he replied. "I contacted the area hospitals. No reports of gunshot wounds since last weekend."

"They wouldn't go to a hospital," Bett said too loudly. "Hospitals ask questions. About everything. Of course, you can always make excuses for somebody with a head injury!"

"You shot him in the back!" Maggie retorted. "And besides…"

"Hold it, now!" The sheriff saw the looks they were giving each other and was startled by how similar it was to other domestic scenes he'd been called to. He knew how to handle those. "Let's go over that part again. You said he got hit in the upper back?"

Maggie's eyes lost some of their brittleness as she turned to him. "He was hurting pretty bad, but there wasn't any blood on his chest. So I don't think the bullet went all the way through, or I'd have caught it, too. I was right in front of him."

Miller could have told her that .22s don't carry that kind of firepower: They do the most damage ricocheting around inside the body.

Maggie continued. "From the bloodstain on his jacket and the way he was holding his arm, I'd say he got hit in the wing bone."

The sheriff glanced at Bett to see if she agreed, but she didn't seem to be listening. In fact, she looked like she was about to keel over. "You all right, Bett?"

Maggie turned, then got up and crossed the room in a stride. "I'll fix that for you." Her voice was almost too soft to hear. And Bett's reply was muffled as the two of them embraced.

The sheriff looked away, concentrating on filling the coffee mugs slowly. Even so, he finished long before they were done hugging. He cleared his throat.

Maggie shooed Bett to the table and then fetched her tea. "When will you get the report back on that gun?"

"Tomorrow. I'll send Brian a copy, but chances are one-in-a-thousand that it's connected to your friend who got pistol-whipped."

"I put the odds closer to two-to-one. Ebert was hit with a gun, not shot."

Bett looked up in surprise. "Tracy?"

Maggie nodded. "Brian says she'll be okay." She turned back to Hugh. "The younger guy, the one who came through the back door, hit Bett with his hand, not his gun. The other guy tried to hit me with his gun. The one you sent to the lab."

"How do you know he was younger?" Bett asked.

"He wore those fancy, white-seamed jeans. The other guy wore work pants. The kind Sears and Monkey Wards sell. From what the guys at the garage wear, the older guy was forty or fifty; the other guy, maybe in his twenties. He had real skinny legs."

Bett giggled. "You're older than that, and you have skinny legs!"

The sheriff shook his head. Some people had crazy notions. As if you couldn't buy any kind of pants in the world. His report included their earlier descriptions. He wasn't going to put the carbons back in to add that stuff. He asked if they could think of anything else, but neither of them could. He gave them a copy of the report to read and sign, then tucked it inside his jacket and rose. "Hate to leave you with a full pot of coffee, but we're busier than usual with this weather."

"Don't worry. Bett packed along a 'poor man's microwave.'"

"What's that?" he asked Bett.

"I haven't the vaguest idea." She looked at Maggie, who was smiling.

"A thermos bottle, of course."

The sheriff chuckled with Maggie, then saw Bett's eyes lighten. Her gaze stayed on Maggie, and her look changed to one he'd seen that afternoon. It was time for him to go.

Maggie accompanied him to the edge of the porch. Gyp went along, always ready to mark the yard.

"You two okay?" Miller asked cautiously. "When I first got here you, uh, seemed to be having a little trouble?" She ducked her head, and he guessed at the source of their spat. "Listen, if it's about staying up here or going to town, I can take the dog for the night."

She shook her head. "We'll be fine here. Thanks, Hugh. It's something else entirely."

"You sure? Bett looked pretty upset about shooting that guy."

"Well, you know that saying about having been around the block? Might be her first time on this street."

"Oh? And you've been down it before?"

She smiled. "Nah. Just taken a few licks." Then she shook her head. "Sears Pants was mad. I've seen guys angry like that before, for no good reason. I don't know what he was mad about, but not everybody's as understanding as you and Matt about my— what do they call it in the Sunday magazines—my lifestyle? Matt's only the second guy I ever met who didn't take it personally. Some guys get mad about people like me and Bett. Berger was torqued like that. Guess he saw something between us."

"And he was still fuming about it today," Hugh added.

She shrugged. "He saw those two flatlanders without their masks, though. If they are the same guys, he should be able to give you a description."

"I thought of that, but he went to Sacramento to testify this afternoon." He looked at Maggie closely. "You don't think he's in on this?"

"No. He's the kind who gets bent out of shape when the world doesn't turn his way. Bett probably didn't help by telling him to bugger off, but I don't think he'd go to anybody else to get back at her."

The sheriff nodded even as he considered her remarks about angry men. He thought about all the ways he'd seen her and Bett in the last few days. "I suppose you two have the same problems as…"

Maggie smiled a little. "Just like real people!" She dismissed his gaffe with a shrug that turned into a shiver.

"You better get inside. It's a mite warmer in there now."

Her smile faded. "We'll see." She brushed his shoulder lightly. "You've been a real friend through all this, Hugh. Thanks."

He touched his hat to her and was thoughtful as he got to his car. He was sure they'd be okay. After all, they were just two people who cared for each other. He knew that much. He just shook his head over the rest.

❖ ❖ ❖

Tracy dozed fitfully all day Tuesday. The nurses stopped their hourly waking regimen by mid-morning, letting her sleep. Around seven a doctor came in to change her dressing and tell her the stitches could be removed in five days. Tracy pointed to the IV in the back of her hand, then to her neck collar, asking if they could be removed. The IV didn't bother her as much as the collar. She would've paid money to be able to shake the kinks out of her neck, but the brace prevented that.

"Maybe tomorrow," he said. "Where does it hurt?"

She outlined her cheekbone.

"Not higher?" He touched her temple lightly.

She thought a moment, then gestured negatively.

He wrote on her chart and told her to rest. Half an hour later, Kessler arrived. He was equally firm.

"Doctor says you can't come back to work until you're free of headaches for at least forty-eight hours." He saw her scowl. "Relax. You'll feel better soon. Think of it as a long weekend."

"Doan' may' me laugh," she retorted. "You fin' Maggie?"

He nodded. "She'll probably be in to see you tomorrow night."

"Check ow' a.m.," she explained in her new, short-word language.

"They're going to want you to stay for observation."

She offered a one-finger gesture at that.

Brian shrugged. "You can always sign yourself out, but you're in a lot of pain. You'll be better off here."

She closed her eyes. She wasn't better off anywhere anymore. She meant to ask if he'd followed up on the break-in at Bett's place, but Kessler was gone. Jim Harley was there instead, looking completely miserable.

"Na' so bad." She asked about work. An easier subject.

He juggled her words briefly, filling in the missing sounds. "Oh! Had today off. I'll ride with Weigert tomorrow."

She pointed at him, then gripped an imaginary steering wheel.

Harley grinned. "Yeah, I drive all the time now. Once was enough to learn that." He told her about his first night with Weigert, who insisted on driving in a downpour with the wipers set on double-time and only their parking lights on. "We drove the whole tour that way. Weigert kept saying 'We're practically invisible!'"

Tracy laughed, then grimaced with pain. Harley started to apologize, but she pointed at her leg. "Sh' be' here when I ga' sha'! Coulda' use a laugh."

After a few more minutes, he left, saying he'd be back in the morning.

Tracy pulled the cord to change the reading light to indirect fluorescent, then closed her eyes and lay still, making minute adjustments to find a comfortable position for her jaw. But the pain just traveled on different angles, radiating from her cheek like energy. They said all they could give her for twenty-four hours was Tylenol. Plain, decaffeinated Tylenol. Jesus Effen Jesus.

She lay motionless, trying to blank out the pain, but knew she wouldn't sleep without some relief from the throbbing. Eyes closed, she reached for the call button.

Instead of plastic, she touched a hand.

In a split second, she gauged her danger, then pulled the hand toward her, twisting it up hard. She opened her eyes. "Elise!"

"And here I thought I had the wrong room!" Elise tried to sound nonchalant even as she held her wrist protectively. "Uh, Tracy…?"

"Wha' you here?" Tracy demanded. She saw shock cross Elise's face.

Then Elise reached out to her. Tracy turned away instinctively, striking the bandaged side of her face. Sudden pain made her cry out, and for a long minute, she couldn't move. When she did turn back, it was only to see the door closing. Elise had left.

She was almost in too much pain to care. But she did care. How did Elise even know she was in the hospital? And where had she gone? Ebert fought tears driven more by emotional confusion than pain. She never wanted anybody to see her when she was hurt. Especially not Elise. Jesus, her cheek hurt. Why had she moved like that?

She gritted her teeth against the ache, but that only made it worse. She pressed the call button, and a nurse came through the door in an instant. Tracy couldn't believe her response time. The nurse checked her over, same as always, then added something to her IV bag.

"This is your last visit tonight," the nurse said. "We won't be waking you every hour like last night, but we still can't give you a sleeping pill. Try to relax and sleep."

Tracy closed her eyes. Give me a break. She wondered how long it really was until 6 a.m. A brief shift in Eternity, maybe.

"Honey…?"

Tracy looked to the foot of the bed. Even with indirect light, Elise's eyes were remarkable. "Wha' you here?"

"Would you…? Do you want me to go?"

Tracy shook her head, then struggled against sudden fuzziness. Everything seemed so slow. And why did Elise sound so hesitant? Tracy had thought about her all day, remembering their time together clearly. Elise's aggressive certitude was what made her so attractive, even before they made love. Tracy knew her airheadedness was an act. Elise noticed everything. There was never a way to hide from her.

Elise pulled a chair over. They were on the same level now. Tracy saw her own pain reflected in Elise's eyes and started to turn away, but Elise dropped her gaze and took her hand, stroking it gently.

"Don't, honey. You'll hurt yourself again."

Tracy grasped her hand firmly.

Elise looked at her, not revealing any sympathy now. "I should know better than to sneak up on a sleeping cop, or a wounded one. My aunt and uncle live near a wildlife refuge. They always warned us when we went on hikes that a wounded animal of any size was the most dangerous. More dangerous than a healthy bear, even a hungry one."

"Tha' me? Wounded an'mal?" Tracy didn't hurt at all anymore. It was wonderful. She was floating with Elise's strokes.

"Of course," Elise replied.

Tracy absorbed that, then pointed at her bandage. "'Cuz of this?"

Elise nodded. "That's the wounded part. But you're an animal, through and through. That's one of the things that attracted me to you."

Tracy's eyes narrowed. "Wha' kind?"

"Oh, I don't know. Probably a cat of some sort, but not a domestic one. A primitive animal. All cops are primitives." Elise tightened her hold. "I'm not putting you down. Just telling you what I think."

Tracy's eyes flashed. "I think, too!" Pain stirred in her jaw as she spit out those words. She softened her enunciation. "Na' an'mal!"

"You don't know much about them, do you? Animals think. All of them do. They just think about the world differently from the way we do; like you think about the streets differently from civvies." When Tracy didn't say anything, Elise continued. "Don't cops mostly have cop-friends?"

Tracy cocked her head as much as the neck brace allowed.

"Do you have cop-friends?"

Tracy nodded. "Par'ner." Then she thought about Kessler. He'd invited her to a cookout at his house once when she was still a rookie. BS Time. She hadn't gone. It didn't seem right somehow. Since then, AS Time, he'd been careful of her. Never too much pressure, but no kid gloves either. Just an underlying assumption that she'd work it all out. "'N Sarge."

"And what about non-cops? Besides me. Any friends who aren't cops?"

Tracy held up a finger in reply.

"A lover?" Elise's casual tone almost hid her interest. But not quite.

If Tracy could have laughed without pain, she would have. Instead she imitated Elise's pseudo-indifference: "Na' a lover," she piped.

"Good!" Elise laughed at her mimicry. "And does your friend see the same things you do on the streets? Take the same precautions?"

Tracy shook her head slightly. She'd tried to warn Maggie, telling her about free-way scams being pulled every day. But Maggie just kept looking for trouble; stopping to help breakdowns whenever she found them.

"And what about victims?" Elise asked. "Do they ever know what hit them? Of course not! Most people don't know they live in a jungle. They think they're safe. You're a guardian. You have to see things differently. That's why your eyes are always alert. That's how I knew you were a cop."

Tracy reached over and lightly massaged Elise's wrist.

"It's okay," Elise said. "I should've known you wouldn't feel safe here. You were sleeping when I came to see you this afternoon, and I…"

"Din' wake me?" Tracy was surprised she'd been there before.

"No. You need your rest, like the nurse said." She smiled. "I want you to get well. I have plans for you!" Then she leaned over to whisper some of those plans.

Tracy drank in her hushed erotica, eyes closed, for as long as she could stand to listen and not act. Elise's words were a heat lamp; their warmth washed through her, relaxing her completely, even her jaw. She wanted to respond more, but all she could manage was to put a finger to Elise's lips. "Promise?"

"Would I lie to a cop?" Elise kissed her eyes closed. "Sleep well, lover. I'll be back tomorrow."

That night Tracy slept without any trouble at all.

⋄ ⋄ ⋄

Bett was at the stereo when Maggie came in with a load of wood. As she watched her stack it on the hearth and adjust the fire, Bett wondered if compatibility was enough. She knew now that she'd overreacted to learning the truth about Maggie's role at M & M. It seemed so obvious in hindsight.

She relived the moment of pulling the trigger, then closed her eyes. The thought of living without Maggie made her heart ache, but the realization that she could have killed her was even worse.

Just then one song ended and piano music introduced Cris Williamson's strong voice singing "Sweet Woman." It gave Bett the courage she needed to go to Maggie and put her arms around her, resting her chin on her head.

"That's nice," Maggie said, relaxing into Bett's embrace.

"Mmm-hmm, it's one of my favorite songs."

Maggie laughed softly and turned. "I suppose someday we'll both be talking about the same thing."

Bett answered simply: She closed her eyes and kissed her. A long moment later, she asked, "Are we talking about the same thing now?"

"Oh, I think so." Maggie kissed her again.

This time Bett broke their kiss. "I'm sorry I yelled at you. I thought you'd set me up. Not told me about M & M for a joke. It made me feel stupid."

"Not stupid!"

Bett drew back at her tone. "Okay then, dumb. I just didn't know."

"Guess we were talking about different things all along," Maggie said more reasonably, "and neither of us knew it."

"Why didn't you just tell me you owned M & M?"

"I thought you knew. Remember that first day on the ridge when I told you Matt's advice about never volunteering anything?"

Bett recalled Maggie's outburst: "At least she wasn't screwing the boss!" She looked up with new awareness. "No wonder you were so mad about that woman. *You're* the boss! You thought I knew that?"

"Well, yeah. Otherwise you'd have thought I was crazy, storming off like I did."

Bett sighed. "I hardly know what to think about you sometimes!" She reached out as Maggie turned away. "Let's start with something easier. What did Brian tell you?"

Maggie gave her his theory that all the events were connected to Scotty's death. They just didn't know how or why yet.

"What if it isn't connected to Scotty?"

Maggie cocked her head. "Then it's a lot of coincidence."

"I'm not saying it's all unrelated. But couldn't these guys be after you?"

"Why me?"

"I'm not sure. A lot of things don't make sense. Scotty was killed Friday night, but that was more than twenty-four hours before those guys tailed us up here. Why the delay?"

"I don't know. But I don't know what I could have that they'd want. We both know it wasn't money."

"Some kind of papers," Bett mused.

"Matt's papers are all here. I checked the secretary myself."

"I know, but the burglars didn't find the stereo, did they? That was closed when you came in, wasn't it?"

Maggie nodded.

"And you said Matt was secretive. Maybe the guy who built that cabinet put in another hiding place for him. He'd tell you, wouldn't he?"

Maggie nodded again, remembering Matt's will.

"Besides, what could Scotty have that was so valuable? He didn't look rich when I met him. Nobody would rub him out..." She saw a flicker of pain cross Maggie's face. "Sorry. I've been talking to Elise. She uses words like that all the time."

Maggie half-smiled. "Ebert, too. That's another mystery. I don't know what she was doing at my place when it was robbed. She hasn't stopped by in more than a year. It sure made Brian suspicious."

"About what?"

"He wanted to know if she was gay. That isn't like him. He kids me a lot, but he was really serious about her."

"Was that when you told him it was none of his business?"

"Yeah, but it didn't help. Brian said that was as good as 'yes' to him. Stuff like that really burns me up. No wonder she never told him."

"Will he hold it against her professionally?"

"He won't, no. But he doesn't know how worried she is about getting hassled. She even went out with a lieutenant one time so the other cops wouldn't think she was gay."

"That's obscene!"

"She only went to a movie with the guy, Bett."

"Still, nobody should have to do that. I suppose he came on to her, too."

"We never talked about it. She stopped coming around after that."

"Why? What *did* happen between you two?"

"She thought she'd do me a favor and check on somebody we hired."

When Maggie paused, Bett asked: "Want to tell me about it?"

She shrugged. "Tracy found out one of the guys did time for drugs."

"Before they changed the marijuana laws?"

"No, it was hard drugs. His wife was in a lot of pain. Dying. The doctors said they couldn't give her anything more for the pain. He was going to try to relieve it himself. He knew it was wrong, but he couldn't stand to see her like that. He didn't know he was buying from an undercover."

"That's horrible!"

"Yeah, it was. They let him out for the funeral. He said he didn't know if that made him more bitter or less. I couldn't say, either. All I know is he's an s.o.b., but I've never met one since without wondering if there was a reason for it." She shook her head. "As for it being related to me or Matt... Nobody ever found trouble like Scotty. I thought maybe you or I had seen something we shouldn't have. But if that was it, those guys would've killed us today for sure."

"Please don't talk like that," Bett implored.

"Sorry." Maggie leaned against the couch. "Brian said your footprint idea was how they made the initial ID, but they need to confirm it with X-rays. I forgot about Scotty breaking his leg."

"You said something about 'walking on logs.' Was he a lumberjack?"

Maggie smiled wryly. "No, he wasn't big enough. He used to say it takes two hod carriers and a moron to make a lumberjack!"

"But he worked in a logging camp?"

"Yeah. He walked the logs, sweeping them with a metal detector. They use them in Oregon to find nails or bullets in felled trees. He said they'd dig out hundreds of them from hunting season. But I don't think that's how he got his leg broken."

"Why?"

"I think he was in another kind of trouble. He called from the hospital and asked me to come and get him. When I got there, he gave me the keys to a real flashy car. Said he won it in a poker game. He had more money than he knew what to do with that time. That was always his problem. No matter how much he had, he'd never have enough."

"Was he lucky at cards?"

"Not so much lucky as fast. Guess he wasn't fast enough that time."

"You mean he cheated?" Bett found it hard to believe that Maggie would hang around somebody she knew was a cheat.

"Probably. He had kind of a blind spot. Thought he was entitled to things because he was so much smarter than everybody else. He might've straightened out if he'd gone to college. Met other people as smart as he was, but he never had the advantages I did."

"I didn't know you went to college."

"Oh, I didn't. I'm not that kind. Besides, I knew what I was supposed to do by then."

"Wait a minute. What do you mean 'not that kind'? And lots of people who know what they want to do go to college. I did."

"I know. You're head-smart, like Scotty. He only ever wanted to be rich."

"I don't think they give degrees in that," Bett said lightly.

Maggie smiled. "I used to think if he'd gone to college he'd have found people who read books and understand them. Maybe money wouldn't have been so almighty to him then."

Bett thought that was a bit idealistic, but she pursued the subject another way. "What kind of smart are you?"

"Hand-smart. I think about things, too, but it's stuff that's already done. I don't imagine things. I'm good with my hands."

Bett raised her eyebrows. "I'll go along with that. But you have a brain, Maggie. You're not stupid."

"I know it." She turned away. "I know where I belong, too."

"Where do you think you belong?"

"In a garage. Teaching little billies. Showing other guys how to fix cars and make a living at it."

"Honey, please. You're not a guy. You're not one of the guys, either!" When she didn't reply, Bett reached out to her. "You use that expression quite a lot, you know."

Maggie turned back. "It sounds better than *flunky mechanic.*"

Bett felt like she'd been slapped. Worse than that, she felt she deserved it. "I'm sorry. Really I am. I know how important M & M is to you. Will you ever forgive me for saying that?"

Maggie tossed her head. "Sorry. It's just that I used to think I was stupid because that's what they told me. I learned it wasn't true, but a lot of little billies get told they're stupid. It takes forever to undo that part of them."

Bett was incredulous. "Who said you were stupid?"

"Doesn't matter." She stood abruptly. "It was a long time ago. I'm going for coffee. You want anything?"

Bett rose with her and hugged her to keep her from leaving. "Will you ever forgive me?"

Maggie relaxed then. "There's nothing to forgive, darlin'. Besides, I'm the one who should apologize. I guess your dad was right, and this trouble with my hands is making me edgy."

Bett drew back to look up at her. "Are they hurting?"

"No. They just tingle a little once in a while."

"I think that's a good sign. But maybe we should stop at my dad's tomorrow and have him look at them."

"Okay. Now let's put the kitchen to rights so we can get an early start. I'll do dishes if you'll thermos the coffee."

"Sure. But Maggie, it's not my 'poor man's microwave'!"

That made her grin. "Well, whose is it then? I found it in a blue knapsack on your side of the cab Sunday morning." She retrieved the bag from a cabinet in the kitchen. "It sure looks familiar."

Bett thought so, too, but couldn't say why just then.

"One of the little billies probably left it in the cab," Maggie suggested. She handed the bag to Bett and set the thermos in the sink, running hot water into it.

Bett examined the knapsack and found the two cassette tapes inside. "You sure these aren't yours? *Nashville's Greatest Hits, Volumes I and II.* They sure sound like tapes you'd own." She saw water overflowing the thermos and went to turn it off. "Uh-oh! It's leaking."

Murky water was indeed dribbling from the base of the thermos. "Liner's probably busted," Maggie said. She shook it, expecting the sound of tinkling glass. But all she heard was the slosh of water. She twisted the top, but her bandages kept her from gripping it tightly enough.

Bett took it from her, imitating her maneuver. "Can you fix it?"

"If the liner's just slipped off the base, we can."

The retainer finally released, and Bett unscrewed it. "Now what?"

The silver liner Maggie expected to see extending from the metal sleeve wasn't there. "Just dump it, I guess. It doesn't look like... Jesus H. Christ!"

Bett felt the small hairs on the back of her neck bristle as four tightly wrapped, soaking wet bundles of money rolled into the sink.

CHAPTER 22.

All the Gold in California

MAGGIE KNEW IT WAS SCOTTY'S. It had his touch: bundles of twenty-dollar bills, random serial numbers, all untraceable.

"Where did it come from?" Bett asked in awe.

"I don't know. A scam of some sort."

"Remember what Scotty said that night about income tax?"

Maggie shook her head. "Not that. Inventory tax. Could be connected, though. Some kind of payoff for illegal goods stored in Nevada."

"What should we do with it?"

"Just put it in the knapsack, I guess."

"Don't you want to know how much it is?"

Maggie smiled at her fascination. "We can dry it in front of the fire."

"There must be a million dollars here!" Bett laid the bills on the oven racks at the hearth, mesmerized by the spread of green-gray ink.

Maggie smiled. "You know how much a million is?"

"No. Not really."

"Neither did I when Matt and I first started. I'll tell you that story, but only if you promise to listen all the way through!"

"Does it have a happy ending?"

"Sure!" She leaned against the couch. "Matt wanted to just put up the money and hire me to run the place for him. But I said a partnership would be better. He didn't know anything about cars, and even if I couldn't bring any money to the table, I had the know-how.

"We started out renting a hole-in-the-wall with a couple pumps, then sold repair contracts to any place big enough to have wheels and too small to do their own work. We'd do upkeep—tune-ups, oil and lube, tire repair—for a flat rate, then got first bid on any bigger jobs that came along. We built our supply contacts and credit line as our customer base grew."

She reflected on those days—months on end without respite. Scheduling their customer needs *and* hers. It hadn't taken Matt long to learn the sales end of things. She'd had to slow him down to keep him from overselling their abilities. It was only her abilities then.

"We agreed to take another look at things when sales topped a quarter million dollars. Decide whether to get a more permanent place or hire help. That was our first marker, anyhow. After we set it, I didn't think about it much. I was pretty sure it was years away. We'd only been open a couple years when I picked him up from a late flight at SFO. I told him the Tyler contract had come in. It was one he'd been trying to land for months.

"He let out a whoop and slapped his hands together. 'That does it, doll!' he said. He was more excited than I expected. I asked what the big deal was. He said, 'That puts us over the quarter-mil mark!'

"I thought he'd been drinking. He couldn't have been, of course, but I'd just looked at the books. 'Nah,' I said. 'No more than two hundred and fifty thousand.' He laughed so hard, I thought he was going to hurt himself."

Bett smiled, but only a little. "And what did you teach him?"

Maggie glanced at her, then began gathering dry bills from the rack. "Oh, different things. We had to get the money business squared away first. He had a funny idea about cars and people who fix them. He laughed when I told him I was a mechanic." She sensed Bett's discomfort but kept on. "He said, 'We live in the Bic Age, the throwaway era.'"

"Did he feel that way about hundred-dollar bills, too?" Bett asked. "What happened to that? Is this the same story?"

"It is, sort of. And no, he didn't feel that way about money. I told him I'd used it to light my girlfriend's cigarette. He kept saying, 'You *burned* it!'"

Bett laughed. "Did you really?"

"No, but I didn't tell him that. He kept spluttering about 'wasting good money.' I told him he'd done that when he tore it up. I said I didn't like being insulted, and he couldn't buy me."

Bett looked at her with new respect. "You knew he was trying to?"

"Sure. Scotty warned me about people with money. I'd been around the block by then. I didn't know much before I ran away…"

Bett put more wet bills on the racks, letting the silence provide some space. "I suppose you're right, and I only listen to half your stories. But sometimes you only tell half a story." She looked up then. "Is that what you meant when you said you left Lange?"

"I suppose you want to hear about that." Maggie didn't know how to talk about seeing Lange for the last time. But she finally did. She knew enough about herself to make it a story. The words came out of her mouth, but she was just the messenger. She kept her feelings wrapped as tightly as the bandages on her hands. And it wasn't until she got to the end that she looked at Bett.

"Don't cry, darlin'."

Bett opened her eyes, unaware that she had been.

Maggie brushed her cheeks. "I knew there was a good reason not to tell you that story."

Bett kissed her fingertips. "You're supposed to cry at the sad parts."

"Is that how it works?" Maggie's smile was thin.

"Yes!" Bett hugged her. "Now tell me where you went when you left. I want to hear all about your adventures."

Maggie shook her head wryly. "Scotty always said I was too naive to be on the road with hippies. He hated them. Said they were all middle-class brats pretending to be poor, feeling sorry for themselves because their parents didn't understand them. After they'd been on the road a while, they'd get tired of being dirty and cold and go home. They all had homes to go to, Scotty said. They weren't like us at all.

"But some of them came from broken homes. Their parents were divorced. I thought they were helpless. Scotty said 'hopeless' was more like it. Kids with divorced parents just got twice as many goodies. He told me about one who got a guitar just for passing geometry. 'Not for getting straight A's, but for *not* getting an F! A Gibson's worth three hundred bucks! We could go all the way to Australia on that much!' Scotty always thought about money. He asked if I remembered a kid from the orphanage called Little Billy." She looked at Bett then. "You know who John-John Kennedy is?"

"President Kennedy's son? Sure. I read he's in college Back East."

"Maybe John Kennedy, Jr., is, but the kid I mean is still standing on Pennsylvania Avenue saluting a riderless horse."

Bett nodded. "I've seen that picture. It's the same guy. What about him?"

"Well, Little Billy had a dream and woke up all excited. He said there was a mix-up at the hospital and that he was really John-John Kennedy."

"Oh, no!"

"Yeah. We tried to explain about the age difference and everything, but it didn't matter to Little Billy that he was seven and John-John was only two or three. He figured if they could send him home with the wrong family, they could've done it early or late. Scotty said that was the difference between us and hippies: 'We're Little Billy, and they're John-John Kennedy. Don't ever forget it. They could buy and sell you with a phone call!' He told me I should help any Little Billies I find, but anybody who volunteers to be poor is really John-John in disguise."

Bett asked if Little Billy had ever gotten over his dream.

"Oh, sure. He's married now. Has two boys and a girl. Didn't name any of them John-John. He tells that story on himself now. He used to, anyway. I haven't seen him in a while."

"Do you keep in touch with many of those kids?"

"Not so much. Scotty always thought I was crazy to."

"Why?"

"Well, at first I was trying to find out why I'd gone back to the orphanage after it had been torn down. Scotty told me I'd set it up with the kids to meet there the first Sunday of every month, out by the back fence where nobody could see us. He said all the kids looked forward to those days, even if they couldn't sneak away every time."

"Why did they have to sneak?"

"Nobody would've let us meet like that. We were like family, but they didn't see it that way." Maggie paused, struck by how angry she still was after so many years.

"So, what did you do on those days?"

"Oh, I suppose we'd talk about our new families. That's what we talked about when we lived together: places we'd lived, or wanted to. Or we'd take a bus to the zoo or go to a park."

"But you were only twelve or thirteen when they found you. No more than a little kid yourself. How could you do all those things?"

"Never little," Maggie said softly. "People always thought I was older. I looked it and acted it. Most of the time it worked to my advantage."

"When was it ever a *dis*advantage?"

"School mostly." Tightness gripped Maggie's voice again.

"What happened there?"

She shook her head. "I don't know for sure. I suppose it was my fault for saying I'd been in school for a long time; kindergarten seemed like a long time to me. I said I was six, but they put me in third grade to start."

"How could they do that? Didn't the orphanage have your records?"

"Not yet. I was living with Gram then. She was sick when school started, so I went alone. It was a different school, and I guess they sort of 'sized me up.' I could read a little and knew numbers up to ten or so." She waved a hand. "It doesn't matter anymore."

Bett knew it did. "Were they the ones who thought you were stupid?"

"They don't call it that in the school records, but 'slow' was a favorite." She tossed her head. "I didn't stay in that grade long. My gram died a little while later. Eventually things got squared away. All but the records. Seems those never change."

Bett knew she was still missing important information. "Maggie, do you remember your parents at all?"

"Sure." She looked up. "You like ancient history, or what?"

Bett smiled. "I like you. And your past makes your present. Don't you know that?"

She laughed. "Not really. You get over a lot of things with time." As if to prove that, she told the story of her parents' deaths with little hesitation.

Despite the ease of her telling, tears filled Bett's eyes. She wouldn't let Maggie brush them aside this time. "I know what it's like to lose a parent. And you lost both of yours!"

Maggie held her. "Ah, darlin'! You were older. Wiser in a sad sort of way. I was only three. I barely knew what happened. Everyday's a brand new day when you're that age."

"But if you remember them...?"

"Shhh. I remember them like pictures in an album. Or how you remember your grandmother. I didn't see my dad much, since he was in the service." She drew a line where her eyebrows used to be. "I got these from him. I always wanted his curly, black hair, too, but I got the red from my mom." She smiled distantly. "She was the most beautiful woman in the world to me. I can still see her. In my head, I mean. She must've loved me a lot for that to be true. But I guess I was all she had, what with my dad gone off to war." She looked at Bett. "Don't feel sorry for me. I got more love in those first three years than most kids get in a lifetime. I didn't even go into an orphanage right away."

"Did you hate it when you did?"

"Not really. I didn't like living with Gram much. She cried all the time. I understand now, of course. My mom was her daughter. Back then it seemed like all she ever did was hug me and wail, 'You poor little thing!' I think I'm six inches taller than I was supposed to be just so nobody would ever call me 'little' again."

Bett sighed. "How did you ever get to be so sanguine?"

Maggie's brow furrowed. "I thought you said I was a Gemini?"

Bett laughed, then drew Maggie close, kissing her smile until it disappeared in response. "You're absolutely amazing. Do you know that?"

Maggie shook her head.

"You are! You've been through hell and come out making jokes about the heat!"

"You take the cards you get dealt, that's all. I was lucky."

"*Lucky?*"

"Sure. Bud gave me all his tools when he retired. Matt and I went into business before prices went crazy. I've been helping out little billies as I find them. What more…?" Her gaze fell on the rack of money.

Bett hugged her. "Don't be so hard on yourself. You did all you could to save him. And nearly got killed in the process. There are limits, Maggie."

"That's what Scotty said about me losing my memory before. He said I had to make my own rules; orphans couldn't live by anybody else's."

"Are rules and limits the same thing?"

"Pretty much. The result's the same when you break them." She grew thoughtful again. "I always thought I'd lost my memory because I'd broken too many rules. Scotty said we'd been meeting behind the orphanage for about a year when the condemnation notices went up. I didn't show up for a couple months in a row, and the kids decided I'd quit coming because of the signs. Scotty knew I wouldn't let that stop me. He figured I got there right after the building had been torn down. And… I just shut down, too." She paused. "Scotty said I always felt too much. That I'd lost my memory to keep from feeling anything. He said I shouldn't try to remember. I should just let the social workers and the shrinks argue their theories. I was better off leaving it alone."

"Did you ever tell… anybody about it?" Bett asked.

Maggie nodded. "I told Matt. I had to tell him why I kept calling all the new guys little billy." Then she smiled. "You and Matt are a lot alike."

Bett rolled her eyes. "Every tick and mouse in my head is now sounding off! How could Matt Graf and I be alike!?!"

"With all your questions, of course." Then she asked: "What did you say about your head?"

Bett explained her internal noises, expecting Maggie to laugh. Everyone else said her logic sounds were hysterical. But she took them seriously.

"That's terrific! How do you get it? From meditating?"

Bett shook her head. "You don't get it from anything. I think it's a congenital defect. I've had it forever. All my life I've tried to get rid of it."

"But why? It'd be so helpful. Like a built-in lie detector!"

Bett smiled. "I wish you could see yourself. You look like a six year old on Christmas morn... Oh, no! Don't close up like that!" Bett hugged her. "You can't run away from me, Maggie. I'll just follow you. Don't you believe me when I say I love you? That I always have? Always will? Whether you're thirty or forty, or six or sixty!" She felt Maggie relax. "I love your special looks of shy delight. As if you taste an idea before you dare accept it. You are an absolute wonder!"

Maggie sighed. "I wish I had your gift for words, darlin'."

"What would you say if you did?"

Her focus grew distant. "A long time ago, Scotty told me he wouldn't be happy until he had enough money. When I asked what he'd do if he had all the money in the world, he gave me a sidelong look and said, 'Anything I want to! Some of it twice!'"

Maggie knew that was how she thought of words: as if there weren't enough in the world to say how she felt. She would never own them the way some people did. She could only borrow them, like books from a library. But the words, like her feelings, would come due before she could understand them all. She'd drop them in a night slot, like books unread. Some books were just too hard to understand. Like her feelings, they took her places she couldn't afford to go.

Still, the feelings would return. The nameless longing to *be with* would flare within her every few months. She'd find herself taking a bath early on a Friday night, dressing in the same old new clothes she always wore to go out. Sometimes she went to the Fox because of a woman she'd seen.

It didn't happen with every woman who came into the shop, but occasionally she'd notice one in the office, standing at ease, weight on one hip, like women do. Or she'd watch a woman put manicured fingers to the back of her neck, sweeping the hair clear of her collar. Such a feminine gesture.

Maggie would turn away, concentrating on whatever part she held in her hand, reminding herself that this was something she could depend on. Its shape and function would stay the same. If it stopped working, she could fix it; repair it or replace it. But sometimes she wanted to hold something softer. Something with a little give to it. And she wasn't thinking of a fan belt.

She never went to the Fox expecting to meet someone. Mostly she just went to be there. To witness the wealth of emotion being spent by women who were like her in some ways. It was amazing how good that made her feel. How richly satisfying it was to

233

be among those women, to look fully into their faces. She couldn't expect Bett to understand that. She didn't understand it herself. And she couldn't explain it anymore than she could explain why she hadn't gone back the weekend after meeting Bett.

Bett had been too good to be true. Maggie knew that; knew she was in over her head with their first kiss. Not because she hadn't connected for a long time. Sometimes six months or a year would go by without meeting someone. But even such intermittent experiences hadn't affected her the way Bett had. She'd never met anyone so eager, so delicate and passionate at the same time. When they made love that first night, it was nothing like her previous encounters. She wanted to be so careful, but Bett's response made her throw caution away. It was frightening to find how easy it was to lose control. Then Bett made love to her, as if she knew her through and through. As if she had been saying: "Touch me here… again… and there…" But she hadn't opened her mouth, except to taste Bett.

No, she knew she couldn't stay that night. And she knew better than to go back the next week. What she'd told Bett was partly true: She would have been disappointed if Bett hadn't been there. But the rest of the reason was: What if she *had* been there? They could never repeat that first night. Things didn't work that way.

She smiled, then shook her head. She didn't know what to think. Matt always said she didn't have enough imagination.

"Where have you been?" Bett asked softly.

She looked up. "Thinking about you. And Matt."

Bett smiled. "Never shake your head when you think about me. Just keep nodding. Saying yes. And what about Matt?"

"Oh, he'd get me thinking about things. Talking about myself. He'd ask a question, then not say anything. Just wait 'til I got things sorted out inside."

"He must have loved you very much," Bett said.

Maggie nodded. "That's what Mary Jo said—Brian's wife. Funny how she understood Matt when I didn't. And I understood Brian when she didn't."

"Brian Kessler? He's one of the most straightforward men I've ever met! What's to understand?"

She shrugged. "I think he was jealous of Matt. He never liked him. Not from the first time they met. Mary Jo was embarrassed by the way he acted around that. Until I told her I was gay."

"Wait. Did I miss something? You told Brian's *wife* you were gay?"

She nodded.

"Why? Hadn't he told her?"

"Oh, no. I was pretty sure he didn't know. That was another reason I told her. So she could tell him."

"Why didn't Brian know? How long had you known each other?"

"A couple years, I guess. I'd known Mary Jo that long, too."

"But if you'd known him that long…!" Bett couldn't imagine knowing anyone a week without telling the person she was gay.

234

"Time doesn't matter. And the men I know don't suspect it. Most of them seem pretty surprised when I say something."

"Do you talk about it with many men?"

"Not so much. I did when I was trying to, um, figure things out." She smiled. "But they didn't know any more than I did, so I sort of gave up."

"Which, um, *things* were you trying to figure out?"

"Oh, you know. Me. The world. Liking women."

"You aren't serious! What did you think they'd know?"

Maggie's brow furrowed. "I never know what other people know. That's why I ask questions. To find out."

Bett shook her head. "You aren't going to tell me you've never talked to another gay woman about that, are you?"

She lit a cigarette. "I wouldn't tell you that."

"But you have, haven't you?"

"Asked them about being gay? Why bother? It'd be like asking somebody why they're left-handed."

"That's not my point. There are hundreds of theories…"

"Theory never helped much," Maggie said shortly. "And I was trying to figure out more than that."

Her tone made Bett pause. "Was that why you went to bed with men?"

"Partly. Thought I'd try it out. But it was sort of like motorcycles." She looked up. "I don't suppose that makes much sense to you, does it?"

Bett shook her head.

"Well, going to bed with a man is like riding a motorcycle. You might ride the same roads, but it isn't exactly… Darlin'? Are you all right?"

But Bett was laughing too hard to answer. If she hadn't been on the floor already, she would have fallen there. Maggie didn't know why she found that so funny, since she'd probably never ridden a motorcycle *or* gone to bed with a man.

"You are too incredible," Bett finally said. "Can I tell Ellen that story?"

Maggie didn't exactly think of it as a story. "If you want to. Are you going to say anything else about, um, me?"

"I'm going to bore her to death about you!" She saw Maggie blush. "Is there something particular you want me to mention? How *did* you figure yourself out. Did you go to therapy?"

"Not since I was in the hospital." She shrugged. "There's not much to figure. I'm really a simple sort of person. You just think I'm complicated."

Bett sighed. "Have I ever told you how incredible you are?"

She grinned. "Not more than once or twice in the last thirty seconds. Now, do you want to make a bet… Sorry." Maggie reddened instantly. "I mean: Do you want to guess how much money we've got here?"

Bett cocked her head. "Don't apologize. It's just a pun."

"No! It's… wrong somehow. Like queer duck. It's… crude." Maggie was relieved to have found the right word.

Bett smiled. "Not if you say it right. Then it's wonderfully suggestive… You're blushing again. What's wrong? Don't you think about 'making a Bett'? 'Laying a Bett'? Don't you think about making love with me? Ever?"

"You aren't going to talk about it, are you?"

Bett almost laughed. "Why does talking about it make you so uncomfortable?"

She only shook her head.

"It isn't making love to me that bothers you, is it?"

"Oh, no!" Maggie touched her face. "You're… wonderful, darlin'."

"So you *do* think about making love to me!"

She sighed. "I try not to. It's been very hard, though."

"But why not? Thinking about making love with you has been one of the most exciting parts of this week. And believe me," Bett persisted, "there's been a *lot* of competition for Most Exciting Event of the Week!"

Maggie smiled at that, but it was a small smile. "I can't think about it or talk about it. It's like hoping for things that might happen. You start making it bigger than what it really is. Then, before you know it, you end up with nothing at all."

Bett tried to grasp that, but it was too foreign. "That's pure superstitious nonsense! Surely your own experience has taught you that!"

"That's exactly what it did teach me! Sometimes I'd meet someone and start thinking we might connect. The next thing you know, she'd be going out the door with somebody else! The same thing happened to you with that woman who apologized all the time. Didn't you say she was disappointing? Well, I don't get disappointed if I don't expect things."

Bett conceded that. "Maybe, but you can't deny your feelings. If you never think about them, you end up only having a sexual experience for a few minutes. You're a sexual being *all* the time."

Maggie chuckled. "Not me, darlin'. I'd never get anything done if I let that happen." She sat up. "C'mon! Let's count this bundle and go to bed. It's been a full day. Tomorrow's going to be a long one, too."

Bett sat back. "Are you serious?"

Maggie stacked the dry bills. "Yeah. It's way past my bedtime. I'm beat."

"No. I mean you really don't think about making love?"

"Nope!" There was finality in Maggie's tone. Then she saw dismay in Bett's face. "I used to. When I was your age. But it just made me sad. Crazy, in a way." She shrugged. "Maybe I made myself stop. Maybe I just outgrew it. Scotty said that would happen. And he was right about a lot of things." She saw that Bett's look hadn't changed. Maggie waited, head cocked.

"A lot of things," Bett repeated, "but not everything."

 CHAPTER 23.

You Can't Get to Heaven from Here

NEVER ASSUME.

Williams knew that. It was a basic tenet of detective work. He also knew it was impossible. You had to assume some things, or you never got past one plus one. He drew concentric circles around the name Fenn, then listed the people he had notes on. Only two of them landed in the circle with Fenn: McIntyre and Delano. He had talked to Delano that morning. She agreed to meet with him later on her work break. McIntyre was still out of town. That left secondary slug work. He checked the file for the forensic report on the victim's car, but there wasn't one. He called Towing.

"What the hell is this?" the dispatcher practically shouted. "I told Kessler, and I'll tell you: Play your hide-and-seek games with somebody else. You call me again about a burned-out Chevy, and I'll write you both up!"

Williams stared at the receiver, then called Kessler. He was teaching a class of rookies and wouldn't be back until 11:30. Williams checked his list again. He considered seeing Officer Ebert at the hospital and decided to wait. She'd still be woozy. The trucker with the fire extinguisher was on the road until Friday. There was still no answer at NoCal Trucking, Fenn's employer. Not yesterday; not today. He might stop there on his way back from Fremont. That left Elise Trinos. There was no answer when he called; maybe he could find her on campus. His final notes included: Fire? Vegas warehouse? Log book? P.O. Hawkins. He called Probation. Joe Hawkins was in court now, but it was a pro forma appearance. He was expected to be back at ten for his weekly paperwork bout. Williams grinned at that, then signed out for Berkeley.

❖ ❖ ❖

"Hey, sleepyhead! Rise 'n shine!" Bett pulled Maggie's pillow over her head and muttered an obscenity.

"C'mon, darlin'. Last train to Oakland is about to leave. You don't want to stay on the mountain by your lonesome, do you?"

"Come back to bed, Maggie. We'll take your truck instead." Bett moved over, lifting the covers in invitation, keeping her eyes closed. She wasn't prepared for a freezing embrace and gasped at the shock of Maggie's hug.

"You're dressed! And soaking wet! Where have you been?" She covered herself as Maggie laughed.

"I fell on the way up the hill. Come on, now. I've got tea here for you, or the last cup of coffee. We'll eat on the road."

Bett kept the bedclothes tight to her chin as she sat up. She hadn't put on a nightgown last night, and this morning, unlike other mornings, she was still naked. She quickly changed thoughts. It was too early for mice chitters.

"Are you always so impossibly good humored in the morning?"

"Every day! But it's starting to wear off. I've been up for hours. I loaded our stuff, packed Tracy's records, killed the fire, locked up the generator, and cleaned up the kitchen. And I'll eat the steering wheel if we don't get to a diner pretty soon, so drink up!"

Bett sipped her tea slowly as real consciousness came over her. Then she asked: "How could you put that big generator away by yourself? Is that how you fell? Are your hands all right?"

"Whoa, darlin'! I can tell that tea's too strong. Already you're starting in on me, and three at a time to boot!" Maggie held up both hands to show they were unharmed. "I didn't do it alone. I used gravity, the morning frost, and a rope. Gyp helped, too. I'm surprised you slept through all that barking."

"I never heard a thing. Why didn't you wait? I could have helped you."

"Had all the help I needed. Except for the cheering crowds. Had to hire them!" She grinned at Bett's sleepy smile. "And I'm only wet because I slipped coming up from the shed. Good thing I tied the rope off, or I'd still be at the bottom of the hill yelling." She cupped her hands and made her voice sound distant. "Helllppp, Betttt! Waaake uuup!"

Bett's smile didn't fade until she thought about getting out of bed. "It's too nice in here; too cold out there!"

"I put some of your clothes on the hearth to warm them up. I'll get them."

Bett caught Maggie's hand as she rose. "Don't you think you ought to get out of those wet things and come to bed first?"

A long minute later, Maggie broke their kiss and stood up. "Guess I did make that tea too strong, didn't I?"

Bett sighed. "It isn't the tea that makes me feel this way! How long will it take us to get back?" She threw off the covers and ran to the main room.

Maggie followed. "Depending on the roads up here and the traffic down there, I'd say three to four hours. Why?"

Bett was already pulling on her jeans. "What time is it?"

"Just past ten. Why?"

Bett's head popped through the top of her shirt, revealing an impish grin. "I'm going to count the minutes until I can make love to you again." She bent down to tie her shoes. "Two o'clock can't get here fast enough for me! I'll pack my toothbrush, and we'll go."

Maggie stepped aside. "You got it all backwards, darlin'."

Bett emerged, suitcase in hand. "We'll see who's backward and who's forward when two o'clock gets here!" Grabbing her jacket, she opened the front door. "Last one to the truck has to drive!" She dashed out.

Her actions mystified Gyp, who woofed and turned to pant at Maggie.

"Oh, no!" she said. "I know for sure your legs are too short!"

⋄ ⋄ ⋄

Jim Harley pushed the hospital room door open a crack, then knocked. A voice replied, and he thought Ebert had gotten a roommate. But the woman sitting on the edge of the bed didn't look sick.

"Sorry. I must have the wrong room."

"Who you looking for?"

Harley couldn't help staring, even if she was white. Ordinarily, he didn't look at white women, except to give them the sketch-glance he learned as a child. But it was an easy lesson. He didn't find white girls very interesting. They had plain, forgettable faces. Unlike black girls, who came in all shades and had such different features. In fact, white women were the only people Harley couldn't recognize. Touring the Far East in the Navy, he'd found it easy to discern both subtle and obvious differences of people there. That helped him on patrol in Oakland, but nothing seemed to help him see white women individually. He knew he'd remember this one, though.

"Ebert," he finally said. "I mean Tracy. Ebert."

"You're in the right place. They took her to X-ray. Said it wouldn't take long, but this is the same place where they say it won't hurt much, too. You're a cop, aren't you?"

That alarmed him. Had he put on part of his uniform out of habit? He resisted the impulse to look. Last night's phone call from Kessler meant too much to him. Maybe Ebert had said something to her. They introduced themselves. "Ebert's partner," he added.

"Me, too," Elise said.

Harley did a double-take. She didn't look more than eighteen or nineteen years old. "You're an auxiliary?"

She smiled. "No. Ebert's partner."

Harley's eyes widened. He only knew one other context for that word.

"Well, speak of the devil!" Elise said as a nurse rolled Ebert through the door in a wheelchair.

Ebert greeted Harley, gesturing to ask why he was out of uniform.

"Special assignment," he said proudly.

They both turned to Elise. She seemed to know what their look meant and took Tracy's bag from the drawer. "I'll run point on getting you out of here."

Harley grinned at Ebert's eye-roll, but he hadn't missed the change in Elise's face when Tracy came in. Apparently she knew the term "partner" the same way he did.

He watched Tracy take her wallet from Elise, their faces unguarded for a moment. He went to the window until he heard the door close and the curtain being pulled around the bed.

"Wha's goin' on?" Ebert asked as she started to dress.

Just what I was going to ask, he thought, still smiling. Then he told her about Kessler's call. "He didn't give me any details, just that he wanted me to tail somebody. I'm ready for anything that doesn't involve Weigert."

Harley heard a mangled but emphatic curse. "What's wrong? It's practically undercover work!"

She swept the curtain back. "Aw'd be mine. 'Cep' for this." She pointed at her cheek.

He sympathized but was hurt she didn't see it as his opportunity. Then Elise came back with a set of papers and a prescription bag. He saw Ebert's eyes soften and turned to hide his awareness. When he looked back, Elise was showing Tracy where to sign the various forms.

"They said there's a cab stand out front," Elise was saying.

Harley offered them a ride. "I don't have to be downtown until noon." He nodded at Elise. "Going to your place?"

The two women replied simultaneously: "Yes." "No."

Elise went on: "You'll rest better at my place. I'll fix you something to eat and read my textbooks out loud to put you to sleep."

Tracy shook her head. "Nee' m' car."

"Are you okay to drive?" Harley asked.

"Probably not," Elise answered for her. "No problem, though. I'll drive."

"Na' aw'matic," Tracy warned.

Elise demonstrated floor shifting. "Vroom–vroom? Like that?"

Tracy rolled her eyes again. "Li'e tha'."

Forty minutes later Harley stopped alongside Ebert's car, still parked on Natchez near Maggie's driveway. As the women got out, he asked for Elise's number to keep in touch with Ebert. He gave the blond a knowing look. "Take good care of her now."

Elise smiled in response.

"Wha' wa' zat?" Tracy asked.

"What was what?" Then excitement overtook Elise as the car responded. "Great wheels, Tracy! Want to go for a ride on the way home?"

Ebert's thoughts of Harley disappeared as Elise pulled onto the main street, wound the 'Z out in first and skipped second altogether to cruise at 40 in third. She relaxed. Anybody who could peel out in first, with a clutch that chattered like hers, knew what she was doing.

"Too fast for you?" Elise asked.

"Jus' look ow' for cops." She closed her eyes.

Elise dropped a hand to Tracy's knee, stroking it lightly. "I'll get you home, draw you a nice hot bath, and fix you some soup. After that, you can nap. I'll curl up next to you while I study. It'll be a nearly perfect afternoon."

Ebert waved a circled thumb and finger. How could it be improved?

❖ ❖ ❖

Williams's visit to the university registrar office was a wasted effort. Elise didn't have class that morning. And she wasn't at her apartment, either. He left his card on her door, then went by Bett's apartment. The door frame had been damaged, but not just by burglars. Someone had added a hasp and padlock, and the screw holes that ranged on either side indicated it had been put on several times. All to no avail, in his opinion. The lock was worthless. Any thirteen-year-old delinquent could open it. The knob lock was intact, but he knew that, to be really safe, it needed a deadbolt.

He saw Hawkins next, but didn't learn anything more than what Kessler had told him. The PO hadn't contacted anybody at the Vegas PD. He only knew what Fenn had told him about the warehouse fire.

The detective headed back to his office, resigned to more slug work.

❖ ❖ ❖

Jim Harley looked through the file Kessler had given him but couldn't get a sense of how things fit together. Finally he asked, "What's the connection between the break-in on Natchez and the garage on Kenning?"

"Same person owns both places." Then Brian told him about the break-in at the cabin. "I still think it all comes back to Fenn, though. Nothing's going on at the M & M yard." He saw Harley's face change. "What?"

"Ebert took me by there Sunday. We found the gate open…"

"The gate was *open?*"

Harley couldn't believe how upset everybody got over an open gate. Had he missed something at the Academy? "We called in the locals, but nothing was missing."

"Something was missing all right," Kessler said. "Did you see a tow truck there?" When Harley nodded, he asked: "Was anything on the hook?"

"No, why?"

Kessler explained the missing wreck as he called the adjacent district. He shook his head as he hung up. "Well, something's going on at M & M. The patrol from last night reported a vehicle turned down the lane behind them. When the driver saw the squad car, he took off." Brian picked up the phone again. "It won't hurt to have Stony hire a guard for a night or two."

"So I won't be doing a stake-out?"

"No. I want you to keep tabs on Maggie. We still don't know if somebody's after her or if something else is going on."

"You want me to be a bodyguard?"

"No, she'd never stand for that, or for protective custody. Your job is to tail her, and make sure nobody else does."

"She's white?" the rookie asked cautiously.

"Unless you count freckles. Why? You prejudiced?"

Harley heard his light tone, but it didn't help. He explained his blind spot toward white women, knowing it was a curious flaw. But he didn't expect the Sarge to find it quite so amusing.

Brian's chuckle finally subsided. "This assignment won't help you with that, but you won't have to worry about losing her, either. You'll see why when she gets here. Better grab some lunch now."

✧ ✧ ✧

It was 1:30 when Maggie and Bett arrived at the Holman residence. Maggie took Gyp to the back of the house for a run while Bett let herself in to track down her father. She came out the back door a minute later. Maggie could see she was unsettled. "What's up?"

"He's here. With a friend." Bett put her head in her hands.

Maggie put an arm around her shoulder. "And...?"

Then Dr. Holman came out the door. He paused when he saw Maggie. "I didn't expect you two to be back... so soon."

Maggie nodded hello. Bett straightened and turned to him.

"Can you treat Maggie's hands?" she asked coolly.

Maggie looked at her again, even more puzzled now.

"Of course. Come in." He led the way through the kitchen and ushered Maggie to the small sink in the bathroom.

When Bett didn't join them, Maggie asked if he knew what was wrong.

He nodded. "I've been seeing someone. I didn't know how to tell Bett." He sighed. "She and her mother were so close."

Maggie took all that in. "We talked about her mom a bit up at the cabin. It must've been really hard for you, too."

He was examining her hands and didn't reply to that, only remarking on how well they were healing. Then he asked, "Have you lost a parent?"

"Yeah, but I was just a kid when it happened. I don't think it's the same when you're old enough to know them as regular people."

He agreed. "It is different for young children. But it's never easy." He applied salve and began bandaging her hands. "I was lost in my own grief for a very long time. Now that I've found someone else..."

Maggie touched his shoulder tentatively. "If you're happy, Bett will see that. It might take some time, is all."

He nodded, then wrapped the fingers on her left hand individually but higher than before, and pronounced her "fit for pushing a pencil."

She rose from the stool. "Wish you'd let me pay for all this treatment."

He only smiled. "We'll work something out one of these days."

"I'll hold you to that."

She went down the hall to Bett's room, where she found her gazing at the photographs on her dresser. Maggie saw her red-rimmed eyes and went to her, holding her close and letting their silent embrace provide comfort.

Finally Bett drew back. "This isn't quite the homecoming I had in mind."

Maggie kissed her forehead. "Maybe we aren't quite home yet!"

Bett hugged her, then wiped her eyes and went to tell her father they were leaving. A few minutes later, they went out the door.

CHAPTER 24.

Coming Home

WILLIAMS FINALLY MADE SOME progress when he connected with a Detective Lowe at the Vegas PD.

"It's filed under Johnson Brothers," Lowe told him. "NoCal's warehouse was adjacent, but it all started at JB's. A year and a week ago: April 14. Report of explosion and fire came in at 2:05 a.m. JB leases tanker-trailers: oil, gas, chemicals—the works. JB claims they were all stored empty, per regs, but the one next to NoCal couldn't have been too empty. It went off like a bomb. They couldn't get near the warehouse until the tanker fires were out. About a dozen, all told."

"Did they ever find the actual cause?" Williams heard Lowe's negative, but he was thinking "explosion and fire" was exactly what had happened in Oakland last week. "What about losses at NoCal?"

"Their inventory listed over twenty million dollars in computers. The insurer verified ten systems, but most of them melted first and then burned. They're still investigating the other forty."

"Isn't fifty computers a lot for a warehouse?"

"They were in storage. Don't you know about April in Vegas?"

"That's different from April in Paris, right?"

"Probably. Here it means warehouses full of inventory from you guys."

"Who's 'you guys'?"

"California businesses. Inventory tax time, you know?" He explained further: California companies shipped finished goods to Nevada to avoid the state inventory tax. The practice was especially popular with computer and other high-end manufacturers, since they had the margin to afford interim freight and storage charges on shipments scheduled for delivery Back East.

"You mean if something isn't physically located here, the company that owns it doesn't get taxed on it?"

"Zap! You're a tax attorney!"

Williams snorted. "Sure sounds like fraud to me!"

"I can see you don't have the true spirit of legal tax evasion. It's kind of a mouse maze for adults. Either that or the teamsters figured it's the best way to keep their trucks rolling. We sure get a load of them coming in six weeks before tax day."

Williams mulled it over but couldn't connect it with his case. Still, being able to evade taxes simply by moving goods over the state line could only invite fraud. He asked for a list of companies that lost systems in the fire.

"Only one. Sheridan Leasing. They filed a claim for all fifty computers; got a partial settlement for two-point-four mil' so far. Looks like the insurer's going to take the full hit, though. The claims agent says the minute Sheridan threatened suit, they cut the first check."

Williams perked up. The stakes had suddenly gotten interesting.

"The claims guy told the bean-counters to settle a year ago and warned them they were begging a suit. But it's a fairly new company—they only got into insurance a few years ago. That's part of the problem. They've never had a loss this big before. And they're worried about the dead watchman, which is why the file's on my desk."

"What's your gut feel on this case, Lowe?"

He paused briefly. "I think something's going on. Some cases are sloppy. This one's almost too clean. There's not so much as a typo in the claim."

"Some folks have a knack for filling out forms." Williams had hoped for a more concrete objection.

"Maybe. But if I had a claim this good, I sure would've put a lawyer on it before now. Partial settlement only went out last week. And…"

"What?" Williams sat forward. "You mean they sent out over two million dollars just last week?"

"Yup. And the claims guy says the demand letter wasn't from any legal-beagle, either. It was from the owner himself: Lawrence Sheridan. Seems to me a company like that would have a raft of lawyers to choose from."

Williams thanked him, then called Sheridan Leasing, where an icy-voiced secretary offered to take his name. Mr. Sheridan wasn't in.

"Where is he?"

"He's unavailable," she said evenly.

"Look, lady, I'm not one of your competitors. I'm with the Oakland P.D. Homicide." He heard her gasp, but it didn't shake her enough.

"He left the country last Friday. I'll give him a message, if you like."

No. Williams didn't want to leave a message. But he knew one was going to be delivered anyhow. Cursing his own clumsiness, he checked his watch and signed out. He had plenty of time to get to Fremont to interview Fenn's girlfriend. There couldn't be any traffic. The whole damn world was out of town!

A few minutes later, his phone rang. Another detective was passing by. Not finding a message pad, he wrote on the desk blotter: "Elise Trinos called. Home all day." Williams didn't find it until Thursday morning when he moved the mail aside.

But by then it didn't matter.

❖ ❖ ❖

As they drove away from the Holman residence, Maggie tried to gauge Bett's mood. Her silence was so uncharacteristic.

"Do you... want to talk about it?" Maggie asked diffidently.

Bett seemed startled and looked at Maggie, then laughed out loud. Finally, she shook her head. "I'm not laughing at you. It's just that we seem to have traded places. Now *I* don't know how to talk about my feelings." She kissed a fingertip and put it to Maggie's lips. "And I can't believe you put up with me asking you that same question every ten minutes for the past four days."

Maggie smiled. "Maybe not quite that often."

"It must've seemed like it." Bett looked out the window, gathering her thoughts. "You know, I think what really set me off isn't that he's been seeing someone." She closed her eyes briefly. "And I should have known something was going on last week-end. He seemed so relaxed. As if he'd taken ten years off."

"Isn't that a good thing? I mean, aren't you happy for him?"

She nodded. "That's what I meant about not minding him... dating. I was okay, until he introduced us. I really lost it then." She shook her head ruefully. "Sarah Davies must think I'm a complete lunatic."

"Who?"

"My dad's friend." Bett sighed. "I just wish he'd found someone named Rose or Jane or something. Sarah... is my mother's name."

Maggie nodded, not entirely sure she understood but glad to see Bett in a more familiar state. She waited a few minutes before saying: "I have to take the money to Brian, then run some errands on the way to the yard. It'll be pretty boring for you, but I don't think you should be alone."

"Then let's go to my place and drop my stuff off. Do you *have* to go to the yard?"

Maggie nodded.

"All right. What about dinner?"

"I'm afraid that's out for tonight, darlin'. I won't be done at the yard 'til seven, and your appointment's at eight."

"We have to eat sometime," Bett countered. Then another idea occurred to her. "Would you come to my session with me?"

"Not on your life! You must think I'm crazy!"

Bett was shocked by her vehemence. "Maggie, we've been through a *lot* this week. We need to talk about where we go from here."

"Maybe so, but it sure isn't to any shrink's office!"

"I don't go to a shrink," she retorted. "I go to Ellen. And not because I'm crazy, either. I go to her for insight and wisdom and to get perspective." She went on more gently. "I love you, Maggie. More than I can possibly say. I love you with my whole heart and soul and body. But even after being with you for a week, I don't understand you."

Maggie tossed her head, not knowing what to say.

"I know: You think you're a simple sort of person, but you're anything *but* simple. You've made a success of your life, despite all kinds of obstacles. You're warm, witty, smart," Bett paused, "and an absolutely ingenuous lover!"

"I doubt it." Maggie glanced at Bett, who seemed startled, then turned her attention back to the road. "And Ellen doesn't know me. She can only give you some kind of sag-couch noise about who knows what. Shrinks only know theory, not people. Besides, she probably wouldn't approve."

"Approve? I don't need anyone's approval, except yours. And I don't always get that when I expect it. That's part of the problem. Not with you," she said quickly. "I mean with my expectations."

Maggie shook her head. "I don't know what you want from me."

"That's not what I'm saying. On the surface, it looks like we have a lot in common. We're both motherless, been in therapy…"

"It's not the same," Maggie objected.

"That's my point exactly. Ellen's been a friend to me. My therapy has been wonderful, but for you, it was some kind of punishment. And you hadn't done anything to deserve it." She added softly, "I don't think you know how angry you still are about that."

"I never get mad anymore, darlin'. It's too easy to lose control when you're mad."

"Is control so important to you?"

"What's that supposed to mean?"

Bett sat back. "I see I've tripped over another of your black holes. Sorry."

Maggie exhaled loudly. "It's not you. Maybe your dad's right about my burns making me grouchy."

Bett opened her mouth, then closed it again and leaned over to kiss Maggie on the cheek.

"What's that for?"

"A peace offering. Will you at least meet Ellen? Just for a minute? I want to show you off, you know."

Maggie smiled. "Maybe. For a minute." She exited the freeway, stopping for a red light. "I don't know why that's so important to you, though. I've only got my own experience to go by. It hasn't always been roses, but nobody's life is. Ellen can't help that. Nobody can. What's done is done."

The instant the light changed, a horn blared behind them. Maggie hit the gas, roaring through the intersection and checking the mirror. It was only an idiot, not a white pickup. But the sudden acceleration had pressed Matt's gun into her lower back, and she relaxed a little more. Then she took Bett's hand and turned onto her street, searching for a parking place.

"I'm sort of set in my ways. I'm not used to taking things—problems, I mean—to anybody else. I've been on my own a long time. Sort of worked it out to where I thought I was happy."

"And were you?" Bett asked.

Maggie slowed to a stop, eye-balling a parking space, then put an arm across the seat and looked out the back window. "I thought I was. Until somebody parked her bike in my truck bed. Since then, nothing's been the same." She glanced at Bett. "It's still there, you know."

"I might not move it. That way you'll have to drive me everywhere!" Bett's eyes sparkled. Then she saw where Maggie intended to park. "You'll never fit in there!"

"Iz'zat right?" Maggie's face lit up at her challenge. "You don't know my secret." She checked the space again, then put the truck in reverse, cocking the wheel. "Parallel parking is just like making rice."

"How so?"

"All you need is precise measuring and careful timing."

"You aren't serious."

Maggie grinned. "Wan'na bet?"

Bett smiled softly. "The real question is, do you?"

Maggie laughed aloud as she backed the truck into place.

❖ ❖ ❖

"Tracy? Can you come here?" Elise was at the front window. She had brought Tracy some juice a few minutes before and knew she was awake. "You won't believe it, but a pickup is trying to park in that space across from us."

Tracy came over and put an arm around her, then gasped something that sounded like, "Sommabish!"

Elise was watching the street. "They'll never fit in there!"

"Hah!" Tracy said emphatically. Then more softly: "'Awtch."

The nose of the truck rolled away from the parked car ahead as the tail end eased into the space. Then the truck slowed.

"Uh-oh! Here comes the backing and filling!"

"Huh-uh. Un time," Tracy declared.

"One time? You're delirious. Cute, but out of your head. Can't be done."

Tracy put a hand out, palm up, making a rubbing motion with her fingers.

Elise laughed. "I couldn't take your money like that."

They both looked out the window, just in time to see the front end of the truck clear the bumper of the car ahead. Then, as the wheels rolled to the curb, the engine noise faded.

"Some a' bitch," Elise breathed in awe.

Tracy tried not to laugh, but she couldn't stop. It hurt like hell and sounded terrible. But, Jesus, it was good to see Maggie again!

CHAPTER 25.

Last Chance Saloon

THERE WERE SOME DUTIES Williams absolutely hated.

"Ms. Delano, we have reason to believe that Scott Fenn is…"

"No!" Lois sat back in the booth.

The detective looked away, only watching her peripherally. Her shock seemed real. Then she smiled thinly, and he wasn't sure again.

"No, you can't be talking about Scott. He's on the road. He took his kit." Her composure slipped then. "He can't be dead. He's just in trouble, right? Somebody else is dead. You just want to ask him some questions, right?"

Williams steeled himself. "Who would Scott want to kill?" He saw her take a sharp breath, shocked by the question; forgetting entirely that she'd suggested it. "Who?" He had to be quick, or she'd start thinking. He could see it in her eyes. Then near hysterical laughter filled their corner of the restaurant. He relaxed. She wasn't hiding anything except fear.

"You guys won't let up on him, will you? He finished probation, but you don't care. You'll frame him again anyway."

"Again" turned out to refer to the B of A robbery. Fenn had given her a real load of bull about that. Williams only half-listened.

"Sure, Scott has a gripe with that cop who arrested him. Is he dead? Of course not. We wouldn't be sitting here if some cop was…"

"Look, we have an unidentified body, found last Friday night behind an exploded car, registered to Scott Fenn. Do you have knowledge of his whereabouts?" He'd shocked her again. Williams saw her scrambling to escape her first conclusion about why a homicide detective would want to see her. Then she found a way out.

"No. Scott drives truck. He's on the road." She nodded, convincing herself. "Call NoCal. They'll know where he is. It's tax time. Every rig in the state is headed for the border or coming back empty for another load."

He smiled a little. "You sound like everybody knows about that tax."

His sudden change of tone distracted her. "Not everybody. Scott knows about it, sure. He drives truck. But he worked at Shazam Computers, and *they* didn't know about it. They stored all their systems right here, year round, like it didn't matter how much it cost in taxes. Scott wrote a letter to the president of the company."

She said the title as if she were talking about the President of the United States. Williams just let her talk.

"…practically in charge of receiving. A friend of his helped him get the job when he was first on probation. Scott learned how everything worked there. They were real smart about some things; real dumb about other stuff. Shazam was like a repair depot. When a system's lease ran out, they'd take it back and refit it, then sell it like brand new. Only, Scott said it was even better than before, because of the new parts. He said they were making a lot of money that way, but they might as well flush it down the toilet for all they were spending in taxes. Even if a lease expired at the end of the year, the dummies would ship the system to Shazam instead of warehousing it in Reno or Vegas. So he wrote that letter. I typed it for him," she added proudly. "And the president himself called him up to thank him. He gave Scott a coffee mug with Shazam's emblem on it and a hundred-dollar savings bond. I thought it was real nice, but Scott was mad as hell. He said Shazam spent fifty bucks to reward him for saving them a million bucks in taxes. He swore he'd…" She caught herself. "I mean, he said he couldn't work at a place that treated him like that. Besides, he wanted to drive truck again. That's why he went to work for NoCal."

Williams leaned forward. "What did Scott swear he'd do?"

Lois kept her eyes averted, twisting her rings. When she did look up, her eyes were full. "Scott's a good man. He was mad for a while, but he got over it. Honest. He gave me the mug and signed the bond over to my two boys. He wouldn't do that if he carried a grudge. I know him. He hangs on to a lot of stuff, but he didn't this time. After he left Shazam, he never said anything more about it."

The detective insisted. "What did he say he'd do?"

"He… said he'd get his money's worth. But he never did anything. I know he didn't!"

Williams shook his head, even as Lois insisted.

"Listen, you don't have to take my word for it. You can ask his friend Maggie. I can give you her number. She helped him get the job at Shazam. When he got arrested before, she talked to the judge. He wanted to send Scott to jail on weekends, but she talked him out of it. She even had her own apartment cut in half so Scott could live there."

She smiled at the detective's raised eyebrow. "I know what you're thinking, but Scott says he and Maggie are like brother and sister. My brother would never do anything like that for me, but I guess she's different. Anyhow, you call her. She'll tell you Scott never did anything to Mr. Sheridan. He just…"

"Who?" Williams sat up.

"Maggie McIn…"

"No! Who's Sheridan?"

"Larry Sheridan. He's the president of Shazam."

Williams asked carefully, "Have you ever heard of Sheridan Leasing?"

"Sure. That's his other company where they ship out the leased computers. I told you: Shazam gets them back when the lease expires and makes them new again. Like a magician's trick, Scott used to say."

Like "Zap! You're an idiot!" Williams silently berated himself for not checking Fenn's background more thoroughly. Everything was starting to come together now. The lines were connecting with the dots. Sheridan was one big dot. Money was another. He asked if Scott had a safe-deposit box.

"Like in a bank? Huh-uh. Why?"

"He showed his probation officer some papers. Claimed they were his alibi for another incident that happened about a year ago. Did he ever talk about hiding papers anywhere?"

She shook her head.

"Do you know where his log book is?"

"He's got it with him," she said firmly. "On a run."

Williams considered telling her the truth then, but without the X-rays from Oregon to confirm the ID, he couldn't. "The log we're looking for is from a year ago."

"Oh, an old one. Scott keeps those in the tin file with our tax returns." A bewildered look crossed her face. "It's gone!"

"What is?"

"The file box. No wonder the closet shelf looked funny. I put the phone books away when the cops left Monday, and there was too much space. It's where the file box sat. Why would anybody want to steal old tax forms?"

"Let the Fremont Police know. They'll amend their report." Damn, he thought. Another dead end. Somebody was at least three days ahead of him. Williams rose, thanking her.

She started to reply automatically, then stopped. "You're wrong about Scott." She quickly daubed her eyes, smiling tightly. "He'll get a big kick out of this when I tell him." She began crying in earnest then.

Williams reached out to her, but she waved him off. He sat in the parking lot until she emerged from the restaurant, holding her head high as she returned to the store where she clerked. It would've been better if he'd been able to tell her Fenn was dead. She couldn't even grieve now. She had to deny the suggested truth. Official word would come to her by way of some uniform knocking at her door. Maybe he'd done her a favor by giving her a chance to prepare for that. He drove out of the parking lot.

Some favor.

❖ ❖ ❖

"Bett!" Elise shouted and ran out the door as soon as she saw her friend getting out of the pickup. She stopped when a small dog charged forward to stand between them, legs braced.

Bett called to him, and he quit growling. "This is Gyp. Our watchdog."

251

Elise crouched to make friends, and Gyp approached with that dual speed of ambling eagerness that marked him as a puppy. Elise laughed as he went from sniffing her fingers to licking her face.

"And this is Maggie!"

Bett's introduction was all but a trumpet blare, and Elise was prepared for someone special, but not to keep looking up the way she had to in order to see Maggie. Reaching for her outstretched hand, Elise's attention was caught by the woman's face, her terribly bruised eye. When their hands met, she felt cloth first and glanced down, seeing the bandages and wondering what had happened. Then she took Maggie's fingers, avoiding the wraps. That triggered her extra sense, and she stood up slowly, absorbing some of the trauma this woman had suffered. The physical pain was muted, though, as stronger core feelings of joy and warmth seeped through to Elise, making her smile.

Maggie withdrew her hand, and they stood together a moment longer, smiling politely and grinning idiotically, until Bett remembered their need to call Brian.

Elise told them about the additional lock on Bett's door. "Winkler has the keys, but he wouldn't give me one. Come up to my place for now." She was walking backwards up the stairs, still talking.

Bett stopped and stared past her, not knowing what shocked her most: seeing Ebert in her friend's doorway, the casual way she wore Elise's robe, or the gauze taped to the side of her head. She didn't know what to say, but Maggie did.

"Hey, guy!" She greeted her old friend with a slow smile.

Tracy nodded slightly, trying to manage a smile.

Elise stared then, too. "You two know each other?"

Maggie spaced her thumb and finger as a measure. "A little bit."

Bett grabbed her arm. "Stop. Can't you see it hurts her to laugh?" Then she turned back. "Ebert, er, Tracy. I can't believe you're... in such pain." She didn't want to make a complete fool of herself and quickly resorted to medical questions. "Didn't they at least give you a collar?"

Ebert stepped back into the apartment as Elise answered for her. "Yes, but she doesn't like wearing it. And her jaw isn't broken. It's a severe bone bruise. They say that's not as bad, but she's still in a lot of pain." Elise pointed Maggie to the phone, then put a bowl of water down for Gyp before settling at the kitchen table with Tracy.

Bett glanced around Elise's apartment, seeing the familiar space and things, all just as they had been when she was last here. Something seemed different, and she looked at Elise for an indication of what had changed. Then she realized it only *felt* like she'd been gone for years.

She sat across from Elise, and the two of them both started talking at once, each eager to catch the other up on events. That's how all their conversations began, even if they'd only been apart for a few hours.

As usual, Bett soon gave up trying to out-talk Elise. She found herself watching Ebert, knowing the two of them were lovers. There was no doubt of that. It was written all over their faces and in how Elise kept a hand on Tracy, never quite letting go. When Bett saw Ebert's focus start to fade, she interrupted. "Tracy, how long have you been up?"

Elise looked at her, too. "Your color's all gone again, honey."

Tracy shook her head slowly, but she let Elise lead her to the couch. Bett watched her lie back, then reach for her cheek and struggle to sit up again. Realizing that the change of position must have increased the pressure in her face, Bett went to her and supported her at a slight angle, briefly explaining to Elise and asking her for several pillows.

When Ebert was settled more comfortably, Bett sat next to her and gently lifted the edge of the bandage, then smoothed it back in place. "You're lucky," she said. "It would've been worse if he'd hit you here." She touched Tracy's head just above the temple. "Your skull isn't nearly as strong or resilient as your cheekbone."

Ebert made a disparaging sound, then saw Elise and forced her words to be clear: "He missed!"

Bett followed her glance and quickly reassured them both: "Of course. And you'll be fine in a few days. But it must hurt like hell. Can't you take something for the pain by now? It's been more than twenty-four hours, hasn't it?"

Elise explained that they'd given her a prescription when she checked out. "But she says it makes her feel sick."

Bett sighed, remembering Maggie's resistance to pain meds. God help us! They're from the same planet! She suggested taking an antacid with the pill, then asked, "Where's your collar? You'll rest better with it on."

Tracy complained that it made talking difficult.

"You don't have to," Elise said. "You can write me notes, like before." She fitted Tracy with the collar before getting her pills while Bett went out to the truck for her medical books.

⬧ ⬧ ⬧

The room quieted just as Maggie's conversation grew loud. "Yeah, well, I just talked to Stony. And you've got some explaining to do, too!" She hung up and went over to Tracy. "Heard you came by the other night. Sorry I wasn't home to offer a warmer welcome."

Tracy looked up. "'S okay. I wan' to say sorry, too. 'Bout tha' deal on Hu'son. Na' my business. Din' know all I should."

Maggie was surprised that she was still upset about something that had happened so long ago. "No, I was out of line. Fighting Matt, not you." She smiled. "Guess we're both pretty hard-headed about some things."

"Na' so hard." Tracy pointed to Maggie's black eye and was about to say more when Elise came back.

She gave Tracy a pill and bottle of antacid before heading to the kitchen to get her juice and a teaspoon. "Can I offer you anything, Maggie?"

"No, thanks. I have to get going."

Bett returned in time to hear that. "So soon? Didn't you talk to Brian?"

Maggie nodded. "And Stony. That's why I have to go." She looked at Tracy. "You still carry a second?" She meant to ask subtly, but her effort at caution was wasted.

Bett asked: "Second what?"

"Gun," Elise answered. "Tracy keeps one in her boot."

Tracy's eyes narrowed at Maggie's question, then widened at Elise's reply. "How you know tha'?"

"It's almost the first thing I checked on you the other night," Elise settled on the couch with her. "I was pretty sure you had one. No, don't smile."

Maggie led Bett to the kitchen, but before she could say anything, Bett pleaded with her to stay.

"Don't go to the yard, Maggie. You can have Brian send somebody to pick up the money here, can't you?"

"I didn't want to scare you, darlin'. I just want to make sure you're safe. And you will be with Tracy here. I'll take the knapsack downtown first. Stony's getting the locks changed, but I still have to run a few errands."

"How long will all that take?"

"I'm not sure. I'll call you when I get to the yard."

"Hey!" Elise said, "Tracy and I want to know what's going on, too."

Maggie nodded. "Listen, can you make your appointment for tomorrow? Or Friday? Brian will need time to…"

"No. If it's safe for you to go to the yard, I can certainly go to the City for a couple of hours."

Maggie realized she wasn't going to budge. "Okay, but I told Brian I'd be right there. I have to go."

"Do you have Elise's number?"

Maggie nodded, then slung the blue bag over her shoulder and went to the door. She told Tracy and Elise: "Bett can explain everything."

"Maggie!" Bett couldn't believe she was just going to leave.

Gyp barked and headed for the door.

"Sorry, I forgot about Gyp. Can you…"

"I'm not talking about the dog! What about *me?*"

"I said I'd call, darlin'." The sound of barely suppressed laughter from the couch made her turn. Tracy managed to hold her laugh in, but Elise was less successful. "What's so funny?"

Tracy waved her toward Bett. "G'wan and kiss her. We won' look."

Maggie felt color rise in her face as she embraced Bett. "Sorry, darlin'. I forgot…"

Bett drew her close. "You'll learn."

Maggie started to smile, then Bett's lips met hers, and she forgot everything else for a long minute.

❖ ❖ ❖

Williams drove north from Fremont on the Nimitz, then exited west on Jackson, toward the San Mateo Bridge. Just before the tollbooths, he turned north again on Industrial and followed the signs marked "Public Scales." He found NoCal Trucking in a cluster of aging, tin warehouses and pulled onto the grassy shoulder between the entry and exit gates. The oversized parking lot was empty, and except for a forklift operating at one end of the dock, the place was dead. Not much of a busy season, he thought, crossing the lot on foot to climb the stairs to the office.

Halfway up, he heard the forklift engine quit. As his eyes cleared the top step, he saw the operator coming toward him—a white kid, early twenties, with greasy black hair and sallow skin. The circles under his eyes were as dark as bruises, and his hands shook slightly when he took out a cigarette and lit it. It dangled from his lips as he asked what sounded like "Help you, bro'?" or "Help you, boy?"

Williams didn't care for either address but kept his features placid. "Words is words," his partner used to say, adding with his throaty chuckle: "You can always off the fuckers later." Williams still missed Beau Jenks at times.

"Looking for the boss. That you?"

The kid snorted. "Boss ain't here. Out sick."

Williams looked at him closely. His eyes were a little too bright, like he'd done too much overtime and was taking something to help him through it. The detective put a foot on the bottom rail of the walkway, as if he had all the time in the world to hear this guy's woes. He'd smoked when he rode patrol. He was thinner then, but never as thin as this guy, who was wearing those fancy designer jeans with white stitches on all the seams.

"Got the flu?"

"Nope. Back trouble."

Williams led him a little. "Hurt himself lifting?" But the kid wasn't the chatty sort.

"He'll be in Monday. Come back then."

Williams was always careful about displaying his badge. He never tried to alarm people. He used it like a shared secret: "Here, this'll interest you!" While they studied the bold numbers and intricately stamped metal, he'd question them. It had worked like a charm once. He'd shown his badge to a wide-eyed perp, then asked softly: "Why did you chop your wife into little pieces, Mr. Dean?" Mesmerized, Dean had told him about all the salt she'd put in his food over the years, trying to kill him with high blood pressure.

The kid wasn't Mr. Dean. He dropped his cigarette and backed away as if the badge were a gun. Then he recovered a little and savagely ground out the butt. "Come back Monday," he said, heading for the forklift. "Ask for Dunston. He'll be in then for sure."

Williams considered going after him. The kid probably knew Fenn. But instinct told him that this guy wasn't behind the recent events. He might know something, but he wasn't in charge. He watched him wheel another load into the truck. Hell! He was barely in charge of the forklift!

He waited until the kid drove into the warehouse, then he tested the office door, found it unlocked, and entered. He could hear the forklift idling deep inside the building, but he kept his eye on the desk phone. When one of the buttons lit up, he hit "hold" then picked up the receiver and unscrewed the mouthpiece to remove the speaker disk. Holding the plunger down, he pressed the lighted button and slowly released the plunger.

His timing was perfect. The kid had finished dialing and was lighting another cigarette. At the other end of the line, jukebox music clashed with TV dialogue. Those sounds mingled with the rumble of balls falling out of a pool table slot and the ring of a cash register. All in all, it was just the sort of place Williams liked to recuperate in himself.

Someone picked up the phone at the other end. "Yeah?"

"Dunston? It's me."

The voice at the bar-end merely grunted.

"Listen, the cops were here."

"Yeah?"

It was such a disinterested reply, Williams's ears perked up.

"Yeah! What should I do?"

"Well, wha'd they want?"

The voice was pure boredom now. Williams wondered why none of them was yawning.

"I don't know. He was looking for you. I told him you were out sick. Said he should come back Monday."

"Who'd he ask for?"

"You, I told you. He said he wanted to talk to the boss."

"Did he ask for me by name?"

"Uh…"

The kid plainly didn't know what to say. Williams felt for him, knowing how much he wanted Dunston's attention. But he was between a rock and a hard place now. He dove for the rocks.

"Yeah! He said, 'Is Dunston here?'"

The detective winced at the lame delivery.

Dunston heard it, too. "Thought you said he asked for the boss."

"Uh, yeah, he did. He said, 'I'm looking for the boss. Is Dunston around?' That's when I told him…"

"Did he say why?"

"Why what?"

"Why he wanted to see me, you asshole."

"Uh, no."

Williams could practically smell the kid's sweat.

"God damn shit-head," Dunston muttered.

"Look, I got scared. He didn't ask anything about Fenn. He just…"

"Shut up, you jerk-off. I told you before. You're probably using the office phone, too!"

"No. No, I'm not. I… I'm at the Mobil station. I closed everything up. Can't you hear the trucks?"

Not a complete moron, Williams thought.

"Aw' right, shut up and listen. Get back to the warehouse and finish loading that trailer. Then tow that car out of there. Leave it in a ditch below the Dumbarton. It'll take them a week to find it. Then pick me up here."

Come on, kid, Williams urged silently. Confirm it for me. "You'll still be at the blankety-blank bar on…"

"Okay. What time?"

Williams sighed inwardly. Not Mr. Dean again.

"Just get here. We're gonna play hardball now."

"Hey, listen…"

"Don't tell me what to do, you little prick. You're in this thing up to your eyeballs. Do what I say. Take the pickup and make sure the tank's full."

"Christ, we're not going back up…"

"We're gonna find those fuckin' waybills, Ross. Don't even think about missing this run!"

Williams heard a phone slam down and the beginning of the kid's curse. Then that connection clicked off, too. He put the phone back together and cradled the receiver. He had enough to pull Ross in now, but he wanted Dunston, too. And Sheridan. The kid couldn't deliver all of them alone. He decided to wait.

It never occurred to him that this was his last chance to stop anybody on this case.

❖ ❖ ❖

Brian signaled Harley when Maggie came through the swinging doors at the end of the room. He had decided against introducing them in favor of just identifying her and letting the rookie take it from there.

Harley saw the tall redhead stop to talk to a couple of uniforms, laughing as they kidded about her shiner and bandaged hands. Her smile faded when she approached the Sarge. Harley listened from a neighboring desk as she laid into him.

"Where do you get off telling Stony to hire a guard? All I asked…"

"Sit down and listen," Brian said evenly. "I've got good reasons." He handed her the patrolman's report about the incident at the yard last night, then gave her the write-up on the impersonation of Ebert.

She muttered "Kids!" at the first paper, but the second one got her attention. "I think I know what they were after at the morgue." She pulled a thermos from the knapsack, then dumped the rest of the contents on his desk.

"What the hell...? Where'd you get all this money?"

"Found it in my truck. Scotty left it when he went to put gas in his car."

"Did you count it?" Brian picked up a flat bundle and fanned it.

"Only one. If they're all the same size, it's about twenty-five grand."

"What about those?" He nodded at the two cassettes.

"I figure they're Scotty's, too. He liked country-western on the road."

"Think he might've recorded something on these?"

"Huh-uh. You can't with commercially made tapes." She pointed at the edge. "Whenever Matt made a tape he wanted to keep, he'd punch out the plastic tabs they put here on blank tapes. That way the 'record' button won't work, even if it gets hit accidentally."

Brian shrugged. She knew more about it than he did. He set the tapes aside as Maggie rose. "Where you going?"

"I've got a couple errands to run, then I'll be at the yard."

"You better wait. Detective Williams wants to ask you a few questions."

"No time now. I'll be at the yard in about an hour. Besides, you've got the money. You don't need me."

"Whoever's after you doesn't know that!"

She grinned. "Ever heard of TV news? You've got plenty of time to get the networks down here. Might be a little late for Live-at-Five, but you can get it on the six o'clock report." She tipped Brian's chin toward the fluorescent lights. "You ought to shave first, though. You know how shadowy you get by dinnertime!" She laughed then, tremendously relieved to have gotten rid of the knapsack and all that it contained.

"They'll want to interview you, too. You're the one who found it."

"No way! I wrapped this part up for you. You take it from here. Besides, I've got a date tonight." She pointed at him. "No wisecracks, hey!" With that as her goodbye, she headed for the door.

Harley joined him. "Think she's right about the threat being over?"

"Only if the bad guys watch TV." He picked up one of the bundles. "This only solves part of the case. Get going now. Let me know where she goes from the yard. Damn it! I don't like this at all. It's too easy."

But Harley liked how easy it looked. Especially now that he didn't have to worry about how to keep track of a certain white female. No wonder the Sarge had laughed so hard. She'd be easy to tail. He could just sit back and figure up his overtime. It was going to be a piece of cake!

CHAPTER 26.

Leaping Lesbians

WILLIAMS RADIOED IN when he got back to the car, first to request a search warrant on NoCal, then to let Kessler know he was going to tail Ross to get to Dunston. Brian told him what Maggie had given him, adding her suggestion of contacting the media about the money-find.

"Good idea," Williams said. "Don't wait for me, though. And don't get specific about any suspects. One of them is still out of the country." He explained Sheridan's involvement and the claim settlement. "I'll follow up on that angle when I bring these guys in." He hung up his radio and absently watched a tractor-trailer in his mirror as it entered the NoCal lot. After jotting down some notes, he saw it again: leaving!

He looked over his shoulder. NoCal's bay doors were closed. Jamming the car into gear, he raced to the back of the warehouse, then cursed aloud. A gate opened onto the road beyond. Ross was gone.

He had been so sure the kid would follow Dunston's orders. All he had to do was tail him. Maybe he still could. The road behind NoCal circled back out to Industrial, and the kid only had a five-minute lead. He'd be easy to spot towing a wreck.

But as he drove past a stack of skids, he realized Ross wasn't towing anything. NoCal's tow truck was there, with what had to be Fenn's burned-out Chevy still hooked to it.

Damn! Now *he* was going to have to call towing!

⋄ ⋄ ⋄

Meanwhile Harley had lost Maggie.

He tried to keep two or three vehicles between them, but missed a crucial red light and couldn't tell if she'd taken the Alameda Tube or gone up the southbound Nimitz ramp. Gambling on being able to spot her on the freeway, he went up. She was nowhere in sight.

He drove to the next exit to turn back to the tunnel and started to radio in. Then he thought about what Kessler had talked about that afternoon. The Sarge hadn't just been shooting the breeze. He'd been giving him details on McIntyre's business.

Harley flipped through his notes, looking for an Alameda address. Ten minutes later, he pulled up across the street from M & M Radiator Repair. McIntyre was there, in front of her truck, talking with some men. The hood was up, and she seemed to be showing them some kind of problem. She leaned into the engine compartment and suddenly staggered back, arms out-flung.

He jumped out of the unmarked car, prepared to blow his cover, when one of the men caught her. Then he realized they were all laughing. Even the redhead. He got back in and watched one man roll a dolly under the front end while another put a pressure gauge on the radiator. She went into the office with the third man. A few minutes later, she came out carrying a thick file folder, spoke briefly to the men at her truck, and drove off.

Harley followed her more closely on the way back through the tunnel. When she turned right on Grove, he dropped back a little but kept her in sight all the way up to 46th Street. By then he figured she was heading for Emeryville. He didn't close the gap, opting instead to cruise past the shop and set himself up for her next direction. But she headed back downtown. He kept two cars between them, which worked fine until she took a shortcut through a manufacturing district. All the factories were closed by then, and suddenly he was the only vehicle on the street with her. When she sped up, he dropped back and took a left, then turned right again, speeding a little to stay parallel with her. They weren't far from Kenning, and as he crossed that street, he glanced toward the yard just as she drove through the gate. He circled back toward M & M and stopped at the far end of the block, out of sight. He waited a few minutes to make sure she didn't leave again. Other vehicles came and went, but no white pickups. He went to the corner phone booth to call Ebert, but the line was busy. He'd try again later. No rush.

✧ ✧ ✧

Maggie was keeping an eye on the gate as she dialed Elise's number. She thought someone had been following her, but no unfamiliar cars pulled into the yard. Then Ebert answered the phone.

"Thought you'd be asleep. Don't those pills knock you out?"

"No more than drinking too much. I know how to handle that."

Maggie knew Tracy sometimes took speed when she drank, claiming it counteracted the effect of the alcohol. "Well, you sound better, but did you ask Bett about taking…?"

"I'm fine," she said shortly, speaking with near normal enunciation. "Wha's taking so long at the yard?"

Maggie let it drop, then explained about having the locks changed. "Did Bett tell you my keys got stolen?"

"Yeah. And you know about the gate chain?"

"I heard. But I'm not even bothering with that lock. Too many of the guys need to drop off cars here. Besides, Brian's arranging a news conference about the money-find. Soon as whoever's chasing us hears we don't have the money, they'll lay off."

Tracy let that pass, then conveyed the directions that Bett had written down about how to get to Ellen's office. "Bett says there's a pizza place across the street next to a Shell station. We'll wait for you there. Will you eat before you come over?"

"Probably not. But it isn't Friday yet, is it?"

Tracy snorted. "Don't tell me you still eat pizza only on Fridays!"

"You know me. I never change. Put Bett on, will you?"

A moment later, Bett spoke into the phone: "When will I see you?"

The invitation in her tone made Maggie's heart skip a beat. She paused to reply casually. "Oh, I'll probably get there before you and Ellen finish."

"Will you meet Ellen?"

Maggie knew how important therapy was to Bett. She also knew what the real question was. "Sure," she said lightly. "But before you tell me what time to be there, you should know that I, um, kind of like me the way I am, darlin'. You might, too, once you get to know me."

"Now *there's* a thought! When can we get started?"

⋄ ⋄ ⋄

Williams was at Brian's desk when he came upstairs from the press conference.

"Don't tell me," Brian said, "you booked both of them, right?"

The detective scowled. It would be a while before he'd forgive himself for losing Ross. He told Brian what happened. "But Hayward PD is helping out. They impounded NoCal's tow truck and Fenn's car and put a watch on the warehouse. If Ross and Dunston show up, they'll get 'em."

Brian tried to encourage him. "Well, we've got evidence all over the place now: Fenn's car, his knapsack, the money, and a lab report from Summit County. They lifted some partials from the gun Maggie took off the thieves. If they match either of the NoCal characters, this case will practically close itself!"

"Maybe." Williams knew murder cases hardly ever closed themselves. He looked over his notes, wondering again about the Las Vegas angle. "You know anything about computers?"

"Not a thing. Why?"

He explained the Sheridan/Shazam connection. "I know a guy who works for Amdahl. Maybe he can tell me something." He dialed information, looking past the money to the thermos. "Is that everything from the knapsack?"

Brian tossed him the cassettes. "These, too. Not bad if you like heavy guitar with a lot of twang and wail."

Williams liked music and favored jazz, but not every kind of jazz. When he got his first in-dash tape player, his kids gave him tapes of jazz artists they liked. Williams thought it sounded more like an aluminum bat being slammed against a cyclone fence than music, but he didn't want to hurt their feelings. He kept the gift tapes in his glove box and played the more mellow artists he preferred.

A fellow detective, the one who had recommended the in-dash, asked why he always listened to the same tape. Williams showed him the gifts, adding: "I know there's better jazz out there. I hear all kinds on the radio, but I can't find them on cassette."

"Why don't you make your own?" asked his friend.

"There ain't no 'record' button on my in-dash!"

"Yeah, you need to get yourself a good at-home deck. You'll be taping over those commercial jobs in no time."

That really irked Williams. He'd already spent more on his in-dash than he'd paid for his first three cars total, only to find he needed a whole n'other machine! As he jotted down the number from information, he asked Kessler if he'd played the tapes yet.

"Huh-uh." Brian glanced up. "You into country-western or what?"

Williams smiled as he made his call. "Just get a tape player down here, Sarge. We'll see what kind of music Fenn liked to listen to." He picked up a cassette and pressed the upper edge, feeling the sticky residue of whatever Fenn had used to cover the cut-out tabs.

We'll see what kind of music Fenn died for.

❖ ❖ ❖

Bett rode in the backseat of Tracy's car as Elise drove. The three of them listened silently to the news until the report of the money-find aired, then Tracy clicked the radio off.

"Pretty sketchy," Bett said. "Is that a standard line about an arrest being imminent?"

Tracy shook her head, wondering what Kessler had besides the money. He had to be close to wrapping up the case, or Maggie and Bett would be in protective custody. Then she felt Elise's hand cover hers. She twined their fingers automatically and saw Elise smile at Bett in the mirror. She flushed at the sudden realization that they'd been discussing her.

Bett touched her shoulder. "Thanks for coming tonight."

She shrugged, speaking slowly. "You and Maggie shouldn't be out on the streets at all until they get somebody behind bars."

"Don't worry so much." Bett turned to Elise. "Maggie told me she and Tracy were alike. I didn't think so, but now I wonder if they both got an overdose of responsibility somewhere."

Elise smiled. "I don't know about Maggie, but Tracy's seen too much. She has the most wonderful eyes… when she isn't watching for perps."

Tracy was thoroughly uncomfortable now. She turned to Bett. "Are you okay? From shooting that guy?"

When Bett didn't respond right away, Tracy faced the road. "There's a reason cops get benched after a shooting."

Bett seemed touched by her concern. "I think I'm just glad to be alive! And we ought to celebrate. Have you been to the *Mais Oui* yet? It just opened a few weeks ago. I asked Maggie, but she said she hadn't been there."

Tracy half-smiled. "Maggie never goes to the City."

"You don't really mean never, do you? She told me she used to pick Matt up at the airport."

"Airport's in South City. And Maggie doesn't like getting much closer than that. She's got funny notions about some things, but she's an ace. Always has been."

"You've known her a long time, haven't you?"

"Yeah, but don't confuse that with knowing her well."

"Do you know anything about her lovers?"

"No. She doesn't talk about that. But I don't think she's seeing anybody." Tracy thought that was safe to say, even if she hadn't seen Maggie for a year.

"Has she ever mentioned a woman named Lange?"

"Huh-uh. Who is she?"

"Her first lover."

Tracy half-smiled.. "Maggie *did* tell me a joke about her one time."

"About Lange?"

Tracy shrugged. "Could be. Anyhow, we were having a few beers after a race one time…"

"I didn't know you ran," Elise interjected.

"She means a car race," Bett said. "Tracy used to drive, and Maggie worked in the track pits. That's how they met."

Elise stopped for a red light. "Did you say *track pits?*"

Bett nodded. "I still don't know what they are, but…"

"Well, I do!" Elise turned to Tracy. "And *you* drove race cars?"

Tracy smiled as much as her jaw would allow. "Green light, honey."

"Hot damn!" Elise breathed.

Bett nudged Tracy. "You were saying?"

"Huh?" Tracy turned from Elise with an effort. "Oh, yeah. I asked Maggie why she didn't try driving. She said there were too many risks on the track, and she hated surprises. But she liked the excitement of the pit, and all she had to do was be good and fast to help somebody win. I made some crack about having had a lover like that once…" She paused to enjoy Elise's chuckle. "Maggie laughed, too, then she said: 'You know, the first time I ever made love to a woman who came, I thought I'd killed her!'"

Elise's laugh drowned out Bett's gasp, but Tracy saw Bett's face.

"She was joking. Or didn't I tell it right?"

Bett shook her head. "I just have a hard time with some of her… jokes."

✧ ✧ ✧

It was 8:20 when Maggie got to the pizzeria. She joined Tracy and Elise in their booth without giving the place or its occupants a glance.

"Any trouble?" Tracy asked as Maggie slid in across from them.

"Not really." Then her brow furrowed. "But what's a reasonable down payment on a bridge?"

Tracy snorted a laugh, causing a brief jolt of pain. She saw Elise's puzzled look turn concerned. "I'm okay. Would you get us another pitcher?"

"I'm about to float away from the first one," Elise said. "But I'll get you both a draft on my way back from the john."

"Go ahead." Maggie rose. "I'll get it."

"No. Sit down. Tracy wants to talk to you alone."

Tracy wondered how she knew that, then turned to Maggie, knowing she had to talk fast, before Elise came back. She plunged in without preamble: "I heard what happened at the cabin. I shoulda' put that gun away, but I was drinking and…" But she couldn't talk about trying to kill herself. She didn't dare think about it for fear the urge would overtake her again.

Maggie couldn't follow her stammered explanation, except about the drinking. "You've been hitting the stuff pretty hard?"

Tracy waved a hand at her beer. "No more than usual."

Maggie shook her head at that and changed subjects. "Uh, Trace, I know you probably don't want to talk about this. I mean, now that you're with Elise."

"She hasn't said anything about my drinking, has she?"

"No, no. I wanted to ask you about Carole."

"My ex? What about her?"

"Well, I know you two lived together for a while…"

"Yeah?"

"Did you know her pretty well?"

"After a year and a half, I should have."

"No, I mean in the beginning. Had you known her long?"

Tracy shrugged. "We met at Fran and Judy's and started going out. Why? What is this? A history test? She split, right when I needed her most. The beginning never matters. Just the end. That's what it all comes down to."

Elise returned and sat down, then popped up. "Oops! Forgot the beer."

They watched her go to the counter.

"Kind of funny," Maggie said. "I mean, Elise and Bett being friends. And you and me."

Tracy was sure she had something else on her mind. "Elise isn't anything like Carole, you know."

Maggie hadn't known Tracy's ex that well. "I wasn't comparing them. I just wanted to know how you feel about Elise. Not how you feel, exactly. I know you like her. But, well, didn't you just meet her?"

Tracy almost grinned. "That kind of time doesn't matter, either. I don't know.

This is different somehow. As for liking her: I'm crazy about her! You don't know what it's like. I've never felt this way about anybody!"

Maggie grinned for her. "Haven't seen your eyes light up like that since the last time you won a race."

Tracy shrugged self-consciously. "I know she's young, and into some weird women's stuff—tarot cards and the goddess. She's out of touch with the real world, but she's still in school. She'll be fine by the time she gets finished."

Maggie cocked her head. "Will you still be with her then? Are you… planning on it?"

"Maybe. I don't know. Have to see if she can stand my being a cop. She really seems to be into it now."

"Is that what happened with Carole? She didn't like you being a cop?"

"Who knows? My whole life went upside down at that 7-11. I was still in the hospital when she moved out. I couldn't even walk yet! Fucking bitch."

Elise returned with the beer. "Who's a fucking bitch?"

Tracy looked up, startled. "Uh, nobody…"

Maggie said, "I don't think it's anybody you know, Elise." She checked the time. "I promised Bett I'd meet her."

Tracy started to get up. "I'll go with you."

Elise put a hand on each of their shoulders. "Stay put and drink your beer. Bett won't be finished for another fifteen minutes at least. And I wouldn't be surprised if her session ran over. A lot's been happening in her life."

Maggie smiled thinly. "Too much." She asked Tracy if anyone had followed them from Berkeley.

"Huh-uh. What about you?"

"No. I thought so this afternoon, but…"

"Why didn't you say so?" Tracy peered out the window. "The same one that followed you up to the cabin?"

"No. That was a pickup. This was a car."

Tracy took out a notepad. "Give me the descriptions."

"I don't have much, Tracy. The truck was a full-size American-make; standard bed, dirty-white, no markings on the door. As for the car, I only saw it in my mirror. The sun was on the windshield, so I can't even give you a color, let alone a make."

"What about size?"

"Too big to be a foreign job. It was probably just my imagination."

Tracy shook her head. "No sense taking chances. I'll check for any vehicles that look out of place, but we better skip going to that new bar and get back to Berkeley. Where's your truck?"

"Found a spot up the block."

"Okay. My car's out back. We'll wait for you two, then follow you to the East Bay. Keep your eyes open."

Maggie nodded, then checked the time again and left.

Tracy watched her until she entered the building across the street.

Elise asked: "How serious is this, Tracy?"

She closed her notebook. "Let's just say I'll feel better when we get back to your place."

∴ ∴ ∴

Ellen glanced at her desk clock. "Before we talk more about Maggie, I need to know you're all right. Are you?"

Bett smiled, then took a deep breath. "I'm fine, I think."

"Do you want to talk about the shooting?"

"No, not yet. I felt so… terrible when I realized what I'd done, but it was… I had to!" She rubbed her face, refusing to break down.

"It's all right," Ellen encouraged. "We can talk about that more at our next session."

Bett was relieved. "Then can you help me figure out why I keep misinterpreting Maggie so thoroughly? Especially when I feel so close to her. I mean, I *do* know how she—or someone in her place—*would* feel. But she doesn't seem to have those same feelings or reactions."

Ellen nodded sympathetically and sat back. "Bett, how much older is Maggie?"

"About ten years. It's not like it's a whole generation!"

"No, but age isn't a factor in a vacuum. You two grew up in very different societies and environments. And, except for two things, your life's been fairly typical."

"What things?"

"Being lesbian. And losing your mother."

"But those are the things I have in common with Maggie."

"Not exactly. Don't forget when those things happened. You were twenty when your mother died."

"And Maggie was just a kid."

"More than that, she was an orphan. She had no family at all. Living in several foster homes made her childhood vastly different from yours, even if she's gotten over the usual insecurities that produces."

"Maggie is the most secure person I've ever met!"

"Still, loss-trauma in childhood or early adolescence can manifest in odd ways. One characteristic is a kind of fatalism. Studies of orphans and relocated children from the turn of the century…"

Bett laughed. "She's not *that* old!" She paused at a sudden thought. "Is that what caused her memory loss before?"

Ellen shrugged. "Adolescent amnesia is common enough and unusual enough to provide material for a thousand Ph.D.s." She saw Bett's eyes narrow angrily, the way they had when she'd described Maggie's initial lesbian experience. "Wait, now. You're very sympathetic toward Maggie, but not toward her first lover. You don't know what it was like to be lesbian before Gay Liberation or female before the Women's Movement."

"I've taken Women's Studies," Bett retorted. "There's just no excuse for the way Lange treated Maggie."

"You can't know that. You don't know Lange or her husband. More important, you don't know what pre-liberation life was like, how limited a woman's choices were. For all you know, it wasn't even Lange's idea to get pregnant." Ellen let that sink in a moment. "Everything didn't change with the first issue of *Ms.* magazine. A lot of women have never participated in the movement. They don't even understand it's theirs."

"Not a *lot,*" Bett protested.

"Are you sure? What about undereducated women? Poor women? Blue- and pink-collar women?"

"Married women," Bett added. "But Maggie isn't some dumb housewife. She's strong, and smart, and… and gay!"

Ellen smiles wryly. "Ah, the Lavender Canonization! Do you only know lesbian feminists?"

"Isn't that redundant?"

"Not all lesbians are feminists. No more than all feminists are lesbian. Your mother, for example."

"My mother was… very unusual."

Ellen nodded. "True. And I think it's wonderful that you've been surrounded by so many strong, unconquered women. Maggie certainly fits that category, but she might've gotten there without the Women's Movement."

Bett was silent briefly. "You don't think she's anti-feminist, do you?"

"If you're not for, you're against? Is everything so black and white?"

"No. But I don't know why she doesn't hire women mechanics."

"Did you ask her?"

Bett shook her head, then told Ellen about the clash they had when she realized Maggie owned M & M. "How could I have been so wrong!"

"How wrong were you? She told you she was a mechanic. Maybe it's how she perceives herself. Or maybe she knows that calling herself 'boss' puts people off."

Bett sighed. "Everything you say makes sense. Why couldn't I see it on my own?"

"You're beginning to," Ellen assured her. "As for why you didn't before, that's a matter of knowledge without experience. One of the hardest transitions a young adult faces is merging formal learning with real life. The more education, the harder the transition. But you're starting to change already."

"How can you tell?"

"When we talked last Saturday, you'd assumed a lot of things about Maggie. Now you seem to be asking more questions, considering her answers instead of refuting them automatically."

"I still don't understand her," Bett said resignedly.

Ellen smiled. "That will happen too, in time. And speaking of time…"

Bett looked at her watch. "Damn! I didn't even get to tell you about my dad. He's… seeing someone."

"This *has* been a big week for you, hasn't it?"

She nodded. "Can I see you on Saturday? I'll need to talk to you before I see him again."

Ellen reached for her appointment book, then heard a sound in the outer office. She went to the door and saw a tall woman standing at the window. "Hello." Then she saw the bandages on her hands. "You must be Maggie."

"Yes. I didn't mean to interrupt. I thought Bett would be finished by now. Is it all right if I wait here?"

"Sure. She'll be out in a minute."

Ellen and Bett agreed on a Saturday time, then went to the outer office where Maggie stood with her back to them, still looking out the window.

"Nobody's chasing us, are they?" asked Bett.

She turned. "No, but something must be going on tonight."

"Why?" Bett joined her at the window. On the sidewalks below, she saw gay couples walking arm-in-arm as well as dozens of individuals alone or in small groups. She tucked herself under Maggie's arm. "What am I supposed to be seeing?"

"The street's full of women like us, darlin'. Lesbians, I mean. See?"

Bett giggled. "Of course I see. Is that all?"

"But what are they all doing here? Where are they going?"

"They live here."

"Not all of them! There's too many! You sure they aren't here for a concert or a convention or something?"

"You're serious, aren't you?"

Maggie nodded, then looked to Ellen.

"How many lesbians do you think there are?" Ellen asked.

"Well, there's probably fifty or more out there now. But they've been coming and going like that for the last ten minutes at least!"

"And how many do you think there are in the Bay Area?"

Maggie spread her hands. "I don't know. Five hundred maybe. That sounds like a lot," she gestured at the street, "but that seems like a lot, too."

"You don't come to this part of the City often, do you?"

"No. I've been to Fisherman's Wharf and Chinatown a few times, but I didn't like it much. It was too crowded." She looked at Bett. "If you keep your mouth open like that, you'll be catching flies to go with your chitters!"

"Are you serious?" Bett asked. "You really never come to San Francisco?"

Ellen spoke up. "She didn't say that, Bett." Then to Maggie, "Did you stand out like a sore thumb in Chinatown?"

"Yeah. The kids thought I was like a New Year's dragon. Bett says I'm from another planet." She glanced at Bett, sharing her smile, then they took their leave of Ellen.

As they went down the stairs, Maggie relayed Tracy's concerns and the decision to get back to the East Bay right away. "I know you're disappointed, darlin', and I don't like it any more than you. But Tracy's a cop. We should follow her advice."

When Bett relented, Maggie looked up the street, seeing a quick flash of lights from a double-parked sports car. As they headed toward her truck, she asked: "Bett, how many lesbians are there, really?"

She laughed. "I never know what makes you change subjects!"

"Well, I see all these women, just walking around together here. It's like the whole world is gay, but I know that can't be. So how many are there?"

Bett paused. "You want to know how many there are in the whole wide world?"

Maggie grinned. "The universe!"

"Two."

Maggie stopped walking. "Huh?"

"Yup! You and me."

Maggie started to lean down to kiss her, then straightened up. "Forgot where we were for a minute."

Bett held her. "Just so long as you remember where we're going!"

CHAPTER 27.

How Many Ways Can I Lose You?

"Slow down, Elise." Tracy adjusted the center mirror for her own use, then reached over and hit the horn to get Maggie and Bett moving again. "Pull alongside her truck." As they waited for Maggie to come around to the driver's side, she drummed her fingers, then hit the horn again.

Maggie finally appeared. "What's up?"

"Did you see that LTD back there? No, don't turn around."

"No. What about it?"

"Somebody's slouched down in the driver's seat." Ebert didn't chew her out for her inattention. Instead she gave her a specific route back to the freeway. "We'll be right behind you, unless this guy follows you. And listen, if anybody *is* on your tail when you get to the entrance, skip the freeway and head for the Embarcadero. Get lost in a crowd."

Maggie frowned. "You know how easy that is for me."

"All I'm saying is, find a bunch of people and get in the middle of them, then flag down a uniform. Got it?"

"Okay. We should be in Berkeley by 10:30, or we'll call and say where we are then. All right?"

Tracy nodded and told Elise to hang back a little. "Let her get to the light." She watched the mirror as the M & M truck moved out. "They'll turn right there." No sooner had Maggie pulled out than the green sedan Ebert had spotted turned on its headlights and moved into traffic.

"Will she know where to go from there?" Elise asked.

"Shit. Who knows? The only friggin' four-door American make in the whole damn city, and she walked right by like it wasn't even there!" Tracy kept an eye on the car behind them as she pulled out her short-barreled .38. "When you get around the corner, slow down. Stop about fifty yards…"

"I got it, Ebert!"

Tracy saw how nervous Elise was by the way she bit her lip. She chalked her tone up to that. "Relax. There probably won't be any trouble, but go through the plan we talked about."

"I stop at an angle to block him," Elise recited, "then run the other way and look for an alarm. If I don't see one, I pound on a door or shout 'Fire!'"

"Right!" Tracy prepared to get out.

"Tracy, could you play the part of my girlfriend for a minute?"

"What do you mean?"

"I'm supposed to be dropping you off. Shouldn't you... kiss me?"

Then Tracy realized that Elise was scared. Her own fear lessened as she leaned over and kissed her, charging herself another way entirely.

A horn sounded behind them. "Hold that thought," she said with a quick smile. That gesture gave her a twinge of pain, reminding her of the fucker who'd hit her with the gun barrel.

She blanked that thought and let her training take over, moving to the back of the 'Z, keeping her gun hand close to her leg, her face turned away from the car behind. The horn blared again. Her anger returned, and she felt herself slow down, unaware that she'd started to limp.

Elise drew forward slowly while Tracy stepped in front of the tailing car. Pacing herself, she turned at the sound of the LTD's engine surge. It started to pass her. She raised her gun. His window was down. He'd hear her, all right.

"Police! Stop, or I'll shoot!"

He never even slowed.

She stepped back, sighting along the barrel to where the bullet would enter the side of his head. She started to squeeze the trigger as he faced her.

Surprise opened his mouth, making his pure white teeth a natural target.

❖ ❖ ❖

"Did you hear that, Bett?"

They were stopped at a light. Bett looked through the back window and saw flashing red lights clearing traffic behind them. Then the wail of a siren reached them. "You mean that fire truck?"

"No." Maggie pulled to the side of the street, but the fire truck turned off. "Guess it was just a car backfiring."

Bett looked out the window again. "I thought Elise and Tracy were going to follow us."

Maggie didn't respond. The fact that the 'Z was no longer behind them, coupled with the distant noise she'd heard, worried her.

"What's going on, Maggie?"

"I don't know," she admitted. "Tracy saw somebody suspicious in a car near the bar. She was going to make sure whoever it was didn't follow us." Maggie pulled back into traffic, joining the line of cars headed up the street.

"Suspicious...?" Bett turned to her. "You mean she was going to roust some guy who was just waiting for his lover?"

"I don't know," Maggie replied. "But I'm thinking maybe we should let the Oakland police put us up for the night."

"*What?* You mean sign ourselves into jail?" Bett was appalled. "No one is following us. I don't want to spend the night in jail. I want to go home and..."

Maggie stopped her. "I just want to make sure we're safe."

Bett sighed. "We're driving through the most civilized city in the country! Has it occurred to you that Ebert is more than a little paranoid?"

Tracy did overreact at times, but Maggie didn't know what to think now. And Bett was right: Nobody was behind them. "All I know is, she was going to stall anybody who tried to follow us. I don't like leaving without them, but I'm not exactly sure where we are."

Bett recognized the area. "Is this the way Tracy told you to go?"

"Yeah. She said it was a straight shot to the freeway. All I'd have to do was turn on Van Ness."

Bett stifled a groan at the string of traffic lights ahead. "That'll take all night! It might be the most direct way, but it certainly isn't the fastest. Even *I* know a closer entrance." Then she thought about that. "But I suppose it makes sense if Tracy didn't want you to get lost. And it might be why they aren't behind us. They went a different way."

"Yeah, once she checked out the LTD and found there was nothing to it, she'd head for Berkeley, knowing we were okay." Maggie slowed for another red light. "And if she stays with Elise tonight, we'll probably be safe enough at your place. I guess we don't have to go to the police."

Bett sighed in relief. "Do you have any plans for tomorrow?"

"You mean after work?"

"Mmm, no. I meant instead of work. You don't *have* to go to the yard, do you?"

"Well, not for the whole day. But I've got that meeting Friday night, and I need to read some reports. Why? What did you have in mind?"

Bett looked out the window. "The weather's supposed to be really nice tomorrow. I was thinking, since our week in the mountains got cut short, and neither of us really planned to be back this soon..."

Maggie smiled. "I suppose I could just go in for a couple hours in the morning." She saw Bett's dismay. "Did you want to go someplace special?"

"No." Bett stroked Maggie's cheek. "I just wanted you all to myself for a day."

Maggie held her hand a moment. Bett's fingers were icy cold. At the next red light, she shrugged off her jacket and slipped it over her shoulders.

"All day, huh?"

"Every waking minute!" Bett put her arms in the sleeves and crossed them, sitting sideways to Maggie and looking like an orphan herself in the too-big jacket.

Maggie turned away. Bett's smile was simply too inviting. She watched the traffic absently, letting her mind wander into the future. The light changed, but she didn't notice.

"You can go now," Bett said softly.

Startled, Maggie released the clutch too fast, killing the engine. She started it up again. "I was, uh, thinking about tomorrow."

"Were you now?" Bett's voice was bright with laughter.

Maggie reddened. "Yeah. I was thinking that if I stop at the yard tonight, I won't have to go in at all tomorrow."

"You better watch out. You never know where radical thinking like that might lead!"

·:· ·:· ·:·

"You goddamn bastard!" Ebert knelt in the street, closing her eyes like a child wishing a nightmare away. "What the fuck are you doing here?" she whispered.

Harley heard the sound of running feet and saw Ebert raise her gun instinctively. He blocked her with his foot, kicking the gun away as Elise arrived at a dead run.

"Are you all right?" she asked Tracy.

Harley turned away. His fear had dissipated, but not his adrenaline. He had to do something physical. He walked around the car, taking deep breaths, not thinking. A knot of bystanders watched from the sidewalk. He shook off one man's offer to call the police. When he got back to the driver's door, he picked up Ebert's gun. A good second, he thought absently. Compact, balanced. It would have done the job. Then it hit him: His job!

"Take care of her, Elise. I'm supposed to be following that pickup." He got in, then heard Ebert groan horribly, her face twisted in a grimace. He paused, knowing his first duty was to assist a downed officer. Incredibly, he heard Elise caution Tracy not to laugh.

Ebert rose. "Safety-tailing them?" At his nod, she cursed again. "Since when?"

"About 4:30. Look, I already lost her once. Kessler's going to think…"

"I know where they're going," Ebert interrupted. She told him their plan to meet in Berkeley and suggested he follow her and Elise back there.

"You sure you're all right?" he asked.

"Yeah." She took her gun back, checked it, then put it away. She looked at Harley. "Listen, Jim," she finally said, "I thought you were the guy who hit me. If I'd known it was you…"

He shook his head slowly. "It doesn't matter who you thought it was. You know procedure. Or is this an unwritten reg?"

"Not unwritten. Just look under *S* for stupid."

"You're sure it isn't *S* for scared?"

She glared at him. "What do you know about that?"

"As a matter of fact, I know a lot about being scared. Comes with the badge. Or did you miss that announcement?"

"Is that what they're teaching at the Academy these days?"

He ignored her tone. "Tracy, you'll never get it straightened out if you try to fix the wrong thing."

She paused a long moment. "I'll think about that."

He and Elise watched her limp toward her car.

"Do you think she's all right?" Elise asked.

"All I know is she's scared." He looked at the young blond beside him, wondering how well she knew Ebert. Did she know what she was getting into? What kind of life cops lead?

"It's the only time her leg bothers her," Elise said.

Then he realized she did know his partner. He'd often seen Ebert limp but had never seen the pattern until now.

"And she acts like she's mad," Elise added.

"That's one way to handle it."

❖ ❖ ❖

Maggie and Bett were nearly at the far end of the Bay Bridge when Maggie mentioned a chat she'd had with the tollbooth operator earlier that night.

"Do you always talk to toll-takers?" Bett asked.

"And here I thought you'd run out of questions tonight!" Maggie grinned. "Yeah, I generally talk to people who wait on me."

Bett had never thought of it that way before. "Tracy's right. You have got some funny ideas."

"When did she say that?"

"On the way to the City." Then Bett remembered what else Tracy had said. "She told a joke I wanted to ask you about, too."

"Don't ask me to explain Tracy's jokes. I hardly ever get them. She told me one about Oakland once. Said some lady told her it wasn't there."

That sidetracked Bett. "What wasn't there?"

"I don't know." Maggie turned onto Kenning and pulled up to the garage yard gate. "Tracy said that was the whole joke." Maggie got out to open the gate. When she got back in, Bett was chuckling. "What's so funny?"

"Tracy's joke. She was quoting Gertrude Stein, right?"

Maggie shrugged. "Who's that?"

Bett searched for an easy answer. "Mmm, she's a poet for one thing. She wrote 'a rose is a rose is a rose'?"

Maggie drew up to the office door. "Poet, huh?"

"Well, she's famous for other things, too, but what she said about Oakland was: 'There's no *there* there.'"

"Sounds like the same joke. I told Tracy to send her down to the yard. 'You tell her I'm there!' I said."

Bett laughed. "You're too much sometimes. Gertrude Stein is dead."

"Well, she missed her chance then, didn't she?" Maggie got out but turned to Bett. "I do love to make you laugh." She leaned across the seat, and they kissed. Their laughter faded. Their kiss lengthened.

She touched Bett's face with new awareness. Kissed her eyes, her ears, her throat. Led by a sudden passion she couldn't resist, she teased the soft swell of her breast, wanting to taste her everywhere at once. She might not have stopped of her own accord, but Bett lifted her chin.

"At the risk of calling you a liar…" She traced Maggie's lips with the tip of her tongue, "…or keeping you from what you're doing…" She lay back, nearly flat on the seat, and smiled up at her. "I don't believe you."

Maggie saw Bett's eyes sparkle, even in the dim light cast by the dome light, and leaned in further to kiss her again. "You don't believe what?"

Bett's smile broadened. "That all you love is my laugh."

Maggie's smile faded. She had once thought "I love you" was a magic phrase, a spell that powered the very center of her being. The day its magic stopped working, she had walked away from that part of herself, mystified at how her feelings had turned on her. How could anything that makes you feel so good make you feel so bad?

Tracy would say that the day after winning a race. Maggie knew she was suffering from all the booze they'd drunk in celebration, but Tracy started connecting winning races with the misery of a hangover. Maggie never realized her confusion was real, until now.

For years her wall had sealed off all feeling. It had worked so well she was sure she'd outgrown any feelings beyond what Matt called "natural yearnings." Yet this was a feeling she'd known before, one that had once made her whole. She thought love had died inside her wall, but it was alive and growing. Only waiting to be acknowledged, only waiting to be set free.

Maggie felt Bett's light touch on her face and realized where they were. What she was about to say.

"You're right. I do love more than your laugh. But this isn't the place to tell you." She grinned. "And you know what they say about timing!"

That seemed to puzzle Bett, but only for a moment. "Some say it's the most important part."

Maggie kissed her again. "Can you wait 'til we get to your place?"

Bett's smile turned into a laugh, deep in her throat. "I'll wait the rest of my life to hear what I'm seeing in your eyes."

Maggie backed out of the cab, pulling her new office keys from her pocket. "It won't take me that long, darlin'!"

Bett sat up and tapped the horn. "Then hurry it up!"

Maggie was still smiling as she fitted a key in the lock. It didn't work, and she used the truck's headlights to find the right one. That one turned easily, and she opened the door just as Bett hit the horn again.

She turned to wave to her when strong arms grabbed her from behind, dragging her into the office. She couldn't even shout a warning.

❖ ❖ ❖

"I don't like this at all," Ebert said.

Harley nodded. Elise looked back and forth between them, waiting for one of them to say more. Neither did. She'd taken Gyp to the backyard for a run while Tracy waited by the phone. But it never rang.

Finally Harley asked, "After 10:30?"

"Five past," Ebert confirmed.

"Well, *now* what are we going to do?" Elise asked.

Harley smiled at her pronoun, but it was no laughing matter. They'd driven from the City in less than thirty minutes. Even if McIntyre hadn't taken the bridge at 70 the way Elise had, she should've been here by now.

"Did you radio in?" Ebert asked.

"Not yet. My relief's scheduled to come on at midnight. I'm supposed to call in at eleven and say where I am."

Ebert nodded. "She might've stopped at the garage. Or her apartment."

"What's more likely?"

"I'd say the yard on Kenning."

He ground out his cigarette. "I'll go there."

"I'll check Natchez, but let's not lose each other." She turned to Elise. "We'll use your phone to communicate."

"But you can't drive," Elise protested.

Ebert shrugged that off as she and Harley checked the time again. "You'll probably get to the yard first, so call here every three minutes until Elise hears from me."

"What phone will you use?" Harley remembered Natchez as a residential street without any nearby stores.

"The one in her apartment. I've got a key."

That startled Harley, who glanced at Elise, but she didn't seem surprised.

"What if I don't hear from either of you?" she asked.

"Hell," he muttered, getting into his car. "Then you better call the cops!"

"You'll hear from us," Ebert said. "But if anything goes wrong, call the work number I left you. Say you're calling for an officer who needs assistance. Be sure to tell them we're out of uniform, working on assignment for Kessler. Got all that?"

Elise nodded.

"If Maggie and Bett show up, don't let them out of your sight until I get back." She reached for her keys. Elise was still holding them.

"Are you okay?" Elise asked.

"To drive? I told you, I'm fine."

"Not just for driving. For any of this." Elise looked into her eyes and found the stare Ebert reserved for perps. Elise gave up the keys but held onto her hand.

"I'm all right," Ebert said coldly.

Elise still didn't let go. "I'm worried about you, Tracy. I saw you take more pills. I know you're hurting. I just want you to be careful, honey."

They were gentle cautions, but Ebert didn't take them well. "Listen, I've got a very high tolerance for pain. And for drugs and alcohol, too. I know what I'm doing."

"That's not what it looked like a half hour ago."

Ebert didn't take that kind of shit from anybody. "Damn it! Get off…"

"You can't fool me," Elise said. "I know when you're hurt. And when you're angry and scared. When you're hurt, you turn it to anger. You try to do the same thing with fear, but it doesn't work. You start to limp…"

"Shut up!" Ebert's eyes were fierce now.

"Tracy, I'm telling you all this for a reason. You can't stuff all those feelings into an anger bag. They don't belong there. You have to let go, or you'll get hurt, really hurt, next time. You can't…"

"I can't walk behind a badge scared. Drop it, Elise. You don't know what you're talking about."

"Yes, I do. You get into situations that call up fear. You can't deny that. Fear is *supposed* to make you more aware. Of everything around you. If you turn it into anger, you focus it. Don't you see? You need a broad scan when you're in danger: to see escape routes, alternatives. You can't see any of that if you're too focused. And that's what happens when you get angry." She took Tracy's arm. It was an iron bar. "Like now."

"I suppose it's okay to be angry now?" Her sarcasm was biting.

"Yes! I'm challenging you." Elise smiled a little. "It's not how I want you to look at me all the time, but we'll talk about that when you get back." Elise hugged her then, using the embrace to rub Tracy's back and physically loosen her. She felt her relax a little and was relieved to see her cold look had changed to something more familiar.

"You've got some nerve, telling off a cop."

"I've got a lot of nerves," Elise said easily. "Hurry back, and I'll let you play with some."

Tracy shook her head. "You're impossible."

"I know. And you like a challenge now and then." Elise kissed her. "Be careful, honey. I really hate visiting you in the hospital."

Tracy shook out her ignition key, then hugged her roughly. "I'll be okay. You just keep yourself busy. Throw Harley's cards for him. I'll be back before you know it."

Elise watched her drive off, feeling slightly reassured. But she wouldn't risk throwing any cards tonight.

⋄ ⋄ ⋄

Bett stared in shock at the office door. Then a man came out. He had a gun in his left hand and awkwardly transferred it to his right: the one in a sling. Bett knew it was Red Mask. Only he wasn't wearing a mask now. He was shading his eyes against the headlights and coming after her.

She thought about using the truck to run him over, but that was absurd. He wouldn't wait for her to master first gear! When he hesitated over which way to approach her, she knew she only had one chance. And she'd have to be damned lucky for that to work.

She quickly closed the driver's door, bringing darkness to the cab. He sneered at the futility of her action and headed for the passenger door. She pulled up on that handle but held the door closed, covering the button lock as if to lock him out. She saw him reach for the outside handle.

"Get outta' there, you dumb cunt!"

Bett shoved the door with both feet, slamming him back. The gun went off, shattering the window. She heard him curse as he stumbled back, then stoop over, searching for the gun.

She used the open door as cover and ran behind the truck, searching for escape. She had to get out of range. The yard gate was too far. She headed for the end of the garage, running hard. She'd never been a sprinter, yet she made it to the corner of the building before he got off the second shot. A sudden catch in her side surprised her, throwing her off balance. She caught the edge of the garage and flung herself around the corner, sprawling headlong in the dirt. She rolled with the fall, knowing she had to keep moving. The pain in her side jabbed sharply, but she knew it would go away. Red Mask wouldn't.

It was pitch dark, and she stumbled, banging her head on something. She slowed down, wary of other obstacles, then arched her back, fighting the instinct to soothe the pain. Experience had taught her that rubbing a side stitch wouldn't help. Funny how it came on her left side this time. It usually hit her on the right.

She tried to remember where things were from last Saturday, but nothing came clearly to mind. It had just been a confusion of rusting metal junk. Her outstretched hands encountered a smooth, chest-high metal plate. It felt just like the tailgate of a truck. She stopped. It *was* a truck, the same one that had followed them up the mountain. She reached into the truck bed for anything that could be turned into a weapon. She only felt a rough canvas tarp. Then she remembered her bike. It was hidden under a tarp just like this one.

Bett knew what she could do then. He'd never find her.

∴ ∴ ∴

Maggie fought, even as her assailant twisted her arm behind her back. Only the pressure of a gun in her ribs made her stop. Then his grip lessened, and she turned to see a second man going out the door. She tried to warn Bett, but the man holding her shoved her, tripping her as he did. She fell on her unprotected shoulder, slamming her bruised eye on the floor. Stunned, she lay still. Then a shot rang out. She jumped as if she'd been hit. "Bett!"

A booted foot came down on her hand, but it barely slowed her. Then the pressure increased. She felt two sharp cracks, and a wave of nausea went through her. But the sound of a second shot made her struggle more. Finally, the man grabbed her by the shirt and put his gun to her neck.

"Damn you! Stop!"

Maggie heard an unexpected tone in his voice. He lifted his foot, letting her cradle her throbbing hand.

"You think he'd keep shooting if he hit her?" he whispered.

Then Maggie realized what she'd heard: It was fear.

He let go of her and backed to the door, looking out on the yard, then flipped the lights on and turned to her. "Do what I say, and I won't let Dunston hurt you. Hear me?"

She nodded.

"Sit up, and back over to the wall."

Maggie looked around as she did. The office was a shambles; the back window smashed. They'd used cutters to remove the mesh guard. Matt always wanted to put bars on that window. She'd argued against it. Putting bars up would only suggest they kept cash there.

But these were no ordinary thieves. All the files had been emptied. And they'd dumped her desk drawers, too. Papers were strewn all over the floor. She didn't know what they were after, only that they were the same ones who robbed the cabin. Their clothes told her that much. And she didn't like what it meant that she could see their faces.

Then the other man came back. Alone.

"Get me a flashlight, Ross."

"What for?"

She closed her eyes, praying that they'd keep arguing. Praying that Bett would find the break in the fence. Run, Bett. Run!

"The little shit got away. I thought I hit her, but the lousy cunt's hiding out back."

Rage surged through Maggie, even as Ross intervened.

"Forget her!" He pointed to Maggie. "She's the one I saw Fenn with that time. If he hid them anyplace, she'll know where."

She shook her head. "Too late. I already gave the money to the police."

"We saw the news," Dunston said. "There wasn't anything about any bills a' lading. What'd Fenn do with them?"

"Bill...?"

He crouched and put his gun to her head. "Don't play dumb with me."

Maggie knew his threat was real. She also knew what a bill of lading was. But the way he said it made it sound like "bill zalading." Of course! That's what he had demanded at the cabin, and Bett heard it as a name.

Dunston jabbed her with the gun barrel.

"You'll never find them if you kill me." Maggie wasn't as calm as she sounded, but she knew she only had one chance now.

Ross came over. "Put it down. I told you she'd know something."

Maggie felt the gun withdraw, then saw Ross grab Dunston's hand before he could strike her.

"Let her talk," Ross insisted. Then to Maggie: "Where are they?"

"Scotty kept a lot of papers in my file cabinet at home. He…"

Dunston hit her then. Squarely, with the back of his hand. Her head banged the wall. He grabbed her as she fell to one side. "We tossed your place," he snarled. "There weren't any files."

"Wrong…" She gasped, dry-mouthed, struggling to complete her reply before he hit her again. "Wrong apartment." She licked her lips, tasting blood. Her upper lip had feeling, but a familiar numbness was spreading from the center of her face. Damn you if you've broken my nose again!

"Let go of her," Ross demanded.

Maggie heard the sound of a gun hammer being set.

"Let her go, I said. She's trying to tell us something."

Dunston did, and Maggie put a hand out to steady herself.

Ross nudged it with his foot. "Don't forget what I said about getting hurt," he reminded her. "Now, show us where to look."

∴ ∴ ∴

Harley whooped in relief when he crossed Kenning Lane. The M & M gate was open, McIntyre's pickup was parked at the office door, and the lights were on. Not seeing any movement in the yard, he made a U-turn at the end of the cross street and pulled up in front of the pay phone. It was only ten to eleven. McIntyre probably hadn't settled in yet. He could radio at eleven, as planned. He phoned Elise but got a busy signal. Ebert must've gotten to Natchez already. Too bad she didn't have a radio. Direct communication sure would make things easier.

He was just reaching for the radio when a white pickup whipped through the intersection ahead. As he pulled away from the curb, an image nagged at him. He slowed to round the corner, and habit made him glance back toward the yard. What he saw made him slam on his brakes: The office lights were on, the gate was open, and the *same truck* was still parked in front.

He looked up the street, but the other pickup was out of sight. He drove into the yard and pulled alongside the truck. He saw the shattered window and drew his gun. He knew by the storage boxes on the bed and the emblem on the door that *this* was her truck. The other pickup was unmarked. He'd almost chased the wrong one.

He got out of the car, listening intently, but the only sound was that of the idling truck. He checked the cab, but it was empty. He switched the engine off and listened again. The yard was quiet. He went to the office. As soon as he looked in, he knew he was too late. It was a wreck. But an empty wreck. He should have followed that other truck. And now it was eleven. He'd be late calling everybody!

Then he saw a bloodstain on the floor. Was it connected to the bullet hole in the truck? He hadn't seen any blood in the cab. Then he spied a phone cord and followed it to the desk. He had to talk to Ebert.

"Harley?" Elise answered mid-ring, sounding frantic.

"Did Ebert call?"

"Twice. She said if you didn't call…"

"Give me her number. Quick."

He didn't bother writing it down or even saying goodbye. He just hung up and dialed, cursing silently the whole time.

∴ ∴ ∴

Ebert was cursing, too. She knew she'd fucked up when Harley didn't call. If they'd gone together in his car and done a drive-by on this place, she wouldn't be pacing an empty, dark kitchen now.

She had entered Maggie's place, gun in hand, checking each room before turning on any lights. The apartment was still in disarray from the break-in. When she saw a rust-colored stain on the rug, it took her a moment to realize what it was. Then she turned off the lights and went to the kitchen for a shot of whiskey. She tossed it down and called Elise, then waited five minutes and called her again. She was pouring a beer chaser when the phone rang at her end. It was Harley.

He told her he hadn't found Maggie or Bett, but somebody else had. She told him to come and get her. She didn't know what to tell him to report to Kessler, and he didn't ask.

Sipping her beer in the dark kitchen, she damned her own stupidity. How the hell would they ever find Maggie now? They couldn't even put out an APB on the truck Harley saw. She scowled, wincing at the pain that cost, and considered taking another pill. She lit a cigarette and decided in favor of another shot instead. It would give her more immediate relief. Before she could pour it, she heard a vehicle pull into the driveway. Knowing Harley couldn't have gotten here that fast, she looked out the window. Then she smiled, not even noticing the pain in her cheek.

∴ ∴ ∴

Maggie saw Tracy's car as they pulled into the driveway. She didn't know how Ebert knew to be there. Maybe Bett found a phone. But how had she known they'd be coming here?

She didn't care how they'd done it, only that Bett was out of danger. And with Tracy here, they'd all be safe soon. Tracy would know what to do. Maggie counted on her for that. It was just about all she could count on.

Ross's promise to keep Dunston away from her was in earnest, but she knew Dunston's type. He would kill her even if he hadn't voiced that threat. What she didn't know was how bills of lading could be so important. They weren't worth money. Or murder. A waybill was just a record of goods in transit or a delivery receipt.

When she asked about that, Ross gave her a sharp look. Dunston laughed without humor. Maggie had heard other men laugh like that. They went through life hating; fueling themselves with it, even as it ate them up. She was always afraid Scotty would get like that. He was headed that way when she went to get him in Nebraska. She was too new to Oakland to help him get a job that time, and she couldn't hire him. It would be too much like hiring family. And Scotty knew himself pretty well. Knew he was best at figuring how to get away with things. Life just didn't challenge him otherwise.

"Which apartment?" Ross asked as they got out of the truck.

"Upstairs. Across the hall from mine."

Ross led the way. As they went up the stairs, Maggie tried to warn Tracy. "Turn left at the top."

Dunston jabbed her with the gun. "Don't try anything," he warned. "I'm right behind you."

"Take it easy," she said. "I don't want that thing going off by accident."

He snorted at that, and Maggie resisted the impulse to look at her own door. If Tracy was inside, she'd heard everything she needed to know.

❖ ❖ ❖

Ebert drew back from the door and went to the phone in the kitchen. She had expected them to enter Maggie's apartment. Given this new situation, she knew she couldn't take them out alone. As she dialed, she wondered where Bett was. The cab wasn't big enough for four. Then the call clicked through. Ebert whispered her name and request for backup. There was a pause at the other end.

"One moment, please."

She stared at the receiver in disbelief. She'd been put on hold! But that was nothing compared to the shock she got a moment later when she was asked for her badge number. She rattled it off to him. "What the hell do you need that for?" she screamed at the top of her *sotto voce* range.

He didn't answer. Just kept talking about police procedure. Then Ebert realized what he was doing. "Shut up and listen! Don't bother tracing this call." She gave him Maggie's address and demanded immediate backup. Controlling herself, she managed to keep from slamming the phone down. But she knew if they didn't hurry, Harley would walk right in on the scene.

Then she thought of Kessler and dialed his number direct, praying for help. Any kind of help. The phone finally stopped ringing, but it seemed like a long time before anyone spoke. "Detective Williams here."

Frantic that she'd misdialed, Ebert whispered as loudly as she dared, "I'm trying to reach Sergeant Kessler."

"He's down to the coffee machine just now. Got a number he can call you back on?" The bored voice made it sound like mid-afternoon break time!

"No! He can't call me!"

"Wait a minute. Here he comes."

She held her breath, only exhaling when Kessler came on the line. There was hope after all.

❖ ❖ ❖

The truck doors slammed shut, and Bett lay perfectly still. They ignored her hiding place this time, too. When she heard a building door close, she pushed the tarp aside. It had been a bone-rattling ride, and she didn't know which hurt more, her head or her back. She was lying on some kind of tool that dug into her with every bump. And each dip in the road caused her head to bang the truck bed. None of that mattered now. Now she had to find a phone. And where the hell was she?

She rolled to one side and pulled herself eye-level with the top of the tailgate. As she recognized her surroundings, a touch of dizziness came over her, followed by weakness. Diagnosing the cause as her adrenaline level returning to normal, she ignored all that and climbed out. Then she felt something shift inside Maggie's jacket. She slipped it off to unzip the duck pocket. Maybe there was something in there she could use as a weapon.

Damn! The whole back of the jacket was covered with something wet. Probably oil from the truck bed. She silently apologized to Maggie, knowing how careful she was with her clothes. Then she felt the object she'd been lying on throughout the ride. She smiled in the darkness. Her hands shook as she took out Matt's gun. She felt giddy with success already.

It was just like at the cabin. Maggie had said the element of surprise was important. She said something about the advantage of being inside, too. Well, they were inside, and was she ever going to surprise them! A tick sounded in the back of her head, but she dismissed that as easily as she dismissed the thought of calling for help. She didn't need help to save Maggie. They'd done all this before!

She took the carpeted stairs two at a time, slowing as she neared the top to catch her breath. The dizzy feeling returned, and she noticed a diffuse white light that didn't seem to have a source. She looked around, recognizing again the slow-motion effect she'd experienced at the cabin. Maybe this was the edge Maggie meant. Everything was very clear, yet very, very slow. The door of the second apartment was half open. Light came from within, but it was dim compared to the aura surrounding her.

Then she heard voices and, as if waking from a dream, knew what she was doing there. She would slip through the door sideways and catch them off guard. Tightening her finger on the trigger, she took a few steps. The odd light seemed to follow her. She shook her head, irritated by the distraction. Then her legs stopped paying attention to her brain, and she walked *into* the door.

Her surprise wasted, she tried to recover. Tried to face the voices. But she couldn't turn. She couldn't tell up from down. The last thing she knew was Maggie's voice, calling her name. She didn't even hear the gun go off when she hit the floor.

❖ ❖ ❖

Maggie tensed at a sound in the hallway. She'd been expecting Tracy to come through the door. She turned obliquely, prepared to dive out of the line of fire. But it wasn't Tracy.

"Bett!" She watched her pitch forward into the room.

The gunshot froze the men momentarily. Maggie didn't hear it. She could only see Bett, lying on the floor in a blood-soaked shirt. She started for her.

"Stay there," Dunston said. "Get the gun, Ross."

But Maggie didn't care what he said now. She'd kill them both with her bare hands if they tried to stop her. Her mind began a litany of no's as she moved toward Bett. No, darlin'. No. You're supposed to be safe somewhere. Anywhere. Not here. You can't be here, covered with… Oh, god! No!

Maggie saw how pale she was. Her ivory skin even whiter than usual, making her hair black in contrast—the color she thought it was the first night they met. Bett looked so fragile then. And now. So delicate, so precious. How could she think these words now? When it was too late. Too late to say how much I love you. Oh, Bett. I never even told you once…

She felt Ross's hand on her shoulder but kept going. She didn't care about their threats. They couldn't hurt her any more than she was already. She could hardly breathe. Her chest ached like a new bruise, like it was caving in on her. She knew it was her heart. Broken now for sure. Forever.

She shrugged him off, and he grabbed her hand to twist it behind her the way he had at the office. That pain got through to her, reminding her of who had done this to Bett. To her. She turned, violently wrenching her hand free, then used her momentum to swing her other arm, windmilling his throat with her fist. The pain in her hand was nothing compared to her rage.

Ross wasn't expecting any of her moves. Stunned, he fell to his knees, gasping for air. She shoved him. He wasn't prepared for that, either. His head snapped back, cracking dully against an iron bed leg. His rasping ceased. He didn't move again.

"So, the bitch has some fight!" Dunston reached for the gun on the desk.

Maggie focused on him then. He was the one who'd shot Bett. Said he thought he'd hit her. Then he'd called Bett names, terrible names. Maggie hadn't been able to do anything then. But that was when she had hope. When she still cared. She had someone to live for then. That was a long time ago. A lifetime ago.

She headed for him. "The bitch is going to kill you."

❖ ❖ ❖

Ebert was answering Kessler's quick, calm questions, when she heard a shot and a muffled shout. She uttered, "Gunfire!" into the phone, then dropped the receiver and headed for the door, pulling her gun out on the way. As she crossed the hallway to crouch at the other door, she heard the thud of a body falling heavily. It could have been the one lying just beyond the threshold of the other apartment. The sight of so much blood appalled her. Then she realized who it was. Jesus, Bett, where did you come from?

She took in all the visuals in an instant, then listened. She heard Maggie's voice. Only Maggie didn't talk like that. Then she heard a more familiar sound: the metallic click of a gun hammer. She kicked the door open. Maggie was walking directly toward a man with a gun.

"*Police! Freeze!*"

Her command was aimed at Maggie as much as the gunman, but only one of them responded. The gunman sighted another armed challenge and fired. Ebert dove left, knowing her only chance was to keep ahead of the bead he'd draw on her. She moved instinctively, changing direction a fraction of an instant before he fired again. Then she stopped, mid-roll, and assumed the position she knew by rote: bracing her elbows, adjusting her aim fractionally, drawing breath. Her finger tightened, then she stopped.

She couldn't shoot. He couldn't, either. Maggie had grabbed his gun arm and was wrestling with him, directly in the line of fire. Maggie wasn't after his gun, though. She was going for his throat.

Ebert shouted, "Stand back!" She could have saved her breath.

Maggie had forced his gun arm up and was clutching his throat, intent on throttling him. He swiped her with the gun, raking the side of her face. She put her head down and butted him, knocking him into the filing cabinet. His shoulder caught the corner, making him howl with pain. He dropped the gun, alternately grabbing at that and swinging at her with his fist.

She didn't seem to notice. She grabbed his shirt, slamming him into the cabinet again. He didn't make a sound this time. He slumped to the floor, his eyes glazed over. She tried to pick him up and couldn't. She looked around the room wildly, then focused on his gun.

"No, Maggie! No!" Ebert rose to stop her but wasn't fast enough.

Maggie picked up the gun and trained it on him with both hands, wanting to make her aim perfect. Deadly perfect.

Ebert smashed a bandaged hand with her gun, just as Maggie pulled the trigger. She never expected to hear Maggie make that kind of sound. Her scream was terrifying an anguish beyond measure.

For a long moment there was silence. Then a siren wailed in the distance.

❖ ❖ ❖

When Harley arrived, he expected to find Ebert near her car. Then he saw the other pickup in the driveway and pulled in behind it. They wouldn't get away this time! His headlights shone on something in the driveway, and he picked up a leather jacket. It was soaked with blood.

Before he could even wonder about that, two shots rang out in quick succession. He dropped the jacket, pulled his gun, and dashed through the door of the duplex. He heard a struggle going on above, then Ebert's shout. He was halfway up the stairs when he heard a third shot, then an awful scream. He stood in the middle of the staircase, too stunned by the scream to move, only knowing he never wanted to hear one like it again. He waited for another sound. One that would erase the terrible echo in his head.

But there were no sounds from above. Just a siren, far away. It was what he needed to get moving again.

At the head of the stairs, he looked each way in the hall. Both apartment doors were open. He swallowed hard, then called Ebert's name.

"Harley?" she called back. "In here."

Something in her tone made him wary. He entered the apartment and saw bodies everywhere. The one just inside the door looked the worst. He put his gun away and surveyed the rest of the victims. A white male lay on the floor at the end of the bed. Another white male looked like he was asleep against a filing cabinet. Ebert was holding the redhead, the woman he was supposed to have protected. It should have been such a breeze.

She must have been the one who'd screamed. She was a bloody mess. Her hands hung limply over Ebert's shoulders. Her bandages had been clean, nearly white, when he first saw her striding toward Kessler. Now they were bloodied and torn. Ebert was trying to doctor a cut on the side of her face. Harley had to look away. Not because of the blood, but because of her eyes. They were eerily vacant.

He didn't know what to say. He couldn't see Ebert's face but knew she didn't want to talk. And whatever had happened, the action was over. Now it was time to pick up the pieces. He knelt beside the girl on the floor and pressed his fingers to her neck, then shook his head and went to the phone.

"I don't guess I'll ever get over it," he said.

"That's what's wrong with being a cop," Ebert said bitterly. "You get all too used to seeing dead bodies."

"Huh-uh. I got used to that part already."

"What then?"

He finished dialing and nodded at Bett. "That anybody can lose that much blood and still live. She looks even worse than you…"

"She's *alive?*"

"'Cording to what they taught me, she is. It isn't exactly a throbbing pulse, but…" He spoke into the phone.

Ebert glanced at Bett in disbelief. "Maggie, did you hear? Bett's alive!" She didn't know if her words got through. She turned back to Maggie just in time to catch her as she slid to the floor.

CHAPTER 28.

Hurts Like the Devil

TRACY AND ELISE WERE at the hospital by mid-morning Thursday. The nurse told them not to stay too long with Bett. She was listed in satisfactory condition but still quite weak.

Bett's first question was about Maggie. "Is she all right?"

"She's fine," Tracy assured her. "We haven't seen her yet, but she's not the one who got shot and lost a gallon of blood."

"Are you sure? They only told me she'd been admitted. They won't let me go see her, she doesn't answer her phone, and she hates hospitals." Bett started crying then, helplessly.

Elise asked Tracy to find out what was happening. "Maybe they won't let her come down without help." She gave Bett a tissue. "There's a guard outside your door. You and Maggie are both in protective custody now."

Bett nodded, wiping her eyes. "A nurse said they were looking for a third man. But they wouldn't keep Maggie away because of that, would they?"

Tracy shook her head as she left.

"I'm sorry to send her away," Bett said. "Not just because I want to know what happened, but… oh, damn! Why am I crying like this?"

"You're probably reacting to the anesthesia," Elise said. "Remember when I had my wisdom teeth pulled?"

Bett giggled through her tears. "You were really goofy!"

Elise took her friend's hand, wondering why Maggie wasn't here at her side.

❖ ❖ ❖

Tracy was thinking the same thing as she showed her badge at Maggie's door. The officer on guard gave her a nod of recognition.

"Heard about you at roll call," the guard said. "Glad you got that back."

Tracy seemed to be the only one on the force who hadn't known her badge was stolen. She entered and found Maggie sitting at the window.

"Hey, guy!" Tracy greeted. Maggie nodded then faced the window again. Tracy joined her and looked out, but the view was just of a parking lot.

"How you feeling?"

Maggie shrugged. "So-so. You?"

"Fine. Tired." She'd never seen Maggie so still and unresponsive. "You sure you're okay? What did the…"

"Ross talked," Maggie said abruptly. "There's another guy involved. That's why Brian posted the guard."

Tracy was startled by Maggie's interruption. This wasn't like her. "When did you talk to Kessler?"

"This morning. I called him."

"So your phone *does* work. Bett tried to reach you…" She saw Maggie turn away. "What's wrong?"

When Maggie didn't reply, Tracy examined her more closely. One eye, the one still multi-colored from last week, was freshly bruised. Her nose was swollen, but the cut on her cheek was faint, just a sharp vertical line. All in all, she'd come through the assault pretty well. "So, you can sit up. Want to walk me to the elevator?"

Maggie started to rise. "You have to leave so soon?"

"No, I thought we'd go see Bett. Tell her…"

Maggie sat down and looked out the window again. "I forgot. They're coming to get me for some kind of test." She glanced up briefly. "She's awake now, huh?"

Tracy's instincts rose. What the hell was wrong? Then she asked the obvious but unimaginable: "Why don't you want to see Bett?"

Maggie's jaw clenched. "Already did," she said tightly. "She was asleep. Needs her rest. The nurse told me."

Tracy knew that was true. Not that anybody could get much rest in a hospital. She cocked her head. "What kind of test?"

"Oh, you know," Maggie said, "doctors always want you to pee in a bottle or bleed in a tube. Just routine." She looked out the window again.

Tracy knew that wasn't the whole truth. Then another thought occurred to her. "You aren't torqued at me, are you? For hitting you last night?"

"Torqued?" Maggie's eyebrows knit again. She looked incredibly like a child trying not to cry. "You kept me from murdering that fucker." Her voice was as tight as her forehead.

"Not murder!" Tracy was shocked at her description. Both parts of it.

"Oh? What do they call it when you lose control and shoot somebody?"

"You didn't shoot him," Tracy said quickly. "And they would have called it self-defense if you had." She was stunned by Maggie's emotional outburst. She was always so self-possessed. Tracy was the one with the short fuse. Maggie fixed things.

"He wasn't shooting at me."

Tracy touched Maggie's shoulder tentatively. "I know. But you probably kept him from shooting me. I owe you." When she didn't reply, Tracy went to the door. "It isn't murder when you shoot to save somebody else. They call that justifiable homicide. You can ask Kessler, but I don't think he'd have locked you up if I'd been a second later."

She left then, still not understanding what was wrong. She stopped at the nurses' station to ask about Maggie's test, telling the nurse she needed to know when to pick her up. Tracy never minded lying for a good reason.

"Well," the nurse hedged, "since it's a patient request... She's going down for an EKG. That'll take about an hour or so."

Tracy was thoughtful as she joined Elise at Bett's door.

"Did you see Maggie? Is she okay?"

"Yeah. How's Bett?"

"In and out of sleep. I told her I'd come in to say good-bye when you two got back. Where's Maggie? Isn't she coming?"

"Not yet."

As they reentered the room, Bett tried to sit up. "Maggie...?"

Tracy hated the thought of deflating her eagerness. Sometimes it galled her to lie. She eased Bett back down. "I saw Maggie. She's fine. She says she came down before, when you were asleep."

"And I missed her," Bett cut in sadly. She closed her eyes, but tears of disappointment escaped silently.

Tracy's short fuse began burning then. How could Maggie do this? It was so little to ask. She took a quick breath. "Yeah, well, she wanted to come down, but they're giving her some kind of test before they release her. And she has to make a statement to Kessler. She wants you to get more rest." Tracy pulled a tissue from the box to wipe Bett's eyes, then took a deeper breath. "She promised to come and see you tonight."

Bett sniffled. "I'm sorry to be such a crybaby. She's right, of course. Learned that from me, you know. About rest, I mean." She kissed Tracy's hand lightly. "Thanks."

"What for?"

"For saving Maggie." Bett released Tracy's hand and closed her eyes. Her words came more slowly: "Elise told me... after I... passed out. Funny how... tried to save Maggie. Then you came... and she..." Bett fell asleep then, and her visitors left quietly.

Tracy stalked down the hall and savagely punched the elevator button, then lit a cigarette, exhaling the first drag just as the doors opened.

Elise stared at her as they got into the empty car. "Honey, you can't smoke in here!"

"Let 'em arrest me." Tracy hit the lobby button.

Elise raised her hands. "Okay, okay! But tell me what's going on. First you lie to Bett, then you yell at me."

The elevator doors opened, and Tracy crossed the lobby without replying. Elise caught up with her at the exit. "I'd better drive. Or do you want to get a speeding ticket all by yourself?"

Tracy finally seemed to hear her. "How'd you know I was lying to Bett?"

She smiled. "If I told you that, you'd change your MO, and I'd have to start all over again!"

Tracy tossed her head but gave Elise the keys. On the drive home, she described her encounter with Maggie.

"Well, she's not as hostile about visitors as some people." Elise watched the road as she stroked Tracy's hand. "What do you think is going on?"

"I don't know. She could be hurt worse than I thought. But she didn't act like this last week, and she was a lot more hurt then. To see her now, you'd think Bett *had* died."

"Don't even think that!"

"Well, you would've thought I was asking her to pick out a casket…"

"Tracy, stop! You'll make me cry if you don't." Elise pulled into a space in front of the apartment. "They've both been through a terrible week. Maybe Maggie doesn't realize it's over yet."

"Maybe." Tracy followed her up the stairs. "Do you know what an EKG is? That's the test she was going to have."

"I've heard of it, sure." Elise unlocked the door and Gyp flew out, leaping up on them to express his joy at their return. She led him down the stairs where they watched him tear around the backyard. "They use EKGs for heart problems, I think."

"Yeah, that's what I thought. But I don't know why she'd be having one. And that's the weird part: The nurse said it was a patient request. No doctor ordered it. Maggie did."

"I don't know, Trace. I always ask Bett about medical stuff. Maybe she's got some kind of condition."

Tracy snorted at that, then whistled for Gyp. As they went back upstairs Elise asked why that sounded so implausible.

"Maggie's healthy as a horse. Besides, she doesn't know a thing about her body. She didn't even know what a pap smear was until I told her."

"You mean she'd never had one?"

"Only after I insisted. But she said she'd never do it again. She'd never had a sick day in her life, and she was going to keep it that way without any doctor sticking cold pliers up inside her."

Elise shook her head. "Bett will fix that."

Tracy shrugged. There was a lot she couldn't convince Maggie of. Maybe Bett would have better luck. She started for the kitchen, but Elise stopped her with a hug that turned into a long kiss.

"Going someplace?" she asked.

A long time later, Elise rested her head between Tracy's breasts. "I love to listen to your heart slow."

Tracy sighed contentedly, then gasped involuntarily.

"What is it, honey?" Elise moved to lie next to her.

"Nothing. A crazy thought."

Elise gently combed her hair back from her bandage. "Tell me."

"Well, at the Academy they warned us not to get involved with victims. Small Eyes even gave us a lecture on it one time. I don't know how Maggie really feels about Bett, but if that'd been you lying on the floor, nobody could've kept me from killing that bastard. She thought Bett was dead. We all did. Even Harley. He was just doing what he'd been taught. He was as surprised as anybody that she was alive." Tracy paused. "Now she thinks she's a murderer. Or could be."

Elise tried to picture what had really happened last night. "I don't think it would have been self-defense," she said, "or justifiable homicide."

"Not murder!" Tracy protested.

"No. But Maggie wasn't saving anybody's life. It was revenge, pure and simple. I think it's what they used to call a crime of passion."

Tracy snorted. "Not Maggie. She told me she wasn't passionate."

Elise giggled through her reply: "And... you... believed... her!"

Tracy protested, "That's what she said."

Elise laughed again. "What did she say that convinced you?"

"It isn't just what she said. I've seen her around women."

"Are you a voyeur?"

"Of course not! But we used to go to the bar together. She only liked to go to the Fox. We went to the City exactly once. I was surprised when she agreed to go last night."

"Well, I know Maggie *can* be passionate. Bett told me about their first night."

Tracy's eyes widened. "Did you tell her about ours?"

"Not yet." Elise grinned. "Bett and I are very good friends. But she's been gone, and you've been here. Don't you and Maggie exchange stories?"

"Not on your life. Not Maggie. In fact, for a long time I thought she might be asexual. But every once in a while, I'd see her leave the Fox with someone. I asked her if she'd ever had a full-time lover. She just laughed and said, 'Sex is sex. It has its place like eating and sleeping.'"

"Oh, god! Poor Bett."

"It's not like she's a nut about celibacy, Elise. She said somebody once told her that it wasn't healthy to go without sex."

"And did Maggie agree?"

"Hard to tell. She said she felt better if she did it once in a while. But then she said, 'That's like believing in taking vitamin C for a cold.'"

"Are you serious?" Elise asked.

"I think she was just kidding. Maggie always jokes like that."

"But it's all so pathetic!"

"Well, yeah, it is kind of sad. But she's normal otherwise."

"If that's normal, what's *ab*normal?"

"Depends on what you measure. She's probably the most successful woman I know. She and Matt built it all from scratch in ten years. But since he died, she's pulled the whole load practically by herself. She works too hard, and I doubt if she's taken any time off in the last few years, so it's not like she's had time to develop any long-term love affairs. This week is probably the first time she's been away from the garage for more than thirty-six hours straight. Too bad it had to be such a shitty time."

"No, that doesn't fit."

"What doesn't?"

Elise sighed in exasperation. "Don't they teach you cops observation? You saw the two of them here yesterday. If they weren't ready to hit the nearest bed, I'll eat my lambda!"

"You can tell that, huh? What exactly are you majoring in, anyway?"

Elise grinned. "And last night, too. I expected them to be here before we arrived, with the lights off already!"

Tracy nodded. "Maggie sure didn't show any of that today."

Elise was recalling her own vigil of worry. Would it repeat itself every night Tracy wasn't safely at her side? She tightened her hold. "You won't get hurt again, will you, honey?"

Tracy cocked her head. "Is that a threat or a question?"

"Don't joke. I'm serious. I…"

Tracy kissed her. "I can't promise that. Last night I did everything by the book. Even Kessler said so. But I was lucky, too. I can't count on that." She covered her eyes with her arm to hide sudden tears. "I'm losing it, Elise. I'm scared. Too fucking…" She rolled away to sit at the edge of the bed.

Elise went around and knelt in front of her. "You weren't just lucky. You were smart. You let your fear work for you instead of fighting it."

"Jesus, Elise, don't you get it? I can't be scared. I'm a cop! Cops aren't supposed to be afraid."

"There are lots of shoulds and shouldn'ts in the world. Women aren't supposed to love women, either. You don't let that get in your way." She was heartened by Tracy's smile. "Can't you talk to Harley?"

"No. He's a good guy. Helluva partner. But he couldn't deal with this. It would just freak him out."

"Why? He isn't freaked out by your being gay, and that's…"

"Nobody on the force knows I'm gay! I'd lose my job if they did. And if Harley knew I was scared…" She paused. "Anyhow, I can't afford to get a rep' for that, either."

"You can't afford *not* to be up front with Harley. He trusts you with his life, every day. Don't you owe it to him to be completely honest?"

"I can't give him something like that to hold over me."

"Do you really think he would?"

She shook her head. "No. He tried to take the heat for everything last night, but he's a lousy liar. Kessler saw right through his story."

"All the more reason for you to be honest with him." Elise sat back. "Maybe I'll invite him for dinner some night. If you two talked with your badges off, you might be surprised."

"Not likely," Tracy said disdainfully.

Elise laughed. "You want to be such a tough guy! You can't convince me of that when you don't have any clothes on." She pushed Tracy back on the bed. "You can try convincing me of something else, though!"

"Try, huh?" Tracy drew her close. "Are you challenging me again?"

Elise grinned. "I think you're up for it!"

⋄ ⋄ ⋄

Brian hardly knew what to think when Maggie arrived that afternoon: She looked awful and sounded worse. He decided not to say anything in front of Williams, and they began taping her statement. It was fairly straightforward, until they got to the part about her seizing Dunston's gun.

"That's all I remember," Maggie said in the same lifeless tone she'd used throughout the interview.

Brian switched off the recorder. "If you're afraid of incriminating…"

"I don't remember anything," she said evenly, "until I woke up in the ER."

Williams spoke then. "If you'll just say that on tape, Ms. McIntyre, we can wrap this up."

She glanced at him. "I always look over my shoulder when anybody calls me that. I answer quicker to 'Maggie.'"

He nodded, and they finished the interview a few minutes later. Williams said he would get it typed up, then asked, "Are you okay, Maggie?"

The corners of her mouth turned up slightly. "Fine. Thanks."

"Good. I'll get on it, then. You probably want to head back to the hospital. I'm glad your friend's going to be okay, too."

Brian saw how quickly her smile disappeared. "You sure you're okay?" He watched her light yet another cigarette. She'd smoked nearly half a pack in the time they'd spent taping her statement.

"I'm fine," she said woodenly. "Will I have to testify?"

"Maybe. Maybe not." He waggled a hand. "Ross's statement marks Dunston for Fenn's murder. Then there's insurance fraud…" He paused as her expression grew more grave. "Listen, I'm going to sign out. We'll go get a sandwich and a beer. I hate talking in these rooms. I always feel like I'm waiting for somebody to confess."

"Let's just get it over with," she said sharply.

In all the years he'd known her, she'd never used that tone with him. He decided to take it another way. "Okay. No argument. I'll let you buy." He thought she was going to refuse. But she only closed her mouth tightly.

At the Last Tour, the noon rush had come and gone, and the four o'clock crowd was still upsetting its collective stomach with machine-grade coffee. They had the place pretty much to themselves.

"I'm not really hungry." Maggie's voice seemed calmer in the dim bar.

"No surprise," he said. "From what Ebert told me, you were in a tough spot last night. I should have put you in protective custody a lot sooner."

"It was my own fault. I shouldn't have stopped at the garage." Her voice was tight again, and she lit a cigarette as the waitress served them each a beer and a shot. Maggie eyed the extra drink. "What's this?"

"Thought we'd celebrate a little." He clinked the shot glasses. "Cheers!" He signaled for another round, then turned to her. "Okay. You want to go first?" When she didn't answer, he prompted: "Let's start with your hands. Your bandages look different. What's the word on those?"

She shifted her left hand self-consciously. "No broken bones. They wrap them thicker at the hospital, is all." She saw his expectant look. "The new skin was damaged on this hand. Might take an extra week to heal."

"What about the right?"

"Same-same."

"You mean the same as the left? Or the same as before?"

"Same as before. Tracy only hit my..." She looked up, then studied her beer again. "How'd you know?"

"I know you," he said simply. "And they didn't give me these stripes just because I'm so handsome." He didn't say what he'd had to go through to get the whole story from Ebert. He hadn't decided what to do with her yet. Despite how messy last night had been, no one had died. He was grateful for that, but still concerned about Ebert's reactions. And now Maggie's.

"What's going to happen next?" Maggie asked.

"Well, we'll order lunch. Have a little chat..."

"To that... to Dunston, I mean. Do you have a case, or is it all up to some sleazeball posting his bail?"

"We have a case." Brian had never seen her so fierce. "You sound like he should be in jail for his own protection."

"Do I?" She tossed her shot. "Don't worry. I won't lose control again."

Brian wondered why she was so angry now. From what Hugh Miller said, she'd had reason, and opportunity, to shoot Dunston at the cabin. In Summit County it would've been self-defense, open and shut. He knew she didn't think in those terms, but he was equally sure she was trying to avoid incriminating herself today. What could have changed so much in a day?

"Can you keep him locked up?" she asked.

He nodded. "Ross's statement makes a pretty strong case for the DA. That wouldn't do it alone, but the slate's loaded on them both—attempted murder, assault, and kidnapping here. And Williams is working with the Vegas PD on arson, insurance fraud, and possibly manslaughter."

He waited for her next question. When she didn't ask more, he opened a menu.

"Beef stew's pretty good," he offered. "And their steak sandwich is worth…" He saw her pale suddenly. "You okay?"

"Sure. Food just… doesn't appeal to me yet."

"Well, you better eat something. You look like you've lost ten pounds. And except for between your ears, you don't have ten to spare." He was glad to see her smile, however thinly.

"Maybe I'll get a burger…" She put a hand to her chest, closing her eyes briefly. "What's the story on the waybills? Why were they so important?"

Brian ordered first, then started with what Hawkins had told him about Fenn's unusual visit, and what Williams had learned from the Vegas PD about the warehouse fire.

By the time their food arrived, he was explaining the arson investigation. "Dunston was trained in demolition. The charge he fixed had a timer on it so Ross and Fenn would both have alibis when it blew. Ross says they planted it on a tanker that Fenn had parked next to NoCal after making sure the rig wasn't quite empty. Ross swears he didn't know there was a guard at the trailer company."

"I still don't get it," Maggie said. "Why would they blow up NoCal's warehouse unless it was overinsured? And wouldn't that be the first thing the arson squad checked?"

"The key's insurance all right, but the building was leased. Think about the contents instead."

"NoCal wouldn't profit from goods damaged in storage. Only the shipper could file a claim for that."

"Right. You know a San Leandro company called Shazam Computers?"

"Sure. Glen Nichols is in charge of shipping and receiving there. He gave Scotty a job… Wait a minute. Glen's not in on this, is he?"

"No, but I wondered who you knew there. Does the name Larry Sheridan ring any bells?"

"Vaguely. Who is he?"

"President of Shazam Computers and owner of Sheridan Leasing. He's the third guy in this circus. He could be the ringleader, but I doubt it."

"Who then?"

"I think Scott Fenn engineered this whole thing." Brian expected a strong reaction from Maggie. But instead of telling him to fuck off, or whatever colloquialism she'd use for that, she only stared at the untouched food on her plate.

Finally she looked up. "So there's more to it than just the money we found in the knapsack?"

He nodded. "Not only more money, but some interesting conversations on those cassettes you brought back."

"But those were commercial tapes!"

Brian nodded. "Williams showed me how they can be recorded over."

"What was on them?"

"Two different talks with Sheridan. Fenn was blackmailing him for a cool million. The money you found in the thermos was his payoff for setting the fire in Vegas. He told Sheridan that fire was 'worth a lot more than a savings bond and a coffee mug.'"

"I knew I'd heard that name before," she mused. "Sheridan was the guy Scotty tipped about the inventory-tax loophole. The savings bond... How did you know what that meant?"

"Lois Delano told Williams about it."

"Aaugh! Lois! I haven't even called her. How is she?"

"She'll be okay. Seems Fenn listened to you once in a while after all. Ross admitted to breaking into their apartment and stealing a file box. Fenn's life insurance policy was..."

"Goddamn him!" she said fiercely. "Who the hell cares about money? You can't buy anybody back to life!"

Brian had never known Maggie to swear, even mildly. And for a moment, he thought she was going to cry. Instead, she tossed the rest of her shot and chased it with a swallow of beer.

"I got to him too late," she said dully.

"Maggie, he was dead before he hit the ground!"

"No, not then. I mean years ago. Back home. I should've married him instead of..."

Brian laughed spontaneously, then apologized. "Look, I don't know what your relationship to Scott Fenn was way back when, but you couldn't have made any more difference by having a marriage license between you. It doesn't work that way."

"Then what does? There must be some way of keeping people from messing up their lives. Doesn't Mary Jo keep you in line?"

"I like to think I keep myself in line." Maggie's perception of marriage surprised him. Was that how she really thought of him and Mary Jo? "Who keeps you in line, Maggie?"

"I do, of course. Some people can take care of themselves. They know what to do, right from the start. But not everybody. Some people need help."

"Sort of like you help the little billies?"

"Exactly!"

"But you don't marry them, do you?"

"No." She shook her head. "Guess that doesn't make much sense, huh?"

Brian smiled gently. "Why was Fenn so important to you? Were you..." He paused. "Lovers" didn't seem like the right word. "Did you go steady?"

"No. But we've known each other forever." She looked away. "He's just my last connection to... people back home."

"Bud and Libby?"

"No, they left Minnesota—retired to Brownsville—right after I came out here."

She picked up her burger thoughtfully but still didn't take a bite. "No, not people exactly. There isn't anybody now. Maybe I just feel rootless with him gone. No past anymore, you know?"

"Has anybody ever told you you've got some peculiar ideas?"

"All the time lately!"

Brian saw her start to grin, then she put a hand to her chest, grimacing.

"What's wrong?"

"Nothing." She moved her hand to her forehead. "I'm just tired."

"We can talk later if you want to go up to the hospital."

"No. Forget it." She looked around. "Where's the restroom?"

Brian pointed to the far end of the bar, and she headed that way, displaying only a slight list in her gait. He thought the drinks had relaxed her. Then the waitress called him to the phone. It was Williams.

"I could bring the papers over," the detective hinted. "The coffee's awful bad here."

Brian smiled. "Okay, but give us another half hour." When he got back to the booth, Maggie had returned.

"What was the blackmail scam?" she asked. "Scotty couldn't very well blow the whistle on the fraud without getting tagged for the arson."

"True, but he knew Sheridan had a lot more to lose than he did. Fenn could disappear without leaving much behind. Sheridan couldn't. Or at least Fenn banked on that. I'm pretty sure he set the whole thing up. On one of the tapes, he reminds Sheridan of who typed up the waybills."

"I still can't figure that out," Maggie countered. "A bill of lading isn't like a bond or anything."

"Right, but let me tell you what Williams found out. Sheridan Leasing is where they build new systems called mini-computers—don't ask me what that means. All I know is that, with add-on stuff, they can sell for a hundred grand and more. Load a few of those in a warehouse, and it doesn't take long to get twenty-five million dollars worth in storage."

She nodded. "Scotty told me some of their special jobs went for even more. But what's the connection between Sheridan Leasing and Shazam Computers, other than who owns them?"

"Shazam refits the systems that come back on expired leases. They clean them up, put in new, state-of-the-art components, and sell them outright. That's how Sheridan competed in the used-equipment market, by offering a low price plus the latest goods."

"So what's his problem that he'd get involved in an insurance swindle?"

"The market for his systems is starting to disappear. Sheridan Leasing is like other mini-computer manufacturers. They sell to all sorts of companies that need computers but can't afford big mainframes like the government uses. So the mini-computer market was a gold mine, until a couple of years ago when IBM put its muscle into microcomputers. Before that, micros were in the toy department or hobby stores. They weren't any kind of threat to mid-size computer companies. Now those little computers are taking off, and the whole ballgame's changing. Sheridan needed the money."

"That can't be it, Brian. I run a business, too. It might not be as big as Sheridan's, but one thing's for sure: he *owes* for those burned up machines. He's already spent—I don't know, probably twenty million—just building them. That's a hell of a lot of risk for not much return. Those computers weren't free!"

"But they were," Brian insisted. "That's why the connection between Shazam and Sheridan was so perfect. One ships new, and the other ships re-fits. Think about it this way: What if they shipped systems to Vegas that they *said* were worth twenty-five million but were really nothing but gutted cabinets? Ones that didn't have anything in them except dead components and some circuit boards to make it look right?"

Maggie got it then. She shook her head. "I'd never make it as a cop!"

He smiled. "Well, I'll never be able to set my points, either."

"And on a Ford, too!" She laughed then, genuinely.

Brian went on. "The claims guy said the fire was so intense they had to use a chemical bath to lift the serial numbers off some of the cabinets. They could never have figured out what was in them, or fought a suit. Sheridan didn't press the claim, though. He didn't want to stir up any investigations. Fenn had picked the insurer, knowing they were new to the business. That was his mistake. Being new, they'd never had to deal with a loss that size. They dragged their feet, delaying payment until about ten days ago."

"So what made push come to shove?"

"Fenn, of course. He told Sheridan to demand settlement on the systems that they'd positively identified. That's on the first tape. He wanted his cut and told Sheridan to threaten suit for the full amount plus damages if they didn't pay up. He predicted they'd at least make partial settlement. If Fenn had been in charge, he probably would've had the whole wad six months ago, but he couldn't exactly file the claim himself.

"Fenn saw Sheridan again last Friday. That's what's on the second tape. He got his payoff for the fire, then set up the blackmail."

"He should've gone to college," Maggie muttered.

"Maybe. Maybe he wouldn't have known about waybills if he hadn't been a truck driver."

"Or a shipping clerk," she said bitterly.

"Cut it out, Maggie!" Brian said sharply. "You can't keep taking the rap for him. He never played anything straight, and you know it. The more he knew about something, the more he'd turn it around on somebody. He used everything and everybody. He might never have used you, but if that's true, you're alone in the world!"

Brian saw the hurt in her eyes. "Sorry, I…"

"Skip it." She finished her drink and lit another cigarette. "Okay. Scotty could've set it up. He thought that way. But whatever he had on Sheridan wasn't just waybills. They only label a shipment or show proof of delivery. You can't make them do more than that. Even Scotty couldn't."

"And he didn't. Proof of delivery was all he needed. He got the list of computers that came back to Shazam, the ones they planned to gut and ship to Vegas, then got tracers from all the carriers that had hauled them brand new from Sheridan Leasing two or three years before. For every system that burned, Fenn had a microfilm print of the signed bill of lading from the original delivery—proof that they weren't new systems, which was what the claims were based on.

"He gave Sheridan one of those delivery copies, then showed him the matching serial number on the insurance claim. You can hear Sheridan practically scream on the tape. He was absolutely caught. Fenn had waited until all the fraud was done, including the first payment from the insurer. He told Sheridan the rest of the waybills were going to the insurer unless he forked over a million bucks."

Maggie smoked in silence for a minute. "Putting a hit on Scotty was a pretty big risk. He could've sent one of those if-anything-happens-to-me letters to somebody."

"According to Ross, Sheridan didn't exactly put a hit on him. He *did* tell Dunston about Fenn's double-cross. Dunston told Ross he was going to get a bigger cut out of Fenn than what they'd get from Sheridan. He rigged Fenn's gas gauge and drained most of the fuel so he wouldn't get far. Ross says they lost him in traffic that night, then found his car on the side of the freeway and waited for him. When he came down the ramp, Dunston went to talk to him. Ross saw Fenn push the gun aside and laugh at him. Dunston hit him with it, and it went off."

Maggie nodded. "He never did use that gun…" She left her thought unfinished. "Then Dunston fired the car?"

"Right. Ross says Fenn didn't have his knapsack when he got to the car with the gas can. After trying to get his personal effects from the morgue, they wondered if he'd left the bag in his car. They got a copy of the accident report and knew M & M had towed it to the yard. They waited until midnight Saturday to go get the wreck and saw you and Bett there. They tailed you, and when you headed east on 80, they were sure you were on your way to Reno to gamble with the cash."

"It all fits," Maggie said. "It was nearly dawn when we got to Eagle Pass. They stuck around trying to find us Sunday, then tossed the cabin until they found the knapsack, but no money or papers. They probably figured Scotty left it in the car after all. So, back to Oakland. Jeez, they must've put a thousand miles on that truck, just chasing back and forth to Eagle Pass."

"They were busy, all right," Brian said. "They took the wreck Sunday night, broke into Lois's apartment Monday, went to Bett's from there, then your place. Dunston was sure you'd hidden the waybills somewhere."

"Tuesday the storm hit," Maggie mused. "Who treated Dunston's back?"

"A twenty-four-hour clinic outside of Sacramento. Bett's shot cracked his scapula. Painful but not life-threatening. Your body-slam broke it clear through." Brian shuddered just thinking about it. But it didn't seem to faze Maggie. Her jaw only shifted slightly.

"So, what did you do to Ross to make him talk so much?"

Brian leaned back in the booth. "Well, Maggie, m'dear, that's another of life's little ironies…"

"You tricked him, didn't you?"

He cleared his throat. "As I was saying, Ross was the first to come to last night. He thought Dunston was dead. He thought you were dead. He…"

"Yeah, yeah, okay. I get the picture."

"He sang like a bird with a lot of I-didn't-do-it refrains. He didn't know every-thing, of course, but from what he said, what's on the tapes, and what Williams put together, we figured out the rest. Sheridan's been out of the country since Friday, but he's due back today. We'll get him, too."

Maggie exhaled loudly. "So it's all over?"

"Until the next time you stop to help somebody on the side of the road. Have you learned your lesson?"

"Boy, howdy!"

Brian grinned, knowing from that expression that she was feeling better.

Williams arrived then and pulled a chair over from a neighboring table. He handed her a sheaf of papers and pointed out where she should initial each page and sign at the end. Then he turned to Kessler.

"Ebert called you a couple times."

"What for?"

"She didn't say. I told her you were finishing the interview here, and since you'd already signed out, you'd probably head home when you were done."

"So I figured I'd better hurry!"

They all looked up as Ebert came through the back door. She and Maggie ex-changed nods. Williams smiled. Brian only shook his head, knowing he was in no shape to deal with her now. But she slid into the booth alongside him as if invited, then helped herself to one of Maggie's cigarettes.

"Besides," Ebert said cheerfully, "I need to know what a real interrogation is like if I'm ever going to pass the Sergeant's exam. Where'd you hide the rubber hose? Or are you still on the second degree? Plying her with drink to make her talk?"

Brian forgot his supervisory role for the moment. He'd never heard Ebert so flippant, or seen her looking like this. Despite her wound, which she'd hidden with a different hairstyle, she fairly glowed. Seeing Ebert with her hair down reminded him of Mary Jo. He'd called her last night, but it had been years since he had worked around the clock. He smiled to himself, remembering how she used to greet him when that happened.

"You should think about detective work," Williams suggested.

Brian looked on as Ebert asked questions on the subject. Her eyes caught his attention now. He saw how deep brown they were and wondered why he hadn't noticed them before. He'd always thought her eyes were small, like olive pits. They weren't like that at all. Then he made himself stop staring. "Got to make a phone call."

Ebert stood to let him out. "I wanted to check with you about coming back to work."

"Not until Monday at the earliest," he said firmly.

"But Sarge, I…"

"Absolutely not. Your stitches won't be out until then."

"I know," she said quickly. "I wanted to take some vacation. Maybe not come back until Wednesday or so."

Brian was puzzled by her change in attitude. Then he shrugged. "Okay."

"Thanks, Sarge. That's great. See you next week." She started to leave as quickly as she'd come.

Brian remembered his position then. "Wait a minute. What about those appointments we talked about?" He wanted a serious answer, but Williams jumped in before she could reply.

"Yeah, don't be rushing off now. You've got time for a beer, don't you? He *will* wait, won't he?"

Brian snickered, tried to stifle it, then headed for the pay phone.

Puzzled by his amusement, Ebert watched him walk away before facing the detective. "He who?"

Williams scoffed. "You might fool an old married man like Kessler, but I've seen vacations come up sudden-like before. I say again: He'll wait long enough for you to have a beer, won't he?"

Ebert tossed her head. "Never knew a man who wouldn't."

The detective's smile broadened as he went to the bar.

"You sure walk the line," Maggie commented.

Ebert half-smiled and asked to read her statement.

"Are you and Elise going out of town?" Maggie asked.

"I don't think so. Why?"

"Just wondering." She lit a cigarette. "I've got things to do. Somebody ought to go and see… go to the hospital."

Tracy looked up from her reading. Maggie was scraping ashes from the tip of her cigarette, her eyes hidden. "I told Bett you'd come by tonight."

"You *what?*"

Tracy didn't understand Maggie's outrage. "I said you promised to…"

"What the hell'd you say that for?"

"What was I supposed to say? That you're too effen busy to drop by and say 'thanks for trying to save my life'? What's wrong with you, Maggie? Bett's a nice kid. And probably the first lover you've had for more than fifteen…"

"*Shut. Up.*" Maggie was white with anger.

Tracy sat back. "Sorry. I shouldn't have said that."

"Forget it." She stubbed out her cigarette.

Brian returned then, whistling amiably. He sat facing Ebert. "So when's your first session?"

"I, uh, haven't set it up yet, Sarge. But I'll get on it first thing tomorrow."

"See that you do. And tell Harley about your vacation, too. You…"

Williams clapped him on the shoulder. "We got trouble. The Mexican police picked up Sheridan."

"What? Why? What happened?"

"I don't know. We had it all set to nab him when he landed here. They were just supposed to keep him under surveillance. Apparently he got wind of what was going on and tried to change tickets."

"Damn," Brian muttered. "I just called home."

"So go. I'll follow up on it. But nothing's going to happen on schedule. It'll be another late night. We might as well meet in your office tonight and finish those reports."

They set a time, then Williams nodded to Ebert. "Have to take a rain check on that beer. Don't keep him waiting too long, now!"

"I'd never do anything like that," she said solemnly.

Williams grinned, then picked up Maggie's statement and left.

Brian cocked his head at Ebert but didn't say anything to her. He turned to Maggie instead. "I know we talked about taking the guard off you…"

"And you agreed," she reminded him.

"That was when we had Sheridan."

"I'll be fine," she said. Then she asked Tracy for a lift to the yard.

When Tracy nodded, Brian relented.

"All right, but tell Bett we'll keep a guard on her until Sheridan's in custody. And we'll take her statement in a few days, after she gets out of the hospital. Okay?"

"Yeah, sure. Fine." Maggie waved him off. "Go get some sleep."

When he'd gone, Tracy voiced his unspoken question but in a slightly different way. "How'd the test go this morning?"

Maggie quickly moved her hand from her chest. "They say I'm fine. Healthy as…"

"A horse. I know. What did you think was wrong?"

She shook her head. "I… I thought I'd had a heart attack."

"Last night, you mean?" Tracy prompted.

Maggie nodded. Last night. This morning. Two minutes ago. She knew she had

302

no defense against losing Bett. When she felt her heart break last night, it made sense. But the ache returned, full force, when she saw Bett lying in that hospital bed, looking as pale and lifeless as she had last night on the apartment floor. There was no escape from the pain. There never had been. Maggie knew that now. Her wall was gone. She didn't know why. She only knew this was no new pain. It was as old as she was. How could she forget? Why did she have to keep facing the same lesson over and over again?

"You'll be all right," Tracy encouraged.

Maggie looked up.

"Really. It'll just be like a bad dream."

She nodded. "I know. I'll forget all about it."

Tracy half-smiled. "Well, you probably won't forget *all*..."

Maggie's eyes tightened. "You don't know how good I am at forgetting."

CHAPTER 29.

If I Live

Bett slept through the rest of the day and woke up around seven. Even before opening her eyes, she knew someone else was in the room.

"Hello, sweetheart."

"Hi, Dad." She closed her eyes, not wanting to reveal her disappointment that he was her only visitor.

"How do you feel?"

"Okay. Thirsty, though."

Dr. Holman raised the head of the bed a few inches and helped her sip some water, then checked her blood pressure.

Bett smiled. "There's probably a nurse lurking outside my door, just waiting to do all that."

"No. They're too scared of me to even come in anymore."

"Oh, Dad! The last time you scared anyone was when I was four and you dressed up as Santa Claus."

Dr. Holman's smile was thin. He had been watching over his daughter most of the day, since late morning when he'd gotten that heart-stopping phone call. He found Bett sleeping peacefully and sat at her bedside, breathing thanks to whatever manner of providence had given him this miracle, a second time. Then he sought out the surgeon of record, a trauma specialist who told him the operation had gone well. The bullet lodged in a floating rib, missing all her vital organs, and they were able to remove it quickly and cleanly.

"Dad?" Bett interrupted his thoughts. "You look pretty grim. Is there something they didn't tell me?"

"No, nothing like that. But there's something you didn't tell me. Like what happened at the cabin...?"

It took Bett a moment to register what he meant. "The shooting?" When he nodded soberly, she sighed. "Actually, I was hoping I'd never have to tell you about that! I thought everything was over when Maggie gave the police the money."

His expression became more severe. "That's another thing. I liked Maggie when I met her, but I can't forgive her for dragging you into this mess."

"Maggie did not..."

"Let me finish, Bett. The police told me that Maggie knows one of the men involved. He has a criminal record. "I'm not saying she did anything wrong, only that she's obviously not the right sort of person for you. You need to consider that before you... get too involved."

Bett stared at him. "You really don't understand, do you?"

"Understand what?"

"What happened to us this week. You don't know Maggie at all. And you certainly don't know how I feel about her, or you wouldn't talk like this." She paused. "I plan to make my life with her, Dad."

"Bett, wait..."

"No, *you* wait. I don't know where you got your version of things, but it's totally distorted. Maggie was a victim, too. Yes, she knew Scotty. She's known him all her life. And she's been loyal to him, no matter what kind of trouble he got into."

"Bett, my only concern is for you. I want you to be safe, not jeopardized by underworld characters!"

She almost laughed. "If you only knew her, you'd see how ridiculous all this is. Maggie knows more cops than you see in a year. She's really wonderful, Dad. You'll..." She stopped as he shook his head.

"I don't want you to get hurt. Can't you see?"

Bett was exasperated. "This isn't going to keep happening! Maggie leads a very quiet life. Too quiet, in fact. I plan to liven it up when we..."

"Stop, Bett. Don't make me say you can't." He went on more gently. "Come home and rest. Put this week out of your mind, and get back to your studies. You'll... find somebody else."

She shook her head in disbelief. In refusal. "There is nothing you can say or do to make me forget this week. And *nothing* will change how I feel about Maggie. Don't make me choose between you, Dad."

"You're my only child, Bett. You're all I have."

"And you're my only parent. But we have more than each other. You have Sarah Davies..."

"It's not the same."

"Only because you won't see that it is!"

Their clash was interrupted by a knock at the door. The guard stuck her head in to say that she'd been called back to headquarters. "They said you'd be okay now." Then she left.

Dr. Holman turned to his daughter. "Will you?"

"I'll be fine. When did the doctor say I could check out?"

"This weekend."

"Not until then?"

"You need rest."

"I can rest at my place!" Bett saw several emotions cross her father's face. "All right. I'll check out Saturday. Okay?"

He looked relieved. "Will you come home?"

"Maybe for Sunday dinner," she said. "And speaking of dinner, I'm starved!"

He smiled at her enthusiasm. "I sent your tray back when it got cold, but I'll call the cafeteria and see…"

"No. All I want is some toast and tea. I can probably get that from staff. You go home. Get some rest yourself." She saw him start to protest. "Dad, please. I don't want to fight. Not about anything."

He gave in then. "Sleep well. Call me in the morning, okay?"

As soon as the door closed behind him, Bett reached for the phone. Then she realized an even more pressing need. She disconnected her now-empty drip, then got out of bed slowly, aware of symptoms she'd only heard about before.

"Patients always tell you how cold the floor feels," her mother had told her. "Everything else is too strange. They don't know if they should mention the dizziness they feel the first time up after surgery, but they always think it's safe to talk about how cold the bathroom tiles feel." Her mother always paid attention to the minute details of life. Larger events never fazed her. Bett knew it was because she'd already checked, and taken care of, all the bits and pieces that made up the whole.

A sudden sadness came over her as she thought of her mother, and then her father. He never laid the law down like that before. He never even tried. Then she realized it was because her mother had tempered him; making him flexible instead of unyielding, the way so many of her friends' fathers were.

Tears stung her eyes. It wasn't their argument or her weakened physical condition that made her so vulnerable, but the realization of her mother's true role. She'd been their translator, their protector and buffer. Not just from the world, but from each other. And now she was gone.

Bett knew she had to help her father somehow. Without his wife's vision of how life *could* be, he was left with only what it *should* be. She couldn't let that continue. She needed him in her life. And her life was going to be with Maggie.

As she left the bathroom, she heard a voice in the hallway. "I guess five minutes won't hurt." A nurse entered, but Bett could only see Maggie, standing just outside the door. Bett started for her.

The nurse stopped her. "What do you think you're doing? Your father would have my cap if he saw you now. Back to bed!"

She did as she was told, never taking her eyes off Maggie.

"He said you were awake and hungry. Then your friend arrived." She glanced at Maggie briefly. "Now, as soon as I get your…"

"No," Bett interrupted. "I want to visit with my friend first. Please. Just for a few minutes." She watched Maggie, trying to fathom what was wrong.

The nurse left then, but Maggie still didn't come any closer. Bett finally said: "I'm not contagious, you know. Come here, honey."

Maggie moved slowly, as if measuring each step, then stopped at the edge of the bed, not reaching for Bett. Not even leaning down to her. She asked, "How are you?"

Bett took a bandaged hand in hers. "If I live, I'll be great!" Too late, she remembered Maggie didn't know Women's Music; the quote was lost on her. If anything, her expression grew more grave. Bett drew her close and kissed her lips. They were dry; unresponsive. The sour aftertaste of whiskey was unmistakable. "You've been drinking!"

Maggie stepped back. "Yeah. Your father noticed, too." She went to the window—her face hidden in the shadows.

"What's wrong?" Bett asked.

"I shouldn't have come tonight. It's late."

"Did you even consider that? Don't you know how much I need you?"

"I know how bad you're hurt." She continued gazing out the window. "I'm sorry. I never... wanted to hurt you."

Bett knew something was very wrong. Maggie's words were too familiar. Then she realized they weren't her words at all. "You talked to my father! Did he try to blame you for this?"

"He didn't have to. I know when I'm in the wrong. I should've taken you home last night."

"You tried."

"Not hard enough."

Bett didn't reply at first, in part because she couldn't believe they were having this conversation. "Come and sit by me, honey. We can't talk when you're way over there."

Maggie moved to the bed but turned the visitor's chair around, straddling it and crossing her arms over the back.

"There's something you have to understand about my dad. He's a sweetheart, but like most men, he doesn't know the first thing about how to deal with his emotions. He gets... well, reactionary, when things upset him. It's like he doesn't know which way to turn, so he turns back." She took Maggie's hand, holding her unwrapped fingers. "He doesn't really mean it when he says we should stop seeing each other. It's like he's in shock."

An odd look crossed Maggie's face. "Is that what he said?"

"Yes, but he's just reacting to... I don't know... a close call, I guess. Give him time."

Maggie withdrew her hand. "What else did he say?"

"What difference does it make?" Bett's alarm increased. "He doesn't decide things for me. I..."

"He's your father!"

"So what?"

"You still depend on him. You have to live by his rules."

"The hell I do!"

Maggie smiled tightly. "You're a lot alike, you know. Both stubborn." Her smile faded. "I told him I'd set it up to take care of your hospital bill, but he took it all wrong." She put a hand to her chest, pressing firmly. "He got real torqued. Wanted to know if you'd... died, would I have paid for the funeral." She stood abruptly and went to the window, leaving Bett to deal with that alone.

She was appalled. "I don't believe it!"

"Don't underestimate his anger, Bett." Maggie shook her head. "And he *is* your father. If he says we shouldn't see each other, maybe we shouldn't. At least not for a while."

Bett was outraged. "I won't stop seeing you for a minute. I love you. I won't give you up. Not for anyone."

Maggie faced her. "It doesn't matter. Not now. You'll be here for a few days. I'll be busy at the yard. I talked to Tracy, though. She and Elise will be in to see you tomorrow. And Saturday. Your dad will be in, too." She paused. "I'll call you Sunday. Let you know if I can get away then. The office is a pretty big mess, but by next week..."

Bett had heard all she could stand. "This is insane! I won't even be here Sunday. I was going to stay until Saturday, just to keep my father happy, but now..." She waited for Maggie to turn, but she kept her eyes on the dark pane. Bett suddenly felt like she had to talk fast. Very fast. She didn't have much time at all.

"Listen, Maggie. I won't even stay that long. I'll sign out tomorrow. You can pick me up. We'll stay at my place until I get back on my feet." She saw Maggie's head shake. "All right, then. I'll stay with you. We can..."

"No, Bett. We can't live together. We can't do anything like that. Not the way your father feels."

"I don't care about that. I only care about you. I love you. I won't let him stop me."

"Will you let *me?*"

Bett didn't know what to say to that softly uttered plea. She was prepared to love Maggie against all odds—prepared to give up her family, her friends, everything, just to be with her. But she wasn't prepared to do any of that alone. "Why... would *you* want to stop me?"

Maggie took a deep breath. "You want to go so fast. Too fast. Maybe we can talk about living together later. Right now you have to get well. Your dad's worried about you. I am, too. You're weak. You need a lot of rest. Quiet time."

Bett smiled. "I can get all that at home. You can help."

Maggie shook her head. "You need..." She faced the window again. "I can't take care of you, Bett."

"It won't be hard," she urged softly.

Maggie didn't seem to hear. "But if you want to go home that soon, I'll get a nurse for you. I owe you that much at least."

Bett refused what she was saying. Refused even more vehemently what she left unsaid. "What happened to you, Maggie? Last night you..."

"Last night was a mistake. A terrible mistake. I... I'm sorry."

308

Bett let those words stand between them a moment. "You're right. We both made mistakes last night. We should've gone to the police; not even stopped at the yard. But everything wasn't a mistake. You started to say something important last night."

Maggie didn't reply.

"We were in the truck. You were kissing me." Bett saw her shoulders sag. She kept her voice low, inviting. "You were going to tell me how much you love me."

"No! I didn't say that!"

"Then what *were* you going to say?" Bett hated sounding so strident, but she had to have the answer to that. She watched Maggie come toward her. Stop on the other side of the chair. Look down.

"I have to go, Bett. Visiting hours…"

Bett reached for her, ignoring the pain that caused. "Tell me what you were going to say last night!"

Maggie finally looked her in the eye. "I was only going to say how much I… like making love to you." She shook her head. "You're in no shape for that now. We can get back to that in a few weeks. Maybe by then your dad will change his mind."

"I don't believe you! You think that's all we have between us? Just sex?"

"Not just sex," Maggie said softly. "Very, very good sex."

Bett's dismay turned to anger. "Listen, Maggie. If I hadn't fainted last night, I would've killed those bastards. I don't put my life on the line because of a good fuck!" She saw Maggie flinch. "And Elise told me that if Tracy hadn't stopped you, you would've…"

"Committed murder! Don't you think I know that?"

Bett heard the anguish in her voice. "Yes. I'm sure you do. All I'm saying is that you acted out of emotion last night. I can't force you to say that you love me, but in case you don't know it, people who just fuck each other…"

"Stop talking like that! I was angry last night. Out of control. How do you know I won't get that mad at your father some day? Or you? You don't know. And neither do I."

"I *do* know," Bett insisted. "I know you. I think I know you better than you do. There are things you don't understand about yourself because you won't think about them. You won't deal with your past. And as far as I can tell, you never analyze your feelings. Do you ever think about *why* you act the way you do?"

For a brief moment, Bett thought she'd won. A reprieve, at least. She saw Maggie nod.

"I haven't thought about anything else, all day long. I… I just can't trust myself with you, Bett. Not now. That's why I can't see you. For a while at least. Maybe in a week or two, after you get back on your feet. Maybe we can have dinner, or…"

"What the hell's the matter with you, Maggie? Are you crazy? I need you *now!* You can't just walk out of here as if there's nothing between us! You love me!"

"No!" She pulled away. "I. Can't. Love. You."

Bett stared at her in wonder. "Don't you know how much that lie costs you? Can't you hear your own pain?"

"It's not a lie." Maggie shut her eyes tightly, keeping her tears back the only way possible. "I don't love you," she whispered hoarsely. Then she couldn't stay any longer. She strode to the door.

Bett stood, holding the back of the chair for support. "You can't run away, Maggie. I know where to find you. And I will."

Maggie stopped. "Don't kid yourself about me, Bett. You'll just get hurt trying to love me. Waiting for me to... love you." She reached for the door, still not turning around. "Maybe it's like what you said about depth perception. That it has to develop right in the beginning. When you're young." She turned then. "Love doesn't work right in me. I can't give you what you need. You need somebody who can... love you back. I'm sorry, dar..."

Bett heard her choked endearment but didn't see her leave. She was crying too hard to see anything.

❖ ❖ ❖

Maggie thought she'd been driving aimlessly for hours, but when she looked at her watch, it was only nine o'clock. And when she registered her surroundings, she knew she'd been going someplace specific all along.

She pulled into a driveway and walked up to a kitchen door: one with small-framed panes, through which warm light glowed. She didn't knock. That hadn't been allowed for years. She simply opened the door and called, "Hello, the house!" Her voice sounded too small to be heard. Then a slight, dark-haired woman came around the corner from the family room.

"Hello, stranger!" Mary Jo Kessler greeted. "Or should I say: Welcome back from the wars? Come in, come in." She gave Maggie a warm hug. Keeping an arm around her waist, she led her to the kitchen table.

"We're running a skeleton crew tonight. The Sarge was home for a little R & R this afternoon but had to go back tonight. And the two privates are on leave up the street. No school tomorrow—some kind of teacher's mental fitness day. So you just get me."

Maggie sat at the table. The pool of light cast by the hanging lamp revealed a small smile in response to the cheerful patter. "I really came to see you. I..." She covered her eyes with a bandaged hand. "I didn't know where else to go."

"Fine." Mary Jo squeezed Maggie's shoulder lightly, then set a box of tissues on the table. "I'd offer you a drink, but you look like you've had your fill of that. How about some coffee?"

At Maggie's nod, she began filling the pot. "And when was the last time you ate? How about some eggs and toast? Over easy? Strawberry jam?"

"That'd be real nice." Maggie's voice was thick with tears.

Mary Jo set the coffeepot on the burner and went to her, cradling her close and stroking her hair.

Maggie had always come here with her emotional pain. Mary Jo never knew why. She just accepted it. Not that Maggie was distressed often. Even when Matt was killed, her first response had been to pour herself into work. It had been six months after the plane crash before she'd come to visit like this—on another night when Mary Jo was home alone. They had talked for hours before Maggie shed any tears at all. Even then, she barely cried. By comparison, tonight she was hysterical.

Mary Jo suggested that she run a cold washcloth over her face. She had an idea of what was wrong. When Maggie returned, she said, "Brian told me what happened. There's no doubt about it being Scotty...?"

"No. It was him, all right." Maggie looked away. "Seems like everybody I know dies."

"Everybody does, sometime or other." Mary Jo set a cup of coffee in front of her. "But nobody did last night."

"Bett will," Maggie said softly.

Mary Jo looked at her sharply. "Who told you that?"

"Nobody. I just know it. She'll die. Someday. Or she'll leave. It's all the same." She covered her eyes again. "I want to love her, but I can't. I just can't. It'll hurt so much worse if I do."

"Seems like it hurts pretty bad now." Mary Jo waited for Maggie to say more. When the silence continued, she went back to the stove. "Tell me about Bett," she said. "How did you meet her?"

Eventually Maggie responded to her more general questions. And by the time she had finished the light supper, she was talking easily, with hardly any prompting.

Mary Jo could see that Bett was someone special. Maggie's eyes would light up and she would smile, genuinely, as she described something the younger woman had said or done. Then, too, she often blushed and shrugged off some part of her story about their week together.

"Brian probably told you what happened last night."

Mary Jo heard the change in her tone. "Yes. He said you were upset." And, she thought, he didn't even see you tonight! "What's wrong? It sounds like you and Bett are getting off to a wonderful start."

"The beginning never matters," Maggie said dolefully. "Only the end."

"Where in the world did you get that?"

Maggie looked up. "What do you mean?"

"That doesn't sound like you at all. And from what you've said about Bett, it's not her philosophy, either."

Maggie didn't reply to that. Instead she asked, "Do you remember when Brian got hurt?"

Mary Jo paused before answering honestly. "Like it happened yesterday."

"Can you tell me how you felt?"

Mary Jo shook her head. There wasn't any way to describe how she felt that day—seeing Brian's partner pull into the driveway in the middle of the day. Alone.

"I think I went into shock. I don't remember the trip to the hospital, or what I did while he was in recovery. I just waited. Endlessly. Then someone took me in…"

She closed her eyes, remembering all too well looking down on Brian: the man she had looked up to all her adult life. He was pale, with a sickly hue that made what he called his "second tour beard" stand out in blue-black relief. She remembered the vision she'd had, just for an instant, of him in his Sunday suit, the one that intensified the luster of his eyes. What a waste, she'd thought, to dress him in that for the funeral. The color would only emphasize his shadowy beard. No one would see his eyes.

She shook off those thoughts. "The first thing I remember feeling was anger. I could've killed him."

"The guy who shot him?"

"No. I mean Brian."

"But…? That doesn't make any sense."

Mary Jo smiled wryly. "You asked how I felt. Feelings are hardly ever rational. But later I figured out why I was so mad. Here was this thirty-year-old father of two, out playing soldier long after he should've been sitting behind a desk teaching rookies how to keep themselves out of the hospital. He didn't have to be on patrol anymore. I knew that. So did Brian. But it was never dull, and he was good at it. He saved more than one life doing that." Mary Jo looked up. "Are you mad at Bett?"

"No," Maggie said automatically.

"You will be. As soon as you finally realize she's going to be all right." Then she asked gently, "How *do* you feel?"

Maggie shook her head. "I don't know. But I could never be really mad at Bett." She paused. "Did you ever think about… leaving Brian?"

Mary Jo nodded slowly. "Did he tell you that?"

"No. It's just that… Well, it just makes sense. I mean, how could you keep loving him? Knowing he might be killed?"

Mary Jo sighed. "The honest answer is I couldn't. And when I figured *that* out, I told Brian. That hurt him. Badly. He depends on my love, you know." She smiled ruefully. "Love's a funny thing. You can't withhold it. It turns into something else if you do. I know. I tried." She spread her hands. "And when that didn't work, I gave him some choices. The same way I did when he asked me to marry him."

"I didn't know you could do that!"

Mary Jo laughed at her child-like awe. "Neither did Brian. But why do you want to know about all this? Bett's a student, not a cop."

She nodded. "I know. But there's more than one way to lose somebody." She studied her coffee. "You know I don't have any education, don't you?"

"I know you didn't stick around to pick up your diploma. I also know that it never got in your way before."

"This is different. Bett and I don't think alike."

"Why? Because she's had more school? I doubt it."

Maggie shrugged. "She doesn't... understand things."

"Oh." Mary Jo considered that a moment. "Well, give her a chance. She's young. If she's anything like the kids I work with at junior college, she's still an idealist. You can help her, the same way you do the little billies."

"No. It's not the same. Those guys understand how things work. And it isn't just that. Bett says I think like a market."

"You what?"

"That's what she said. She called it 'bazaar thinking.'"

It took Mary Jo a moment to process that, then she smiled. "You mean your thinking is bizarre."

"Yeah. That's what I said."

"It's not exactly the same." Mary Jo spelled the words, then explained their differences.

"Jeez," Maggie muttered. "How dumb can you get?"

"Don't be so hard on yourself. Words like that would be confusing for anyone as auditory as you are."

"What's that mean?"

"Auditory? It means you get all your words by ear instead of by sight. You still don't read much, do you?"

"No. Would that help?"

"It might. Does Bett use many words you don't know?"

She shrugged. "I didn't think so, but then I didn't know there was more than one kind of bazaar." She was silent a moment. "Is there a word that sounds like ingenious but means something else?"

"Well, there's ingenuous."

"What's that mean?"

"Naive. Innocent. Or very open. It depends on the context. How did she use it?"

Color rose in Maggie's face, and she got up for more coffee. "It's no good," she said, returning to the table. "I can't go through life asking 'What's that mean?' every five minutes."

"Maybe you could just go out with her for a while and learn all the words that way."

Maggie smiled, knowing she was being teased. "I, um, sort of suggested that, but Bett wants us to live together."

"And...?"

She shrugged. "It doesn't matter what she wants. Her father said we shouldn't see each other anymore."

313

Mary Jo considered that a moment. "I don't know her father, of course, but from what you've told me about Bett, I think you might be overrating his influence. You don't have any point of reference for that, but take it from me: After a certain age, children pretty much do what they want, whether their parents like it or not."

Maggie drank her coffee in silence for a while, then said in a low voice: "Bett says she wants to marry me. I don't have any point of reference for that, either."

Mary Jo smiled and got up to make a fresh pot of coffee. They were in for a long night. She didn't mind in the least.

CHAPTER 30.

The Rock Will Wear Away

"CHRIST!" TRACY MUTTERED as she and Elise wheeled Bett out to the parking lot. "It's easier to break out of jail!"

Bett didn't reply. She'd exhausted herself telling doctors, nurses, and clerks that she knew what she was doing and took complete responsibility for her action. Then she signed the liability waiver. Any other time she would have laughed at the part about not suing if she died, but by then she was too fed up to be amused.

Tracy parked the wheelchair alongside her sports car as Elise crouched next to Bett. "Do you feel sick?"

She shook her head. A silent lie. She was suffering a kind of shock-queasiness. Then she felt Tracy's hand on her shoulder.

"You'll be okay," Tracy said gently.

Bett's eyes filled at the gesture. "Sure. Why don't you... go have a cigarette or something. I just need to sit for a minute." But she couldn't help watching as Tracy led Elise to a bench a few yards from the car. It was the same bench she and Maggie had shared a week ago. How much we've all changed, she thought. Last week Tracy would have barked at her to return to the hospital and quick-marched her to the door.

But now Tracy seemed to have forgotten Bett. She was taking out a cigarette, asking Elise for a light. They gazed at each other, not the least bit interested in the cigarette, except as a means of being able to touch each other in public. Tracy never even put it to her lips. She leaned toward the lit match Elise held, then blew it out, threw the cigarette over her shoulder, and kissed her.

Bett quickly looked around, but no one else was in the parking lot. She couldn't believe Tracy's abandon. Then she knew she'd been wrong about Tracy—utterly, 180 degrees wrong. She'd worried about all the wrong things, too. Maggie and Tracy could never have been lovers. Not because they were so much alike, but because Tracy was a risk-taker. Maggie never took risks.

Bett heard footsteps and turned to warn her friends. But Tracy was already at her side, unlocking the door and offering an arm to help her in.

"Watch your head!" She smiled at Bett's double-take. "Sorry. I usually say that to perps." She tossed the keys to Elise and left to return the chair.

Elise unlocked the driver's door and got in the backseat. "Tracy's worried about Maggie. She went out looking for her after you called last night."

Bett refused to let her hopes rise. "She didn't find her, did she?"

"Not exactly. She called the CHP when I told her Maggie had been drinking, but no accidents with white pickups were reported."

Bett had to know what "not exactly" meant. "What *did* she find out?"

Elise hesitated. "Stony found a note at M & M this morning."

"What did it say?"

Tracy returned in time to hear Bett's question. She glanced at Elise in the mirror and shrugged as she started the engine. "Not much. Something about canceling tonight's meeting."

"What else?" Bett wasn't fooled by her nonchalance, and when Tracy reached for her sunglasses, she caught her hand. "Tell me!"

"It just said not to expect her in."

"For how long?"

"A few days." Then she added: "No more than a week."

Bett let go and turned away, wondering how far Maggie could run in a week. Then wondered why she still cared.

They rode home in silence, none of them willing to make small talk. As they parked in front of the apartment, they heard a dog yelp.

"Gyp!" Bett had forgotten about him.

They all saw Winkler, the apartment manager, at the same time. He was looking for the source of the bark. A second bark led him to their building, and by the time the three of them got out of the car, they could hear the man pounding on Elise's door.

She went ahead to try to mollify him as Tracy and Bett followed more slowly. She was already coming back down the stairs when they got to the front door. "Winkler won't even let me open my door. Will you come and flash your badge before he calls the cops?"

"Sure," Tracy said, then turned to Bett. "We talked about taking care of Gyp for you. Just until you're feeling better."

Bett nodded her thanks as she took her overnight bag from Tracy and her keys from Elise. "Now I think I'm going to go and pass out." She declined Elise's offer of help and headed down the hall, hearing their exchange as she did.

"Your badge, Tracy. Just your badge. Not your gun!"

"I was just checking it. Jeez, lighten up, would you?"

Bett smiled. Maybe she hadn't been entirely wrong about Tracy. She picked out the new, silver key on her ring, only to find she didn't need it. They'd either forgotten to secure the padlock, or decided not to use it. But the standard lock was intact, and Bett used her more familiar key to let herself in. She closed the door, resting her forehead against the cool wood as she reached for the chain lock. A sudden quiver of fear went through her: She sensed another presence in the apartment.

She drew breath to scream, then heard a deliberate step. She turned, and Maggie stepped out of the shadows.

"Hello, Bett."

Her knees weakened as her terror faded. She leaned against the door, letting several emotions wash over her. Relief was first, mixed with joy and surprise. Despite everything Maggie had said last night, she was *here*. Then hurt overwhelmed her again. "How did you get in here?" she demanded.

"I, uh, sort of broke in." Maggie held up a key.

Even from where Bett stood, she could see it wasn't the same shape as the new key Elise had given her.

Maggie gestured at the door. "That's not a very good lock. Scotty gave me this key years ago. He filed the middle notches off both sides. It'll work on any of those kinds of padlocks now. I kept it because he promised me he was finished with all that stuff. Kids' stuff, he called it."

"Scotty always lied to you, didn't he?"

"Not really. He did give that up. He just went on to… more adult crimes, I guess. And I never faced the truth about him before."

Bett didn't say anything. She was still trying to process Maggie's presence. Last night she thought she'd lost her forever, knowing that once Maggie made a decision or learned a lesson, it became a rule in her world; some kind of immutable law she would never think about again. The fact that she was here, of her own volition, gave Bett a glimmer of hope. For both of them.

"I didn't expect you to come home," Maggie said. "When I called the hospital, they said it was 'out of the question' for you to leave today."

Bett almost smiled at that. "Why did you come here, then?"

"I wanted to bring you something."

"But you didn't want to see me?"

"No. I mean, yes, but I didn't think you'd want to see me." She took a breath. "You have every right to hate me for how I treated you last night. I was trying to protect myself." She grimaced in frustration. "I was going to leave you a letter, to explain everything. I figured, after you read it, if you wanted to see me, you'd call."

"What if I didn't?"

"I don't know what I'd do. Probably write you again. And again. Until I got the words right. Or," she turned one hand palm up and let it fall, "until you told me to stop."

Bett closed her eyes. Who was this woman? Was this the Maggie who never took chances? Who never had expectations for fear of disappointment? No, this was the other Maggie, the one who took risks all the time without knowing it. This was the woman who helped little billies build faith in themselves; who hired an ex-felon despite even Matt's opposition. This was the Maggie who kept trying to reform Scotty, long after he'd proved it couldn't be done.

When Bett opened her eyes, the room was spinning. She reached out instinctively. Maggie was there to catch her and guide her to the couch. She knelt beside Bett and gently wiped her tears away.

"Do you hurt, darlin'?"

Bett shook her head. "No. I'm crying and dizzy for the same reason I've been so hostile. They're classic, textbook examples of why people shouldn't leave a hospital early!" She touched Maggie's face, not daring to let go of her. "You look terrible."

Maggie smiled wryly. "Well, I haven't had much sleep."

"You didn't go home, did you?"

"I couldn't. And Mary Jo says I probably shouldn't."

Bett raised an eyebrow at that. "Why not? And who…? You mean Brian's wife?"

"Yeah. She said I should stay with you." Maggie ducked her head. "Or if that didn't work, come and stay with them. Until you're well."

Bett's other eyebrow went up. "Only until then?"

"No." She shook her head as dismay creased her brow. "I told Mary Jo I wouldn't be able to explain it all. Writing you a letter was her idea."

Bett had forgotten about that. "I'd like to read it."

"It isn't finished. I only…"

"That doesn't matter," Bett interrupted. "Let me see what you've written so far." She wouldn't listen to any objections, and Maggie fetched it.

"I didn't say much yet," she offered in apology.

Bett took the single sheet of paper from her. "Do you know how much it means to me that you wrote anything?"

Maggie shrugged. "I just don't want you to be disappointed."

Bett smiled knowingly and turned to the letter. But she studied it far longer than the few words on the page required. She looked up. "What…?" She stopped herself and read the paper again. Maggie had written "Dear Bett" at the top. At the bottom of the page, in the same careful hand, she had written "Love, Maggie." The space in between was blank.

"I knew where I wanted to start," Maggie said softly. "And what I wanted to say at the end."

Bett wondered aloud, "Was everything else going to fit in between?"

"I thought it would. If I could find the right words."

"Oh, Maggie!" Bett hugged her and didn't let go until she was sure she wasn't going to laugh. Or cry.

"I wanted to tell you I love you," Maggie said.

"Then that's all you had to say. It's just that simple."

"But it isn't. I mean it wasn't. And I can't promise it will be."

Bett's heart constricted again. "Are you taking it all away? Past? Present? Future? Just like that?"

"No, darlin'. I don't know how much… I don't know if I can love you enough. All I can do is try."

"That's all I ask." Bett cupped her face. "We can talk about it. Just tell me you won't go away again…?"

Maggie took her hands and kissed her fingertips. "I won't go away unless you tell me to."

As Bett's eyes filled again, Maggie brushed the tears from her cheek. "You can't keep crying like this, darlin'. I won't know what to do."

Yet, that wasn't true. She leaned over and kissed Bett, almost like she was kissing her for the first time, not knowing what to expect. And much like kissing for the first time, the moment was its own reward. She drew back then, smiling shyly. "I wanted to put that in my letter, too, but I didn't know how."

"Even poets learn to draw the line somewhere!" Bett said. "Now, tell me what else you were going to write."

Maggie opened her mouth, but no words came out. She spread her hands. "The problem is, I don't know where to start."

Bett knew what that was like from her sessions with Ellen. She held Maggie's hand and leaned back gingerly. "You said you acted the way you did last night because you were trying to protect yourself. What did you mean?"

Haltingly, Maggie told her about the ache in her chest: when she'd first felt it, and how it kept recurring. "I asked the doctor to see if there was something wrong. He gave me a test, but I guess hearts don't really break, do they?"

Bett sighed. "Not medically speaking, no. But not being able to measure pain on a machine doesn't make it any less real. Why didn't you tell me all this last night?"

"I was sure I couldn't love you. Not yet anyhow. Mary Jo says that kind of *can't* really means *won't*. She thinks I'm afraid because everybody I ever loved got taken away. My folks. The kids at the orphanage. Then Matt. And now Scotty."

Bett absorbed that thoughtfully. "Don't forget Lange."

"She didn't get taken away. She just changed her mind."

"Are you sure?"

"I told you what happened!"

"Yes, but you lost her the same way you lost all those other people."

"It's completely different," Maggie said tightly. "Lange had a choice, and she made it."

Bett was silent, knowing instinctively there was something wrong with that conclusion, but not knowing what it was. "What else did you and Mary Jo talk about?"

"I asked her how she felt when Brian got hurt a few years ago. I wanted to know if she'd put governors on her feelings."

"Governors?"

"Yeah." Maggie tossed her head. "Regulators. You put them on engines to keep drivers from going too fast."

Once she understood the term, Bett was staggered by the concept. "Why would you ever want to do that with your feelings?"

"I know how much it hurts to lose someone."

"But you didn't lose me," she said firmly. "And you aren't going to. I told you I love you. I always will."

Maggie nodded. "I know that's how you feel now. I also know how beautiful you are. How different our worlds are. And when you go to medical school, you'll meet people. Other women…"

"Where's all this coming from, Maggie? I never said I was going to medical school. How did you know I was even thinking about it again?"

"Remember all those books you brought up to the cabin?"

"Of course. I knew I'd miss some classes. I wanted to keep up with my reading."

"You didn't even open those, darlin'. Every time I saw you reading, it was that book your dad gave you. I know you were finding out how to treat my hands, but whenever you talked about my burns…" Her voice grew soft. "You should see how your eyes light up when you talk about medical stuff. Like there's nothing else in the world so important."

Bett knew all that was true. "I have been thinking about medical school, but being a doctor isn't all that matters to me. Right now you matter more. And what's all this other-women noise? Do you think I'm fickle?"

"No. I'm just telling you what Mary Jo said. Before she and Brian got married, they talked about being faithful. It turns out she didn't really have to worry about that, but it got them talking about other things. From then on, they agreed to talk to each other about what they were most afraid of. She says it's the only way to deal with fear. Sharing it means you don't face it alone. It might be all in one person's head, not a real problem at all. Or maybe it *is* real, but the other person doesn't know it yet. I'm probably not explaining it very well, but Mary Jo can tell you it's the best rule they ever made. None of the others mattered."

Bett was beginning to see things from Maggie's perspective. "So how did my lack of fidelity get to be such a big fear for you?"

"You've… had other lovers."

Bett cocked her head in challenge.

Maggie nodded. "I know. Me, too. But it isn't the same. At least, not for me." She looked down at her hands. "I used to have rules about making love. I thought if I was careful, it wouldn't get old. And that seemed to work. It never got old, anyhow. But it's never been like this before, either." She looked up. "I've never wanted anyone like I've wanted you. All this week. Even when I thought we couldn't…" She glanced away. "I used to be able to keep feelings like that in check before, but my wall is gone."

"Your wall? I thought that was only for physical pain."

Maggie shrugged. "I don't know what it's for or what happened to it. I only know it's gone, and I can't think. All I can do is feel." She took a deep breath. "As much as I want you, I don't know if I can make you happy. You know a lot more about loving, and I'm afraid you'll want more, or different kinds, than I can give you."

"Oh, Maggie…"

"No, listen, Bett. Things got all mixed up this week. I know I short-changed you at least once. Maybe more. I didn't mean to, but I don't know how some things work. I just need a little time to figure it out. Then, if you'll give me a chance, I can… learn to love you the way you deserve." She took her hand. "There's nothing I want more than that, darlin'. I know I can take care of you every other way, but if that's not enough for you, if you want someone else…" She shook her head. "I don't know what I'll do. I can't lose you. Not again."

Bett didn't say anything for a long minute as she sorted out all of the inner realities Maggie was sharing: the need to protect herself mixed with self-doubt; equating loving someone with protecting that person; hope for the future overwhelmed by the pain of the past. She decided to start with what she knew best.

"I love you, Maggie. Now and forever. And I never want to do, or say, anything to make you question that."

"I know," Maggie said softly.

"You doubt something, though. What don't you trust in me?"

"It's not you, darlin'. It's the world. Things change outside of us, and then we have to change, too."

"Change isn't all bad, is it?"

"No, not so long as what's important stays the same. But you could change your mind. Suddenly realize what a mistake you'd made. I don't have any control over how you feel." She took Bett's other hand. "If there's anything I don't trust, it's love. One minute it's there, and the next it's gone. That's why I want to take it slow in the beginning. Make sure it's what you really want before we get too involved."

"What about what you want?"

She smiled. "You don't have to worry about that."

"You mean I should just trust that you love me, but you need some kind of test of time to make sure I love you."

Maggie shook her head. "I only know what happened with Lange."

Bett thought again about Maggie's story, piecing it together with Ellen's comments. Finally she said: "I wonder if you do. Did you ever find out what what's-his-name knew about you two?"

"Tom. No. Why? What does that matter?"

"What if *he* changed her mind?"

"What do you mean?"

"Well, from what you said, he probably felt pretty threatened. Not only is Lange bright and successful, but one day he suspects she's having an affair. He gets rid of you, at least temporarily, then decides to make that permanent by getting Lange pregnant."

Maggie heard her out, then said, "You're making this all up."

"In a way. But it fits, doesn't it? He could have played on Lange's feelings of guilt—started talking about having a *real* marriage. Lange was probably vulnerable to that. Maybe she thought having a baby would straighten her out somehow. She wouldn't be the first gay person, male or female, to think that."

Maggie shook her head again. "Lange's not gay."

"Why? Because she's married?"

"No. She divorced Tom years ago. And she never remarried, but she never lived with anyone after that, either."

"That doesn't mean…" Bett stopped. "How do you know all this?"

"Scotty told me. He kept in touch with her. I never knew why."

Then the phone rang.

"Want me to get it?" Maggie asked.

"No, it's probably my dad." Bett had left a message with his service, asking him to call her tonight at home. He'd be furious with her for checking out of the hospital early. "But I'm definitely going to need some tea. Would you put water on to boil?" She picked up the receiver, but it wasn't Dr. Holman.

"Hi, Elise. No, you didn't wake me. What's up?" She looked across to the kitchen, where Maggie was filling the tea kettle, and smiled into the receiver. "I don't have to guess whose truck is parked out back." Her smile faded. "Tell Tracy not to do any such thing. And who the hell is Harley?… Well, tell him to *stop* looking for Maggie *or* her truck. She's here." Bett listened again. "I suppose Ellen's taking new clients." She recited her therapist's number from memory. "When you talk to her, would you tell her I'll call next week instead of seeing her tomorrow?" Bett was thoughtful as she hung up and rose gingerly to join Maggie in the kitchen.

"Is Tracy keeping tabs on me again?" Maggie asked.

"What do you mean?"

"She used to do that a lot."

"Did you ever ask her why?" When Maggie shook her head, Bett asked, "Did Scotty keep tabs on Lange for you?"

"Not for me," Maggie said quickly. "He never said why he did."

"And you never asked?"

"No. And none of that matters now. It all happened a long time ago. It's over and done with. Lange might as well be dead."

"But she isn't," Bett said. "And neither are your feelings for her."

"Don't you understand? I can't be wrong about Lange. Everything I did… everything I've done…" She turned away. "No, Bett. I can't afford to be wrong about that. There's no way to fix it." Then she turned back. "Forget Lange. Forget I ever mentioned her."

Bett shook her head. "It doesn't work that way, honey."

"Sure it does. All you have to do is concentrate on other stuff. After a while it gets to be automatic. You just... forget."

"And what do you do with your feelings?" Bett asked softly.

She shrugged. "After a while, they go away, too."

Bett knew that wasn't true. She tried "forgetting" when her mother died. She tried pretending that she was just away on a trip, or that they'd see each other on the weekend. But none of it worked. There'd been too many reminders. Too many people... She looked up with new awareness. "You couldn't forget, either. Scotty wouldn't let you, would he?"

Maggie's brow furrowed. "What do you mean?"

"He kept in touch with Lange. He kept her alive for you."

"You make it sound like he was doing me a favor."

Bett knew he had been. She also knew Maggie wasn't willing to see that yet. She decided to take another approach. "Maggie, have you ever tried to fix a car and not been able to?"

"Well, sure. But what's that..."

"How do you do it? What steps do you take?"

Maggie shrugged, then explained using trouble-shooting tests and talking with the owner. "There's a lot of different ways to figure it out."

"Do you always find the problem?"

"Not always. Especially if it's intermittent."

"So when that happens, and you really can't fix it, you don't say there isn't a problem, do you?"

"No, of course not."

"And you don't just forget about it, do you?"

Then Maggie realized where she was heading. "It's not the same."

"Maybe not," Bett conceded. "But somehow I don't think you'd walk away from a car you couldn't fix just because..."

"Cars are different," Maggie interrupted. Then she added more gently: "I won't walk away from you, darlin'."

Bett shook her head. "But you do, honey. You hide inside yourself, behind your wall. Or you just leave physically." She reached out to her. "I know you're not really leaving *me*, but I'm the one who gets left behind. Don't you see?"

Maggie took a deep breath. "I know, and I'm sorry. I just don't know what else to do."

"Are you so afraid I'll hurt you?"

"No, darlin', it's not you. It's me." She drew Bett close, not knowing what to say, and just held her gently for a moment.

The tea kettle began rattling its prelude to readiness. Maggie switched off the element, then suggested that Bett lie down while she fixed her tea. "I'll bring it over when it's ready, okay?"

Bett nodded and went to the bed, kicking her shoes off and stretching out on her side to avoid disturbing her wound or its bandage. Her back was to Maggie now, and the sounds in the kitchen—the tea kettle's dying whistle, the rustle of waxed paper in the tea box, the water splashing into the mug—should have comforted her. Instead, she found herself fighting tears of disappointment. She wanted Maggie to understand so much more than she seemed willing to.

Maggie's eyes were on the steeping tea, but she didn't see the water change from pink to rosy to deep red. Her thoughts traveled inward as she tried to make sense of her feelings. As she tried to understand the source of her emotional conflict.

She'd built her defenses instinctively, without thought for where that might lead. All she'd known in the beginning was that she needed some kind of shield. And that had worked for a long time. The vague dissatisfaction she'd experienced with previous physical relationships hadn't been enough to challenge those defenses. But there was nothing vague about the feelings Bett instilled in her. What made her hesitate? What *was* she so afraid of? Was it just the unknown? Was it not being sure how things would turn out? Then she thought of Matt's reaction to her cautious nature that night so long ago when they were planning what to do with M & M next.

"You're like an old woman!" he'd shouted. "All you think about is how bad it'll be when it doesn't work. Don't you ever imagine things working right? How can you fix cars with thinking like that?"

"I know how cars look and sound when they work right," she'd retorted. "I don't know what M & M is supposed to look like or be like. I've never done this before!"

Matt had laughed then. Not at her, but at her limited vision. And they had talked, long into the night, about M & M and what it meant to each of them. He thought of it as a game. A gambler's game. Nobody gambled just to break even, he told her. You gambled to win, or you didn't bother to play. What was the point otherwise?

That terrified Maggie. M & M wasn't a game to her. It was her life. She couldn't imagine treating it like a roll of dice. Then she had thought about it further and realized that Matt would never take risks like that, either. He'd never pilot a plane the way he said he ran M & M.

She had taken a step back, examining how he acted, not just what he said. And she began to see how careful he really was: how he'd study an idea or a plan, looking for its weakness, then figure out a way to counter it. Sometimes it was just a line in a contract, or an offhand remark to a banker. But she began to see, and learn, all of his tricks, internalizing his subtle processes until they were part of her way of doing things, too.

Their conversation that night had made its impact in other ways, too. She had changed from being a kind of sidekick in their venture to becoming a full partner. She had felt herself growing in that new role. It had been scary at times, but she knew she had to learn a new way of being, or M & M would always feel like a wild ride.

She looked over at Bett, resting on the bed, and knew with certainty that they would never get anywhere unless she could get rid of the ever-present fear of losing her. She knew she had to change. Again.

"If that tea steeps any longer," Bett called out, "I'll have to chew it!"

Maggie quickly fished out the tea bag and brought the mug to the bedside. "Sorry," she said. "I sort of got lost in thought."

Bett raised herself on one elbow. "What were you thinking about?"

Maggie pulled over the desk chair and sat next to her. "Lots of things. My wall, Matt, M & M…" She took a deep breath. "I think I'm going to have to forget about getting my wall back."

Bett was taking a sip of tea and nearly choked on it. "What? Why? *Really?* I mean, that's… What does that mean?"

Maggie chuckled at Bett's onslaught and her confusion. She took the cup from her and set it on the bedside table.

"Maybe you should rest for a while first. What if I promise to tell you all about it when you wake up?"

Bett saw the wisdom of that. "Only if you'll join me," she said.

Maggie agreed, and they giggled softly as they settled side-by-side on the bed, taking care not to disturb each other's wounds.

Bett sighed deeply in the comfort of Maggie's arms and smiled at the promise of waking up in them. Then another thought occurred to her.

"Maggie, will you always have stories to tell me?"

"Darlin', so long as you have questions to ask, I'll have stories to tell."

Acknowledgments

Charlene B.: You have been my champion and my critic and my guide and my friend through the final birthing process of this novel. Your patience has been as boundless as your enthusiasm, and it is only because of you that I have been able to think of myself, out loud, as a writer.

Karen S.: You have been my audience and my muse from time immemorial. Since there is no way to give back all the spirit and grit that you have modeled for me, I'll just keep bringing you coffee beans and writing words and stories, knowing that you will be at the far end of the page.

Women singers, songwriters, and musicians: You have given voice to all matters of the lesbian heart. I chose your songs as chapter titles not only to reflect the music of the era in which this novel is set but also to describe the essence of each chapter. Playing women's music during the creative process helped me to weave your wisdom into the end product that became this book. Thank you for all you have given me through your art.

About the Author

SHEILA J. CONNOLLY lives in Milwaukee, Wisconsin, where she is a psychometrician, developing tests for people who work in Quality. She has been employed in various industry sectors and has lived in regions all over the United States. She cites Dorothy L. Sayers, Josephine Tey, and Nevil Shute as the storytellers who most influenced her own style and the writers she wants to emulate. This is her first novel.

CPSIA information can be obtained
at www.ICGtesting.com
Printed in the USA
FFOW03n2021170615
14323FF

9 780984 657056